What others are sa

"Compelling storyline with characters you'll grow to care about. Don't wait to read this book!"

~USA Today Bestselling author Christy Barritt

"How much would you be willing to forgive? How far would you go to restore a broken relationship? How much would you risk to bring an evil man to justice? Mikayla and Jax will have to answer all of these questions in *Forged*, Book 4 of the Night Guardians series. This story will take you from Canada to Puerto Rico with a few stops along the way and danger lurking at every turn. And if you start to think you know what will happen next, trust me, you don't! *Forged* is a thrilling and satisfying conclusion to the Night Guardians series and you do not want to miss it!"

~Lynn Blackburn, bestselling romantic suspense author

"A story of faith and healing, with characters so well-crafted that they come alive with every turn of the page. This book is a reminder that even in the quiet, pain-filled moments of our lives, God is with us."

~C.C. Warrens, author of The Holly Novels

"Sara Davison delivers an emotionally charged, tension-filled, entertaining story I couldn't put down. *Driven* is the perfect balance of romantic suspense coupled with a well-delivered message of faith that will keep readers on the edge of their seat until the very last page."

~Natalie Walters, author of Carol award finalist Living Lies and the Harbored Secrets Series.

Forged

The Night Guardians Series

Book One: Vigilant
Book Two: Guarded
Book Three: Driven
Book Four: Forged

Forged

The Night Guardians Series

By

Sara Davison

MBI

Forged
Published by Mountain Brook Ink
White Salmon, WA U.S.A.

The Author is represented by and this book is published in association with the literary agency of WordServe Literary Group, Ltd, www.wordserveliterary.com.

ISBN 9781-953957-03-0

The Team: Miralee Ferrell, Kristen Johnson, Tim Pietz, Cindy Jackson.

Cover Design: Indie Cover Design, Lynnette Bonner Designer

Mountain Brook Ink is an inspirational publisher offering fiction you can believe in.

Printed in the United States of America

Dedication

To my mother, who once gave me a book on
writing with no idea that it would change my life.
Thank you for making all your friends read my stories.

And, always and above all, to the One who doesn't always choose to deliver us from the fire but walks through it with us every step of the way.

Acknowledgments

Writing a book at any time is difficult. Writing during a pandemic is an extreme challenge. So, I owe a deep and heartfelt thanks to all who have encouraged me to carry on in the midst of the craziness that is life on this tiny, fallen planet.

As always, to Michael, for his unwavering love and support. And my kids, whose return home may have distracted me from my writing but in the most wonderful way. Despite the cause, I am grateful for the gift of extra, unexpected time with all three of you.

To my author friends and members of my writer's groups, I am so thankful for the technology that allows us to continue to meet virtually and urge each other on in this calling that God has given us. May your work and words bless and impact countless others as they have me.

To readers who have read the books in this series or others of mine and let me know through messages or reviews that God has somehow used my stories to bless them, you are the reason I do what I do. I love and thank God for each one of you.

To my agent, Sarah Joy Freese, and to Greg Johnson and the rest of the team at WordServe Literary. Your support of authors and books—including mine—has the power to change the world, so thank you for believing in our stories.

And to Miralee Ferrell and everyone at Mountain Brook Ink, what a joy it has been to work on this series with you. I am deeply grateful to be part of this wonderful literary family!

If we are thrown into the blazing furnace,
the God we serve is able to deliver us from it,
and he will deliver us from Your Majesty's hand.

But even if he does not …
(Daniel 3:17-18a)

Chapter One

Jax Rodríguez maneuvered the last box into place and slammed the trunk of his Porsche 928 closed. The hot early-June sun beat down from a cloudless sky, and he swiped his bare arm across his forehead. A car parked at the curb half a block up on the other side of the street caught his eye. The silver Matrix had been sitting there for a couple of hours as he loaded his car. Not that unusual, except that the engine had been running the whole time. Two men, both fairly large from what he could make out, sat in the front seats. Were they watching him? He frowned. No idea why they would be.

Could the attention be racially motivated? Chase Washington, his former partner in their PI firm, had been helping him move today, and it wouldn't be the first time he'd been profiled that way. Or that Jax had, for that matter. Although, now that he thought about it, he'd seen that car parked along his street before, always in a different spot. That likely meant that he was the one in their crosshairs, not Chase. Jax squinted, trying to make out the license plate, but the distance and the glare of the sun made it impossible.

The headlights of the Matrix flashed on briefly before dying out. Chills shivered across Jax's skin despite the humid day. For some reason, that had felt like a warning. But a warning of what?

A hand clapped down hard on his shoulder, yanking him from his musings. "Still can't believe you're abandoning me for the big city."

Jax whirled around. "Sorry, Chase. But you know how it is."

Chase shot a look at the apartment building Jax was vacating. "Yeah, I know exactly how it is."

Jax followed his gaze. His girlfriend, Mikayla Grant, exited the building, a garment bag filled with his dress shirts and pants folded over one arm. A smile crossed his face. He hadn't abandoned his partner for Toronto—he'd abandoned him for the opportunity to live in the same city as the woman he loved. Not to mention the chance to join his friend—former cop and Mikayla's brother-in-law, Daniel Grey—who had recently started his own private investigation agency in Toronto.

Being in the city would also allow Jax to be close to his mamá. Which was a good thing, given that his dad had left them to return to Puerto Rico when Jax was a kid, and his older brother Diego had disappeared twenty years earlier after becoming deeply involved in the drug world. Jax and his mother were on their own.

Jax had dedicated the last ten years to searching for Diego with no success. The failure stung, not only because he desperately missed his brother and would give anything to know if he was dead or alive, but also because Jax's specialty as a PI was missing persons. He'd been able to track down dozens of lost people over the last decade and bring them home to their families. He didn't begrudge them their happiness, but every joyful reunion he witnessed was a painful reminder that he might never find his own brother.

Jax punched Chase lightly in the arm. "Pete is a great PI—he will be a good partner for you. And you can come visit me and Daniel any time. Toronto is not that far away." Although it had certainly felt like it when he'd made the two-and-a-half-hour trip every weekend for the past year to see Mikayla. And it had felt even farther when he was driving away from her after a couple of way-too-short days together. Not that it hadn't been worth every second and every cent he'd spent on gas.

Their eyes met and she smiled. The sight weakened his knees a little, and he braced himself with a hand on the trunk of the Porsche. Chase elbowed him in the ribs. "You gonna put a ring on her finger or what?"

The thought of the black velvet box he'd tucked into his overnight bag before fitting the bag carefully into a spot on the floor behind the driver's seat flitted through his mind. "Definitely thinking about it."

"Better get my goodbye kiss in before you do then." Chase shot him a mischievous grin before striding up the walkway.

"Do not even …" his friend had already reached Mikayla and flung his arms around her, "… think about it," Jax muttered.

"Goodbye, Mik. When you come to your senses and dump this guy, you have my number."

"I'll keep that in mind." The laughter in her voice sent warmth rushing through Jax's chest.

His former partner planted a kiss on Mikayla's cheek before taking the garment bag from her and carrying it to the car. He slipped the hangers over the hook in the back seat then closed the door.

Mikayla walked over to stand beside Jax, and he wrapped his arm around her waist. Chase stopped in front of them. "Seriously, man, I'm going to miss you." He held out his hand.

Jax clasped it. "I will miss you as well. Good luck with everything, *amigo mío*."

"You too." Chase dipped his head toward Mikayla. "Take care of each other."

She slid an arm around Jax. "We will."

Jax watched his friend as he strode along the sidewalk and climbed into his car. After he'd driven past them, Mikayla came around in front of him and rested her hands on his hips. "You okay?"

He tucked a strand of short blonde hair behind her ear. "Yeah, I am okay. Change is good but hard at the same time, no?"

"*Sí, es difícil.*"

Hearing his native language on her lips did something to him deep inside. Her pronunciation needed a little work and she often used the wrong words, but Jax loved that she was trying. He framed her face with his hands and leaned in for a kiss. Before his lips could touch hers, a burst of music stopped him.

A sheepish look crossed Mikayla's face. "Sorry. I left my ringer on because I asked Nicole to call me if Christina went into labor."

Jax lowered his hands. "Better get it then." Their friends Holden and Christina had lost a baby a year and a half ago and had struggled with a grief that had driven them apart. After months of processing their loss, they had finally found their way to each other and to a stronger faith in the God they both realized had not turned His back on them. Now they were expecting another child any day, and Jax could not be more thrilled for them.

"Okay, great. Thanks for letting us know. We're on our way." Mikayla's face had lit up as she talked to her twin sister. She hit the disconnect button on the phone. "Holden and Christina have gone to the hospital."

Jax retrieved the car keys from the front pocket of his jeans. "Let's go."

"I just need to grab my water bottle." Mikayla rounded the trunk of the car and reached for the handle of the door behind the driver's seat.

A movement down the street snagged Jax's attention. The silver car had pulled away from the curb and was accelerating toward them. His heart rate shifted into overdrive as the Matrix veered over to their side of the street. "Mik!" Jax lunged around the back of the car, grabbed her elbow, and yanked her behind his Porsche and out of the path of the oncoming vehicle. The Matrix roared past, close enough to the rear door, still hanging open, that it rocked a little on its hinges.

For a few seconds he and Mikayla stood in stunned silence, watching the vehicle until it had squealed around a corner and disappeared. Then she turned to him, her green eyes wide. "What just happened?"

"A couple of punk kids out for a joyride, I guess." He drew her into his arms. "Are you all right?"

She nodded, her head brushing against his burgundy T-shirt. "I'm fine. Thanks to you."

Jax held her a moment longer, until the violent thudding in his chest eased. If the headlights flashing hadn't been a warning, Mikayla nearly being run down definitely was. Who had issued the warning and what were they trying to tell him?

"We should get going." Mikayla stepped back.

Reluctantly, Jax let her go. Even if someone *had* been watching him, he was about to leave this town for good and they wouldn't have any idea where to find him. Whoever it was would have to find someone else to target.

Mikayla retrieved her water bottle from the back seat before stumbling around to the passenger side door, clearly still a little shaken from her close encounter. Jax's jaw clenched. If anything had happened to her, it wouldn't have mattered to him in the slightest how big those two guys were. He would have hunted them down and—

"Ready to go?" Mikayla's voice pulled him back to the present.

Jax shifted his attention to her. She'd swung open her door and was resting her arm on the top of it.

"Yeah, sorry. I would like to check my mailbox one last time. It will only take a minute."

She waved the water bottle through the air. "It's fine. Go."

Jax peered in the direction the Matrix had disappeared. Should he leave her alone? He stepped onto the sidewalk. Given the speed it had been traveling, the car had to be long gone. And the mailboxes for his building lined the wall inside the front door—he'd be able to see Mikayla the whole time. Plus, she had proven on more than one occasion that she was capable of taking care of herself. She would be fine. Still, uneasiness swirled through him as he jogged along the front walk to the entrance of the building.

He slid the tiny key into the box, yanked open the metal door, and grabbed the few items inside, likely all flyers and bills. He didn't take time to sort through the pile as he dropped the key into the superintendent's box and hurried out of the building. The street was quiet, and he took a deep breath as he made his way to the driver's side of the car.

Mikayla set her water bottle in the cup holder as he slid behind the wheel and stuck the key into the ignition. "Anything interesting?" She nodded at the pieces of mail he still clutched in his left hand.

Jax checked the rear-view mirror. The urge to leave the neighborhood gripped him, but he didn't want to alarm Mikayla any more than she already was. He sifted through the pile quickly. As he'd suspected, two bills, a pizza flyer, and a coupon for twenty-five percent off duct work. Nothing too … The final piece of mail snagged his attention. His brow furrowed as he tugged out a postcard with a picture of a brilliant sunset over the ocean, palm trees silhouetted against the orange, pink, and red sky. Who would send him a postcard? He searched his memory but couldn't come up with anyone he knew who might be vacationing in a tropical paradise right now.

Jax set the rest of the mail on the console and flipped over the card. He scanned the back of it, his chest tightening.

When he raised his gaze to meet Mikayla's, his heart pounded against his ribcage as wildly as it had when he'd pulled her out of the path of the silver car.

"It's from my brother."

Chapter Two

"Diego?" Mikayla stared at him. "What does it say?"

Jax flipped the postcard around to show her the back. "Nothing."

"Then how do you know it's from him?"

"Remember I told you the two of us once got lost in the woods for four days when we were Boy Scouts?"

She nodded. "What does that have to do with this postcard?"

He half-turned the card toward him and tapped the bottom with his finger. "See this?"

Mikayla leaned forward, squinting a little. "Is that a fish?"

The tiny creature had been scratched in black ink next to the description of the beach in the photo, so discretely most people wouldn't notice it. "Yeah. We survived that time in the woods by catching a rabbit and a few trout from a river. From that time on, when we wanted to send private messages to each other, Diego would sign his with a fish and I would sign mine with a rabbit. He called me that too, *conejito.* Little Rabbit."

Memories of that time breached the wall Jax had erected around his mind to keep from thinking of his older brother too much, of reliving the pain of his loss over and over. Despite the trauma they'd experienced when their parents split up and their father had kidnapped them and taken them to his native Puerto Rico for two years—or maybe because of it—the two of them had been inseparable during their growing up years. It had been the two of them against the world until they'd been returned to their mother in Canada, and Diego, already starting down the path toward alcoholism that their dad had led him along, had gotten deeper into drinking and dealing drugs.

Jax had heard increasingly terrifying stories about Diego's

activities and, to keep his brother from getting hurt or worse, Jax told their mother. She and Diego had fought, then Diego took off and they hadn't heard from him since.

Mikayla took the postcard and flipped it over. "It's from Venezuela. Do you think that's where he is?"

Jax turned the key in the ignition. "I doubt he'd make it that easy to find him, since he's obviously still trying to avoid detection." He slid the transmission into drive and pulled onto the street.

Mikayla held the card up as though an invisible message might appear if the sun shone through it. "Then why would he send it?"

"To inform me he is alive, maybe."

"That's good to know, right?"

"I suppose."

She frowned. "You don't sound too sure."

Jax expelled a long breath. "Of course I am glad to know he is alive. But if he is being so secretive, he must be in danger. Now it bothers me even more that I have no idea where he is. If I did, I might be able to help him."

"He clearly doesn't want to put you in danger too."

"I suppose not." After searching for Diego for so long, Jax would gladly risk his life to try and find him. Bring him home to their mother who still grieved her elder son's loss. He reached for Mikayla's hand. At least, he *would* have gladly taken any chance before he'd met her. Now he had a lot more to lose.

His thoughts whirled like the debris tossed in the hurricane winds that had decimated Puerto Rico a few years ago. Why had Diego contacted him now? And who had sent the card? Jax's name and address hadn't been written in his brother's handwriting, not unless it had changed in the last couple of decades. If someone else had sent it, who was it and how much did they know about Diego? Jax braked for a red light. The card hadn't been forwarded; it had been mailed directly to the apartment he'd lived in for only the last five years. How did Diego—or whoever had addressed the card—know where he lived? Or had, until today? Had his brother kept track of him?

Mikayla squeezed his fingers. “What are you thinking?”

“I am wondering what we should tell my mamá tomorrow when we see her. I think it would be best not to mention that Diego may have contacted me. Not until I have more information to give her.”

“You don’t want to get her hopes up.”

No, he didn’t. Not when he might not be any closer to discovering where his brother was than before he got the postcard. “Exactly.”

When she didn’t respond, he shot her a sideways glance. “What are *you* thinking, Grant?”

She smiled at the old nickname, but it didn’t quite reach her eyes. “I’m wondering how you’re going to get that information you mentioned. Any idea where to start?”

Jax let go of her and signaled to get on the ramp leading to the highway. “I will have to give that some thought. Although, I don’t think it is how I would go about gathering that information that you are worrying about, is it?”

She sighed. “All right, I guess what I’d really like to know is what you will do if you figure out where your brother might be.”

The ring in the bag behind his seat flashed across his mind. Before he’d seen the drawing of the fish on the back of the card, all he had wanted was to ask Mikayla to marry him, for the two of them to start their life together.

The postcard had changed everything. If his brother had taken a big chance by reaching out to him, then maybe he really was in danger and needed Jax’s help. If Jax could do a little research and somehow manage to pinpoint Diego’s location, he wouldn’t have a choice.

Jax reached for Mikayla’s hand again and held it tight. “If I think I know where he might be, then I will have to go and find him.”

Chapter Three

Mikayla stood in front of the vending machine, her brain unable to take in all the colorful selections on the other side of the glass. After a couple of minutes, someone plucked the two-dollar coin she'd been clutching between her finger and thumb and slid it into the slot. Jax stabbed a button. The ring twisted and a bag of chips dropped to the bottom of the machine. He scooped the change out of the slot and then bent to push the door open, grab the bag, and hold it out to her.

She smiled as she took it. "How did you know that was what I wanted?"

"Salt and vinegar chips are your thinking food."

That was true. Even after a year, it amazed her how well he could read her. How he so often seemed to know what she needed before she did. "How do you know I'm thinking about something?"

He ran a finger over the v grooved into the center of her forehead. "I can see it, here." He cupped her face with his hands. "You are worrying about me and Diego, no?"

"Not worrying. Just processing what it might mean, you getting that postcard from him."

"I don't want you to be concerned. It is unlikely I will be able to find him based on that card, but if I do, we will talk about what I should do next, okay?"

Her shoulders relaxed a little. "Okay."

"Good." Jax leaned in closer.

"She's here!" Their friend Holden's cry stopped Jax from kissing her.

His dark eyes met Mikayla's. "That baby has seriously bad timing."

She laughed as he let go of her. Grasping his hand, she tugged him along the hospital corridor. "Come on. Let's go meet this little one."

They joined Mikayla's brother-in-law and twin sister, Daniel and Nicole, in the waiting room. Holden's face glowed as he gestured for them to follow him. When they walked into the room, Christina was glowing too, her long, auburn hair flowing over her shoulders as she leaned against the pillows. She cradled a tiny bundle in her arms. Nicole headed straight for the two of them. Mikayla stopped at the bed rail, next to her sister. She and Nicole leaned over to peer at the sweet little one.

Christina smiled and tugged the blanket away from her daughter's face. "This is Ciana."

"Ciana." Nicole said the name softly as she touched a finger to the baby's cheek.

"It means *light*." Christina lifted the bundle a little. "Do you want to hold her?"

Nicole didn't wait to be asked twice. She took the baby in her arms and swung a little to the side so Mikayla could see her. Ciana. The name was perfect for the little doll with the pink cheeks and long, reddish lashes. This child was an answer to prayer—the light of morning that had followed a long, dark night for Holden and Christina.

After a moment, Nicole held her out. "Your turn, Kayla."

Nicole and Daniel's daughter, Elle, was seven months old, so both Nicole and Mikayla had experience holding a little one. Even so, as her twin set the precious bundle in Mikayla's arms, a thrill of joy shot through her. Every baby was unique and special and every birth cause for a celebration. And this birth seemed more special than most, poignant, even. Holding the bundle securely with one arm, Mikayla brushed a soft red curl from the baby's forehead.

She looked up, searching for Jax. He stood at the foot of the bed next to Holden, his eyes fixed on her. The expression on his face emptied all the air from Mikayla's lungs. For a moment she couldn't tear her gaze away. Then, her cheeks warm, she contemplated the little one in her arms again. Ciana waved a tiny hand in the air. Mikayla gazed at the fingers, the perfect little nails, the wrinkled red skin around the knuckles. When the little one yawned, her strawberry lips stretching wide, Mikayla's heart was lost.

She carried the baby to the foot of the bed and stopped in front of Jax. "Are you comfortable holding her?"

Something akin to panic flared in his eyes. Still, when he spoke, his voice oozed the self-confidence he was famous for. "Of course. I am excellent with babies."

"Really. When was the last time you held one?"

"Umm …"

"Have you ever?"

When would he have? Diego, his only sibling, had been gone from his life since he was seventeen and Jax was fourteen, so Jax had no nieces or nephews that he knew of. He and Mikayla had visited Daniel and Nicole occasionally, the weekends he'd driven to Toronto, but she couldn't remember him ever holding Elle. Obviously, it was way past time for this particular first.

"I don't think so. But how hard can it be? She cannot weigh more than five or six pounds."

"Six pounds, eight ounces, to be exact." Holden hovered on the far side of Jax, clearly not too sure about his daughter being the test subject for Jax's assertion that he was *excellent with babies*.

Jax bent his arm and Mikayla set Ciana carefully in the crook of it. Swaying slightly from side to side—how did he know to do that?—he gazed at the sleeping child. She understood now what had been in his eyes when she'd caught him watching her—a glimpse into the future the two of them might have if they got married and had children of their own. Assuming, of course, that he didn't end up going after his brother and walking into unknown peril.

The vision of their future faded a little around the edges. Jax nudged her gently in the arm with his elbow. When she forced herself to meet his eyes, they held a question. Clearly, he'd felt the chill that passed over her. She shook her head slightly. He didn't press her, although she knew he would, once they were alone. Letting go of something he believed was bothering her was not Jax's MO.

Holden gave Jax a minute before taking his new little daughter from him. Daniel peered in from Holden's other side and slapped his friend on the back. "Congratulations, man. I'm really happy for you and Christina."

"Thanks." Holden smiled but didn't take his eyes from the baby.

Jax's shirt was slightly wrinkled at the elbow from holding Ciana, and Mikayla rested her fingers there a few seconds, drawing comfort from the baby's lingering warmth. "We should go. Let Holden and Christina get some rest."

"We're going too." Nicole leaned over the rail and kissed Christina's forehead. "Good job, Mama," she murmured.

Christina's hazel eyes glistened as she smiled at her sister-in-law. "Thanks so much for coming."

"Of course. We had to see this little one. I'll call you tomorrow."

Christina nodded, her attention already snagged by her husband who was walking toward her holding their daughter close.

Mikayla followed Daniel and Jax to the door. Just before stepping into the hallway, she glanced back. Holden had settled on a chair pulled close to the side of the bed. As Mikayla watched, he slid an arm around Christina's shoulders and tugged her closer to press his lips to the side of her head. The tableau of the three of them burned into her brain, Mikayla turned away.

Jax grabbed her hand. "Exciting, no?"

"Very."

He tightened his hold on her fingers. "We will talk about it when we get to the car."

"Talk about what?" She attempted an innocent expression, although she'd never, not even in the early weeks after meeting him a year ago, fooled him with it.

He didn't bother replying, only leveled a look at her that confirmed he wasn't buying it. Mikayla repressed a sigh. Being involved with a man whose naturally intuitive nature was only heightened by his PI training could be a challenge. Especially when she was trying to hide something from him. Like her fear of never seeing him again if he went after Diego. A fear she thought she had dealt with after losing her adoptive parents in a car crash a couple of years ago. Apparently not. The thought of facing life without Jax was nearly crippling. *Father, give me peace and strength. Help me to remember what you have proven to me over and over—that even if I lose every person in the world I love, I will not be alone. You are always with me.*

The apprehension eased a little as peace trickled in.

Someone touched her arm and she smiled at her sister.

"Are you okay?" Nicole's eyes held the same concern as Jax's. Was Mikayla that easy to read?

"I'm fine. Tired. But so happy for Holden and Christina."

"So am I."

It was strange to see her sister without either of her kids. Mikayla's niece and nephew held a special place in her heart. Mikayla had been abducted from a park as a toddler and raised by people she believed were her parents. She'd only discovered she had a twin sister a year and a half ago and flown from Chicago to Toronto to meet Nicole and her son, Jordan. Shortly after they had reconnected, Jordan was kidnapped, and until Daniel, a police detective at the time, had rescued him from a cold-blooded killer, she'd thought she might never see Jordan again. Since then, she hadn't taken a moment with him or any of her family for granted.

When Elle was born a few months ago, Nicole had named her after Mikayla. At least, after the name Ella, which her birth parents had given her before her adoptive ones changed it. Elle Hunter Kelly Grey, meaning the little one not only shared a name with Mikayla but her and Nicole's surname at birth and Nicole's two married names. Sorrow and joy, loss and hope were all interwoven through the names of this young child. So, her niece was special to Mikayla as well. What would she do if anything happened to either…

Mikayla shook off the thought impatiently. God and Jax had

been working on her—encouraging her to let go of the past and trust them with her future—and she really was trying to do that. "Who's watching Jordan and Elle?"

"If he had his way, it would be Jordan. He tried very hard to convince me he was perfectly capable of baby-sitting his little sister, but I'm not quite ready for that yet."

Mikayla chuckled. While her nephew did often act far older than his eight years, it was likely a good choice for Nicole not to leave him alone with his seven-month-old sister. "Did Connie come over?" Connie and Joe, who had owned Nicole's diner before passing it along to her, had been surrogate parents to Nicole since she had started working for them after college, although Joe had passed away several years ago.

A shadow passed over her sister's features. "No. She hasn't been doing well lately. Definitely doesn't have the energy to keep up with Jordan, let alone a baby. We hired a sitter, Ashley McKenzie, from church." The shadows deepened. "Mom and Dad offered, but I'm not quite ready for that, either."

Mikayla got that. After she'd been abducted, their birth parents had traveled the world for their father's engineering job, essentially abandoning Nicole to the care of a string of nannies. They claimed they hadn't had a choice—that their dad's work had compelled them to go—but Nicole and Mikayla suspected that their inability to be around Nicole when she was a constant reminder of the identical twin they had lost was much closer to the truth. Their parents had been reaching out, tentatively, since Mikayla had returned to Toronto, even moving to the city to be closer to the girls. The four of them were civil to each other, but they had a long way to go in building any kind of relationship.

"I don't blame you."

"Speaking of which, we should probably get home. Ashley has school tomorrow, so I don't want to keep her up too late."

Rats. Mikayla had been hoping her sister might suggest the four of them go out for a late dinner or coffee, anything to delay the coming discussion with Jax. She peered at him. A slight amusement tempered the intensity in his eyes. Of course he'd figured out she'd been wishing for a reprieve. "Ready?" He tugged on her hand, guiding her along the hallway.

Ready for a talk that would no doubt lead to him ferreting out every doubt and anxiety she was wrestling with, much as she'd like to hide them from him? Not really. Mikayla trudged after him. Since he was clearly not offering her a choice, probably better to get it over with and pray that the peace she'd felt earlier would not dissipate as they discussed the possibility of Jax taking off and possibly disappearing into the unknown.

Just like his brother had done.

Chapter Four

Mikayla was scared. The trepidation in her eyes hurt something deep inside Jax. He hadn't seen that since he'd taken her to the do-over prom, under the stars, that he'd set up after she shared her horrific prom experience with him. Jax had asked her for more that night—more than those three weeks they'd had together, more than the friendship he already valued above any other in his life. And he'd watched the struggle play out, witnessed her fighting with the terror of letting herself love someone else she could lose like she had her parents. With God's help, she'd wrestled that terror into submission and peace had filled those beautiful green eyes. A peace that had rarely left them in the year since.

The postcard from his brother had jolted her, enough that Jax was tempted to rip it up and pretend he'd never received it.

Problem was, he couldn't. Not even for her. He'd searched too long for Diego, seen hope flare and then flicker and die out in his mother's eyes too many times, to walk away from this lead, meager as it was.

If it were up to him, Mikayla would never know a minute of fear or pain or hurt. It wasn't up to him, though. Not entirely. Although he'd do whatever he could to ease that fear as much as possible. Starting with getting her to talk about how she was feeling, even if that was not her strong suit.

Jax touched the small of Mikayla's back lightly as they exited the hospital into the parking lot. She knew how important this was to him and would never want to stand in his way or make him feel badly about whatever he chose to do. Still, it was her life too, and he had to make it clear that she did have a say in his decision.

When they reached his Porsche, Jax opened the passenger door and held it until Mikayla settled onto the seat. She talked almost non-stop on the way home—mostly about the baby and how perfect she was and how happy she was for Holden and Christina. Incessant talking was unusual for her, and although Jax loved the sound of her voice and shared her sentiments, he understood what she was doing.

The apartment building where she lived wasn't far from the hospital. Fifteen minutes after they'd left the maternity ward, Jax turned into the lot, found a parking spot, and switched off the engine. "I'll walk you to the door." Her building was situated in a rougher part of town. He didn't love her living there, but as Toronto was one of the most expensive cities in the country to live, he did get it. After they were married, they could move somewhere safer.

Jax reined in those thoughts as he pressed the button to release his seat belt. They were a ways away from being married, as much as the thought was on his mind these days. He climbed out of the car and rounded the hood as Mikayla stepped onto the pavement, her water bottle clutched in one hand. The sight of it reminded Jax of how close he'd come to losing her earlier that day. The heat that rose in his chest gave him a deeper understanding of how she felt about him leaving her to head into a potentially perilous situation. He reached for her hand as they walked between rows of parked cars in the dimly lit lot.

She said something as they approached the front doors that got lost in the muddle of thoughts whirling through his head. "I'm sorry, what?"

Mikayla let go of his hand and faced him, her back to the brick wall next to the double glass doors of her building. "I said I thought Ciana's red curls were the cutest thing I'd ever seen."

"I agree with you that she might be the most adorable baby ever born. And I could not be happier for Holden and Christina, after all they have been through. But Mik," Jax took a step closer, "what I really want to hear is how you are feeling about this situation with Diego."

"*Estoy, uh, por ti alegre. Verdaderamente.*"

As much as he appreciated her telling him she was happy for

him, her saying it in Spanish—even with the words out of order and the pronunciation of the final one butchered a little—caused him to lose his train of thought. Likely her intention. "I know what you are doing."

Her smile deepened. "*¿Qué?*"

She knew exactly what he meant. Jax pressed a hand to the brick wall on either side of her head. "Grant." He attempted to inject a warning tone into his voice, but the heightened amusement in her eyes suggested he hadn't been successful.

"*No estoy—*"

It had been a long, tumultuous day, and he only had so much willpower. Jax lowered his hands to slide his fingers into her hair and capture her mouth with his.

The faint aroma of her lilac shampoo drifted around him. The scent and feel and taste of her were so comforting that, after he ended the kiss, he pulled her into his arms and held her close.

After a couple of minutes, she rested her hands on his upper arms, her fingers warm on his skin beneath the sleeves of his T-shirt. "Okay, here's the thing. I really am happy for you." She wrinkled her nose. "Was that what I said?"

He grinned. "More or less. I knew what you meant."

"How do you say it?"

"*Estoy verdaderamente feliz por ti.*"

"One of these days I'm going to get it."

"You're doing great."

She lifted her shoulders. "It did throw me, you getting that postcard out of the blue after so many years. And it scares me a little, the thought of you going after Diego. After what happened with my parents, it would nearly kill me, losing another person that I ..."

He ran a thumb over her cheek. "Another person you what?" Mikayla was much more reserved than he was when it came to expressing her feelings. Jax had told her weeks ago that he loved her, but she hadn't said the words to him yet, one of the main reasons he hadn't asked her to marry him. He wasn't worried about it. Not much, anyway. Whether she intended to or not, she said a lot more with her eyes than she did with her words, so he knew how she felt about him. Still …

"That I love." Mikayla squeezed his arms. "*Te amo, Jax*."

If her speaking his native language to him hadn't completely swept him away, hearing her say, for the first time, that she loved him definitely did. He kissed her again. "Thank you for that. I love you too."

"I know." Her lower lip trembled slightly. "That's why it's so hard for me, the thought of anything happening to you." She reached for his hands and held them. "But I know how much it would mean to you and to your mamá, finding Diego, and I would never want to keep you from that. I was reminded today of the lesson I learned over the last couple of years of grieving for my mom and dad, that if the worst happened and the people I care about are taken away, I'll still never be alone. So, I want you to do whatever you need to do to find your brother. If I can help in any way, you only have to ask."

Jax searched her eyes. The apprehension he'd seen in them earlier had faded. "*Gracias, preciosa*." He pulled her to him again, cupping the back of her head when she rested it on his chest.

He held her until she yawned, and it struck him what a tiring day it had been. "You should get some sleep."

Her eyelids drooped as she gazed up at him. "You too. See you tomorrow?"

His mother had invited the two of them to lunch to celebrate his move to Toronto. "*Sí*. I will pick you up at eleven."

"*Buenas noches*." Mikayla pulled open the front door and entered her building. Jax contemplated her through the glass as she unlocked the inside door and stepped into the hallway leading to the elevator. When the heavy doors slid closed, he forced himself to turn and head for his car.

The minute he finished following this slim lead regarding Diego's whereabouts—no doubt to yet another dead end—he was going to propose to Mikayla.

The sooner they were married and he could stop having to watch her walk away from him, the better.

Chapter Five

"Mikayla!" Jax's mamá held out both hands as Mikayla walked into her condo. Mikayla grasped the warm fingers in hers and leaned forward as his mother kissed her on the cheek. "*Bienvenida.* Welcome."

"*Gracias, Risa.*" Using Spanish with Jax's mother, who had grown up in Puerto Rico, was intimidating, but Risa always tried to use her English with Mikayla, so Mikayla was determined to show her the same respect. The enticing aromas of meat, cheese, and spices swirled through the air, and she closed her eyes, breathing them in.

"*Hola, Mamá.*" Jax kissed his mother before closing the condo door.

"*Hola, hijo.*" Risa smiled at him before slipping her arm through Mikayla's and guiding her toward the living room. "Lunch is almost ready." She glanced over her shoulder. "Jax, why don't you set the table? I have something to show Mikayla."

Jax stopped in the doorway of the living room. "What do you have?"

"Just an old photo album."

"Um, I do not think Mikayla would be interested in seeing a bunch of ancient pictures."

His mother's laugh was gentle and teasing. *Risa* meant laughter, and the name suited her perfectly. As difficult as her life had been, the soft lines around her eyes suggested she had never lost her ability to smile. "I am thinking she will be very interested in these."

"Mamá."

She waved a hand in the direction of the dining room. "Table."

Jax exhaled loudly. "Fine. But none of me in the bathtub." He pointed a finger at his mother.

His mamá didn't answer, only offered him a *no promises* smile before she and Mikayla settled on the couch. A blue album, its cover worn along the edges as though she lifted it often to peruse the photos, sat on the coffee table. Risa reached for it and slid it onto her lap.

"Are these of Jax?"

"*Sí.* And Diego." Sadness flitted across her gentle face. Mikayla couldn't imagine how painful it must be to have no idea where your child was or what he was going through.

The first pictures were mostly of the two young brothers playing various sports. Soccer, of course. And baseball. And one of the two of them tossing a football with a man. Was that their dad? Mikayla bent closer. Juan Miguel senior was extremely handsome, with dark hair on the longer side, although not as long as Jax had kept his until recently, when he'd cut it short enough that he could no longer put it in a ponytail. Between Risa and their father, Mikayla could see where Jax got his looks. The two brothers strongly resembled each other, so no doubt Diego was equally attractive. If he was still alive.

The thought that he might not be filled her with an unexpected tinge of grief. Would Risa want to know if that were the case? Did the hope that one day she might see him again keep her going, or would it be easier for her and Jax to know the truth so they could find closure?

They flipped through several pages, Risa offering commentary. Mikayla smiled at the one of Diego and Jax in Boy Scout uniforms. Probably the year they'd gotten lost in the woods and Diego had told Jax nothing bad could happen if they were together.

Except bad things *had* happened to them, largely because of Diego's poor choices.

Risa turned another page, to a photo of Diego, Jax, and a third boy who appeared to be Diego's age, arms slung around each other's shoulders. Mikayla tapped the tip of her index finger on the photo. "Who is this?"

"His name is Ernesto Rivas. He and Diego were best friends. They were very good to Jax, let him tag around with them wherever they went. He idolized them both."

Mikayla studied the boy's face. Had he gone down the same path as Diego? "Where is Ernesto now?"

"I'm not sure. I lost touch with him after Diego …" she exhaled, "… after he left. Ernesto's grandfather owned an international real estate development firm that Ernesto's father ended up taking over. I assume Ernesto also went to work there, although I lost touch with the family when they moved home."

Diego's friend might have turned out all right then, if he had gotten involved in his family's company. Had Jax kept in touch with him? "Home?"

"Yes, they were from Caracas, and the firm was based there."

Caracas. It took Mikayla a minute, then her eyes widened. Caracas was the capital of Venezuela. If Diego hadn't sent that postcard himself, like Jax suspected, could his friend have sent it for him? And did that mean Ernesto knew where Diego was?

Her pulse pounded in her neck, and she kept her head low and her eyes focused on the page so Risa couldn't see Mikayla's reaction to that bit of information.

Jax wandered into the living room. "The table is set. Should we …"

When Mikayla met his eyes, his gaze had zeroed in on her. She shook her head slightly. Jax had been about to speak, but he closed his mouth before shifting his attention to his mother. "Shall we eat, Mamá?"

"Of course." Risa closed the album and returned it to the coffee table. "Please, sit at the table. I will get the food." She rose gracefully and crossed the living room to the kitchen.

Mikayla trailed after her. Jax stopped her in the doorway with a hand on her arm. "What is it?"

"I'll tell you on the way home."

He hesitated as though he didn't want to wait that long, but when his mother carried a platter of enchiladas to the table, he followed Mikayla to the dining room. Risa filled their plates. After handing Jax his, she waved a hand through the air. "*Buen provecho.*"

They both returned the traditional greeting—which Jax had told Mikayla was equivalent to the French *bon appetit*—before digging in. The food was delicious, and Risa kept them entertained with stories of the kids at the school where she worked as a special needs teacher. Although Jax sent Mikayla more than one furtive glance, the three of them spent a lot of time laughing and talking.

Two and a half hours flew by before Jax offered to help his mother with the clean-up. When they waved Mikayla out of the kitchen, she returned to the couch and flipped through the photo album again. She drank in every photo of Jax growing up, but her gaze returned to Ernesto over and over. Was it possible he was the key to Jax figuring out what had happened to his brother?

For a few brief seconds, she contemplated not telling him what Risa had said, but she shoved that thought away. *Enough.* She would not break her promise to help him discover what had happened to Diego.

It would be up to Jax to decide what to do with the information once she had given it to him.

Chapter Six

Jax waited until they were on their way to Mikayla's before he broached the subject. Although he'd been biting his tongue all during lunch, something had stopped him from pushing her to share whatever it was that had put that expression on her face when he'd walked into the living room earlier.

He knew her well enough to grasp that it was something big. Did it have to do with Diego? He couldn't imagine what else she might have seen in the photo album or that his mother might have told her that would have such an impact.

Jax steered the Porsche around the curve of the on-ramp and onto the highway before glancing over at her. "Are you going to tell me?"

He didn't need to specify what he meant. She shifted a little on the seat to face him. "When your mom and I were going through the pictures of you and Diego, I asked her about the boy who was in a lot of the pictures with you."

"Ernesto."

"Yes. She said he and Diego were best friends."

"They were. They did everything together. I am sure I drove them crazy, following them around, but they usually let me hang out with them."

"That's what she said. Have you kept in touch with him?"

"I talked to him a few times after Diego took off. For a while Ernesto kept tabs on him through mutual friends, but then his family moved away, and I didn't hear from him again."

"Do you remember where they moved to?"

He thought back. Did he? His family was involved with some big company, and they'd moved so his father could take it over from his grandfather. But where had they gone? South America, somewhere. He drew in a sharp breath. "Venezuela."

"That's right. Your mother said their company was headquartered in Caracas."

Hmm. Jax gripped the steering wheel. Was it possible that Ernesto had kept in touch with Diego? "Interesting."

"Would you have any idea how to contact him?"

"Did my mother mention the name of the company?"

"No. I didn't want her to get suspicious, so I didn't push her on it, but she did say it was an international real estate development firm."

"I can't see it being that hard to find. His last name is Rivas." He reached for her hand. "Thank you for telling me. It is a good lead."

"Of course. Your mother seemed really sad today when she was talking about Diego. I understand why you want to find him, for your sake and for hers. And I meant it when I said I would help any way I could."

"That means a lot to me." Thoughts spun through his head. As soon as he got home, he would do a little digging, find out the name of Ernesto's family's company. "No bathtub photos, I hope."

Mikayla laughed. "Sadly, no. A lot of you and Diego playing sports, and a great one of the two of you in your Boy Scout uniforms, which reminded me of the story you told of the two of you in the woods."

A pang shot through his chest at the memory of those four days with his older brother. Of the worry that quickly gave way to triumph as they foraged for food, set up shelter, found clean water to drink, and made a fire. He never would have believed, after the closeness the two of them had shared while lost and alone, they could ever find themselves here, with no idea where the other one was.

He pushed away the melancholy before it could overtake him. Mikayla's building loomed ahead, and he slowed to turn into her parking lot.

"You can drop me off at the door."

"Are you sure?" They had talked about doing something

together this afternoon, although they hadn't made firm plans.

"Yes." She picked up the bag she'd set on the floor. "We can hang out later this week. I know you're dying to get home and start researching how to contact Ernesto."

He couldn't deny that was true. And as much as he wanted to spend time with her, maybe it would be better to follow up on this new information so it wasn't taking up too much space in his head. He parked in front of her building. "Maybe you're right."

"Maybe?" Her smile was teasing.

"Okay, definitely." Jax slid a hand to the back of her head and pulled her toward him. "Which is not to say it's easy to let you go." He pressed his lips to hers.

When he straightened, she ran her fingers lightly across his cheek. "Let me know what you find out."

"Of course."

Mikayla pushed open the door. "Thanks for today. I enjoyed spending time with your mother."

"She is crazy about you."

"And I am crazy about her. She's a remarkable woman."

"Yes, she is. You both are. I am blessed to have the two of you in my life."

She leaned over the console and kissed him before climbing out of the car.

"Mik?"

She rested a hand on top of the door frame and ducked her head to peer into the vehicle. "Yes?"

"I want you to know that, if I never do find Diego, that is enough for me. You are more than enough."

Her smile was slightly shaky. "That's good to know."

Had she doubted that? Jax mentally kicked himself for ever making her feel that way. Another reason to rule out this latest lead and then move on with his life. Ask Mikayla to marry him and start making plans. Plans that did not include his long-lost brother.

Maybe twenty years of searching, of putting his life on hold for someone who clearly did not want to be found, was long enough.

Chapter Seven

Jax stared at the laptop screen. It had taken a little digging, but he'd found the website for Buena Tierra Trust, the Rivas family corporation. President and CEO, Ernesto Rivas. Well. Diego's friend had certainly done well for himself. Of course, it helped if your grandfather and father set up a wildly profitable company and then simply handed it to …

Jax snapped off that thought before it could take root. Ernesto's family had worked hard for everything they had. Ernesto likely did too. From what Jax could remember, Ernesto was a great guy. Even though he'd come from a lot of money while Jax and Diego lived with a single mother who struggled to earn every penny, he'd never made them feel inferior.

Was he still that same great guy? How would he react to Jax calling him out of the blue? Jax reached for his cell. Only one way to find out. The phone rang four times before a professional-sounding man picked up and said, in Spanish, "Buena Tierra Trust. How may I direct your call?"

"Could I speak with Ernesto Rivas, please?" Was it possible to simply call up the company and ask to speak to the president? Would there be protocols to follow? Safewalls to try and breach?

"May I ask who is calling?"

"Juan Miguel Rodríguez. I'm the brother of a friend of his, Diego Rodríguez."

"One moment, please."

Jax waited through several minutes of elevator music, tapping his fingernails on the desk with increasing force. Finally, a male voice, vaguely familiar, if deeper than he remembered, came over the line. "Jax?"

"Ernesto, hi. Yeah, it's me."

"Wow. It has been a long time. *¿Cómo estás?*"

"*Estoy bien, gracias.*"

"And your mamá?"

"She's fine too. The reason I'm calling is that I'm trying to locate Diego. I know the two of you are friends, and—"

"Let me stop you right there, Jax. Yes, Diego and I were friends. But I haven't seen him in years. I can't give you any information about him."

"Can't or won't?"

He waited through a pause on the other end of the line. When Ernesto finally spoke, his voice had lost all the lightness it had held earlier. "My advice to you is to let it go, Jax."

"Let it go? He's my brother. I need to—"

"What you need to do is listen to me. Let it go. Take care of yourself and your mother. It was good to hear from you."

The line went dead. Jax pulled the device away from his ear and stared at it in disbelief. *Are you kidding me?* He tossed the phone onto his desk and grabbed the back of his neck with one hand, using his fingers to work out the knots that had formed there. What kind of a response was that? If Ernesto had simply lost touch with Diego and truly had no idea where he was now, why wouldn't he say so? Instead, he'd issued what sounded an awful lot like a warning. Why?

He contemplated the phone. Should he call again? Given the firmness of Ernesto's response, he'd no doubt instructed whoever had answered the phone not to let Jax through. Still, he had to try. He snatched up the device and hit redial.

The same young male picked up. When Jax asked again to speak to Ernesto, the man hesitated, then said, "I am sorry. Señor Rivas is in a meeting and not available to speak to anyone."

"Let me guess. He is planning to be in meetings for the foreseeable future. Specifically, every time I call."

After another pause, the man said, "Señor Rivas is not available to speak to you. *Lo siento.*"

Jax bit back the angry words threatening to spill out of his mouth. It wasn't this man's fault that Ernesto refused to speak to Jax. Whoever this guy was, he was only doing his job. Which apparently didn't include even offering to give his boss a message. "I am sorry too."

He disconnected the call without bothering to wait for a response. Even if it wasn't the guy's fault, Jax's empathy didn't quite extend to ending the call pleasantly.

Now what?

He leaned back in his chair and kneaded the knots in his neck that had only grown tauter during the two short conversations. Clearly Ernesto was keeping something from him. But what?

Jax lowered his hand. It was useless to speculate. And to make any more attempts to reach Ernesto by phone. Even if he could convince the guardian of the phone line that he was someone else, someone safe to put through to the head of the company, it would be a waste of time. It was a whole lot easier to cut someone off on the phone than if they showed up in person and …

Jax straightened, his chair snapping into place. That was it. He needed to go to Caracas. Confront Ernesto either in his office or, if he couldn't get in the door, in the parking lot or at his home. Surely Diego's old friend wouldn't refuse to talk to Jax if he was standing in front of him.

Would he?

Jax pushed to his feet. He wouldn't give Ernesto that option. Not without doing everything in his power to find out what he knew about Diego.

And if that threw Jax directly into the path of danger, well, that was a chance he was going to have to take.

Chapter Eight

Mikayla peered out the windows of the CN Tower in downtown Toronto as they ate, catching glimpses of the changing skyline and Lake Ontario below. Whoever had thought of creating something like the 360 Restaurant that rotated slowly as patrons ate, offering a panoramic view of the city, was brilliant. The place was pricey but perfect for a special occasion.

And although it wasn't an anniversary for her and Jax, tonight felt like a special occasion. He hadn't made the official pronouncement yet, but she suspected he was working his way around to letting her know he was leaving. After he'd called to fill her in on the disastrous phone call with Ernesto Rivas a couple of days ago, frustration evident in his voice, Mikayla had reconciled herself to the fact that Jax wouldn't be able to let this go. He'd need to travel to Venezuela and confront Ernesto in person.

And, while he didn't need her permission to go, she had to give him her blessing.

She contemplated him as he speared the last piece of his steak with a fork and stuck it in his mouth. He'd been uncharacteristically quiet during dinner. Was he worried about sharing his plans? She'd made it clear she wouldn't object to him doing what he had to do, hadn't she?

Mikayla reflected on her initial reaction to the postcard and the thought of him possibly putting himself in an unsafe situation to help his brother. Maybe she hadn't. Not clear enough, anyway. She set her fork on the plate next to what was left of her Cornish game hen. Well, that was what tonight was about. Ensuring he knew that, whatever he decided, he had her full support.

Mikayla reached across the table and touched the side of her hand to his. "Want to tell me what you're thinking about?"

He tugged the burgundy linen napkin out from under his fork and unfolded it. After swiping it across his mouth, he tossed it onto the table. "Why don't we walk?"

She'd paid for the dinner package online, so she nodded and reached for her bag. "Should we check out the observation deck?"

"Absolutely." Jax took her hand, and they headed out of the restaurant and rode the elevator up to the observation level. After they'd walked around the circumference, gazing out at views across the city of Toronto as the sun trailed ribbons of pink and orange across the horizon over the lake, Jax nodded at a sign on the wall advertising the level below, the one with the glass floor. "Are you up for that?"

"I am if you are."

He grinned, the weight he'd been carrying throughout dinner appearing to slide off his shoulders. That ability to shake off whatever had temporarily brought him down was one of the first things she had noticed about Jax, and one of the things she admired—and envied—the most. "I accept your challenge." Tightening his hold on her fingers, Jax tugged her toward the stairs.

On the floor below, they stopped at the edge of the panes of glass built into the floor. A sign attached to the wall announced that, when it was first installed in 1994, the floor of glass was the first in the world. Now, apparently, they had become a feature at many of the world's natural and manmade sites, including the Grand Canyon. The one in the CN tower offered a view of Canada's largest city from eleven hundred feet above the ground.

Although Mikayla knew it had to be safe, it did ease her mind, reading about how the glass was tested every year and was five times stronger than it was required to be for weight-bearing floors.

"Can you do this?"

She tore her gaze from the plaque on the wall and met Jax's dark eyes. He was studying her intently, as though asking more than the words and their current situation suggested. Memories of all she had been through the last couple of years flashed through her mind. She had faced terrible loss and the spectre of being completely alone in the world. Except that she never had been alone. God had proven faithful. He had never left her, and He never would.

That truth—and the feel of Jax's strong, warm fingers wrapped around hers—drove away any remaining wisps of doubt. Even if she wasn't entirely sure what he was asking her, the answer was clear. "Yes."

They stepped together onto the glass floor. Mikayla stared at the cars and people that appeared little more than toys from this height. Instead of trepidation, exhilaration billowed through her. "Amazing." She breathed the word, unable to tear her gaze from the busy city streets lined with golden lights snaking between rows of towering office buildings. Viewing them from this height felt a little like flying, and for a few seconds the absurd urge to spread her arms like a bird gripped her.

When she looked up, Jax was still watching her. Mikayla swallowed. "Aren't you going to admire the view?"

"I am." His voice was low and husky. "It's breathtaking."

She glanced around. It was getting late, and most of the tourists had gone for the day. An older couple pointed out sights to each other through the glass fifteen or twenty feet away, but otherwise they were alone. Jax let go of her hand and stepped closer. "Mik." He rubbed a strand of her hair between two fingers, his knuckles brushing against her cheek.

When he didn't say any more, she nodded. "I know. You're going to Venezuela."

He exhaled. "I don't want to, but I feel like I need to go, talk to Ernesto in person."

"I get it. I think you should."

"You do?"

"Yes. This is the best lead on Diego you've had in a long time. You have to follow up on it or you won't be able to live with yourself."

"You are truly okay if I do this?"

"I mean, I don't want you to go away. And I really don't want you to put yourself at risk. But yes, I'm okay with you doing whatever you feel you have to do."

Jax leaned in and pressed his lips to hers. Then he wrapped his arms around her and pulled her close. "Thank you. That means more to me than I can tell you."

"I could go with you," she mumbled into his pale blue dress shirt.

"I appreciate you offering, but I think it would be better if I went alone. If you were there, I'd worry about you." He let her go and slid his hands along her jawline, framing her face. "And I'd definitely be distracted."

She smiled faintly. "If I'm not there, I'll worry about you."

His thumbs stroked her cheeks. "Don't. I'll be fine. This is what I do. And I promise I'll come back as quickly as possible." He contemplated her a moment, his dark eyes intense, until Mikayla drew in a shaky breath.

"I feel as though you are taking one last picture of me."

The corners of his mouth twitched. "I am taking a picture of you. But not the last one." He kissed her on the forehead. "I will see you again, I promise. Before you know it."

"When will you go?"

"Tomorrow, if I can get a flight. The sooner I go, the sooner I can come home."

Mikayla rested her head on his chest, and he wrapped his arms around her again. His heart beat strong and steady beneath her cheek. *This* was home to her. She closed her eyes. *Father, help me to let him go and trust you to take care of him.* Peace flowed through her, as strong as the panes of glass beneath their feet.

As piercing as the thought of anything happening to Jax might be, Mikayla trusted that God would go with him wherever he needed to go, and that whatever happened, He would not abandon either of them.

Chapter Nine

Jax stood on the sidewalk, staring up at the towering glass skyscraper. The headquarters of Buena Tierra Trust. He'd known that Ernesto's family had done well, but he hadn't fully grasped until this moment how well. It might not be as easy as Jax had thought to get to Ernesto if the CEO didn't want to see him. He tipped his head to gaze at the upper floors. How had the Rivas family managed to survive the virtual collapse of the country a few years ago? Clearly, they had not only survived but continued to thrive. Their international business must be strong.

Through the front doors, he could see one security guard standing inside the entrance, next to a metal detector. Jax wasn't worried about that. He didn't have a weapon on him, although he almost wished he did. Not that shooting his way inside would be a good idea—no doubt he'd be dead before he ever reached the elevators.

Another guard sat at a massive desk, behind a bulletproof shield. The one standing near the door had a sidearm strapped to his waist, and Jax could only assume the other man did as well. And they likely represented a team of security guards monitoring every floor throughout the massive structure. Were disturbances commonplace here? It certainly seemed as though the company was prepared for any eventuality, any person who might cause trouble.

Caracas did have a high crime rate. A lot of petty theft, but it also had the highest per capita murder rate in the world. Traffic flowed like a river behind Jax, the constant hum punctuated by the periodic beeping of car horns. Few vehicles stopped at red lights, and never for long, likely so drivers could avoid being robbed. Any police officers Jax had seen appeared not to notice when cars carried on into the intersection, narrowly avoiding collisions.

An interesting place to base a multi-million-dollar corporation. Although, when Ernesto's grandfather had started the company, Venezuela would have been one of the richest countries on the planet, thanks to their oil and gas industry. How it had gone from that position to having one of the worst economies in the world was mind-boggling.

Jax raked his fingers through his hair. What should he do? If he went inside and requested an audience with Ernesto and was refused, he'd tip his hand. Ernesto would know he was in the country and his guard would be up. Literally.

Jax couldn't have come all this way for nothing. Clearly Ernesto knew something about Diego. Now that Jax knew that, he couldn't simply walk away. He had to get that information. According to the clock tower in the large stone church across the street, one of many in the downtown area, it was 3:30 in the afternoon. When did Ernesto finish for the day, five? Or did the president of a huge company like that routinely work ten or twelve-hour days?

Likely the best thing for Jax to do was put in a bit of time, then return shortly before five and wait, hoping to catch Ernesto leaving the building. Confronting him face to face had to be his best shot at getting the guy to talk to him.

A warm breeze drifted past him, trailing the aroma of hot grease with it. Jax drew in a deep breath. His stomach rumbled in response. They hadn't offered food on the plane, so he hadn't eaten anything since the granola bar he'd grabbed on his way out the door to the airport, hours ago.

He scanned the area. A young man in a burgundy golf shirt and jeans sat on the edge of a fountain, clutching a cardboard container in one hand. As Jax watched, the man took a bite of something that resembled a taco. His gaze collided with Jax's over the food, and he nodded. Whatever he was eating, it smelled amazing.

Jax wandered over, stopping a few feet in front of the man. "*Hola.*"

"*Hola*." The guy nodded again.

"What is that you are eating?" Jax asked in Spanish.

The man cocked his head. "*No sos de aquí, ¿cierto?*" He popped the last bite into his mouth and swiped a napkin across his face.

No, Jax wasn't from here—was it that obvious? "How did you know?"

"If you were from here, you would know what a cachapa was."

Ah. A cachapa. The man was likely right, and he would have recognized the Venezuelan specialty if he was from the country. Jax had heard of cachapa but had never tried it. "Where can I get one?"

The man gathered up his garbage. "I will show you."

Jax hesitated. As much as he appreciated the offer, it wasn't smart for him to go off with a stranger, especially one who knew he wasn't a local.

The man gestured down the street. "The stand is right there. Lots of people around. And police." He held up both hands—one still clutching a crumpled napkin and grease-streaked paper—as though he got Jax's concern. "You will be safe."

Jax peered in the direction the guy had pointed. He could see at least three men in black, blue, and beige camo—*Policía Nacional Bolivariana* patches on their shirts and the yellow, blue, and red striped Venezuelan flag on the sleeves—standing around the square. It likely was reasonably safe to walk along the crowded sidewalk with this guy. His stomach growled again. That cachapa *had* smelled incredible. If he ended up leaving the country without seeing Ernesto, at least he could say he'd tried some of the food. "*Bueno. Gracias*."

The man stood, swiped crumbs off the front of his jeans, and started along the sidewalk. He tossed his garbage into the first can they passed. Jax fell into step next to him, the gaping hole in his abdomen growing in correlation to the aroma of frying food that intensified as they walked. The people they passed appeared as worn and weary as the graffiti-covered buildings. A little chipped and broken from years of battering and tumult, like the stone streets threading through the city. Still, something drew Jax to them. They were beautiful, strong and resilient like their country.

About fifty yards down the street, the guy stopped in front of an open stall. "*Hola, Fernando.*"

A wide grin crossed the face of the middle-aged man in a full-length white apron behind the counter. "*Hola, Rubén.*"

The two of them chatted for a moment before Rubén gestured to Jax. "*Una cachapa para mi amigo.*" He glanced over at Jax. "*¿Y una botella de agua?*"

Jax repressed a smile. His friend? He studied Rubén's open, friendly face. Yeah, okay. He could live with that. "*Sí. Por favor.*" Water would be good. It wasn't unbearably hot, but when the rays of sun broke through the low-hanging clouds, the air definitely grew warm. "Can I get something for you?"

"*No, gracias.*" Rubén smiled and patted his stomach.

Fernando piled toppings on something that looked a little like a large pancake, rolled it up, wrapped it in paper, and set it in a cardboard container to hand to Jax along with a bottle of water. The same amazing smell that had hung in the air when Rubén was eating filled Jax's nostrils, and he reached under his jacket and navy T-shirt to unzip the pouch where he kept his bank card and a bit of cash. "*¿Cuánto es?*" he asked. How much?

"*Seis dólares.*" Fernando held up six fingers then lowered them quickly, as though quoting the price in American dollars could get him in trouble.

When Jax had gone to the currency exchange that morning on his way to the airport and asked about getting Venezuelan Bolivars, the woman at the counter had shaken her head. "Just take American money," she'd advised him. "The Bolivar is pretty much useless—you'd need thousands or millions of them to buy anything. Most places in Caracas will take American dollars now, even if a few years ago they wouldn't have." Apparently, the woman had been correct.

Jax tugged a ten-dollar bill free and handed it to Fernando. The man rifled through the bills he carried in a bag tied tightly around his waist. Jax held up a hand. "*Déjeselo, amigo*." He didn't want the change. The fewer bills he carried around, the better.

"*Gracias*." Fernando flashed him a brilliant smile as Jax zipped up the pouch and tugged his shirt over it.

Jax held up the cardboard container and spoke in Spanish. "Thank you for this. It smells incredible." He scanned the area for the nearest place to sit and eat.

"There." Rubén gestured to a bench in the shade.

"Would you join me?" As Rubén was the first person Jax had talked to in the country, he wouldn't mind chatting with the man while he ate, maybe learning a bit more about Caracas as he contemplated his next steps.

Rubén hesitated before nodding. "*Sí*."

He and Jax strolled over to the bench. The wall beyond it was covered in a huge mural, as most of the walls and fences in the city seemed to be. This one was of a massive sun painted on a sky-blue background. The words *Convivir Para Vivir* were printed above the sun. *Living together to live*. Jax mulled that over as he settled on the bench. Was that how the people here survived? By following that mantra and helping each other through each day? Given how helpful Rubén had been and how friendly Fernando was, it was entirely likely.

Jax took a bite of the cachapa. When the tastes of pork, spices, and cheese exploded on his tongue, he nearly moaned in pleasure.

Rubén beamed. "*¿Esta buena, no?*"

Jax swallowed the bite. "*Muy buena*." Either he was hungrier than he'd thought, or it really was one of the best things he'd ever tasted. Mikayla would love it. Maybe someday he would bring her here. Jax had only arrived a few hours earlier and already Venezuela had captured his heart. The thought of sharing it with Mikayla warmed him even as it sent pangs through his chest. He missed her already. What a sap he had turned into. Jax smiled and took another bite of the cachapa.

Rubén chatted away to him in Spanish as Jax ate, telling him about the city and everything Jax should take in while he was there. After a few minutes, he shifted to face Jax. "What are you doing in Caracas?"

Jax washed down his last bite of lunch with a swig of water before wiping his mouth with the napkin. "I was hoping to meet with someone, but I don't know if he will see me."

"Someone from Buena Tierra?"

Jax stared at him. How did he know that?

His new *amigo* lifted a shoulder. "I saw you watching the building. You seemed very interested in it."

What harm was there in telling him who Jax was there to see? Maybe Rubén would have some advice for him. "I was hoping to meet with the president of the company, actually." He took another drink of water.

Rubén's dark eyebrows rose almost to his hairline. "Señor Rivas?"

Jax lowered the bottle to the bench. "You know him?"

"Everyone in Caracas knows him. His family, anyway." The smile he offered Jax was grim. "Good luck trying to see him if you do not have an appointment. The building has very tight security and his home is a fortress."

"You know where he lives?" Hope ignited inside Jax. Even as he'd studied the towering skyscraper, he'd known that it would be nearly impossible to get to Ernesto that way. No doubt the parking was underground and he rarely, if ever, emerged from the building. But if he could wait outside his home …

"*Sí.* I make deliveries to Señor Rivas sometimes."

"Deliveries?" Jax studied the guy. Like the contraband kind? Had Ernesto gone down the same path as Diego after all?

"Yes. Groceries, prescriptions, that kind of thing."

Ah. Jax nodded, his mind spinning. "Could you show me?"

Rubén shook his head. "No. I am sorry. If Señor Rivas knew I had taken you there, he would not be happy. He would no longer call me when he needed something. The Rivas family values its privacy above everything."

"I get it." Jax crumpled the napkin in his hand, trying not to let his disappointment and frustration show. Of course he wouldn't want to do anything to put his new friend's livelihood in jeopardy.

Still …

"Where are you from?"

Jax tossed the napkin into the empty cardboard tray. "Canada."

Rubén's face lit up. "Ah. Where the Toronto Blue Jays play, no?"

"That's right." Jax had forgotten how crazy they were about baseball in this country. "I live in Toronto, actually."

"*¿En serio?* Do you ever go to the games?"

"Sometimes, yes." He and Mikayla had taken her nephew, Jordan, to a game a couple of weeks ago, in fact.

Rubén sighed. "*Increíble.* Someday I would like to go to Canada."

"To live?"

"No, not to live. To visit. I would like someday to go to all the major league ball parks. Then I would come home." Sadness drifted across his features. "Many people have left Venezuela, it is true. But I cannot. I love my country. And my family is here. Even though life is not easy, especially in the last few years, I could not leave them."

"I get that. Family is the reason I am here too."

"How do you mean?"

"My brother, Diego, has been missing for twenty years. Ernesto Rivas was his best friend when they were growing up. I came here to see if he could give me information that might help me find him."

"You could not call Señor Rivas?"

"I tried, but he wouldn't talk to me. He made it sound as though it would be risky to keep searching for Diego. But he is my brother. I have to do everything I can to find him, to see if he is okay."

For a moment, Rubén didn't answer. Then he blew out a breath. "I have a brother too. Luis. After Luis Aparicio, my father's favorite ball player of all time. Two years ago, he moved to Spain. I have not seen him since."

Something twisted in Jax's chest. How many people walking

by them could tell the same story? "*Lo siento, amigo.*"

Rubén straightened as though he'd made a sudden decision. "All right. I will take you to Señor Rivas's home. Tonight, when it is dark. But you must promise not to tell him who showed you where he lived."

Excitement poured through Jax, although he did his best to keep it in check. Even if he did go to Ernesto's home, there was no guarantee he would be able to talk to him. But maybe. "I promise."

Rubén peered around, as though worried someone might have heard him make the offer. "Meet me here at 10 o'clock. And be very careful. Stay aware of what is going on around you. It is not a good idea to be out after dark, but I cannot take the chance of anyone seeing me."

"I understand. I will be careful."

"I have to go to work now." Rubén stood and took a step toward the street. "I will see you tonight."

"Yes." Jax touched his arm. "Thank you, my friend."

"You are welcome." When Rubén met his gaze, his face had gone completely serious. "I only hope that neither of us regrets it."

Jax watched him until he had disappeared into the crowd of pedestrians on the sidewalk. Then he stood and carried his garbage to a can a few feet away, under a palm tree. Rubén's last words hung in the air, and Jax pondered them as he started in the direction of his hotel. Whatever happened at Ernesto's house, Jax would not regret going.

If he didn't get the information he was searching for and had to give up his quest, at least he would be able to live with himself, knowing he had done everything he possibly could to find his brother.

Chapter Ten

Mikayla toyed with a sugar packet as she waited for the dinner crowd in Joe's Diner to die down so Nicole could join her. Jax had been gone less than a day, and already Mikayla missed him enough that, when she'd woken a few hours ago after painting most of the night, she'd decided she couldn't stand being in her apartment alone.

She glanced at her phone. Almost seven pm. His plane was supposed to have landed at the Simón Bolívar International Airport in Maiquetía, about twenty kilometers from Caracas, shortly before two. Had he found a way into the city? Jax had assured her the airport was the main mode of international travel into the country and he would be able to take public transportation from there into Caracas. Would it be that easy, though, with everything that had happened in the country in the last few years?

If he had managed to get to the city, had he found Ernesto's building? Had Diego's friend agreed to see him?

Mikayla tossed the sugar packet on the table and reached for the white ceramic mug of coffee Nicole had filled for her before going to give the people at a nearby table their bill. The rich scent of mocha calmed her a little. Jax was a big boy. He'd traveled extensively and knew how to take care of himself. He'd be fine.

Hopefully he would contact her as soon as he was able to pick up a disposable phone, let her know how everything was going. If he hit a dead end, maybe he'd even come home tonight.

A thrill shot through her. Once Jax either got answers or felt able to set his search for Diego aside, would they be free to talk about their future? Mikayla suspected the thought of the two of them getting married had crossed his mind, as it had hers, although they had never discussed the topic. Maybe when he got back from—

"Ready for a refill?"

Mikayla's head jerked. Her sister stood at the end of the table, a half-full pot of coffee clutched in one hand. "Oh. Sure." Mikayla slid the mug closer to her sister.

Nicole splashed steaming coffee into it, filled the empty mug at the place across from her, then set the pot on the table and slid onto the red leather bench. "You were a million miles away. Or a couple thousand, anyway." She grinned.

Warmth crept up Mikayla's neck. "Yeah. I guess I was."

"Have you heard from Jax?"

"Not yet. I'm sure he'll call later, let me know how it went with Ernesto."

"I'm praying he gets answers about his brother."

"Thanks. Me too. I—"

A phone buzzed. "Sorry." Nicole fumbled in her apron pocket and tugged out her device. "It's Connie. She wasn't feeling great last night, so I'd better get it."

"Of course." Mikayla wrapped her fingers around the mug as her twin hit the button.

"Connie? How are you … oh. Hi. Sorry, I thought …" She listened a moment then her gaze, swimming with alarm, met Mikayla's.

Connie's husband, Joe, had died before Mikayla reconnected with her sister, so she'd never met him, but from the sorrow in Nicole's voice whenever she talked about him, Mikayla knew she had never quite recovered from his loss. Had something happened to Connie?

"I'll be right there." Clutching the phone, Nicole slid to the end of the bench. "Sorry, Kayla. I have to go."

Alarmed by the way the color had drained from her sister's face, Mikayla grabbed her bag. "I'll come with you."

Nicole stopped briefly at the cash register and told the young woman behind it that she had to leave on a family emergency.

The woman reached across the counter to touch Nicole's elbow. "Of course, Nic, go. We'll be fine."

Mikayla followed her sister out the door and onto the busy Toronto sidewalk. "What's going on?"

"That was the hospital." A gust of wind swept down the street and Nicole swiped the hair from her face. "Connie's had some kind of a cardiac incident."

"Oh, Nic. I'm sorry. Here." Mikayla tugged the keys from the pocket of her jacket. "We can take my car." Nicole nodded and followed her to the blue Sonata Mikayla had parked at the curb half a block from the diner. They jumped in and Mikayla waited for a break in the heavy downtown traffic before pulling onto the street. "Did they say how she's doing?"

Nicole's knuckles had gone white around her phone. "No. They just said to come. It sounded urgent." She drew in a shuddering breath. "She hasn't been doing well for a while. I've been hoping and praying for a little more time." Her voice broke and she rested her head against the side window.

Mikayla veered around a cab double parked outside a towering bank building. "I'm so thankful you had her and Joe."

Her head still pressed to the glass, Nicole nodded. "Me too."

Mikayla's phone vibrated and her heart rate picked up. Jax. She scanned the Bluetooth screen set in the dash and her shoulders slumped. Their mother. "It's Marion. I'll let it go to voicemail."

"No, don't." Nicole waved her free hand at the screen. "She's been trying to call me too. We have to talk to her at some point."

"Are you sure?"

"Yes. At least see what she wants."

Mikayla hesitated then hit the connect button on the screen. "Hello?"

"Hi, Ell … er, honey. How are you doing?"

Mikayla gritted her teeth a little at the term of endearment. As far as she was concerned, her mother hadn't earned the right to that level of intimacy. Not yet. At least she hadn't called her Ella. Not quite. The first few months after Mikayla returned, both her parents insisted on calling her by her birth name on the rare occasions they spoke. She'd yet to hear either of them say *Mikayla.* She got it, but she had no connection to the name Ella, and their insistence on using it felt like a deliberate attempt on their part to wipe out the years she had been missing from their lives.

Denial. Their go-to reaction in any negative situation.

"I'm okay, but Connie isn't doing well. Nicole and I are on our way to the hospital right now."

"Oh, I'm sorry to hear that."

Mikayla shot a sideways look at her sister. That had sounded sincere. Since coming into their lives again, their mother had gotten her back up whenever Connie's or Joe's names were mentioned, as though she resented the older couple for taking the place in Nicole's life that she and their dad had abdicated.

Nicole had straightened but otherwise wasn't revealing how her mother's words were affecting her.

"Thanks. Nic's pretty worried."

"Of course she is. Am I on speaker?"

"Yes."

"Nicole? I'm terribly sorry to hear that Connie is ill. We'll be thinking about you both. And … praying."

Nicole's eyebrows rose. As far as Mikayla knew, her parents had never mentioned praying or anything else to do with faith. Was she only spouting words that were customary in a situation like this? Trying to soften up Nicole by acknowledging the faith they knew was such an integral part of her life?

"Thanks, Mom. I appreciate it." Nicole's voice trembled slightly.

"Please let us know how Connie is after you see her."

When Nicole didn't respond, Mikayla said, "We will. Thanks for calling," and hit the disconnect button.

They drove in silence for a couple of minutes, until Nicole shifted a little in her seat to face Mikayla. "That was weird."

"They do seem to be trying lately."

"I suppose." Nicole released her death-grip on her phone and set it in the cup holder between them.

"Too little, too late?"

"I don't know. I mean, I believe in redemption and second chances, and they do seem to feel remorse over their past choices, but I'm struggling to forgive them for leaving me on my own all those years."

"I don't blame you."

"But you don't agree."

"I didn't say that. You have every right to feel the way you feel. And I'm on your side, whatever you decide to do about them. It's just …"

"What?"

Mikayla kept her eyes on the busy street ahead of her. "I know what it's like to feel as though you have lots of time to work these things out and then, without warning, that time can suddenly run out."

"I know you do. And I get that. When Joe had his heart attack and died, all I could think about were the things I meant to say to him or that we were supposed to do together and put off. I would have given anything for even a few more days with him."

"Exactly." Those kinds of thoughts had consumed Mikayla for months after her parents' car crash. "I'd hate for you to have to live with those kinds of regrets."

"I don't want that either. And I know I'm supposed to forgive them, that God doesn't want me carrying around this bitterness and resentment. Still …"

"It's hard, I know. I feel that bitterness too, for how they treated you. I think all you can do is pray that God will give you the ability to forgive them since, humanly speaking, it's too hard." An empty parking spot caught her eye, and Mikayla touched the brakes. They were a few blocks from the hospital, but this was likely as close as they could get without having to pay for the expensive parking in the lot.

If something happened to Jax, would she regret anything she hadn't said to him? She shook her head slightly. Maybe she'd been a little slower about it than he had been, but she'd been honest with Jax. She'd opened herself up and told him how she felt about him, and she had encouraged him to do what he had to do to find Diego.

Mikayla eased her car into the space. Even if pursuing this lead on his brother's whereabouts ended up costing Jax, she wouldn't have done anything differently.

She had given him to God, and now all she could do was trust.

Chapter Eleven

Mikayla followed her sister to the cardiac floor. The sharp, clean scent of antiseptic accompanied them as they walked along the corridor leading to Connie's room. When they reached it, Nicole rapped lightly on the partly open door before walking in. Connie lay in the small bed, rails raised on both sides, pale and tiny against the white pillow and the sheet that covered her thin body. Although Mikayla hadn't known the older woman nearly as long as Nicole had, and they didn't have the same relationship, the IV running from the blue-veined hand to the bag and the quiet beeping of the machines hooked up to Connie's body still bothered her.

At least she was alive. Nicole might have a chance to talk to her if she regained consciousness. Mikayla should give the two of them a little time. "Nic, I'll go to the waiting room down the hall."

"No, don't go."

"Are you sure?"

Her sister nodded. "Yes. I want you here."

"All right." As she settled onto a teal plastic chair in the corner, Mikayla offered up a brief, silent prayer that Connie would wake up and be able to assure Nicole that she was okay.

Nicole stopped next to the bed and gripped the rail. The sorrow etched deep in her face made Mikayla's chest ache. If only there was something she could do to make this easier for her twin. The price of love was high, as Mikayla well knew. Still, love was worth it. She knew that too. Her months of darkness and pain after the death of her parents had taught her that. Despite what she had gone through, she wouldn't have traded a moment she'd had with them, not even to ease the grief of losing them.

The legs of a chair scraped across the cream-colored tile floor as Nicole dragged it closer to the bed. "Connie?"

The older woman stirred slightly before her eyes fluttered open. A faint smile creased her lined cheeks. "Nicole."

Nicole brushed a silver curl from Connie's forehead. "How are you feeling?"

"I'm fine, darling girl. Not quite my time yet." She touched the back of her free hand to Nicole's cheek. "Soon, though."

Mikayla clasped her fingers in her lap. Connie was likely right, and before many more weeks, maybe days, passed, she would leave them to join Jesus and Joe in heaven.

What would her loss do to Nicole? She contemplated her sister. Nicole would be okay. Her faith was strong, and if Mikayla knew anything, it was that God was faithful in the midst of grief. She doubted she would have made it through the incredibly dark days, weeks, and months following the sudden, shocking death of her parents if God hadn't been there, holding her close.

And He would be there for Nicole. So would Daniel, and Jordan and Elle, and Mikayla and Jax and Holden and Christina and all the other people in her life who loved Nicole. And she could cling to the truth that one day she would see Connie and Joe again.

Mikayla relaxed a little in her chair. She had that hope too, about her parents, and was incredibly thankful for it.

Nicole and Connie talked quietly until Connie's eyes drifted shut. A few minutes later, the announcement that visiting hours were ending crackled over the loudspeaker. Nicole placed the elderly woman's hand on the sheet reverently. "I guess we should go. Let her rest."

Mikayla slung the strap of her bag over her shoulder. She crossed the room and held the door open for her sister. "We can come back in the morning."

Nicole stepped into the hallway. "I'll bring the kids to see her."

"She'd like that." They walked to the elevators halfway down the corridor. After they'd stepped inside, Mikayla slid an arm around Nicole's shoulders. "Are you okay?"

"I am, actually. I've been preparing myself for a while for her to go. It's not easy, though."

"I know it's not."

When they walked out of the building, dusk had fallen over the city, and the streetlights and buildings had lit up. Mikayla gazed at a skyscraper whose top floors disappeared into a low bank of clouds. Only the odd star and a thin sliver of moon broke through the cover. Was Jax gazing at those same stars? The idea comforted her, made her feel connected to him even though he was two thousand miles away.

If Ernesto gave him information about where Diego might be, would Jax follow it, even if it took him around the globe? If he did, she wouldn't blame him. If Nicole was missing and Mikayla had information that might lead to her, nothing would keep her from going after her sister.

Someone brushed by Mikayla, shoving her a step backwards. Nicole whirled around. "Hey, watch it," she called after the guy's retreating back.

"It's fine. I'm sure it was an accident." Mikayla peered at the guy over her shoulder. A half a block behind them, he pointed something at a silver car parked at the curb. The lights blinked on and he pulled open the driver's door. One hand on the top of the frame, he glanced at Mikayla and their eyes met. A cold smile crossed the man's face, and he offered her a mock salute before sliding behind the wheel. Shivers tingled along her spine.

Had he bumped into her on purpose? Given his bizarre behavior, the jostling now felt threatening. Her gaze shifted to the license plate, but the guy had parked a distance from a streetlamp, and in the murky half-darkness, exacerbated by the light fog drifting on the air, she couldn't make out any numbers or letters.

The driver merged with the downtown traffic. As he passed beneath a light, she tried again to see his license plate, but could only catch a few letters—A, C, R. Was that enough to pass along to Daniel, see if he could identify the owner? Likely not. And the man had done little more than give her a creepy feeling, nothing they could put him behind bars for.

Now that the vehicle was closer, she could see there was a second man in the car, sitting in the passenger seat. When they drew even with Mikayla and Nicole, the driver slowed the vehicle, although he kept his focus on the road ahead. She tried to catch a glimpse of the license plate on the back of the vehicle when it crawled by, but something had been smeared across it and she could only make out the A and the R.

Nicole grasped Mikayla's elbow. "What's wrong?"

Mikayla opened her mouth to reply, to ask her sister if she'd seen the same thing Mikayla had, then closed her mouth without speaking. Her sister had enough to deal with right now. Likely that guy had only smiled at her as an apology for shoving her earlier. Although it hadn't felt like an apology.

The vehicle turned right at the next corner and disappeared. A little of the tension eased from her shoulders. "Nothing. I was just thinking about Jax." She started along the sidewalk again, shivers crawling over her skin like ants on spilled sugar.

Nicole fell into step beside her. "Of course you were." Her voice was teasing, and more of Mikayla's angst dissipated in the night air.

"Are you two going to get married or what?"

Mikayla's cheeks warmed. "We haven't talked about it."

"You should." They reached a corner and stopped at the orange *don't walk* hand flashing in front of them.

Maybe they should. A verse from Exodus that her adopted mother had quoted her often—even given Mikayla a key chain with the words printed on it when she got her driver's license—drifted through her mind now. "The Lord will fight for you; you need only to be still." As it always did, the promise trailed peace along with it like the glowing tail of a comet.

Although it also dragged a question into her mind.

What battle, exactly, lay ahead of her, and what would she face when she found herself in the thick of it?

Chapter Twelve

Dampness seeped through Jax's light jacket. A breeze swooped through the square, sending a paper cup tumbling end over end across the empty pavement in front of him. Jax sat, his back to a low stone wall, watching the cup until it caught on a grate. For a large city, one beaten down by economic hardship, whoever was charged with keeping the streets of Caracas clean did a remarkably good job. Very little garbage littered the sidewalks. Even the graffiti was, for the most part, tasteful and artistic, adding to rather than detracting from the charm of the city.

A group of five or six people, older teenagers maybe, appeared at a corner a block from him, coming off a side street. Jax held his breath, but they turned and ambled in the opposite direction. A police car drove by slowly. Could its occupants see him? If they did, they must have figured he wasn't anyone to be concerned about, as the vehicle continued along the street. Only a couple of people had walked past the spot where Jax sat on the hard cement, mostly hidden in shadow. No one looked in his direction.

Everything in him wanted to reach into his shirt pocket and snatch the burner phone he'd picked up after arriving in Caracas and call Mikayla. She'd manage to get it out of him what he was up to, though, and he didn't want to worry her. He'd call her when he returned to his hotel room, let her know what he'd found out from Ernesto.

If anything.

From a few blocks away, a siren disturbed the unnatural stillness of the city. Jax tried to imagine Toronto ever being this quiet and couldn't. Clearly the locals knew enough to stay inside after dark. Likely he should have as well.

Another breeze drifted by him, slightly cooler now that the sun had set over Venezuela. Jax slid up the zipper on his jacket and peered at the lit-up clock tower on the corner. 10:15. Had Rubén chickened out? Although Jax would be disappointed, he wouldn't blame the guy. Jobs were precious here, and he'd never want to be the cause of Rubén losing his and maybe bringing suffering to his family. The thought sickened Jax. He was the one who should chicken out, not ask a stranger to take such an enormous risk. Even asking him to travel around the city after dark was too much. If Rubén didn't show up in five minutes, Jax would go, not put the man in any further peril.

The seconds ticked by as he sat, peering into the dark alleyways or the shadows beneath the rare downtown tree for any movement. Not only because he was searching for Rubén, but because he was deeply aware of how vulnerable he was out here, alone and unarmed. Something moved in the shadows next to a building, and he straightened. Rubén stepped into the glow of a streetlamp, and Jax's shoulders relaxed slightly. He pushed to his feet and met his new friend halfway across the square.

Rubén stopped in front of Jax. "*Disculpas por llegar tarde.*"

Jax waved a hand. "*No te preocupes.*" Rubén certainly didn't owe him an apology for not showing up on time; Jax was just relieved he had shown up at all. Lines grooved into the man's forehead showed a little strain, but he didn't appear frightened, only cautious. "Are you still okay to do this?"

Rubén pushed back his shoulders. "*Sí.*"

"*Bueno.*" The lingering aroma of spices from the market and food trucks hanging in the air from earlier in the day drifted up Jax's nose. "*¿Vamos?*"

Rubén jerked his head toward a side street. "*Vamos.*"

Jax nodded and followed Rubén. *Yes. Let's go.* The sooner they got to Ernesto's, the sooner Jax might be able to get information that could lead him to his brother.

He half-jogged to keep up with Rubén as the young man led him along numerous streets, so many that Jax was soon lost. Was he trying to confuse Jax? To throw anyone who might be following them off their trail? If Rubén abandoned him, Jax would have to call a cab to return to his hotel, and he had no idea how safe it was to take one of those this late at night.

Without warning, Rubén grabbed Jax's elbow and hauled him into a dark alleyway.

His heart rate rocketed. "What—"

Rubén let go of him and held a finger to his lips. Jax clamped his mouth shut. Rubén jerked his head toward a dumpster halfway down the alleyway and the two of them crept toward it. They'd barely ducked behind the metal bin when the sound of voices shattered the stillness.

Several men, clearly angry, argued in Spanish at the opening between the two buildings. When the sound of a fist smacking flesh assaulted his ears, followed by a cry of pain, Jax tensed. Should they do something?

Rubén grabbed his arm again and shook his head vehemently.

The pungent smell of garbage drifted on the air. Jax shifted slightly to get more comfortable, and a paper takeout bag crumpled beneath his running shoe. He froze, but the raised voices drowned out the noise. Even so, in the near darkness, he caught Rubén's glower. The scuffle intensified. Another cry split the night and Jax pressed a damp palm to the dumpster, prepared to leave their hiding place and head into the alley if it sounded as though someone might be getting seriously injured.

Rubén tugged him closer, his fingers digging into Jax's elbow. "If you go out there, I will leave and you will be on your own," he hissed in Spanish.

Jax tugged his arm from Rubén's grasp, nodded curtly, and lowered his hand to a tight fist at his side. Unless he was convinced someone's life hung in the balance, he'd wait it out.

After what felt like forever, the scuffling stopped, and the voices gradually died away. Rubén peered around the edge of the dumpster. "*Ya se fueron.*"

Jax released a breath. The men, whoever they were, had gone. He followed Rubén to the opening. A few dark patches on the cement tightened his chest, but no one lay in the alley. Whoever had been on the receiving end of the blows had clearly survived. Or been carried away.

They didn't pass anyone else, and after twenty minutes of traversing through a maze of Caracas streets lined with houses that grew farther and farther apart, Rubén skidded to a halt. "There." He jutted his chin to their right. Jax studied the property he'd indicated. A tall stone wall stretched along the edge of the street for the length of a city block, two strings of barbed wire attached to the top of it.

A metal gate, wide enough for a large vehicle but not by much, was set into the stone wall ten feet from where Jax stood. He took a step toward it, but Rubén clapped him on the shoulder. "What are you doing?"

"I need to get inside."

"You think they will open the gates and welcome you in?"

Jax contemplated the barbed wire at the top of the wall. Yep, the gates seemed like the best bet. "I have to try."

Rubén's fingers slid from his shoulder. "I must go. I cannot afford to be seen here."

Repressing a wince at the thought of trying to find his hotel in the middle of the night without a guide, Jax nodded. "*Entiendo*. I understand." He stuck out a hand. "*Gracias, mi amigo*."

Rubén clutched Jax's fingers briefly before spinning around and striding away. Jax watched him until he disappeared into the night. He was on his own.

He sidled along the stone wall until he reached the metal gates. His back pressed to the stone pillar on one side of the opening, he peered cautiously around the edge. Ernesto's home was set about fifteen yards back from the street. The massive lawn was dotted with trees and light poured from nearly every window onto the neatly manicured flowerbeds below.

A large black SUV was parked in front of a four-car garage set on an angle to the right of the house. Nothing moved in the yard or circular driveway. If Jax could get through the gates, he might be able to make it to the front door and ring the bell before anyone stopped him.

Abandoning caution, he strode to where the two heavy gates

met, grasped a bar on either side of the opening, and tugged. Although he had known they wouldn't, he was disappointed when the gates didn't budge. That would have been too easy. He scrutinized the far post. A security pad reminiscent of something out of *The Matrix* was mounted there. No doubt it would take a fingerprint and possibly an ocular scan to get the massive barriers to swing open.

Jax eyed the barbed wire on top of the wall again. If he managed to climb over it, he'd have to drop the ten or so feet to the grass below and—

Something dug into his spine and he froze.

"Hands where I can see them." The Spanish words were as hard and cold as the object digging into his back. Clearly the man behind him would brook no arguments.

Jax held up his hands. "I need to speak with Señor Rivas."

"What you need is to keep your mouth shut." That was a different voice. Two men, then. At least. No sense trying to overpower them. "Turn around. Slowly."

Jax complied. "*Por favor*. I …"

The man holding the gun on him cocked it. Jax closed his mouth. Both men were huge, well over six feet, and dressed completely in black. Ernesto must offer a gym membership in his benefits package, a benefit the two standing before him clearly took full advantage of. The second man hadn't pulled his gun out of the holster strapped to his chest. Not yet, anyway. Instead, he held a walkie talkie to his mouth as he strode to the panel on the stone pillar. After pressing his thumb to the pad, he leaned closer to the screen. An ocular scan, as Jax had suspected. When the guard straightened, he issued orders into the walkie talkie, speaking too low and too close to the device for Jax to make out what he was saying. The gates slowly swung inward. The black SUV in front of the garage roared to life. The driver wheeled it around and drove for the opening.

Jax's heart sank. Were they planning to take him somewhere? If so, it was likely to be a one-way trip. What was one more suspected intruder dumped in an alleyway in the middle of a city with one of the highest murder rates in the world?

Through the open gates, he scrutinized the house. Someone stood in front of one of the windows, peering out.

Was that Ernesto? Would he hear Jax if he called out? Probably not, between the distance and the closed window. The likelihood was too low to take the chance, anyway. Given the efficiency with which the men in black were carrying out the process of removing Jax from the premises, they likely dealt with trespassers on a regular basis and knew exactly how to dispense with them. Jax might not get out more than a word or two before the man with the gun used it to shut him up.

A movement caught his eye. Jax squinted. Framed in light, the man's features gradually came into focus. Not the boy of his memories, but the man whose face graced the Buena Tierra Trust website. Ernesto had raised something to his mouth. Words rose from the walkie talkie in the hand of the man by the security panel, too staticky for Jax to discern. Still, hope flickered. The guard was communicating with Ernesto. When the big man pressed the button on the side and held it to his mouth, Jax knew this was his one chance to reach Diego's former friend. The only opportunity he might be given to save his own life.

Before the guard could speak, Jax called out, "Ernesto. It's Jax."

The SUV screeched to a stop next to him. The driver jumped out, rounded the front of the vehicle, and grabbed Jax's arm.

"Get him in," the man with the gun yelled.

The one holding the walkie talkie strode over and grasped Jax's other arm, and the two of them hauled him toward the SUV. The gunman transferred the weapon to his left hand so he could yank open the back door. Jax shot another look in the direction of the house. Ernesto still stood in the window, his head lowered, the walkie talkie pressed to his forehead. Had he heard Jax over the static and the sound of the approaching vehicle? If so, he didn't appear to be making any attempt to do anything about it.

One of the men forced Jax's head down before they shoved him onto the back seat. Right before the door slammed behind him, Jax caught the curt command that came through the walkie talkie.

"Wait."

Chapter Thirteen

"You can leave us."

The man who'd held the gun on Jax tilted his head. "*¿Está seguro, Señor Rivas?*"

Ernesto's dark eyes met Jax's. "*Sí.* I am sure. He is a friend."

The other two guards still clutched Jax's arms, but when the first man nodded at them, they let him go. The three of them headed for the door leading out of the living room.

"Wait in the hall."

Jax frowned. Was Ernesto keeping his options open? Would he have Jax hauled away somewhere if he refused to leave without getting what he'd come for? Because that was Jax's plan.

The last man out of the room pulled the French doors closed.

Ernesto's gaze hadn't left Jax's. When he spoke in Spanish, his voice was as cool as his nearly black eyes were heated. "I thought I made it perfectly clear to you on the phone that I had no information about Diego."

Jax's arms throbbed where the two men had gripped him, and he barely resisted the urge to rub them. "That wasn't exactly what you said."

"No? Then what did I say? Exactly."

"You said that you *couldn't* give me information about my brother, not that you didn't have any."

"Semantics."

"There's quite a difference."

Ernesto stared at him a moment before shaking his head. "Same old Jax. I never could win an argument with you, even when you were a kid." His features softened slightly as he held out a hand toward two armchairs facing the crackling fire in the stone fireplace at the far end of the room. "Since you've come all this way, might as well sit." He started toward the chairs but stopped at a wheeled cart that held a tray filled with various bottles of liquor. "Scotch? Brandy?"

"*No, gracias.* Although I'd love some water." Jax hadn't had a drink since he'd left his hotel room, and he was parched. He walked across the thick Oriental rug toward the fireplace. Between the rich furnishings and warm glow from the fire and the sconces mounted along the walls, the room felt like a sanctuary. Even so, the tension humming between him and the owner of the house undermined any sense that Jax had found refuge here.

Ernesto poured himself a drink then filled a water glass from a crystal pitcher and carried both drinks over. He set them on silver coasters on the round table between their two chairs. "You never did share your brother's vices, did you?"

Jax rested one elbow on the plush arm of the chair and reached for his glass. "I have my own, believe me."

Ernesto lowered himself onto the other armchair. "Considerably less destructive than Diego's were, I'll bet."

"Were?" Jax pulled back his hand without grasping the glass.

"Were. Are. I don't know." Ernesto lifted his drink, the amber liquid sloshing around in the glass as he did. The movement pulled his jacket tight across the left side of his chest, revealing a bulge. He was carrying? Did he seriously consider Jax's unexpected appearance at his home that much of a threat? Why?

Jax shook away the questions so he could focus on trying to get what he had come for. "What *do* you know?"

Ernesto set the glass on the table with a thud. "First things first. Tell me how your mamá is."

Jax gritted his teeth. As far as he was concerned, finding out about where Diego might be *was* the first thing. Ernesto was calling the shots here, though. Quite literally, if he had changed enough to order his men to take Jax out and kill him if Jax pressed him too hard. "Physically, she is fine. She is a very strong woman, but she still grieves for Diego. I see it in her eyes every day. Which is why …"

Ernesto held up a hand. "In time, Jax." The flickering firelight reflected in his eyes. "When you called me at the office, hearing your voice reminded me of when we were younger. You were determined to come with Diego and me, whatever we were doing. Nothing could ever put you off. I see you have not changed so much."

Was that what this was, payback for being a pesky kid? "*Perdóname*. Forgive me if I bothered you back then."

"That is the thing; you didn't. I mean, by the time we were teenagers, we had to act as though we didn't want you tagging along after us. The truth is," Ernesto leaned forward and clasped his hands between his knees, "we did. You were the best of us, Jax. When you were around, Diego wanted to be better. He tried to be. I was always thankful that he had you in his life even if, in the end, all that did was delay the inevitable." He straightened and reached for his glass again. "Addiction is a terrible thing. It is bondage, pure and simple. I know you tried to help him. I did, too. In the end, though, no one could have helped Diego except Diego. And God."

God. If only Jax had known then what he knew now about God and what it meant to be in a relationship with Him. Maybe he could have shared that with Diego, and everything might have been different.

"It was not your fault, Jax. I promise you there was nothing you could have done to save him."

Jax had always blamed himself for not being able to help his brother. Was it possible he couldn't have done anything more? Could he lay down this terrible burden he'd carried for twenty years? "I appreciate you saying that."

"I mean it." Ernesto took a sip from his glass.

A knock sounded on the French door and both men swiveled toward it. Ernesto set the glass on the table. "¿Sí?"

A soft voice answered, "*Soy yo, Ernesto*."

His face lit up. "*Es mi esposa, Camila*."

His wife. Somehow Jax hadn't considered the possibility that Ernesto might be married, have a family.

Ernesto rose, slid a hand beneath his jacket to tug the weapon out of the chest holster, and shoved the pistol into a drawer in the drink cart before continuing toward the door. "*Pasa, mi amor.*"

Jax stood too. As happy as he was to meet Ernesto's family, the desperate need to find out about Diego gripped Jax. He forced himself to tamp down his impatience and smile as the door opened and a tall, slim woman with short dark hair stepped gracefully into the room. Ernesto took her hand and pulled her closer to kiss her on the cheek. "*Lo siento.*" He reached past her with his free hand to push the door closed. "I had an unexpected guest and didn't tell you because I thought you were asleep."

"No, not yet," she answered in gentle, lilting Spanish. "I was waiting for you and, when you did not appear, I decided to come in search of you."

Ernesto tucked her hand into the crook of his arm and led her toward the fireplace. "Camila. This is Juan Miguel Rodríguez. Jax. Diego's younger brother."

"Ah. Diego." She smiled, but Jax didn't miss the slight shadow that passed over her face. "It is a pleasure to meet you, Jax."

"It is a pleasure to meet you as well. I did not realize Ernesto was married."

She laughed lightly as she rested her fingers on her husband's chest. "You mean I was not the first thing he mentioned as soon as you walked through the door?"

Ernesto captured her hand in his and pressed it to his mouth.

It would be more accurate to say Jax had been shoved through the door by two of Ernesto's hired guns than that he'd simply walked into the house on his own, but Jax kept that to himself. "No, although we have not been talking long. I haven't yet had a chance to ask him about his personal life."

"Then I will leave the two of you to catch up." Camila slid her hand from Ernesto's arm. "It is good to have you here, Jax. You are welcome to stay as long as you like. Diego's family is our family."

"*Gracias.*" Her words moved Jax deeply. Then the shadow he'd seen wasn't anger or resentment toward Diego. What had it been, sadness? Why? Did she know something he didn't? His fingers curled into fists at his sides. It was beginning to feel as though, when it came to his brother, everyone knew something he didn't. Weren't he and his mamá the ones who should know the most?

Hopefully, in the next few minutes, Ernesto would share something with him that would help. Clearly, he would only do so in his own time. Like it or not, Jax needed to respect that and be patient.

Ernesto watched his wife until she had crossed the room and disappeared out the door. Only after it closed behind her did he turn to Jax and hold out a hand, inviting him to sit again.

Jax settled on the plush navy chair. "Your wife is lovely, Ernesto."

A warm smile crossed the man's face. "Yes, she is. And we have twin eight-year-old girls, Marisa and Viviana, equally lovely."

"How does she know Diego?"

"He came here once, several years ago. Stayed a few days. He and Camila hit it off immediately."

"So he seemed …?"

"Stable? Yes, actually. He appeared to be doing fairly well. As you know, though, with addicts that can change in a moment. I tried to talk him into staying in Venezuela, but he said he couldn't." Ernesto reached for his drink. "I should have tried harder to convince him. Maybe if I had …" He stared into the contents of the glass. "Who knows what might have happened?"

What did that mean? What *had* happened? Jax clenched his jaw until it ached, trying to stem the flood of questions.

Ernesto looked up. "How about you, are you married?"

"No, but I started seeing an incredible woman, Mikayla, a year ago, and I am thinking about proposing."

"If she is a good woman, then do it. Married life is truly a gift." His gaze drifted to the door. "My family is far more than I deserve."

"I doubt that is true. You have always been someone I

admired, an incredibly loyal friend to my brother."

Ernesto's smile faded. "Diego was an amazing person. The alcohol, the drugs, those were not him. They were thieves, stealing him from us one bottle, one hit, at a time."

Was. Jax's stomach tightened. "That is the second time you have referred to him in the past tense. What do you know, Ernesto? Tell me. Please."

Ernesto's shoulders slumped. "You will not like it."

"Anything is better than knowing nothing."

"Maybe you are right." Ernesto rested the glass on the arm of his chair. "All right. Here is what I do know. When he stopped by here, Diego was on his way from Canada to Puerto Rico."

Puerto Rico. That made sense. Diego had been born there, like their parents had been, and he and Jax had lived there for a couple of years when they were pre-teens. Because of that, the country had been on Jax's radar the entire time he'd been looking for Diego. "I've considered searching for him in Puerto Rico, put out a few feelers, even went there a couple of times, but I never got the slightest hint that he was there."

"No, you wouldn't have."

"Why not?"

Ernesto ran a finger around the top of the glass. "I don't know who or what Diego got involved with there, more drug-dealing maybe. From the little I could gather the rare times he did get in touch with me, it was something extremely dangerous. Then, about three years ago …"

"What?" Jax gripped the arms of the chair, bracing himself.

"All communication with him abruptly stopped. I made a few calls, got in touch with a mutual friend in Puerto Rico with whom I have dealings occasionally." Ernesto swiped away a bead of sweat that had started down one temple. "I don't know anything for sure, only that I have heard rumors that Diego …" He met Jax's gaze. "That he is dead."

Although Jax had long known that was a strong possibility, hearing the words out loud struck him hard, and he closed his eyes and bent forward slightly to ease a sudden pain in his midsection.

The warmth of the fire couldn't touch the cold that spread all through him.

"I am sorry, Jax."

Jax opened his eyes. The sorrow on Ernesto's face appeared as deep as his own. "Me too. You are not certain, though?"

"No, not certain. But my friend confirmed that he had caught the rumors from more than one credible source. And as I have not heard anything from Diego since then, I cannot think of any other explanation."

"Will you give me the name of this friend?"

Ernesto hesitated. "As I said, whatever Diego was involved in, it was clearly unsafe. Deadly, even. That is why I did not want to tell you anything about him; I knew you wouldn't be able to let it go, that you would want to go after him." He swirled the amber liquid around in his glass absently, as though he didn't realize he was doing it. "I am not sure my friend will be willing to talk to you. And I do not think I should give you his information. But I will do this. I will get in touch with him and, if he is willing to talk to you, I will have him contact you. Do you have a number where you can be reached?"

"Yes. I picked up a burner phone after I arrived in Caracas."

"Good idea." Still clutching the glass of Scotch in one hand, Ernesto crossed the room to a large desk against the far wall. He set the drink on the wooden surface and grabbed a phone.

Jax gave him his number and then reached for his water glass and took a long swig. The cool liquid alleviated the dryness in his throat but did nothing to wash away the intense ache inside.

Ernesto turned and leaned against the desk. "I'm sure you wouldn't tell me if I asked, so I will not push you for details on how you managed to find out where I lived."

"You're right, I wouldn't, so thank you."

"What made you think to come to me after all this time?"

Jax reached into his jacket pocket. He withdrew the postcard he'd gotten in the mail the day he moved to Toronto. "I received this a few days ago, postmarked Venezuela. I'd forgotten that was where you moved to, but Mamá was showing Mikayla some pictures of when we were kids, and you were in a lot of them. Mikayla asked about you, and Mamá said she'd lost touch with you and your family when you returned to Venezuela. That's why I called you."

"Ah." Ernesto pushed away from the desk and strode over to take the postcard from him. After examining it a moment, he held it out. "Diego sent this to me in an envelope about four years ago, asked me to forward it to you so you couldn't trace it to him. I did mail it, but postal service in the country has been notoriously unreliable since the economy collapsed. I am sorry, but not shocked, that it took this long to find its way to you."

Jax stuck the card into the inside pocket of his jacket. "If you have nothing else to tell me, I will go. You don't want to keep your wife waiting any longer."

Ernesto grinned. "No, I do not." He rested a hand between Jax's shoulder blades as they crossed the room. When they reached the double French doors, Ernesto stopped. "I wish I could have given you better news, my friend. I loved Diego like a brother."

"I know you did. And he loved you." Jax hid a wince. He hated talking about his brother in the past tense. He wouldn't do it again. Not until he knew for sure. He held out his hand.

Ernesto gripped it. "Despite the welcome you received when you called me and when you arrived at the gate, which I apologize for, it was very good to see you again, Jax."

"You too." Jax released him and touched his upper arm, which still hurt. "Your security team is very … efficient."

"I should hope so, given what I pay them." A sheepish look crossed Ernesto's face. "I know this fortress business is ridiculous, pretentious, even. But it isn't for show, Jax, or even for comfort. It is for safety. There is nothing I would not do to keep my family safe."

"*Entiendo.* I understand."

Ernesto studied Jax a moment. "Which is why you are going to Puerto Rico."

"*Sí.* You were right. I cannot let this go, Ernesto. I have to find out what happened to Diego."

Ernesto nodded. "If you discover anything, you will let me know?"

"*Por supuesto que sí.* I will."

"And I expect an invitation to that wedding of yours."

"Of course. You and Camila will get one. Mamá would love to see you."

"And I would love to see her." Ernesto reached for the brass doorknob. "I will have one of my men drive you to your hotel."

"You don't have to do that."

"I do. I owe it to Diego not to let his little brother wander the streets of Caracas alone at night." He clapped Jax on the shoulder. "You may even sit in the front seat this time."

Jax managed a weak smile. "*Gracias*." Although he'd offered a feeble protest, Jax was relieved not to have to try and find his way through the maze of streets to his hotel, especially now that it was past midnight.

Ernesto pulled him into a hug. "Be careful, Jax. I do not want to be the one to have to call your mamá and tell her—"

"I will be careful." Jax couldn't even think about that. Couldn't contemplate what a call like that, the news that both her sons were dead, would do to this mother.

Ernesto slapped him on the back a couple of times before letting him go. He issued instructions to the man who had driven the SUV through the opening in the gates. The man nodded and strode for the front door.

Jax followed him outside and over to the large black vehicle. As the man didn't appear inclined to engage him in conversation, Jax spent the ten minutes it took them to reach his hotel running over everything Ernesto had told him. The news that Diego was likely dead hung around his neck like a heavy weight, making it difficult to draw in a breath. A faint hope flickered though, deep inside. Ernesto and this mysterious friend of his were only repeating rumors they'd heard, not facts. Neither of them had seen a body or knew for sure that the rumors were true.

Until Jax saw his brother's grave for himself, he would cling to the possibility, however slight, that the rumors were false and that, somewhere in the world, Diego still lived and breathed.

Chapter Fourteen

Jordan pushed Elle's stroller along the hospital corridor. Mikayla smiled, watching him from a couple of steps behind. Even in the year and a half since she'd met him, he'd grown so much, already losing his little boy appearance. And he adored his baby sister, always available to take her from Nicole and hold her or keep an eye on her while Nicole was at the diner and Daniel was cooking dinner. No doubt Jordan would watch over his sister all her life. Lucky girl. After growing up believing she was an only child, Mikayla envied Elle the presence of a doting, protective sibling in her life, although Mikayla wouldn't wish anything else for the sweet little girl.

As they approached Connie's room, voices drifted into the hallway. Mikayla reached the opening and peered around the doorframe. What was their mother doing here? She swung around to face Nicole and mouthed the words, *it's Marion*.

Nicole's eyes, identical to Mikayla's down to the gold flecks in the irises, widened. "Seriously?"

Mikayla lifted her shoulders, as flummoxed as her sister. As far as Mikayla knew, their mother had never talked to Connie, although Nicole had shared with both their parents what an impact Joe and Connie had had on her life.

A frown creased Nicole's forehead as she stepped around Jordan and the stroller and strode to the door.

Mikayla rested a hand on her nephew's shoulder. "Jord, can you wait here with Elle for a minute?"

A perceptive child, he could clearly tell his mother wasn't happy about the presence of his grandmother in his surrogate grandma's room. He kept his eyes on Nicole, a slight frown on his face. "Sure."

She rapped on the slightly open door a couple of times before stepping into the room. “Mom? What are you doing here?”

Mikayla trailed after her. Their mother patted Connie on the hand before rising. “I’ve been chatting with Connie. She’s feeling better today.”

Nicole shifted her attention to the woman in the bed. “Are you really?”

Connie’s face softened in a warm smile. “Much better. The doctor says I can likely go home in a day or two.”

“That’s great news. I brought the kids to see you.”

Connie’s blue eyes lit up. “Bring those sweet babies in here. They’re exactly the medicine I need.”

Marion touched the top of the bed rail. “I’ll go, Connie. Let you have a visit. It was good to see you.”

“You too. Thanks for coming by, Marion.”

“I’ll walk you out.” Mikayla followed her mother into the hall.

Nicole stopped in the doorway. “Bring Elle in to see Grandma Connie, Jord,” she instructed her son.

He waited until Marion had pressed a kiss to the top of his head and touched a finger to Elle’s cheek before wheeling his sister into Connie’s room. Nicole closed the door behind the three of them.

Mikayla and her mother stood in the hall in awkward silence for a few seconds, until Mikayla gestured toward the bank of elevators. “Shall we?”

Her mother nodded and trudged next to her along the cold tile floor. Neither spoke until they had entered the elevator and the car lurched downward. Then Mikayla propped a shoulder against the back wall. “I didn’t realize you knew Connie.”

As usual, their mother was impeccably dressed in a pinstriped navy suit and cream blouse. Her short silver hair was cut in a bob around her face, a similar style to Mikayla’s, and small gold hoops dangled from her ears. “I don’t know her, other than the little Nicole has told me. But after I heard she was in the hospital, I felt the need to come see her.”

"Why?"

"To thank her for being there for my daughter when I wasn't."

"Oh." Mikayla hadn't expected that.

Her normally implacable and perfectly in control mother twisted her ringed fingers together, as anxious as Mikayla had seen her. Not that she'd spent a lot of time in the woman's presence. Marion Hunter was nearly as much of a stranger to her as she was to Connie.

When her mother stopped fidgeting and shoved her hands into the pockets of her dress pants, she met Mikayla's gaze. "I don't need to tell you that, after you were taken, your father and I made a lot of mistakes. Mistakes we can never make up for. We … *I* was such a coward." She tugged one hand free from her pocket and lifted it in the air. "I don't even know how to begin …"

The elevator slowed and Mikayla pushed away from the wall. Everything in her wanted to steel herself against the helplessness in her mother's eyes. Their parents had hurt Nicole so badly. Only the grace of God—and the love of Connie and Joe—had kept her from the kind of life that young girls with no family to protect them often fell into.

Were she and Nicole supposed to forget all that? Forgive their parents simply because they seemed so broken and remorseful over their past actions?

Something did give a little in Mikayla's chest, a slight melting of the glacier that had settled there after she'd reunited with her sister and learned what had happened to her after Mikayla disappeared. "You acknowledging how important Connie is to Nicole is a good first step."

The doors slid open. Two men in scrubs waited outside the car, so Mikayla left it at that as she stepped out, her mother at her heels. They didn't speak again until they reached a set of large revolving doors. When Mikayla stopped at the entrance, her mother clutched the strap of her Prada bag tightly. "I know there's nothing I can say or do to make up for the past. But I want you to know how sorry I am. I hope that one day Nicole will be able to forgive us, although I won't blame her if she can't."

"I'll talk to her." The words that spilled from Mikayla's mouth caught her by surprise. Judging from the jerk of her mother's head, they'd surprised her too.

"You will?"

"Yes. But don't expect too much." Mikayla held up both palms in her mother's direction. "You both hurt her deeply. I don't know if she will ever be able to move past that, and I won't push her if she isn't ready."

"Of course not. I wouldn't expect you to." Her mother reached out, tentative, and touched Mikayla's sleeve before almost immediately withdrawing her hand. "Thank you, Mikayla."

Hearing her mother say her name for the first time touched something deep inside Mikayla. In that moment, she understood a little of how Jax must feel when she tried to speak to him in his own language. Her determination to learn more Spanish settled into a rock-hard commitment.

Words mattered. Languages did too. And using the ones that showed you knew the person you were talking to, that you understood them, allowed you to connect with them on a soul-deep level. But sometimes those words had to be earned. As touched as she was that her mother had used her name, Mikayla couldn't bring herself to call Marion Hunter *Mom*. Not yet. Maybe not ever, since she still considered Rose Grant her real mother and always would. "You're welcome."

Neither of them moved for a moment, then Mikayla surprised herself again by doing something she couldn't ever remember doing. She wrapped her arms around Marion and hugged her, briefly, before stepping back. "Drive safely."

Given her mother's state of mind, Mikayla was a little concerned about her getting behind the wheel of a car, but she wasn't about to offer to drive her home. It would take an hour to get there and back in the heavy downtown traffic and she couldn't leave Nicole that long.

"Your father drove me. He's waiting in the car."

That relieved Mikayla's mind a little, although the events of the past few minutes still had thoughts whirling through it like debris on a windy day in Toronto. "That's good."

Her mother took a step toward the door.

"Say hi to him for me."

A faint smile, the first she'd managed since Mikayla had seen her in Connie's room, crossed her mother's face. "I will." She stepped into the revolving door and made her way outside. A white Mercedes-Benz glided to the curb in front of her.

Mikayla watched through the thick glass as her mother walked toward the vehicle. She pulled open the passenger door, lowered herself gracefully onto the seat, and closed the door. The car idled there a moment, then her father leaned forward a little, his gaze connecting with Mikayla's. He raised a hand and dipped his head slightly. A lump rose in her throat as Mikayla waved back. A weak smile crossed his face before he gripped the wheel and eased the car into traffic.

She spun around and headed for the elevator. What had she agreed to? Getting in the middle of the conflict between Nicole and her parents was not something she'd ever wanted to do. She was firmly on Nicole's side, no matter how sorry her parents were or how hard Nicole dug in her heels about forgiving them.

Still, her sister's words from the day before, about how God would want her to forgive them, if not for their sake, for her own, echoed through Mikayla's mind. She wouldn't push Nicole to do anything she wasn't ready to do, but she didn't want her twin to have to carry a load that might weigh her down for the rest of her life, either.

They'd both need to do a lot of praying about this situation, because, without God's help, it was possible she and Nicole would never be free of that burden.

Chapter Fifteen

Although Jax tossed and turned for hours, his brain going over every detail of his conversation with Ernesto, he finally managed to fall asleep. When he woke a few hours later, sunlight streamed through the window and the sound of traffic blared through the thin glass. Caracas had come awake.

Jax reached for the phone he'd left on the bedside table. No texts. Disappointment and frustration formed a hard ball in his gut. Had Ernesto even contacted his friend yet? If he had, why hadn't the guy messaged Jax? He tossed the phone onto the table and flopped against the thin hotel pillow. If Ernesto and this mutual friend of his and Diego's were so convinced it was too risky to even talk about his brother, years after he had supposedly died, possibly it was. Maybe Ernesto was right and Jax should let it go.

The idea coiled around his gut like a hissing cobra. As he'd told Ernesto, he couldn't. After two decades of wondering and worrying and searching, he and Mamá needed closure. They couldn't go on like this any longer.

To distract himself from those thoughts, he reflected on his call with Mikayla the night before. Although it had been well after midnight when he'd gotten to his room, he'd known she would likely be up working. He texted to make sure, and she called right away. After he had told her about his conversation with Ernesto, she'd responded with so much love and care that the two thousand miles between them had felt more like a million. In the end, he wasn't sure if the call had made things better or worse. Although she'd offered him unwavering support and encouragement in continuing his mission, hearing her voice had filled him with such an intense longing to see her that he'd nearly called the airline and switched his destination from San Juan to Toronto. Even now, his chest ached at the thought of how far away she was, how long it might be before he could see her again. As they'd ended the call, sometime in the early hours of the morning, she'd told him again, in Spanish, that she loved him. A smile played across his lips at the memory. He'd never tire of hearing those words from her lips. As his former partner, Chase, had told him, he really needed to put a ring on her finger. Sooner rather than later.

Jax stared at a small water stain on the ceiling above the bed. Now what? As soon as Ernesto's man had deposited him at the hotel, Jax had used one of the public computers in the business area to book a flight to Puerto Rico. The earliest available one didn't leave until 8 pm, and there was a two-hour stopover in Punta Cana, so he wouldn't get to San Juan until after midnight. He hissed out a breath of air. So much of the private eye game involved waiting, the least favorite aspect of his job. This time it was even harder since it was personal. Jax turned onto his side and punched up the pillow beneath his head.

Despite the rumors Ernesto had heard, which, if true, would mean there was no particular rush to get to Puerto Rico, Jax was filled with an inexplicable urge to be on his way. Maybe that was only because of what he'd told Mikayla—that the sooner he got the answers he was searching for, the sooner he could go home to her—but it felt like more than that.

Jax's stomach growled and he sat up. The honking of car horns rose above the steady buzz of traffic. The city was as noisy now as it had been quiet the night before. He stood and tossed the sheets and thin blanket up over the pillows. He'd go grab a coffee and something to eat, which would not only fill his stomach but use up a couple of the hours he needed to put in before he could throw everything in his backpack and head for the airport. Which he planned to do even if he didn't hear from Ernesto's friend.

Jax set his pack on the bed and dug through it for a clean T-shirt. The phone on the bedside table caught his eye. Should he take it with him? He couldn't chance having it stolen. If he did, he'd have lost his connection to the contact in Puerto Rico. And Mikayla would have no way to reach him until he could get another one.

Since he'd paid an extra day for the room, it was likely best to leave the phone and anything else he couldn't afford to lose here, like he had the day before. Not that there was any guarantee this place was secure. It was probably slightly safer than carrying those items around with him, though. He unzipped the front pocket of the backpack and tugged out his wallet and passport, the two things he needed if he wanted to continue his journey. Or return to Canada, for that matter.

Jax took a few bills out of the wallet and shoved them into the front pocket of his jeans before carrying the phone, passport, and wallet over to the corner of the room. He'd noticed last night, when searching for a place to leave his valuables, that the brown floral carpet had come away from the floor slightly in one corner. He shoved the chair he'd dragged over aside and crouched in front of the spot. It took a bit of effort, but he managed to work all three items under the carpet and then maneuver the armchair into place. That should do it. Anyone searching the room in a hurry was unlikely to investigate the corner beneath a chair.

His only other option was to sit here waiting for it to be time to go to the airport, his stomach protesting the lack of food as he stared at the four walls closing in on him. He'd take his chances with the makeshift hiding place.

Jax headed out of the room, checking to make sure the door was locked behind him before making his way to the front desk in the small, poorly lit lobby. The hotel was clean and comfortable, but the décor was outdated and so was the key system. They still used old-fashioned metal keys that were handed in at the front desk on the way out and picked up by guests when they returned, which suited Jax today. On the off chance he did have an encounter with a pickpocket, no need to advertise that he was a tourist.

He handed his key to an older woman in a burgundy polyester jacket and skirt, who took it with a nod before hanging it on the wall of hooks behind her. Outside the hotel, the sidewalks were crowded with pedestrians, a stark contrast to his solitary journey through the city after dark. Since he didn't know anywhere else to go for food, he started for the place Rubén had taken him for lunch the day before. A block from the market where Fernando's stall was located, the competing aromas of coffee and hot grease filled the air, and he quickened his pace.

As he approached the stall, Fernando, still wearing his full white apron, leaned over the counter a little and a huge smile crossed his face. "*Buenos dias.* Rubén's friend, no?"

Jax grinned. "*Sí.*" At least, he hoped he was still Rubén's friend after putting him in a vulnerable position last night. His grin faded. "Have you seen him this morning?"

He held his breath until the big man nodded and replied in rapid Spanish, "Yes. He stopped for coffee on his way to work."

Rubén was okay, then. Excellent news. Although, without him there to make recommendations, Jax wasn't sure what to order. He studied the offerings through the plexiglass that lined the top of the stall. Fernando used the spatula he clutched in one hand to tap a tray of what looked like croissants. "*Cachitos. Deliciosos.*"

They did smell good. Jax nodded and held up three fingers. "*Tres, por favor. Y un café.*"

"*Muy bien.*" Fernando used the spatula to shovel the croissants into a paper bag, then he crumpled over the top of it and handed it to Jax, along with a paper cup of coffee.

"*Gracias.*" Jax paid, held the cup up in the man's direction, then moved out of the way as more customers pressed toward the counter. Half a block from the stall, he found a low wall in the shade. After setting the coffee next to him and unrolling the top of the bag, he pulled out one of the croissants and took a bite. The pastry was filled with a mixture of meat—ham, maybe?—and cheese. Fernando hadn't exaggerated—they were *deliciosos.* He made short work of the three cachitos, washing them down with swigs of the strong, hot coffee. When he finished, he carried his garbage over to a can and dumped it in.

He wandered the streets of Caracas for a couple of hours, glad he was wearing a T-shirt as the temperature had risen from the day before. Now that he had time to study them, he was struck again at how artistic much of the graffiti covering almost every available wall was. Political slogans too, and angry rants on the state of the country with language he wouldn't have repeated to his mother but that were interesting in the context of what had happened in Venezuela in recent years.

His thoughts strayed continuously to the friend of Ernesto's he was waiting to hear from. Had he texted yet? Finally, unable to stand the suspense any longer, Jax started in the direction of his hotel.

His thoughts returned to Mikayla. If they did get engaged when he got back, they could start planning their wedding, hopefully have a reasonably short engagement, and then—

Someone slammed into his shoulder. Jax had been so lost in thought that he hadn't seen anyone coming and couldn't regain his balance fast enough to prevent whoever it was from driving him through the opening between two buildings.

He stopped before running into a wall of four young guys, all wearing shorts and dingy T-shirts, ball caps on their heads and menacing expressions on their faces. Jax glanced over his shoulder, but three more men had followed him into the alley and stood blocking the exit. Really? In broad daylight? Was this what had happened to that guy he'd heard getting beat up last night? Jax's heart thudded, but he forced himself to breathe deeply. The intake of oxygen, even thick as it was with stale air and the smell of rotting garbage, calmed him a little. He half turned, his back to the wall, so he could keep an eye on both groups. "*¿Qué quieren?*" Not that the question was helpful. Even if they told him what they wanted, it was unlikely he'd have it on him.

A smirk crossed the face of a young man who stood a foot or so in front of the others, clearly the leader. Despite his worn clothing, a thick gold chain hung around his neck, over tattoos that extended from his chest to the base of his throat. Jax's gaze dropped to the kid's fingers. A blade flashed in his hand, and Jax's mouth went dry.

"That depends," the kid answered in Spanish. "What do you have?"

If whether or not he got out of this alleyway depended on

what he had on him, Jax was in serious trouble. Maybe he should have brought his valuables with him—at least then he'd have a little bargaining power. Although, outnumbered as he was, and decidedly out-armed, even that might not have given him as much power as he would have liked. "Only a little money," he said.

The guy with the knife held out his free hand. Jax hesitated. What would happen after he handed over everything? Before he could decide, the guy lunged forward, planted his hand on Jax's chest, and shoved him against the cement wall of one of the buildings. The tip of the knife dug into Jax's throat. "*Ya*," he said. Now.

The guy was a little shorter than Jax and only seventeen or eighteen, but he was surprisingly strong. Even if Jax's gym-honed muscles could compete, the knife gave the kid a pretty big edge in their confrontation.

He couldn't lower his head without driving the blade in deeper, so he felt for the front pocket of his jeans, dug around in it, and pulled out all the bills he'd shoved into it earlier. No use trying to hold anything back. That would only make them mad, and he hadn't brought that much cash with him anyway. He held out the money.

Without loosening his grip on Jax, the kid jerked his head, and one of his cronies stepped forward and snatched the bills. He rifled through them then announced, "*Quince dólares.*"

Fifteen dollars. Would that be enough to purchase his life? Jax's eyes met the kid's, which roiled with anger and desperation. On some level, Jax did empathize with him. He understood that kind of desperation. When their father had kidnapped him and Diego and taken them to Puerto Rico, he'd fallen into drinking, essentially leaving the two of them to fend for themselves. They were young, eight and eleven, and they did whatever they had to do to get food. Including stealing. Neither of them had ever used a weapon, though, or dragged anyone into a dark alley and threatened to kill them if they didn't give them something.

Jax gritted his teeth. He couldn't die. Not here. Not like this. Not when he was so close to finding out what had happened to

Diego—and to marrying the love of his life and having children and growing old with her. The thought of his life ending suddenly and violently with all that unfulfilled sickened Jax, but there was little he could do about it. Not on his own. *Dios, ayúdame. Help me. Get me out of this, please*. He sent the fervent prayer upwards, his eyes still fixed on the kid's.

"*¿Qué más tienes?*" the kid spat out.

What else did he have? Only the clothes on his back. "*Nada.*"

The knife edged in deeper. "*¿Teléfono?*"

"*No.*"

The kid jerked his head again. Another guy strode to his side and patted Jax down, even checked the pockets of his jeans. Jax gritted his teeth, suppressing the urge to resist the thorough inspection, knowing that would only make things worse for him. After a minute, the guy stepped back and flapped his hand. "*Nada. Mátalo*."

Jax's heart beat painfully against his ribs as several of the other gang members chimed in, supporting the guy who had advised their leader to kill him. For a long moment, the kid holding the knife to his throat stared at Jax, as though debating whether to listen to his followers.

Dios, ayúdame, por favor. Jax repeated the silent plea over and over, deeply aware that, with a flick of his wrist, the kid in front of him could end his life.

After what felt like an eternity, the guy lowered the knife and shoved Jax hard against the wall. "It's not worth it. Let's go," he muttered in Spanish before pushing through the group and storming toward the opening of the alley. His gang fell into step behind him. In seconds, Jax was alone. He slumped against the wall, his legs trembling slightly. His neck stung, and he swiped his fingers over the spot where the knife had dug in. A small amount of blood smeared his fingers when he held them up. No major damage then. Could have been much worse.

Gracias, Dios mío. He shot a look toward the sky, a startling blue that Mikayla had told him once was called *celeste*. So much beauty shimmering above all the ugliness below.

Jax pushed away from the wall and made his way toward the sidewalk. Pedestrians passed by in a constant stream. Had no one seen or heard what was happening in the alleyway? Maybe they'd learned not to get involved. Given the high crime rate in the city, most of its citizens were likely fairly desensitized to it. And he couldn't blame them for not wanting to take on an armed group of thugs.

Jax stumbled over a brick lying on the ground a couple of feet inside the opening. He caught himself by pressing a palm to the cold, hard wall of one of the buildings. The close call had shaken him. It had certainly reminded him not to walk around unfamiliar streets in a country he didn't know lost in thought. He was usually a lot more aware of what was going on around him than that, like he'd been trained to be. He wouldn't make that mistake again.

But he wouldn't give up his quest, either. What had happened had reminded him of something even more important, something that sent an uncomfortable but well-deserved twinge of conviction through him. Jax hadn't spent enough time in prayer over this trip, either trying to figure out if he was supposed to come here or in asking for God to watch over him as he did. Even so, God had saved his life today. He'd shown him that He would go with Jax, watch over him, wherever he went. That promise was everywhere in the Bible, and Jax clung to it now as he stepped out from between the two buildings.

Something told him that, whatever happened in the next few days, he would need to remind himself over and over that he wasn't doing any of it alone.

Chapter Sixteen

Shivers tingled across her skin, and Mikayla rubbed her arms. What was that about? As far as she knew, everything was okay. Still, a breath of cold air, like a cloud drifting across the face of the sun, had passed over her, leaving a chill in its wake. Was Jax all right?

The thought that he might not be paralyzed her for a few seconds, before she straightened on the stool at the island in Nicole's kitchen.

Her sister had been filling Mikayla's cup with steaming orange and ginger tea, the enticing aroma drifting on the air around them, but she stopped and set the pot on the island. "What is it?"

The glib response—*nothing*—sprang to Mikayla's lips, but she bit it back. Although it might very well be true, it wasn't the answer her sister was seeking. And although they'd only been reunited a year ago after being apart most of their lives, their twin connection was strong. Nicole would know if Mikayla was keeping anything from her. "I'm not sure. I felt a cold chill, as though something might be wrong."

"With Jax?"

"Maybe." Who else's life was so tightly interwoven with hers that she might sense it if he or she was in trouble or hurt? Nicole, for sure, but she was clearly fine. Jordan or Elle, maybe, but they were here in the condo. Elle was sleeping, and Jordan was in the living room watching one of the Laurel and Hardy DVDs Daniel had brought with him when he and Nicole got married.

A little of the color drained from Nicole's face. "I'll check on the kids." Her train of thought had clearly followed the same tracks as Mikayla's.

"Of course, go." Mikayla waited until her sister left the

kitchen, then she slid off the stool and reached for the bag she'd set on the kitchen counter. After rummaging around in it, she pulled out her phone. Maybe Jax had called or texted. When he phoned last night, he'd sounded okay. Physically, anyway. Torn up over the news Ernesto had given him that Diego might be dead, of course. Had he heard from the guy Ernesto said might contact him?

No new messages. Nicole pushed through the swinging doors, and Mikayla lowered the bag to the counter. She returned to the stool, setting her phone on the island where she could keep an eye on the screen.

"The kids are fine. And I called the hospital. Connie's all right too. Resting. The doctor does want her to stay one more day, but she sounded confident that she'd be able to go home tomorrow."

"Good." Mikayla took a sip of the spicy tea. The fragrance and the soothing heat of it drove away the last of the chills. "Sorry to worry you."

"Don't be. If anything's going on, or might be, I want to know." Nicole slid onto the stool across from her and reached for the tea pot. "Have you heard from Jax?"

"Yes, he called from Caracas last night."

"And?"

"He managed to find out where Diego's friend Ernesto lived and went to the house. Ernesto told him that Diego had gone to Puerto Rico a few years ago but …"

"What?" Nicole set the pot on the island and rested her forearms on the countertop.

Mikayla traced the patterns in the marble with the tip of her index finger. Fresh sorrow washed through her. "He'd heard rumors that Diego was dead." She couldn't imagine how that news had impacted Jax. The urge to be with him, to wrap her arms around him, comfort him in some small way, was so strong that she ached with it.

Nicole drew in a sharp breath. "Kayla, that's awful. Poor Jax."

"I know. Not surprisingly, he sounded really sad on the phone. Ernesto didn't know for sure if the rumors were true, so I think Jax is going to fly to San Juan, see if he can get concrete information."

Nicole covered Mikayla's hand with hers. "Daniel and I are praying for Jax, that God will keep him safe and that he'll be able to find the answers he needs. We'll keep praying until he's home again."

"Thank you. I appreciate that, and Jax will too."

"Let me know if you hear anything." Nicole pulled back her hand.

"I will." Mikayla took another sip of tea and wiped a drip off the side of the mug. "Did you speak to Marion?"

Nicole grimaced. "No, but Connie and I did talk about her a little after the two of you left her room yesterday."

"Did she tell you what the two of them discussed?"

"She said Mom came to thank her for being such an important part of my life."

"Yeah, that's what she told me on our way out of the hospital."

"How did that conversation go?"

Mikayla sighed. "Awkward and stilted, as usual. Slightly less each time, so maybe we're making progress. It's going to take time, though."

"For me, too."

Mikayla studied her twin. Nicole had so much more right to be angry with their parents than she did. In fact, most of the animosity Mikayla felt toward them was on behalf of her sister. "Do you think you can get there?"

"To the point where we can be close?"

"Yes."

"I don't know." Nicole grabbed the pot and poured a little of the hot liquid into her cup, even though it was nearly full. "Did you know Mom and Dad have been going to church?"

Mikayla blinked. "No. Did Connie tell you that?"

"Yeah. She said Mom told her they'd both arrived at the place where they realized they couldn't deal with everything that had happened on their own."

"Only twenty-five or thirty years late."

Nicole offered her a wry grin. "I know, right? In any case, they've been going for a few months now."

Ah. That did explain why her mother had told Nicole over the phone that she would be praying for them. "Interesting."

"I thought so. It helps, somehow."

"That's good, Nic."

Her sister grabbed a dishcloth from the sink and swiped it over a small puddle of tea on the counter. "I don't know what the future holds, but I'm praying too, for the strength to forgive. And for the healing of our family. I would love it if we could get to the place where I was good with my kids—and yours—spending time with their grandparents."

Mikayla nearly choked on a sip of tea. She set her mug down so abruptly a bit of the hot liquid sloshed onto the island. "What are you talking about? I don't have kids."

"Not yet." Nicole raised the mug to her lips, but not before Mikayla caught a glimpse of the mischievous smile that crossed her face. "I'm guessing Jax would like that to change before too long."

"Nicole." The flush of heat deepened, and Mikayla pressed a hand to her cheek.

"What?" Her sister laughed. "The man is clearly head over heels in love with you. It's only natural that he would be thinking about the two of you getting married, starting a family. Aren't you?"

"Of course not."

Nicole gazed at her steadily.

"All right, fine. Maybe the fleeting thought that Jax and I might get married and have children someday has passed through my mind."

"Fleeting."

"That's right."

"So that look on your face when he was holding baby Ciana

was …?"

"Exhaustion. We'd spent all day moving his stuff to Toronto, you know."

"Whatever you say." Nicole grinned as she wiped up the tea Mikayla had spilled. "But if I were you, I'd start thinking about it a little more seriously. When Jax gets home, I'd bet a lot of money it won't be long before the topic comes up."

"We'll see."

"Yes, we will." Nicole hopped off the stool. "In the meantime, I'm going to start supper. You'll stay, right?"

"Sure." What did Mikayla have to rush home to? Only an empty apartment that had felt even more silent and lifeless since Jax had left for Venezuela. Although he didn't live there, for the past year he had spent so much time at her place that she felt his absence like a warm blanket torn off her in the middle of the night.

That made this separation so much harder. Since the night he had recreated her prom for her—redeeming that terrible experience and replacing it with one of her most cherished memories—she'd always known, when she was missing him, that they would be together again within a few days. Now, she had no idea when she would see him again, and that thought, in the rare moments she allowed herself to dwell on it, was ripping her apart.

"I'm going to ask Jordan to set the table."

Mikayla nodded as she carried her empty cup and the tea pot over to the sink to rinse them out. If this separation from Jax was teaching her anything, it was that she was more than ready to commit her life to him. She grabbed a loaf of French bread and a knife and carried them to the cutting board.

The chills that had skittered across her skin earlier passed over them again, and the knife clattered onto the board. Something was wrong; she could feel it. Mikayla pressed her palms to the cool marble island. *Father, watch over Jax. I don't know what's happening or if he's okay, but you do. Keep him safe. Help him to find out about his brother and then bring him back to me. Please.*

A slow warmth crept through her, driving away the chill. Mikayla's muscles relaxed. Whatever was going on with Jax, it was out of her control. She had to trust that if he was facing any kind of peril, God was with him.

The haunting voice of doubt that had assailed her in the deepest valleys of grief echoed inside her now. Although she knew it had no real power over her anymore, and although she rushed to bar the entrance, the raspy whisper filtered in like a deadly cloud of smoke curling beneath the door.

Will that be enough?

Chapter Seventeen

Jax snatched his backpack off the rollers and slung it over his shoulder. His plane left in an hour, and he still hadn't heard from Ernesto's guy. While he had to follow the unrelenting urge to go to Puerto Rico, he had no idea what he would do if he landed in San Juan and still hadn't received a message. The very real possibility that he never would threatened to derail his resolve, but he hiked the strap of his pack a little higher on his shoulder. He needed to keep moving forward and praying that somehow it would all work out. God had to be the one behind the pull to follow his brother's trail, or Jax wouldn't have made it this far.

He stuck the passport he'd retrieved from under the carpet in his hotel room into the front pocket of his pack and made his way to the gate. He kept his phone on as, thirty minutes later, the first call to board crackled over the loudspeaker. He glanced at it repeatedly as he strode through the tunnel leading from the terminal into the aircraft and scanned it every few seconds after taking his spot next to the window. The hint of jet fuel clinging to the wall of the plane hit him as he stowed his backpack beneath the seat.

When they were instructed to fasten their seatbelts, he reluctantly switched the device to airplane mode and stuck it into his pocket. As he hadn't slept much the night before, Jax rested his head against the window and dozed as they flew to the Dominican. No messages came during the two-hour layover at the airport in Punta Cana, and once again he dropped the device into his pocket as they prepared to take off for the last leg of the journey to San Juan.

When the wheels touched down in Puerto Rico, he snatched his phone and checked again. Still nothing. For several minutes after he'd gotten off the plane, Jax stood in the middle of the busy terminal, contemplating his few options. The most appealing one was finding a hotel and getting a few hours of sleep so he could start fresh in the morning.

He picked up the rental car he'd arranged for ahead of time and drove to a hotel he had stayed at in the past, in Luquillo. The first time he'd flown to Puerto Rico as an adult, Jax had sat in the parking lot for a long time, considering which town to make his home base while he was in the country. His father had lived in Arecibo, west of San Juan, when Jax was a kid. Still did, as far as Jax knew. When he finally pulled away from the airport, Jax headed east, ending up in the coastal town of Luquillo.

Although it was a bit of a drive from the airport, Jax felt the need to get away from the city and begin his search in a quiet, familiar town on the coast. Until he heard from Ernesto's friend, one place was as good as another for him to wait. Might as well be somewhere with a view.

It was past midnight, but traffic was still heavy around the airport, and it took him an hour and a half to get to his destination. He found a spot in the parking lot and climbed out of his car. At the sound of waves hitting the shore, Jax halted, halfway to the hotel entrance. Standing between two strange cars, he inhaled one briny, salt-laden breath after another. This was the smell, the sound, that he associated with his country; this was what called his heart here even though Canada had always been his home.

Several minutes later, fortified and freshly motivated, he strode toward the building. After closing the hotel room door behind him, he checked the phone he clutched in one hand as he had since debarking from the plane, even while driving.

A red dot above the text icon notified him that someone had messaged him, but he fought the rush of excitement. Likely it was Mikayla, checking to see if he had arrived in Puerto Rico. Not that a text from her would be a disappointment. Still … Taking a deep breath, he tapped the icon. Unknown caller. His adrenaline level rose as he scanned the words.

¿Estás aquí?

Was he here? Jax scanned the room. Was the sender asking if he was here in Puerto Rico? Likely Ernesto had told him he would be coming from Venezuela but not when he would arrive, so that was a logical question.

He tapped a response with his index finger. *Sí.*

Nothing happened. His eyes fixed on the small screen, Jax pushed away from the door and crossed the room to drop his backpack on a chair next to the bed. *Come on. Come on.* Was the guy having second thoughts?

After another minute of gazing at the blank screen, Jax set the device on the bedside table, zipped open his pack, and yanked out track pants and a T-shirt. He was completely at the mercy of Ernesto's friend and his timetable. No sense driving himself crazy trying to force something to happen. He needed sleep. Hopefully he'd get a text before he went to bed so he'd know what the plan was for the next day. If not, he'd check again in the morning.

Jax grabbed his bag with toothbrush, soap, and razor and headed to the washroom for a shower. When he came out fifteen minutes later, there was still nothing new on the phone. He tossed the covers back and crawled into bed. He hadn't thought he'd be able to quell his whirling thoughts enough to sleep, but when the sound of a low-flying airplane jolted him out of oblivion, dull light glimmered through the crack in the heavy brown curtains on the hotel room window.

Jax rolled over and snatched his phone off the table. 6:20 am. Another red notification lit up the text icon and he hit the button and blinked a couple of times until the screen came into focus.

Lirios. Iglesia Primera. 1900.

Not exactly Shakespeare, this guy. Jax blinked again, but the message didn't become any clearer. He sat up and threw the covers off to swing his legs over the side of the bed. It took a couple of minutes, but he was able to connect to the hotel internet and do a search for *First Church, Lirios, Puerto Rico*. When a blue stucco building flashed across the screen, the excitement he'd been keeping a lid on since getting the first text threatened to erupt, but he forced himself to keep it in check. 1900. Did that mean he was supposed to meet this guy at 7 pm at a church in Lirios? That did make sense, even given the cryptic message.

He researched the distance from Luquillo to the church. Google advised that it would take a little more than an hour to drive there, but Jax knew this country. He'd allow three hours at least in case road conditions were poor or they had to stop for animals meandering across the street. Even so, he had most of the day to wait. Again. Jax typed *bueno* in response to the text before tossing the device onto the table.

The desire to hear Mikayla's voice gripped him, and he reached for the phone and then hesitated. Not a great time to call her. She'd likely only gone to bed an hour or two ago. Maybe less if, as she often did, she'd painted until the first rays of sun slid between the slats of her blinds to fall across her canvas and draw her back to the real world. It would be several hours yet before she was ready to crawl out of bed and stumble to the kitchen for coffee. If he called and woke her now, she would struggle to return to sleep, and her day would be shot.

Desperate to talk to her, he almost called anyway, his finger hovering over the first number, then he leaned over and dropped the phone onto the side table. That would be selfish. He'd call her after he met with Ernesto's friend. That way, he could let her know what he'd learned. If, as he suspected, the guy only confirmed what Ernesto had told him, that Diego was dead, he could also let her know he would be flying home soon.

Or maybe, given that this quest had sunk its claws deep into him and appeared determined not to let go until it had wrung everything out of him that it could, his message to her would be completely different. Jax might be calling to tell her that Ernesto's friend had sent him down another path, and he had no idea where it would lead or when he would ever see Mikayla again.

Chapter Eighteen

Jax steered the rental car along PR-30. Traffic was heavy, and he was glad he'd allowed plenty of time to get to Lirios. According to the GPS, he was only a few miles from the small town, a barrio of Juncos, which lay a little south of the El Yunque National Forest. Jax hadn't been to the rainforest since he was a kid. When all of this was behind him, maybe he and Mikayla could take a trip here too. He'd show her around his country, and they could explore the natural wonders of the forest together.

He touched the brakes as taillights lit up the highway ahead of him. Regular rush hour traffic or an accident? He tapped his fingers on the steering wheel. It was only 6:15, but if he got stuck here for any length of time, practically a stone's throw from his destination, he could easily miss his appointment. Judging from the lengthy time between messages, the man might not be willing to take another chance on meeting with him. Jax suspected this would be his one and only opportunity to find out about his brother. If he had to abandon the rental and walk to Lirios, he'd do it.

Brake lights slowly flicked off, one by one, as the vehicles in front of him picked up speed. Two minutes later, they slowed again. Ducking his head, Jax peered down the highway as far as he could. Lights flashed ahead. An accident then. Could he get around it if he got off the highway? He read the sign he was crawling by. The cut-off to Humacao. Jax had never been to Humacao, although Chase, an avid golf fan, had mentioned the Palmas del Mar resort and its famous golf courses to him a few times.

Something about the place called to Jax. If he got off here, he should be able to travel along the outskirts of the city, bypassing the accident on the highway so he could get to Lirios in time. Jax flipped on his signal and eased into the exit lane.

He drove for several minutes, passing through the southern edge of the barrios of Candelero Abajo and Candelero Arriba before crossing into Mariana, the barrio at the western tip of Humacao. Should be safe to return to the highway now. Jax watched for the signs that would direct him to the route he'd been on before he'd taken this detour. Thick smoke poured from the chimney of a concrete-block building on his right, and Jax slowed the vehicle as he approached. Various pieces of metalwork hung on the wall on either side of the door, and one large piece was propped against a chair on the porch. What was that, a blacksmith shop? Did such a thing even exist anymore? For machinery parts and for horseshoes, maybe, since there were a lot of horses in the country. Someone appeared to use this place to create intricate works of art, though. Jax admired them briefly before pressing on the gas again, anxious to reach his destination.

He followed the signs to the highway. On the far side of the accident, traffic flowed at a steady sixty-five miles an hour, and he reached the outskirts of Lirios with minutes to spare. A few houses, all painted in various pastel colors, lined the road on both sides, palm trees waving in front yards and along the street. According to his research, Lirios had a population of just under seven thousand people. Had his brother lived in this area? Likely not if, as Ernesto had suggested, he'd been involved in the drug trade in Puerto Rico. A bigger city like San Juan or Bayamón would make more sense. So why was Jax here?

The GPS directed him onto the street where the church was located. When he spotted the blue stucco building, Jax pulled over across the street from it and killed the engine. Now what? Was he supposed to go inside? Wait in front of the building? He peered at his phone. 6:50. He'd wait here five more minutes and then, if nothing happened, get out and walk around the property.

At 6:55, with nothing going on either inside or outside the church that he could see, he climbed out of the car. Shoving the keys into the front pocket of his jeans, he crossed the street and walked up the uneven stone walkway to the front door. Locked. Jax pursed his lips. Was he at the right place? Maybe he'd read the message wrong, or he was supposed to come another day. He glanced at the sign on the front lawn. *Iglesia Primera.* The line below it read *de 1 Samuel 22:2.* What verse was that? When he arrived at whatever hotel he was staying at tonight, he'd go online and find it.

Movement in his peripheral vision caught his attention, and he watched as a black Lexus glided past the church and turned into the parking lot on the far side. The windows were tinted, so he couldn't see inside. Was that his 7 o'clock appointment? The car continued along the side of the church until it disappeared. Jax scanned the street, but no one appeared to be around. Should he head into the parking lot around the back of the building where no one would see him? A memory of the gang that had shoved him between those two buildings in Caracas slammed through his mind, and he touched the spot on his throat where the tip of the blade had dug in.

This clandestine meeting felt a little like a higher-class, more sophisticated version of that encounter, heading into an out of the way area to meet with at least one stranger, maybe more, whose intentions Jax really didn't know. He trusted Ernesto, but Diego's childhood friend hadn't shared how he knew the man in the black car. This whole meeting felt a little off. What did this guy do, anyway? He clearly had money. Jax knew Ernesto well enough to believe he'd earned his legitimately—through an inheritance and hard work. What about his friend? If he'd known Diego, were they in the same line of work?

Jax started along the side of the church. What choice did he have? If he wanted to find out what happened to his brother, talking to this man was his only option.

Stifling the warning signals blaring in his brain, Jax walked the length of the building. He reached the back corner and stepped onto the gravel parking lot. Something pressed against his temple and he stopped. A man as massive as any of Ernesto's henchmen stood in front of him, dressed in a navy Polo shirt and dress pants. A second man who could have been his twin held a pistol to Jax's head. Had they brought him back here to kill him? Why? Because he was Diego's brother? What in the world had his brother gotten himself into here?

It appeared as though Jax might not live long enough to find out.

"Turn around," the man in front of him commanded in Spanish, his tone of voice suggesting that he wouldn't tolerate disobedience. If Jax had been considering such a thing, the increased pressure against his temple helped him decide that cooperation was likely his best recourse, even if turning his back on this goon seemed a highly questionable thing to do.

The man with the handgun pulled it back an inch or so and circled the barrel in the air, emphasizing the request. Repressing a sigh, Jax turned and faced the church.

"Hands against the wall. Feet spread."

They wanted to frisk him? As unappealing as the idea was, it gave Jax hope. If they planned to rob or kill him, they likely wouldn't search him first; it would be easier to take whatever they wanted after he was dead.

Jax only hesitated a second. As tired as he was of being manhandled by everyone, he needed to do whatever these men told him to if he wanted to meet with the one who'd contacted him. Probably he'd instructed them to make sure Jax wasn't armed. Which did make sense, especially if he was someone high up in the drug world or even a legitimate enterprise.

Jax planted his feet shoulder-width apart and pressed his hands to the wall, the stucco pricking into his palms. Let them do their worst. He needed to find out about Diego, and if this was the price he had to pay, well, he'd pay it. He gritted his teeth as the man stepped closer and patted his chest and down to his waist. Then he reached into Jax's front pocket and tugged out the remote to his rental car.

"Hey," Jax protested. He had nothing else on him except the phone in his back pocket, which the man searching him didn't appear to have any interest in. Jax had brought the rest of his valuables with him this time but left them in the trunk of the car. Which they now had full access to. He grimaced.

"Insurance," the gunman grunted, sounding almost amused.

A massive spider sat in the center of a web that started below the overhanging roof a couple of feet above Jax's head and continued down the wall, ending under the fingers of his left hand. Jax focused on the eight-legged creature—a weaver, not venomous, thankfully—on the intricate design of the web, the lower half shimmering in the sunlight, and on a tiny fly, buzzing as it struggled to free itself from its gossamer prison. The man continued his search down one leg and then the other, crouching behind Jax to feel around his ankles before straightening.

"*Date vuelta*," he demanded again. Turn around.

Jax brushed bits of the spiderweb clinging to his fingers off on his jeans as he faced the man who'd frisked him. Now what?

"*Levanta tu camisa.*"

Lift his shirt? The men who worked for Ernesto's contact were thorough, Jax had to give them that. Checking to see if he was wired confirmed Jax's suspicion that either their boss was a kingpin in some organization or Diego had gotten himself tangled up with all the wrong kinds of people. Both, probably.

Jax exhaled as he grasped the hem of his T-shirt and raised it to his shoulders. He held it there for a couple of seconds before lowering it again. "*¿Ya?*"

The man didn't bother to respond, only jerked his head in the direction of the black Lexus, idling in the middle of the empty parking lot, before whirling around and starting toward it. "*Ven con nosotros.*"

Oh, Jax was going with them, all right. No way he was submitting to an inspection like that without getting something out of it. He fell into step behind the man, his partner encouraging him to keep pace by periodically prodding Jax's back with the gun, something Jax was beginning to suspect he did more for fun than out of any real need. After all, Jax was the one who'd requested this meeting. What did they think he would do, bolt before he had a chance to talk to the man he'd asked to see? He couldn't even drive away, since they had his keys.

The man behind him directed Jax to the passenger side of the vehicle. The other one strode to the rear door on the driver's side and rapped on the window. When the glass slid down a couple of inches, the man informed whoever was inside that Jax was clean.

"Let him in, then wait outside." The orders were issued in terse, authoritative Spanish before the window closed again.

The man with the gun brushed past Jax to yank open the back door. He directed Jax inside with a wave of the weapon.

Jax slid onto the seat, barely getting out of the way before the door slammed behind him. He shifted to face the man on the other end of the bench seat. Half-hidden in the shadows of the dimly lit interior, the man gazed at him without speaking. Then he nodded, curtly. "You remind me of your brother," he said, in Spanish.

"Do I?"

"*Sí.*" The man chuckled, but the sound lacked any real mirth. "He was far more handsome than he had a right to be too."

"I wouldn't know." Bitterness gave Jax's voice a slight edge he hadn't intended. "I haven't seen him in twenty years."

"That must have been difficult."

Past tense again. Was the man about to confirm Jax's worst fear? "It is."

The man continued to scrutinize him. As Jax's eyes slowly adjusted to the dim lighting in the vehicle, he could make out his features. Intense eyes. Slightly larger than average nose. Glasses. Who was this guy? "You know who I am. Do I get to know your name?"

"No."

Jax waited, but the man apparently felt no compulsion to elaborate further or defend his failure to be forthcoming. His jaw clenched as he endured the ongoing inspection or evaluation or whatever it was. Thirty seconds later, the man reached for a button on the door handle and lowered the glass. The thug on the other side leaned closer as the man issued a sharp order. "*Vámonos.*"

"*Sí, Señor H.*" The security guard stepped back as his boss closed the window.

Go? Jax's eyes narrowed. Was he suggesting their conversation was over? "I won't get out of this car without answers."

"Get out?" Mild surprise flickered in the eyes that met his. "Why would you do that?"

Both front doors opened and the two men who'd been waiting outside climbed in.

"You mean you're taking me somewhere?" Jax wasn't too sure about this situation. Once again, he was outnumbered and outgunned, trapped in unfamiliar territory with strangers he had no idea he could trust not to put a bullet in his head and dump him into a ditch.

"Yes." The man rested his arm casually along the top of the seat, as though they were two friends about to go for a Sunday drive in the country. "I am taking you to your brother."

Chapter Nineteen

They drove in silence. After five minutes, the distance between houses lengthened, and they left the small town of Lirios behind and headed into the country. Jax's heart pounded as he watched the landscape stream by his window in ribbons of brown and green. Was this man, whoever he was, actually taking him to Diego? A million questions swirled around in his mind, but something told him his companion was unlikely to answer a single one. He'd have to wait until they reached their destination, when hopefully everything Jax wanted to know would be revealed.

It didn't take long. Fifteen minutes after they'd left Lirios, the big man driving the Lexus turned into a tiny, rutted parking lot and bounced to a stop. Jax stared out his window. All he could see were rolling hills dotted with weeds and palm trees. Where were they? More importantly, where was his brother?

"We will get out here," the man informed him.

Get out? Was this it, then? Had they brought him out here to murder him? Maybe Ernesto was right, and Jax had asked one too many questions about the fate of his brother. "I …"

The man pushed open his door as the two men in the front seats exited the vehicle. "Now, please."

What use was there in arguing? If Jax didn't get out on his own, they'd simply drag him out and there would be nothing he could do to stop them. *Mikayla.* The face he loved, blonde hair blowing around in the breeze until, laughing, she caught it back with one hand the way she had the night they'd dined at the CN Tower, drifted through Jax's mind. He fumbled for the door handle.

The man who'd held the gun on him waited as Jax stepped onto the rough parking lot. He'd holstered his weapon, but Jax was pretty sure that at any misstep on his part it would reappear quickly. The man gestured to the back of the car. When Jax started in that direction, the guy trailed after him. The other two men stood on the far side, so Jax rounded the rear of the vehicle. As soon as he did, he caught sight of the field in front of him. A wave of dizziness struck, and he slapped a hand on the trunk to keep himself from going down.

Several rows of headstones stretched out before him. Jax concentrated on drawing in one ragged breath after another. Ernesto's friend walked over and stopped in front of him, a frown creasing his forehead.

"*Lo siento mucho*. I was under the impression that Ernesto had given you the news Diego was dead. No?"

"He said he'd heard rumors that he might be. I was hoping you might tell me …" Jax's voice grew hoarse, and he cleared his throat. "I was hoping Ernesto was wrong."

The man shook his head. "He was not wrong. Diego was killed three years ago." He half-turned to point in the direction of the graves. "His stone is in the last row, at the southwest corner of the cemetery." He faced Jax. "I thought you would want to see it, but if it is too difficult, we can—"

"No." Jax pushed away from the trunk. "I do want to see it."

"Then please …" The man stepped out of his way and held a hand toward the field. "Take as much time as you need."

Jax walked by him and made his way on shaky legs past the rows of headstones, many chipped or broken. Weeds grew up around the stones, and several of them had toppled over. Most cemeteries in Puerto Rico had raised plots, but whoever had been assigned this final resting place had been buried underground. The cemetery was situated on a high hill, so water levels shouldn't be a huge issue. Still, what kind of a graveyard was this? One where they tossed the bodies of those who'd lived their lives on the wrong side of the law, maybe.

Heat rose in his chest. Whatever he'd done, Diego didn't deserve to end up in a place like this. Could Jax have his body moved somewhere? He reached the last row. The headstones had ended. The graves in this section were commemorated only by small, rectangular stones set into the ground and largely overgrown.

Jax bent to brush weeds from the top of the stone in the southwest corner. When he'd cleared it enough to read the words engraved on it, he closed his eyes for a few seconds. His brother's stone. He dropped to his knees and rested a hand on the small marker. This couldn't be happening.

A few years into the search, Jax had learned to no longer get his hopes up when he thought he'd discovered another lead. Except maybe he hadn't learned that lesson as well as he thought he had, since hope had billowed inside him the moment he'd flipped over that postcard and seen the fish etched on the back. How could he have allowed himself to believe he might see his brother again, even manage to find out where he was—or had been—only to discover that Diego was dead? And he'd died three years ago? Ernesto had told Jax he'd mailed the card from his brother four years ago, but it had gotten held up or lost until now. If Jax had received the postcard when he should have, he could have come to Puerto Rico and found his brother before he was killed. Maybe even talk him into coming to Canada, so whatever had happened to him wouldn't have happened. What kind of cruel twist of fate was that?

Jax tipped his head and stared at the darkening sky, pinpricks of light starting to poke through. *Really, God? Is this the answer to all my desperate prayers over the past two decades? Would it have been that hard for you to have led me here a few years ago?*

He lowered his gaze to the stone. This wasn't God's fault. Diego had made his own choices. He'd left the family and willfully gone down the dark path that had brought him here, to this makeshift cemetery. Jax ran his fingers over the cold stone, the numbers etched deep. The year of his brother's birth, only thirty-seven years ago. That pathetic hyphen meant to somehow encapsulate a person's life on earth. Who they were. What they'd done. Who loved them. How could a small straight line possibly hope to convey the slightest hint of any of that?

His fingers stilled on the year of Diego's death. What month had he died? Had it been an accident? A murder? Illness? The lack of information was enough to drive Jax nearly out of his mind.

The words engraved in the stone haunted him. *Diego Rodríguez*. Nothing more. No inscription that would let future passersby know he'd been someone's son, someone's brother. That he'd been deeply loved. Which, despite everything, he had been. Was, even now.

Tears burned, and Jax pressed his palms to his eyes. The tears came anyway, and he dropped his hands and let them flow. Tears for Diego and the life he'd chosen. For his death at way too young an age. For all the time with him that Jax had missed out on. And for their mamá. His chest squeezed. How could he tell her that her firstborn son was gone? She never had given up hope, he knew. Would the loss of that hope be more than she could endure?

Jax studied the stone. It was plain and unadorned. Weeds still covered part of it, and he reached down and yanked them out by the roots. A flash of metal caught his eye as he tossed the weeds away, and he leaned in closer. A two-inch diameter circle of scrolling metal artwork was set into the stone to the right of Diego's name.

He rested the tips of his fingers on the metal. The handiwork was exquisite, all vines and tiny leaves winding over and around each other. Jax reached back to tug the phone from his pocket and snapped a picture of the stone and the metal piece.

Wait. He'd seen something like this recently, only on a larger scale. That blacksmith shop he'd passed by in Mariana had similar pieces. Could that be a coincidence or was the same artist who'd created the pieces he'd admired also responsible for this one?

He stuck the phone into his pocket. Before he left the area, Jax needed to talk to the artist, find out who had commissioned him to make the piece for Diego's stone. If the person who had done the metalwork didn't know what had happened to his brother, maybe whoever had hired him would. Finding out as much as he could about Diego's life over the last two decades and maybe even who had killed him and why were all that Jax could do for his brother now.

He traced the outline of the round metal piece and his brother's name and the dates of the beginning and the ending of his life once more. "*Que Dios te acompañe, mi hermano.*"

Tears threatened again, but Jax blinked them away as he pushed to his feet and wiped bits of grass and dirt from the knees of his jeans. *I need Mikayla.* The thought sideswiped him, and he nearly sank to the ground again. He'd give anything to see her, hold her in his arms.

They weren't married yet, and they'd never slept together. Even so, over the past year they had become one, and a deep, driving need to hear her voice thrummed through him. As soon as he got to his car, he would call her.

And then he would investigate his brother's death a little more. He couldn't walk away, not yet. Not before he did everything possible to uncover the details surrounding Diego's demise. Even if what had happened to Diego had been a result of his poor choices, Jax still felt the need to do this. Maybe he didn't owe his brother anything, but after everything she had been through, Jax owed their mother as much information as he could possibly scrounge up.

And Jax would do whatever he had to do to get it.

Chapter Twenty

When Jax arrived at the car, the two security guards had returned to the front seats and closed the doors. Ernesto's friend had been leaning against the side of the Lexus, his arms crossed, but he straightened as Jax approached.

Jax swiped away the last of the moisture beneath his eye with his thumb. The other man winced. "I truly am sorry for your loss. I loved him too. Diego was an extraordinary man."

Extraordinary? That seemed a strange adjective to apply to a drug dealer who'd likely met his end during a deal gone bad in an alley somewhere. Jax contemplated the man. He was tall and lean, with hazel eyes and, somewhat surprisingly, blond hair cut short in a military style. With his wire-rimmed glasses, he resembled an academic more than a drug kingpin, but appearances could be deceiving. "Do you know how he died?"

The man's features hardened slightly. "Those kinds of questions are dangerous."

Which wasn't a no.

"If you hope to leave Puerto Rico alive, you won't ask any others."

"Not ask questions?" Jax's voice rose. He didn't buy for one second that the man in front of him knew nothing about Diego's death. Those eyes that weren't quite meeting his were too keen, too astute. Everything in him wanted to grab the man by the arms and shake him until he shared what he knew. "How am I supposed to find out what happened to Diego?" He took a step forward.

Immediately, the passenger door of the Lexus cracked open. Without looking back at the car, the blond man held up a hand. After a couple of seconds, the door closed. The man walked over and clapped a hand on Jax's shoulder. "Maybe it's time to accept that you can't and move on with your life. There is nothing you can do for Diego now."

Jax mulled that over. Ernesto had given him the same advice. Could he take it? He shook his head. "I can't do that."

The man grimaced as he lowered his arm. "Ernesto warned me you were stubborn."

Jax lifted his hands, palms up. "Diego was my brother."

Behind the wire-rimmed spectacles, something flickered in the man's hazel eyes. He glanced at the car before resting his fingers between Jax's shoulder blades and directing him a few feet away. When he spoke, his voice was low and, for the first time, the words were in English. "For Diego's sake, I will tell you one thing. But you must swear you will tell no one where you heard it."

"I swear." What would Jax tell anyone if they asked? He knew nothing about the man next to him, not even his name.

The man leaned closer. "Diego had friends who worked in a restaurant in Candelaria. *El Pescado Rojo.* Maybe they can tell you more." He spun around and started for the car. "And now we must go."

Jax followed him. A faint, ghost-like version of the hope he'd felt earlier shimmered inside him. Another lead. So, he couldn't leave the country yet. As soon as he returned to his rental car, he'd drive to Candelaria, which wasn't far from the airport anyway. Would these friends of Diego be as secretive and wary as Ernesto and the blond man?

As soon as Jax slid into the back, the big man behind the wheel half turned to reach his arm over the seat. The remote for Jax's rental car dangled from one finger, and he reached for it and shoved it into the pocket of his jeans.

The ride to the church was quiet. Questions he knew there was no use asking flitted through his head. Trying to find answers felt as futile as the struggling of that fly in the web clinging to the wall of the church.

Was that what Jax was to these people? Given both Ernesto's and this man's reaction to his request for information, clearly his questions were, to them, the irritating buzz of a pathetic, condemned fly. A fly caught up in something he was unwilling or unable to free himself from despite the looming threat advancing toward him.

What that threat was, Jax had no idea. But he intended to find out.

When the driver pulled the Lexus into the parking lot and around to the rear of the church, Jax reached out a hand to the man next to him. "*Gracias*." The word was too small to convey how much he appreciated Ernesto's friend taking him to his brother's grave and giving him the information about the restaurant in Candelaria, both clearly at risk to himself.

The man grasped his hand firmly. "I hope you get the answers you seek, and that you are then able to find peace. Diego would have wanted that for you and your mother."

Jax nodded before climbing out of the car. As soon as he stepped onto the gravel and closed the door, the car began to move. Jax watched until it reached the street, turned right, and disappeared on the far side of the church. *The answers he sought*. Why were they so hard to come by?

Each bit of information about Diego was like a word on a Scrabble board. Only one word was spelled out clearly, in the center of the board. DEAD. All the other words surrounding that one were scrambled, as though someone had tossed them onto the board where the letters had landed in random order. How could Jax possibly put enough words together to form an accurate picture of what his brother had gone through?

Jax strode toward his rental car, hit the remote to disengage the locks, and snagged the phone from his pocket before sliding behind the wheel. He needed to talk to Mikayla. After dialing her number, he hit the speaker button and set the device in the cup holder. Then he started the car and pulled onto the quiet street.

The phone rang four times before Mikayla answered with a breathless, "Jax?"

Her voice, even that one word, wrapped around him like a winter jacket he'd pulled on to ward off the cold night. "*Hola, preciosa*."

"*Hola. ¿Cómo estás?*"

Where did he even begin? "I just came from Diego's grave."

"Oh, Jax. I'm so sorry."

The compassion in her voice nearly undid him. Unutterable weariness swept over him. The only thing he wanted was to drop onto a couch, pull Mikayla to him, her head resting on his chest, and fall asleep with his cheek pressed to her silky hair.

Through the line, she drew in a shuddering breath. "I wish I could hold you."

Jax managed a wry grin. "You are reading my thoughts."

"Will you come home?"

He hesitated. Now, listening to her in the stillness of the car, the lights of Puerto Rico streaming past his windows, coming home to her sounded like the only good idea in the world. This quest still tangled him up like that fly in the spider web, though. Why? Diego was dead. As the blond man had reminded him, he could do nothing for his brother now. So why couldn't he wipe away the cobwebs of this case as easily as he had swiped the bits of web off on his jeans earlier? All he knew was that he couldn't. "I would like more details about what happened to Diego. I am hoping that will help both Mamá and me find peace."

"Then you should try to get them. Do you have any idea how?"

"I have a couple of leads to follow up on. One likely won't be that helpful, but there was a small round bit of metal set into Diego's stone, a piece of artwork with scrolling leaves and vines. Really beautiful, actually. I took a picture of it that I'll send you. I noticed a blacksmith shop in a town about forty minutes from the cemetery that sold similar work, so I thought I'd stop in there and see if the piece in Diego's stone had been made by the same artist and if he or she can tell me who commissioned it. If so, I'll follow up, see if they know anything about what happened to him."

"That makes sense."

"It's a long shot, but I also found out that Diego had friends who worked at a restaurant in Candelaria, which is about an hour and a half from the blacksmith shop. I'm going to drive there after I stop at the shop, try to find them. Hopefully they will be willing to share with me anything they know."

"That sounds promising. You'll be careful?"

"Always." No need to tell her about being robbed at knife

point by a gang in Caracas or a gun being held to his head today or the warnings both Ernesto and his friend had issued him about the riskiness of asking about Diego. Some time he would, but not now. Not when there was nothing she could do from Canada except worry.

"Will you call me after you talk to Diego's friends?"

"Of course. I don't think I will see them until tomorrow, but I will call right after. I promise." Hopefully from the airport where he was waiting for a flight that would take him straight to her.

"Okay. *Te amo*, Jax."

He seriously would never get tired of hearing her say that. "*Te amo, mi corazón*." Reluctantly, he hit the button to disconnect the call. The idea of stopping at the blacksmith shop didn't seem that great now; everything in him told him to get to Candelaria as quickly as he could, and Humacao lay in the wrong direction. Still, it wasn't that far out of his way. If he didn't plan to visit *El Pescado Rojo* until tomorrow, he could afford the little amount of time tonight that it would take to drive to Mariana in Humacao, find the place, and ask a few questions.

He retraced the route he'd followed to Lirios. After exiting the highway, he braked to allow a flock of chickens to hop across the street in front of him, a couple of them flapping their wings indignantly when he stopped the vehicle too close to them. When they'd made their way to the far side of the road, clucking and pecking at the ground, he continued on into the barrio of Mariana.

Smoke hung in the air over the building he'd driven past earlier. Hopefully that meant the artist was still at work.

Jax parked at the side of the road. He wouldn't stay long. Given how secretive everyone was when it came to giving out information about Diego, it was quite possible that whoever worked here would refuse to speak to him. As Mikayla had suggested, the restaurant sounded like a more promising lead. While he was thinking of her, he grabbed his phone and sent her the picture he'd taken of Diego's gravestone.

Then he killed the engine and tugged the remote free of the ignition. For all the good it would do him, it was time to go be a pesky fly once again.

Chapter Twenty-One

A faraway knocking sound drew Mikayla slowly from the world she had retreated to in her head. She blinked and dropped the paintbrush into a jar of water on the ledge of her easel. Was someone here? Twisting her wrist, she glanced at her watch. Nine pm. Late for a visit.

Mikayla snagged a rag off a chair as she strode toward the door. Likely Mrs. Thompkins from down the hall wondering if Mikayla had seen her wayward cat. The mischievous tabby did sometimes appear on her balcony, mewing to be let inside, but she hadn't seen or heard any living creature out there this evening. Not that she would have, necessarily, when she was as deep into her work as she had been.

At the door, Mikayla paused and leaned close to the peephole to peer into the hall. Daniel, Nicole, and Jordan. A small smile crossed her face as she reached for the doorknob. As happy as she was to see them, it was a little unusual for them to drop by this late, even on a Friday night. Was everything okay? Did Daniel have news about Jax? Her stomach twisted as she pulled open the door. "Hey, you guys. This is a surprise."

A wide grin lit up Jordan's freckled face. "Hi, Aunt Kayla." He threw his arms around her waist.

Mikayla pulled him close. How much longer would he submit to hugs from his aunt? Might as well take as many of them as she could get before he decided he'd outgrown them.

Daniel stepped into the apartment behind Nicole and Jordan and closed the door. "Hey, Mik." He kissed her on the cheek.

Nicole slid her arm around Jordan's shoulders. "Sorry to drop in like this. I tried calling a few times and didn't get an answer, so we thought we'd stop on our way home from Jordan's soccer practice and check on you."

Mikayla waved the rag she still clutched in one hand through the air. "I'm glad you did. I was working and didn't hear the phone." Panic wormed its way through her chest. Had Jax tried to call her? She walked over to the table next to the easel and tapped her phone screen. The picture she'd been studying earlier, of Diego's stone, filled the screen, and she hit the button to clear it. For some reason, she wasn't ready to share it with Nicole or Daniel yet.

She checked the phone history. Three missed calls. All from her sister. No news was good news, right? Somehow the silence from Jax, even though he'd called recently and had promised to call again the next day, felt ominous.

A few drops of blue paint on the floor beneath her chair caught her eye and she used the damp rag to swipe them away. A smile played across her lips. The last time Jax had been here, he'd carried a cup of coffee over to where she was working on a painting of a pair of birds swooping through the branches of a tree. Her eyes focused on the canvas, she reached for the cup, unaware that she still clutched the brush, laden with sky-blue paint, in one hand. Jax had pulled the cup away in time to keep the paint from falling into it, but not fast enough to avoid having a few drops hit the side of his shoe and splatter onto the tile floor. As usual, he'd teased her about her creativity-induced oblivion before kissing her, handing her the cup, and going to the kitchen for a paper towel to wipe up the drops. Obviously, he'd missed a couple that had landed beneath her chair.

Mikayla shook her head a little to pull herself from the memory, from the warmth that drifted through her chest at the thought of him being here, in her apartment. She gestured to the living area. "Want to sit?"

Nicole slid off her jacket and hung it on a hook behind the door. "Could we put something on for Jordan to watch while we talk in the kitchen?"

"Sure." Mikayla grabbed the remote and turned on a twenty-four-hour kids' channel. Likely Jordan was a little past those shows, but he didn't complain, only plopped onto the couch.

"I'll boil the kettle." Mikayla led the way into the kitchen. A small table with four chairs sat in front of the window, and Daniel pulled out one of the chairs.

Nicole opened the cupboard where Mikayla kept her tea bags and grabbed a couple boxes as Mikayla carried the kettle to the sink and filled it. "Where's Elle?"

Her sister leaned a hip against the counter. "She's with Mom and Dad, actually."

"Really."

"Yeah. I'm still not sure how I feel about them being around the kids, but Elle had a slight fever earlier and I didn't want to bring her out, so we thought we'd try it for tonight."

"Baby steps."

"Exactly."

Mikayla set the kettle on the burner and turned it on. "Is Elle okay?"

"I think so. Probably teething."

While her sister settled on the seat next to her husband, Mikayla rested her hands on the back of the chair across from them. "So, what's up? Is Connie okay?"

"She's better. I'm picking her up tomorrow afternoon and we're bringing her to our condo for a few days."

"That's good news."

"I hope so. She insists she doesn't want to stay long, that she'd prefer to be home, but I'm nervous about her being on her own."

Daniel rested his arm on the back of her chair, his fingers cupping her shoulder. "She'll only be a phone call away."

"I know." Nicole smiled at him.

Mikayla watched the two of them together. They had been through a lot, even broken up briefly before they were supposed to get married the first time. But they'd made it through every challenge and come out stronger. Would the same be true of her and Jax? "Not that you need a reason to come by, but was there something specific you wanted to talk to me about?"

Nicole blinked as she tore her gaze from her husband, the way Mikayla had when they'd knocked on the door. "We were wondering if you'd heard anything from Jax."

"I have, actually. He called me an hour ago." Her chest squeezed at the memory of the sadness in his voice. "He found out his brother is definitely dead. In fact, he'd just been to his grave."

Daniel winced. "Oh man. I'm sorry to hear that."

"Me too." Sorrow drifted through Nicole's eyes. "Poor Jax."

"He sounded pretty broken up on the phone. He knew that was a strong possibility, but he was hoping it would end another way."

The kettle whistled, and Mikayla walked over to slide it off the burner. She grabbed the pot and tossed a couple of peppermint tea bags in.

"I'll get the mugs." Daniel crossed the kitchen to the cupboard next to the sink.

Nicole clasped her hands on the table. "Is he coming home?"

"He wants to do a little more investigating into how Diego died, but he'll likely catch a flight soon."

Daniel set a blue and white striped mug at each of their places. "I wish he'd let me go with him."

Mikayla dropped the lid on the pot with a clang. "You offered?"

"Yeah, when he first told me he was going. I would have been happy to keep him company, but he said this was something he needed to do himself."

She grabbed a box of cookies from the cupboard and carried it and the tea pot to the table. Daniel was such a good friend. If she and Jax ever got married, he'd be an amazing brother too, like he was to her. No one could replace Diego, but maybe Daniel could help fill the void Jax would feel more keenly than ever, now that any hope of reuniting with his older brother had vanished.

She filled Nicole's mug, inhaling the aroma of warm mint as she poured. "I appreciate you offering, Daniel. I'm sure it meant a lot to Jax."

Daniel moved his cup closer to her. "You'll let us know if

you hear any more from him?"

"Of course." Mikayla filled his mug and then her own. Another cold chill worked its way through her, and she wrapped her fingers around the warm ceramic. Why did that keep happening? When she'd talked to Jax earlier, he was upset, but it didn't seem as though he was in immediate peril. Caracas was one thing, but he knew Puerto Rico. And she'd checked the distance from Lirios to Candelaria after she'd spoken to him. It wasn't that far, only about forty miles. After he talked to Diego's friends, he'd be close to the airport where he'd catch the flight home. What could go wrong?

The niggling feeling that something might, that maybe it already had, wouldn't leave her. From the looks Nicole kept shooting her way, she was picking up on Mikayla's angst. Still, her sister didn't push her, which Mikayla appreciated.

Daniel's offer echoed the thought that had scrolled through her mind on an endless loop—like a news bulletin across the bottom of the TV screen—ever since Jax had told her he was going after his brother. *I should go to him. I should go to him.*

When they'd finished their tea, Nicole carried the cups over to the sink. "We better head home. I don't want to leave Mom too long with the baby."

"Of course, go." Mikayla walked them to the door. "Thanks for caring so much about Jax."

Daniel shrugged. "He's family." He hugged her. "Everything's going to be okay, Mik."

"I know." Although she didn't, really. More shivers skittered across her skin and Mikayla rubbed her forearms absently. *Father, if this feeling is from you, show me what you want me to do.*

Daniel headed to the living room to get Jordan. Nicole lasered in on Mikayla's hands and Mikayla lowered them to her sides. Lines of concern etched her sister's forehead. "I know you're heartbroken for Jax, but this is something more, isn't it?"

No use trying to deny it. "It is, although I don't know what. I keep getting this sense that something bad is going to happen. Or has happened. Silly, right?"

"You know all those years we were separated, when we didn't remember the other one existed?"

Nicole was such an intrinsic part of her life now that Mikayla could barely recall a time when she wasn't. "Yes."

"I'd feel sad sometimes, for no reason, or afraid, or really happy, and I'd wonder why. After Daniel brought you back to me, I understood. Although we were far from each other, we were still connected. And I know that's a twin thing, but you and Jax have an incredibly deep connection too. So no, it's not silly. It's a sign of how much you love him, that even from thousands of miles away you can feel his pain, sense what he is going through. But Kayla …"

"What?"

"Don't do anything crazy."

She offered Nicole a weak smile. "Who, me?"

"I mean it."

Mikayla wrapped her arms around her sister. "I know you do." She couldn't bring herself to make the promise. *Would* she do something crazy? Maybe, if she truly believed Jax was in danger.

Nicole stepped back. "What can I do?"

"Pray."

"You know we are."

Jordan bounded over and wrapped his arms around Mikayla's waist again. "'Bye, Aunt Kayla."

She ruffled his hair. "Good-bye, little man." The words tripped over her tongue a little as they spilled from her mouth. Why did they feel so final? "Take good care of your little sister, okay?"

"Kayla." Nicole's voice held uneasiness, as though the words had sounded final to her too.

Mikayla repeated Daniel's words. "Everything's going to be okay, Nic. I promise. Just pray."

Her sister was clearly not convinced, but when Daniel rested a hand on her back, she allowed him to guide her into the hallway. "Call me tomorrow?"

"I will. Thanks for coming. I love you guys."

She'd meant to say the words casually, but they came out

more like a farewell than an expression of affection. She bit her lip as Nicole half-twisted to peer behind her. Mikayla forced a smile, trying to set her sister's mind at ease.

Likely it hadn't helped, but Nicole did continue down the hall with her husband and son. Mikayla watched them until they entered the stairwell. *Will I see them again?*

She frowned as she closed the door. Of course she would. And she would see Jax again too. *Father.* She stopped, not sure what to ask for this time. Maybe she didn't have to know. God knew what she needed, even if she couldn't put it into words. And He knew what Jax needed too.

Watch over him, please. Keep him safe. Bring him home to me. The words had become a mantra, the liturgy that was keeping her sane as she waited for Jax to let her know he was boarding a flight for Canada. Would she get that message tomorrow? If not, Nicole's concern might prove to be well-founded.

Mikayla might end up doing something crazy after all.

Chapter Twenty-Two

Jax rapped on the heavy door. Although smoke poured from the chimney, he couldn't detect any movement inside, even when he knocked again and leaned his ear closer to the door.

Should he come back tomorrow? He contemplated the silent neighborhood. He had no place to stay in this town and little desire to try and find one this late at night. Candelaria was only about a forty-five-minute drive—barring unforeseen delays—and he'd much prefer to spend the night there if possible so he could head to the restaurant first thing tomorrow. Besides, someone had to be up around here. Surely whoever owned the place wouldn't leave the fire blazing all night. Would they?

Jax tried the handle. It turned easily in his hand, and he opened the door slowly. "*¿Hola?*"

No response. He stepped inside. A roaring fire blazed in the forge in the center of the shop. Beads of sweat formed on Jax's forehead, and he swiped them away with the sleeve of his T-shirt. Despite the massive fan hanging above the flames, drawing the heat and smoke up the chimney, the acrid smell permeated the place. Would the blacksmith mind him letting himself in? It was a shop, after all, and not a private home. And no hours were posted on the door.

A wall of metal artwork, each piece unique but similar in style to the ones mounted on the outside wall and the smaller one on Diego's gravestone, caught his eye. Jax slid the backpack off, dropped it to the cement floor behind the door, and wandered over. He studied the pieces for several minutes. Whoever had made them was a true artist. Like the small one in the cemetery, the metalwork was intricate and detailed, down to the spines on the leaves, and a different scene had been crafted in the center of each one. A mountain range, a lighthouse on the shore of a roiling sea, a group of children running and playing. He couldn't imagine the concentration required to melt the metal until it was pliable enough to stretch thin and weave in and through other strands to form the designs.

He leaned closer to study one of them. How much would a piece like this cost, anyway? Mikayla would love one, and she'd appreciate the artistic detail. Would they let him take something like this on a plane? Maybe if he—

An arm slammed across his upper back, shoving Jax against the wall and pinning him in place so firmly that the side of his head pressed against metal.

"*¿Qué está haciendo aquí?*" The man holding him in place hissed the question in Jax's ear.

For a few seconds, Jax couldn't remember why he *was* there, his head spun so wildly. Finally, he remembered that he was after information about someone and managed to get that much out. "*Busco información sobre alguien.*"

Without loosening his grip on Jax even slightly, the man twisted around. When he straightened, he clutched a metal rod in his fingers, the end glowing red from the flames. He held it to Jax's face, a few inches away but close enough for him to feel the heat against his skin.

"*No nos gustan los entrometidos aquí.*"

Yeah, Jax had already figured out they didn't like nosy people around here. And in case he'd forgotten, the heat from the poker was driving the point home incredibly well. He planted his hands against the wall and attempted to push away from it. Whoever stood behind him had a couple of inches and likely a good thirty pounds on him, all muscle forged through bending hot metal to his will for hours every day. The pressure between Jax's shoulder blades increased until it felt as though his spine might crack in two. He gave up and lowered his hands.

"Who do you want information on?" the blacksmith barked in harsh Spanish.

Jax hesitated. Given the man's obvious hostility, should Jax tell him? What if he knew the people who had killed Diego? Maybe even worked for them.

The poker dipped closer. Whatever might happen to Jax if he told the truth was unlikely to be worse than what would happen to him if he didn't. "Diego Rodríguez."

The faint hope that the man might let him go if he told him faded as the man shifted closer and spoke in Spanish again, the red-hot tip of the poker swinging treacherously close to Jax's eye. "Diego Rodríguez is dead."

Not a revelation, although it hurt hearing it now as much as it had the first time. The skin below Jax's left eye stung beneath the heat of the hot metal. "*Sí. Yo sé.*" He ground out the words. "I need to know what happened to him."

"*¿Por qué?*"

Why? Might as well go all in. "He was my brother."

The man knew everything now. If the blacksmith was committed to keeping the details surrounding Diego's death a secret, Jax might very well have sealed his own death warrant.

For several agonizing seconds, the man didn't move, then he tossed the poker behind him where it landed on the stone fire pit with a clatter. He spun Jax around, gripping his forearms in his large hands. "Jax?"

Jax's heart thudded in his chest. No. It couldn't be. "Di—"

His brother stopped him with a sharp shake of his head. "Diego has been gone for three years. I am Tomás Santiago." He released Jax's arms.

Stunned, Jax slumped against the wall. His brother was alive?

Diego strode to the door and locked it before returning to stand in front of Jax. For a few seconds, the brothers only contemplated each other. Then Diego let out a short laugh and pulled Jax to him. When he slapped Jax on the back and released him, so many questions spun through his mind he had trouble pinning one down.

"How …? Why …?"

Diego laughed again and grasped Jax's elbow. "Come. Sit. You look like you have seen a ghost." He directed Jax to a small

Formica table in a corner of the room.

"I am not convinced I haven't." Jax sank onto a paint-chipped white chair. His feelings were as muddled as his thoughts. He was happy to see his brother alive and well and standing in front of him, but darker emotions assaulted him as well. Why was Diego pretending to be dead? And since he wasn't lying in that grave Jax had visited, why hadn't he made more of an attempt to contact Jax than sending him some cryptic postcard?

He tamped down his rising anger. Time enough for that later.

Diego grinned, his teeth flashing white in the glow of the fire. "I assure you I am flesh and blood." He patted the bulging biceps on his right arm. Not that Jax needed to be reminded of how decidedly un-ghostlike they were, not with his back still throbbing. As if he could read his brother's mind, Diego grimaced. "*Perdóname.* I am sorry for that greeting. I need to be very cautious these days."

Why? The question flitted through Jax's mind, but he suspected the answer would be more involved than he had the mental capacity to process tonight.

Standing across from him, Diego pressed his hands flat on the tabletop. "Let us start with this. How is Mamá?"

"She is okay." He met his brother's dark eyes. "Still grieving."

Pain contorted Diego's face as he lowered himself onto a chair. "I knew you would take good care of her."

"I didn't have a choice, did I?" All right, maybe he'd make a little time for the anger to come out tonight. After all, he'd wept—wept!—at his brother's grave only an hour before.

Diego dipped his head, acknowledging his brother's fury. "How did you find me?"

"I got your postcard a few days ago and flew to Venezuela to talk to Ernesto. It took a little persuasion, but he finally told me that you had been in Puerto Rico. He also warned me it would be dangerous to come here after you."

"He was not wrong about that. Although I have to admit it is incredibly good to see you." Diego leaned across the small table to punch Jax in the upper arm. "You have grown up, *conejito*."

Little Rabbit. Jax hadn't heard that nickname in years. It sent mixed emotions coursing through him. "It has been a long time." He did expend a little effort to try and keep the bitterness out of his voice, but not quite enough to manage it.

A shadow flickered across Diego's features. "Far too long, I know. I have much to explain and much to atone for. But …" He eyed the door. "Maybe not tonight. Or here."

Jax ran his fingers across his forehead. His brother was probably right that now was not the time to get into everything that had happened since he'd disappeared. Maybe it was the exhaustion, but the feelings spiraling through him were not the ones Jax had expected to have when he finally reunited with Diego. He'd assumed, naively, that if the moment ever arrived, all he would experience was joy. The joy was there, sure, but threaded like veins of gold through the rocks of rage and fear and resentment. Rocks that had been building up like layers of strata since Diego had left. Clearly it was going to take time and work to mine it free.

"Do you have a place to sleep?"

Jax lowered his hand to the table. "I was planning to get a motel room."

"You should not travel this late at night. Stay here, with me."

The house Jax had seen next to the shop was pretty small. "Don't you have a wife or kids? What will they think of a stranger—"

Diego held up a hand. Something roiled in his eyes that Jax was far too exhausted to try and decipher. "I am alone. Stay. Get some rest. We can talk in the morning." He rose and crossed the room to the forge to turn off the blower.

Jax was too tired to argue. Pressing a palm to the table, he pushed to his feet and trudged across the shop after his brother. When he reached the backpack he'd dropped on the floor, he bent down, grabbed one strap, and slung it over his shoulder. Diego inched the door open and peered out before opening it wider and stepping outside. Jax frowned. Why was his brother taking so many precautions? And why had he reacted so strongly to Jax's presence in his workshop? Was Diego's life in danger? Was Jax's, since he was staying here? He wouldn't particularly care at this point, not enough to abandon his brother after finally reuniting with him, except that everything in him rebelled at the thought of Mikayla getting a call with the news that he was dead.

The thought sickened him, but Jax shelved it in the back of his mind. For now, he needed sleep. Tomorrow, he and Diego would talk. As glad as Jax was that his brother was still alive, he was going to demand that explanation—and maybe that atonement—Diego had admitted he owed him.

And Jax wouldn't leave the country until he had received it.

Chapter Twenty-Three

The aroma of brewed coffee pulled him from sleep a few hours later. For several minutes after he'd pried his eyes open, Jax lay staring at the ceiling, one arm flung across his forehead, the thin blanket Diego had given him tangled around his legs. Had he been dreaming or was he actually sleeping on his newly resurrected brother's couch?

The thought infused him with a jolt of energy stronger than any coffee, and Jax sat up. He folded the blanket and tossed it over the arm of the couch then took a quick shower in Diego's small bathroom before heading for the kitchen. A note stuck to the faucet caught his eye. *Do not drink! Boiled water in fridge.*

Really? Was this town still under a boil water advisory this long after Hurricane Maria had struck? In any case, Jax had every intention of following Diego's instructions. He grabbed a blue ceramic mug from the counter next to the coffee maker, filled the mug nearly to the rim, and then returned the carafe to the hot pad.

Was Mikayla having her first cup yet? He glanced at the clock on the stove. 7:40 am. Not likely. Jax had hoped to call her last night, after Diego got him set up on the couch and left him, but he couldn't get a good connection. Not that unusual for Puerto Rico. Still, he'd tried for half an hour before giving up in frustration and grabbing a few hours of sleep. He'd call her later today, let her know that somehow, miraculously, he'd found his brother.

The house was silent. Likely Diego was already in his workshop. Jax hefted his backpack onto his shoulder. His plans were very up in the air, no telling when he might need it. The nutty scent drifting from his mug swirled around Jax as he stepped outside.

The trail leading to his brother's shop was little more than a worn dirt footpath. Still, the grass was neatly cut, and several flowering bushes lined the freshly painted metal fence that surrounded the property. Even if, for reasons that Jax was becoming increasingly desperate to hear, Diego was living under an assumed name and presumably in hiding, he appeared to be taking good care of his place.

Jax reached the end of the path and knocked lightly on the door before pushing it open. A blast of heat greeted him when he stepped inside. His brother glanced at him through his safety glasses before bringing the anvil down on a piece of metal he'd pulled from the fire and set on the stone edge. Jax dropped his pack behind the door where he'd set it the evening before. He stood a safe distance away until his brother finished and came around the forge to greet him, pulling off his gloves and shoving them in the pocket of his coveralls as he walked.

"*Buenos días*, little brother." Diego tugged off his glasses and swiped an arm across his forehead, leaving a streak of black.

"You're at it early."

"Early?" Diego shot him an amused look. "It's nearly 8 am."

"I don't remember you ever crawling out of bed before noon on weekends when we were kids."

The amusement in his brother's eyes faded as he took a slow, measured breath. "As you said last night, that was a long time ago. Things change, Jax. People change."

Do they? Jax kept the cynical thought to himself by taking a gulp of steaming coffee.

When he lowered it, his brother was watching him, his dark eyes swirling again with emotions Jax couldn't decode. Before he could ask Diego what he was thinking, his brother stripped off his coveralls and jerked his head toward the small table. "Come. Sit."

"I don't want to take you away from your work."

"It will keep." Diego pulled one of the wooden chairs out from under the table. Jax set his mug on the surface before taking the seat across from him. Red curtains with stripes that might have been white at one point but were now an ash gray from the fire hung on either side of the window next to the table. Purely for looks, since heavy blinds covered the glass, keeping any natural light from penetrating the room.

Although, given his brother's furtive behavior the night before, it was more likely prying eyes Diego was trying to block out.

A basket of quesitos sat in the middle of the table, the cream-cheese-filled pastries drawing Jax back to his childhood and baking with his mamá on Saturday mornings. The ones in the basket smelled good, but not as good as the ones she still made for him when he visited on the weekends. Jax studied the small pastries. Did his brother bake now? That certainly would be a change.

Diego pointed to the basket. "Help yourself. They're from the market down the road. Best in town."

Ah. That made more sense. Jax reached for one but didn't take a bite, only gazed across the table at Diego. "Is this a better time?"

A phone sat on the table, and Diego slid it closer to the wall with the edge of his hand before grabbing a quesito from the basket. "For what?"

"That explanation you mentioned last night."

His brother set the pastry on the table. "Not much for small talk, are you?"

"I am, with people who haven't been missing from my life for two decades."

As he had the night before, Diego eyed the door. Who did he think would hear the two of them talking over the roar of the flames? "I will tell you everything, I swear. Only …" The phone he'd moved away from him vibrated, and Diego looked down. His jaw tightened. "We need to get out of here."

"What? Why?"

"They're coming." Diego typed a lengthy response into his phone before shoving the chair away from the table.

"Who's coming?" Jax pushed to his feet.

"I can't get into it right now. But you need to go. Where's your stuff?" Diego strode to the forge and hit the button to turn it off.

"My bag's behind the door." Jax stared at his brother, trying to process what was going on. "Where are we headed?"

Diego snagged a backpack from a hook near a work bench attached to the wall and brushed off the top of it. "Not we, me. You need to go to the airport."

What is happening? Jax watched as Diego opened a drawer in the work bench. He withdrew an object—a gun?—and tucked it into the backpack. "The airport? Why?"

"So you can go home."

"What are you talking about? I'm not going home. Not before we have a chance to talk."

Diego yanked the zipper closed on the backpack. "I can't talk now. As soon as I am somewhere safe, I will call you and tell you everything you want to know. I promise." He tossed the backpack over his shoulder and started for the door.

Jax stepped into his path, blocking him from reaching the exit. "You are kidding me, right? I finally track you down after twenty years and suddenly you're kicking me out?"

"I'm not kicking you …" Diego huffed out a breath. "Fine. I am kicking you out. Now go." He took a step forward.

When Jax didn't move, his brother stopped again, inches from him. Jax met his heated gaze steadily. "I'm not going anywhere until you tell me what is going on."

Diego's jaw worked. "That text was a warning from a friend. He was letting me know they're coming. They are forty miles out of town and heading this way fast."

"Who's coming?"

"People I can't afford to have find me."

"You or Tomás?"

"Either. And we are wasting time standing here talking."

"Let's go, then. Come to the airport with me. We will fly to Canada and figure this out when we get there."

"I can't fly. Diego Rodríguez is dead, and Tomás Santiago doesn't have a passport. Now are you going to move, or do I have to move you?"

Something told him if he let Diego walk out of here, Jax would never see him again. No way he was letting that happen after all he had gone through to find him. He snatched his pack off the floor, unzipped the small front pocket, and yanked out his passport. Stepping around Diego, he strode to the fire and tossed it in. “There. Now I don’t have a passport either.”

“That was extremely stupid.” Diego glared at him, both hands fisted at his sides. “Are you trying to get me to slug you? Because I will.”

Was he? Part of Jax did feel the need to have it out with his brother. Likely not the right moment, though. “Remember when we were lost in the woods that time? You told me that nothing bad could happen as long as the two of us were together. I believed it then and I believe it now. So, I am going with you.”

Diego glared at him a few more seconds before his shoulders slumped. “Jax. I don’t want you involved in this.” His voice held a desperation Jax had never heard in it before.

He refused to relent. “I am your brother. I’m already involved.”

Diego sighed. “Do you have a phone?”

“A disposable one.”

His brother held out a hand, blackened from his work.

Jax hesitated before digging around in the front pocket again and producing the device. As soon as he placed it on his brother’s palm, Diego crossed the shop to the table, snatched the phone he’d left there, and tossed them both into the fire. Jax flinched. His phone and passport—his only two lifelines to Mikayla—were gone. Now the fact that he hadn’t been able to get through to her the night before stung even more. He slid the straps over both shoulders. He’d find another phone as soon as he and Diego were away from whoever was coming after him, let her know what was going on. She’d understand.

Diego kicked off his safety shoes and snatched a pair of hiking boots sitting on the floor near the door. He yanked them on and then glanced at Jax’s running shoes. “Here.” He strode to a cupboard near the workbench, his long laces flopping against the cement floor. After flinging open the door, he produced another, more worn, pair of hiking boots and tossed them toward Jax. "This will not be like strolling along the shore of Lake Ontario, city boy."

The boots landed near Jax's feet, and he toed off his running shoes and tugged them on. A little big but not too bad. "I can keep up with you." He had no idea whether he could keep up with his brother, but if it killed him, he would expend every bit of energy trying.

"We'll see." Diego finished tying his laces with a loud snap and rose from a crouch. "I am reserving the slugging option for a time in the very near future," he muttered as he pushed past Jax, shoving him to the side with his shoulder.

Yeah, that was definitely going to happen. But first they needed to get somewhere safe. Jax tied his own boots before scrambling out the door.

Hopefully Diego knew where that might be, because Jax had absolutely no idea.

Chapter Twenty-Four

Diego didn't speak as they tromped down his driveway. They'd nearly reached the road when two figures slipped out from behind a tree. Jax glanced at his brother, but Diego barely slowed his pace as he dug into the pocket of his jeans. After tugging out a set of keys, he tossed them to one of the men who caught them in his cupped hands. "*Gracias, mi amigo*."

The man nodded as he pulled open the door of Diego's old Ford Ranger. "*Ten cuidado,*" he called out before sliding onto the front seat.

Obviously a friend, since he wanted Diego to be careful.

"*Siempre*." Diego slowed a little, half turning in Jax's direction. "Do you have your car keys?"

"Why?"

He inclined his head in the direction of the second man. "My friend will return it to the airport for you. That may throw our pursuers off your trail, temporarily, anyway."

How would that work? Didn't Jax have to be the one to bring it back? Would the man actually return it or …? He gave his head a shake. What did any of that matter now? He slid the pack from his shoulders and dug the keys out of a side pocket. The dark-haired man, who appeared to be about their age, held out his hand when Jax reached him. Jax set the keys on his palm. "*Gracias*."

The man nodded and strode toward the rental car. Maybe he would have a big fine to pay when he and Diego reached their destination, but at this point, Jax didn't much care.

From what he had seen, Diego hadn't lied to the first man when he'd told him he was always careful. Extremely careful. And yet someone had managed to hunt him down. Who was it and what did they want with his brother? He half-jogged to keep pace with

Diego. "Why is he taking your vehicle instead of us?"

"Too easy to trace. He will drive it toward the men coming for me and leave it abandoned on the side of the road before they reach it. Hopefully it will throw them off. Buy us a little more time."

Clearly this escape had been well thought out. "Where are we going?"

"You'll see when we get there. In the meantime, I'd save my breath if I were you."

So they were what, going to jog away from the people coming after Diego? In hiking boots? Jax pressed his lips together to hold in a myriad of questions. His brother was likely right, and he should concentrate on breathing and keeping up.

After ten minutes of rapid, military-style hiking, the short beep of a horn sounded behind them. Diego stopped at the edge of the road and held up a hand.

An old pickup truck that had been forest-green at one point, judging from the odd strip of color still clinging to the rusted metal, came to a stop, brakes screeching as though the pads were as old as the vehicle. A loud bang sent his adrenaline into overdrive, until Jax realized it was only the ancient vehicle backfiring.

"That's our ride." Diego started for the truck, sliding his pack off as he walked.

"Seriously?" Jax was pretty sure they were safer and would get farther on foot than that old truck could take them.

Diego glanced at him over his shoulder. "You were expecting a limo, maybe? We are not going to the prom, little brother."

God, help us. Jax was getting a little tired of trying to figure out this whole madcap adventure. Might as well go along for the ride and hope and pray that all would go well.

Diego yanked open the passenger door and climbed into the cab. Jax followed him, pulling the door shut then reaching for the seatbelt. His fingers closed around air. No seatbelts. Good combination with the inadequate brakes. The aroma of greasy takeout burgers and fries hung in the air of the cab. Blowing out a breath, Jax leaned against the seat as the driver, an old man with sprigs of white hair shooting out in all directions from below his San Diego Padres ballcap, grasped the gear shift. Jax gritted his teeth against the grinding sound the transmission made before the vehicle leapt forward.

His brother's mention of a limo stirred the memory of his do-over prom with Mikayla, just the two of them under the stars. He might have smiled if their lives weren't so clearly at risk. And now from more than one source. The truck hit a pothole and bounced wildly. No shocks, either. Great. Jax pressed a palm to the roof of the vehicle to keep from being knocked out against the window.

Warm thoughts of that evening with Mikayla slowed the rush of adrenaline that had pumped through Jax since Diego had received the text at breakfast. Or maybe since the moment he'd gotten that postcard in the mail and started to believe his brother might still be out there somewhere, alive. Which he was—they hit another pothole that threw Diego into Jax's side, sending him crashing against the door—although he was beginning to have serious doubts that either of them would be much longer.

He planted both palms on the roof of the vehicle. "Exactly how far will we be driving in this truck?"

Diego didn't miss a beat. "Seven hundred miles."

Jax shot him a dark look. "We're on an island that's a hundred and ten miles long."

His brother laughed. "Oh, sorry. I thought you asked how far it would *feel* we had driven."

Seriously? Joking, at a time like this? Jax had forgotten how his older brother could always make him laugh. When he was clean and sober, anyway. Which meant that him cracking jokes now was probably a good sign. He'd take time to appreciate both that and the humor once the two of them had safely arrived at—

The driver spun the wheel to the right suddenly, hurtling them into a shallow ditch and up the other side. Jax let go of the roof with one hand and shoved it against the window to keep from being flung against the glass. Although he suspected he would regret not eating more at breakfast before this day was over, he was grateful he hadn't at the moment. Even empty, his stomach was threatening to mutiny, and he drew in a few deep breaths, trying to keep a surge of nausea at bay.

"Do not throw up. Jorge is very particular about his truck."

Hands still bracing his body in place, Jax scanned the vehicle. A thick coat of dust covered the dashboard, the windshield had so many cracks running across its surface it resembled a topographic map, and crumpled takeout bags and oil-streaked rags covered the floor. Jax ended his visual tour of the truck at his brother's face. Although he wasn't smiling, Diego's dark eyes gleamed with mischief.

The truck bounced its way across a twenty-foot section of tall weeds before Jorge brought it to a skidding, grinding halt. When Jax lowered his hands, his prints remained firmly in the heavily pilled fabric of the roof. "I see what you mean about the seven hundred miles."

Diego glanced at the outline of his hands then shot him a sardonic grin. "Actually, that was better than in our drills." He slapped the old man on the shoulder. "Well done, Jorge. Only felt like six hundred miles today."

Jax managed a small laugh. If his brother was joking around, they couldn't be facing as serious a threat as he'd thought. Could they?

The elderly driver offered Diego a toothless smile. "*Gracias*." His grin faded. "*Que Dios los acompañe, amigos.*"

Diego squeezed his friend's arm before inclining his head toward the door. "If we're not out in ten seconds, we'll be returning to Mariana with Jorge."

That was a serious threat on its own. Whatever waited for them outside the truck couldn't be a worse fate than the one that awaited them if they stayed inside. Jax grabbed for the handle and, when the door didn't move, shoved against it, nearly falling into the weeds when it flew open.

Diego grabbed his elbow to steady him, then followed Jax as he stepped out into knee-high grass. His brother had barely slammed the door before Jorge revved the engine, spun the truck around, bounced down and up over the far side of the ditch, and hurtled away in a cloud of fumes.

"Come." Diego slung an arm around Jax's shoulders and guided him toward the edge of a massive stand of trees.

"Where are we?"

They entered the dark forest, and Diego stopped. "This is El Yunque."

"Ah." Jax had been here once before, on a class trip in the fifth grade. From what he could recall, the rainforest was massive, twenty-five or thirty thousand acres. They'd done a short hike on a well-marked trail that day, but the teachers had warned them not to stray off it as El Yunque could be a treacherous place. Somehow, he doubted he and Diego were about to take a stroll along the public walkways to admire the scenery. So why had his brother brought them here?

"Look, Jax." Diego faced him, his dark eyes deadly serious now. "I know I've been joking around, but you need to realize that these people who are after me—"

"Us."

He blinked. "What?"

"They're after us, not just you. We're in this together now, whatever happens."

"All right, us. In any case, these people aren't fooling around. If they catch us, they will kill us." He grasped Jax's forearm, the desperation that had crept into his voice earlier threading through the words again. "I'm the one they want. They may not know about you yet, so it's not too late to back out. I would not blame you."

Jax shook his head. "I'm not going anywhere, except in there with you, so you can stop trying to get rid of me." He adjusted his pack higher on his shoulders. "And the longer we stand here arguing about it, the closer those guys are getting."

Diego hesitated then blew out a breath. "All right then. We'll have to go carefully, stay off the trails and make sure no one sees or hears us. Follow my lead and try to keep up." He strode deeper into the trees.

Jax fell into step behind him. The air was thick and warm, and his T-shirt soon clung to his back. For an hour or so, they did follow a rough trail, nothing like the smooth, worn one he'd traveled as a kid. With every thud of his boots on the hard ground, another question pounded through Jax's head, but he bit his lip to keep from blurting it out. Other than the sound of their footsteps, only the trilling of birds and the odd chirp of a coqui—the tree frogs that were native to the country—broke the heavy stillness of the forest.

They descended a small hill, pitted with holes and criss-crossed by tree roots. Halfway up the other side, his brother stopped. In the distance, voices intruded on the natural tranquility of the place. Diego jerked his head to a group of trees a few feet off the path, and he and Jax crept around to the far side of them. His brother lowered his pack to the ground before sinking next to it, his back to a trunk. Jax did the same. He waited, barely breathing, as the voices grew louder. Had they been found already?

The sound of a woman saying something followed by her laughter, mingling with a man's, eased the tightness in his chest. Whoever these people were, they didn't sound like professional trackers. More like locals, or tourists, maybe, enjoying a day in nature.

Neither of them moved as the couple approached, laughing and talking in English as they hiked past them on the trail. Tourists then. A light scorn accompanied that thought, but Jax extinguished it immediately. Really, he was almost as much a tourist in this country as anyone else. He was definitely relying on his brother's knowledge and expertise of the area to get them through this crazy flight through the forest to whatever destination Diego had in mind.

They sat there until the couple's voices and footsteps had long faded in the distance. Then Diego unzipped his pack, pulled out two bottles of water, and handed one to Jax. "Use it sparingly. We can refill these when we come across a spring, but it could be a while before we reach one."

Jax accepted the bottle and took a couple of swigs before screwing on the cap and sticking it in his pack. "Are there no mosquitos here?" If they'd been hiking in Canada on a hot, humid day, they'd have been eaten alive by now.

"No, none. There's no standing water in the park, it's all constantly moving, so mosquitos can't live here."

Something to be thankful for, anyway, although based on what they encountered in the rainforest, Jax might be wishing all they had to face were a few annoying mosquitos before their journey was over.

Diego pushed to his feet. "Ready to go?"

"Are you going to tell me where we're headed?"

"It's better if you don't know. But settle in—it will be a long hike."

"Long as in hours or days?"

"Days." His brother stuck an arm through the strap of his backpack. His eyes met Jax's. "Okay?"

Jax nodded, although *okay* wasn't exactly the word he'd use. He wouldn't be able to communicate with Mikayla for days. After assuring her he would call today and likely be about to head home, what would she think of this sudden, deafening silence? She'd be worried, of course. What would she do, tell Daniel? That made the most sense. Knowing Daniel, he'd jump on a plane. Jax's stomach twisted. Except for Mikayla coming here, Daniel flying to Puerto Rico, leaving his family to put himself in peril for Jax's sake, was the last thing he wanted.

He fell into step behind his brother again. Frustration over not being able to communicate with either of them sent fissions of discomfort hissing through him, like the slight, warning pain of a dentist drill venturing a little too close to a nerve. He kicked a rock out of his path, hard enough to send it crashing into the trees and earn him a dirty look from Diego over his brother's shoulder.

"Sorry," he muttered. Maybe they'd get through the forest faster than Diego had predicted. Until then, his only option was to keep going, one slogging step at a time, listening to the crickets and the calling of birds and praying that he and the brother he had finally reunited with would make it out of this rainforest alive.

Chapter Twenty-Five

Don't do it, Mik. It's not safe.

Mikayla grabbed her jacket, shoved her arms into the sleeves, and zipped it up to her chin. She couldn't stay in this apartment another minute, not without losing her mind. The convenience store a couple of blocks away was open until eleven. She'd go there, grab a soda, and come straight back. Hopefully a brisk walk in the chilly night air would help blow off a bit of steam. Mikayla dug through her purse for her wallet, then tugged a five-dollar bill out of the slot and tucked it into the back pocket of her jeans.

Foregoing the elevator, she took the stairs five flights to the lobby of her building. Jax would freak out if he knew what she was doing. *But Jax isn't here, is he?* Which brought up an excellent point. Where *was* Jax? He'd promised to call today, and he'd never left her waiting for his call before. Not even when he was only a couple of hours away and she had no reason to worry that anything might have happened to him.

How could he fail to get in touch with her, when he had to know how concerned she would be if she didn't hear from him? Had he made it to the restaurant in Candelaria? Found Diego's friends? It was possible that they'd welcomed Diego's brother into their midst. Maybe, even now, they were all sitting around a big table, enjoying drinks and food and reminiscing about Jax's brother, telling stories and sharing memories of all the great times they'd had with him.

She would understand that. In fact, she'd love to know that Jax was getting the closure he was seeking that way. But why couldn't he slip away for two minutes to call and let her know that was what was happening?

Mikayla stopped and slumped against the brick wall of a

clothing store, its interior dark and silent. Because that wasn't what was happening. She rubbed the heel of her hand over the place in her chest where all the cold that had been skittering across her skin the last couple of days had settled into a hard ball of ice.

Jax wasn't getting hold of her because, for some reason, he couldn't.

That was the only explanation. The question was, what could she do about it? A cool breeze swooped along the sidewalk, sending debris tumbling past her tennis shoes in swirls of ripped packaging and napkins smeared with ketchup. At least, Mikayla hoped it was ketchup.

The sinister thought sent a shudder through her body, and she pushed away from the wall and kicked her foot free of a paper bag. A block away, the neon sign above the convenience store glowed through the branches of a tree that swayed in the wind, sending shards of light and shadow dancing along the sidewalk.

She strode toward the light. A couple brushed by her, heading in the opposite direction. Absorbed in each other, neither seemed to notice Mikayla as they passed by. The intimacy between them, as though they were the only two people in the world, made her feel even more alone.

Shaking off the sensation, she stepped into the small store to the accompaniment of a shrill tinkling of bells. The older man behind the counter peered over and nodded, then returned his attention to a tall guy with disheveled, sandy-brown hair who stood with his back to Mikayla, checking his lottery numbers. She wandered over to one of the floor-to-ceiling drink coolers and surveyed the selection. Too many choices. Where was Jax when she needed him?

Her wry grin at the memory of him helping her choose a bag of chips in the hospital faded quickly. What would she do if something happened to him? Could she go on? Would she want to?

A gentle chiding in her soul stilled her raging thoughts and she pressed a palm to the glass. Losing Jax would be incredibly painful, but her life wouldn't end. God would be with her, and He was with Jax too, wherever he was and whatever he was going through. She might not be able to do anything for him from so far away, but she could trust that he was under God's protection.

Forgive me, Father. When am I going to learn?

She pushed away from the glass, tugged open the door, and reached for a diet cola. By the time she had wended her way around a spinnable greeting card stand and a cardboard display of DVDs, the sandy-haired man had finished paying and turned to go, clutching a fresh batch of lottery tickets in one hand. His bloodshot eyes grazed over Mikayla before he started for the door, weaving a little as he strode to the exit. Warning bells jangled in her mind as clearly as the bells on the door as he stepped outside.

Mikayla shook off the unsettling interaction as she set the cola on the counter.

The cashier rang up her purchase. "That'll be a dollar fifty."

She tugged the five out of the pocket of her jeans and laid it next to the can. He took it, rang up her purchase, scooped change out of the tray, and dropped it into her outstretched hand. "Careful out there."

Mikayla frowned slightly. Why would he say something like that? "I will. Thanks." She stuck the change into her front pocket, snagged the can, and strolled past a long row of chip and nacho bags to the door.

The couple she had passed by earlier was long gone, and Mikayla couldn't see anyone else walking along the sidewalk between the store and her building. Likely a good thing. She'd go straight home, turn on a mindless television show, drink her pop, then head for bed. By the time she woke up, Jax would likely have called or texted to let her know that everything was fine.

Maybe his phone had died, or someone had taken it and he hadn't had a chance to replace it. Really, that was the most likely scenario.

Just in case, she pulled the phone out of her jacket pocket and checked the screen. Still nothing. *He is under God's protection*, she reminded herself sternly, refusing to allow apprehension to regain the footing it had lost in the store.

Mikayla trudged toward home. One of the streetlamps was out, leaving a massive black slough stretching between poles. Her heart rate quickened. Maybe it hadn't been the brightest idea, coming out here alone. Jax wasn't the only one who would not be happy if he knew she had. Nicole wouldn't be either. Or Daniel.

She clutched the soda can tighter. It was only eleven, not the middle of the night, and she was an adult, perfectly capable of taking care of herself. After all, she'd survived being abducted—twice. Once as a toddler and then again, a year ago, when she and Jax and Holden had gone to Chicago in search of a missing child. The organization that had taken Matthew Gibson from his bed at night, believing they were rescuing him from his abusive father, was not thrilled when the three of them unearthed Matthew's location. Two of their members had kidnapped Mikayla and taken her to a warehouse where she'd been locked in a basement. She'd managed to escape, proving she could take care of herself. Which, if Jax found out about her nighttime trek to the store tonight, she would remind him.

Father, please. Bring him home so we can have that conversation. I— Someone stepped around the corner of a building and stopped in front of her. In the deep shadows, Mikayla could barely make out the man's features, but she suspected from his height and build that it was the same man who'd scrutinized her before walking out of the convenience store.

Dread flickered, swallowed up almost immediately by the burst of heat that shot through her chest. Couldn't she walk a couple of blocks without some idiot harassing her? "Excuse me." She injected as much iciness into her tone as possible as she started to step around the man.

He grabbed the sleeve of her jacket, stopping her. "Where do you think you're going, blondie?"

Blondie? Really? She yanked her jacket from his grasp. "Touch me again, and it will be the last thing you ever do."

The man swayed a little. The breeze rustling past him carried the acrid smell of whiskey with it, and Mikayla wrinkled her nose. He seemed to shrink a little, as though he hadn't expected her to stand up for herself and wasn't sure what to do now that she had. Typical bully. "Take it easy." The words slurred a little as they came out of his mouth. "I was only trying to have a little fun."

"Well, fun's over."

"Okay, okay." He waved a hand through the air before turning and stumbling in the direction he'd come, along the side of the building.

"Are you all right?"

Mikayla whirled around. The cashier from the convenience store stood a few feet behind her.

"I saw that guy notice you before he left the store and was a little worried he might try something."

"He did. But he backed off when I told him to."

"I saw. Guess I didn't need to worry."

"I appreciate you checking." And she did, even though he hadn't needed to intervene.

"No problem. Do you have far to go?"

Although she doubted he had questionable intentions, what had just happened, coupled with the fact that the two of them were out here in the semi-darkness alone, left her hesitant to tell the man where she lived. "Not far, no. I'll be fine. But thanks again for coming out to make sure." Hopefully he'd take the hint and leave her alone.

The older man touched the side of his hand to his temple. "All right, then. Have a good night." He turned and headed in the direction of the store.

She bit her lower lip as she watched him go. The man in the silver car had offered her the same salute. Was it simply a gesture of farewell, then? Had it meant nothing? It hadn't felt like nothing. Still, whoever the man who'd bumped into her was, he'd moved on and was no longer a threat.

Although the cool breeze had died down, Mikayla shivered. Her emotional turmoil over Jax's lack of communication was likely spinning recent events into far more ominous happenings than they were.

She started for home. No doubt she would hear from Jax later tonight or tomorrow, and he would offer a logical explanation for not contacting her sooner. Then she could reflect on this time and laugh at how she had allowed her overactive imagination to convince her there was far more going on than there actually was.

As it had in Chicago, when they'd brought Matthew home and Holden and Christina started the process of adopting him, everything would turn out well.

Chapter Twenty-Six

The sky was clear and the moon bright, so Diego kept hiking even after twilight had descended over the forest. For the last few hours, Jax's feet protested every step. Finally, his brother stopped walking. A wooden shelter stood a few feet from the trail. Only a roof and four corner poles, but it beckoned to Jax as strongly as any luxury hotel.

Diego shone his flashlight around the shelter, where thick foliage encroached over the edges of the cleared space.

"What are you checking for?"

"Fire ants."

Of course. That would be fun to deal with in the middle of the night. "Is that the biggest concern?"

Diego shone the light at the base of a patch of plants. "Definitely in the top ten."

Ten? Jax wasn't sure he wanted to know what the other nine might be. Thankfully, there were no venomous snakes in El Yunque. Spiders, though. Possibly other poisonous insects. And bats, of course. They'd been swooping through the air around them ever since the sun had dipped below the horizon. Jax repressed a shudder. He'd never been a fan of the flying rodents.

Diego switched the flashlight off and stuck it into his pack. When he stepped out from under the shelter and started breaking off large fern branches, Jax joined him. His brother shook each branch before tossing it onto the cleared patch of ground.

Jax did the same. "Spiders?"

"Among other things, but yeah, tarantulas, mostly."

Oh right. Tarantulas. Jax had forgotten about those. Really not something he wanted to share his bed with. Even if that bed was nothing more than a pile of ferns. They worked until they had a decent pile under the shelter. A winged creature fluttered by him. A moth. In the light of the moon, Jax could make out a number of them flitting around the undergrowth. "What's the best way to protect ourselves from insects while we're sleeping?"

"Cover up every bit of exposed skin you can." Diego separated the ferns into two piles with his boot. "We might still get the occasional bite, since this place is an insect paradise after dark, but hopefully not too bad."

"I'm tired enough it likely won't matter." Jax crouched to loosen the laces of his hiking boots.

"Good. If you sleep, maybe you can walk faster tomorrow. Keep up with me."

Jax looked up. "What are you talking about? I never fell behind."

"Only because I slowed down like I used to do when you were a kid. I'd be much farther along now if I hadn't had to wait for you."

Heat surged through Jax's chest. He'd traveled thousands of miles in his quest to find his brother. Now he was risking his life to accompany him through the wilderness, and this was the thanks he got? He abandoned his efforts with the boot and straightened. "You did not slow down for me today, and you never did when I was a kid, either. Come to think of it, I've spent my whole life chasing after you, and right now I am having a hard time remembering why."

"I never asked you to tag along after me. Not then and not now. In fact, why don't you leave in the morning. Go home to Mamá where you belong."

Clenching both fists, Jax stepped closer to his brother. "I would not bring Mamá up if I were you."

"Oh, right. I forgot what a mama's boy you are."

"One of us had to be, since you left and broke her—"

He didn't see his brother's fist coming, so the shot to his jaw sent him stumbling to one side. Jax recovered quickly. He wasn't a big fighter, but twenty years of pent-up grief and anger launched him toward his brother. He couldn't have cared less that Diego was taller or stronger than he was. He landed blow after blow on his face and torso.

Half blind with a fury he'd never experienced before, it took Jax a minute to realize that not only was Diego not hitting him again, he wasn't making any attempt to block Jax's punches. When that truth finally punctured the haze swirling around him, Jax planted his palms on his brother's chest and shoved him back a couple of steps before stomping over to a corner post and lowering himself to the ground.

Diego came over and sat next to him. Neither of them spoke for a moment, until his brother nudged him in the arm. "Feel better?"

His jaw and knuckles throbbed, but Jax gritted his teeth and ground out, "Yes, actually. You deserved that."

"I know I did. That and much more."

Which was why Diego hadn't fought back. And likely why he had picked that fight in the first place. The rage that had been fueling Jax seeped away. He bent his legs, propped his elbows on his knees, and lowered his forehead to his fingertips. "Why didn't you get in touch with us sooner, let us know you were alive?"

"I wanted to, I swear. I came close, many times. But then something would happen that put me in danger again, and I could not bring myself to draw you into it."

"At least we would have known you were alive. We didn't have to get drawn into anything. You could have told me to stay away and I would have."

His brother cocked his head and contemplated him.

All right, he wouldn't have stayed away. But his brother hadn't been around him since they were teenagers. He couldn't possibly be as sure about that as he seemed. "Maybe you don't know me as well as you think you do."

"Or maybe I do." Diego wrapped his arms around his knees. "I know it's been twenty years and you were a kid when I left, but you haven't changed that much, little brother. You were always the most loyal, selfless person I knew. The fact that you came to Puerto Rico to find me and that you are here now, risking everything to stay with me, tells me that you are still those things."

Jax raised his head. "How can you say that when I am the one who told Mamá what you were involved in, which led to the fight that drove you away?" The guilt he'd always carried for that pressed on him more heavily than his backpack had when they were hiking, and he rested his temple on one palm again.

"Is that why you think I left? Because of you?"

"Of course. I have always thought you must hate me and that was why you didn't get in touch, even with Mamá."

"Oh, Jax." Diego drove his fingers through his tangled hair. "I never blamed you for that. I knew you were trying to help me the only way you could. I didn't stay away because I *hate* you; I stayed away because I *love* you. You and Mamá both."

The rewriting of the history Jax had always believed to be true was more than his brain could comprehend. "Where did you go?"

Diego reached for a twig. "When I first left, I moved in with a few friends. Not the brightest idea, but I was pretty lost at the time. They were all into drugs too and most of them dealt, so for a long time I got sucked deeper and deeper into that world. Did two years in The East, which was hell, although it turned out to be the best thing for me because it scared me straight."

Jax felt sick. His brother had been in jail in the same city where Jax lived, and he'd had no idea. "But you still didn't contact us."

"No. I did not want you to come see me in prison. Then, when I got out, some people who had no interest in me switching to the straight and narrow path came after me. After being beaten up in an alley one night, I decided it would be best to leave the country until things cooled off. Since Papá was in Puerto Rico, it made sense to me to come here, see if I could find him."

"Did you?"

"Eventually." A shadow passed over Diego's features. "I spent a little time with him but couldn't stay because he was still drinking heavily. One night he convinced me to share a whiskey bottle with him. The next morning, I packed up and left. It was only through the grace of God that my life did not spiral out of control again after that. Another incident that scared me enough to keep me on the right path." He ran the twig aimlessly through the dirt floor of the shelter. "That was six years ago, and I have not spoken to him since."

Jax hadn't spoken to their father since he was a kid. The sorrow of that—of all the time lost with his father and brother—drained him of the little energy he had left. He needed sleep or he would hold up his brother even more tomorrow. "I'm sorry if I slowed you down today."

Diego waved the twig through the air, sending bits of dirt flying. "I only said that to make you mad. You actually did pretty good for a city boy who spends his days …" He shifted to face Jax, interest sparking in his eyes. "What *do* you do for a living?"

Although Diego's story was clearly not finished, Jax accepted the subject change. He had enough to absorb for one night. "I am a private investigator, specializing in missing persons cases."

"Ah." Diego's face softened. "You really never have stopped searching for me, have you?"

"Never."

His brother lifted his massive shoulders. "See? Loyal and selfless. I do know you."

Blood trickled slowly from a cut on Diego's face and Jax winced. "Do you have a bandage for your cheek?"

Diego swiped off the blood with his fingers and leaned back to clean them on the grass. "I will be fine. Although I have to admit you have a meaner right hook than I had anticipated."

"Sorry."

"Don't be. As you pointed out, I deserved it. I feel better now too." Diego tossed the twig away and slapped his thighs. "We should get some sleep."

Jax stood and brushed the dirt off the back of his jeans. "Yeah, especially you, old man. I might have had to hustle to keep up with you today, but you're going to run out of steam at some point."

"You can only hope."

Jax took a step toward his backpack, but his brother grabbed his elbow to stop him. When Jax met his gaze, Diego's face had grown serious. "Thank you for never giving up on me, Jax."

"I never will."

"I hope it doesn't cost you."

"It would cost me a lot more to walk away."

Diego let go of him. "That is true. Walking away does carry a terrible price."

Jax's chest clenched. He hadn't meant that as a dig against his brother. "I'm sorry. I was talking about myself, not you."

"I know. But if you had been talking about me, I would have deserved it as much as I deserved for you to hit me before."

The remorse in Diego's voice evaporated the last of the anger that had been clinging to Jax's insides like the moisture that coated the wall of a cave. Clearly his brother had believed he was protecting his family by not contacting them before now. And given his story so far, maybe he was right. Jax would reserve final judgment until he'd heard the rest of it.

He clasped his brother's shoulder. "*Buenas noches, hermanito*. Sleep well."

Diego managed a weak smile that Jax barely caught in the light filtering through the leaves of the trees. "You too."

Jax let him go and made his way to the pile of branches. His jaw and knuckles still hurt, but the far more intense pain he'd carried around for as long as he could remember had eased a little. Enough that he could draw in a deeper breath than he'd taken in a while.

Something in Diego's story had sparked questions in Jax's mind, but he couldn't dig his way through the exhaustion enough to remember what it was. He changed into track pants and, even though the temperature had barely dropped, tugged a hoodie over his head before stretching out on the makeshift bed. The hood did little to block out the loud singing of the coqui and the occasional hoot of an owl, but it might help ward off any insects that invaded their quarters in the night.

Hopefully he'd remember what his brother had said so the

two of them could discuss it before they reached the end of this insane journey. Or before whoever was chasing them caught up to them and the two of them were separated again.

Permanently, this time.

Chapter Twenty-Seven

The trails through the rainforest Diego led them along were so rough that calling them trails at all was misleading. Every muscle in Jax's body screaming at him after the intense hiking the day before and an uncomfortable night on the ground, he picked his way carefully up and down hills, stepping over rocks and roots. Several times he and his brother had to duck below the branches of a tree that had fallen across the pathway. At times the path was a little more well-defined, which Jax was thankful for as they often found themselves traversing a narrow walkway with a steep drop into a tree-covered ditch to one side of them.

Diego seemed to have a sixth sense about the presence of other people, and would gesture for Jax to step off what little path there was. They would crouch or lie behind bushes or trees until whoever it was had gone by. At the moment, they were hunkered behind a fallen log, their backs pressed to the wood as they ate a protein bar from the stash in Diego's pack. Jax swiped an arm across his forehead. He'd expected it to be hot, since it was nearly summer. But he hadn't been prepared for the humidity that sucked the oxygen from his lungs and left him breathing heavily at every incline. Not that he would let Diego see that.

He tugged the bottle of water from the side pocket of the backpack and took a few swallows. He had no idea when or where he would be able to refill it, so he forced himself to stop and screw the lid back on.

The voices of the people who had passed by them a few minutes ago had nearly faded completely, muted by the mist drifting through the trees.

"The park closes at six, so we'll be able to make better time after that—until it gets dark. Then we'll need to find another place to spend the night." Diego screwed the plastic cap onto his own water bottle and shoved it into the pocket of his pack.

"Good plan." It was hard enough to make their way along the rough trails in daylight; Jax had no desire to try and hike through darkness. One of them would end up with a sprained ankle or broken leg for sure. They might anyway, but sticking to walking during the day was their best bet. Even if it did increase the chances of them being seen.

Jax shoved that thought from his mind as he planted a hand on the log and pushed himself upright. He took a step forward, but Diego shot out a hand. "Watch."

"What?" Jax scanned the foliage in front of him.

"*Manzanillo de la muerte.*" Diego nodded at the plant with small green leaves and tiny round fruit.

Apple of death tree? That did sound like something it would be wise to avoid. "Poisonous?"

Diego nodded. "One of the most toxic plants in the world. If it touches your skin, it could burn and blister. It can even cause temporary blindness." He got to his feet as Jax skirted carefully around the plant. The rainforest held any number of menaces that he knew little about. Good thing his brother was with him or Jax might not survive long enough to get wherever it was they were going. "Should we—"

"*¡Ay bendito!*" Diego swiped at his right forearm, attempting to brush something away.

"What is it?"

"Black widow."

"Did it bite you?"

"*Sí.*" His brother twisted his arm to study the top of it.

Jax leaned closer. Two small red marks dotted the skin of Diego's forearm. "What do we do? Should I cut it and suck the venom out?"

Diego let out a short laugh. "As fun as that would be to watch, I do not think it will be necessary. Black widow bites are rarely fatal."

Rarely? Jax couldn't tear his gaze from the red marks. Was

the poison spreading already? What would he do if Diego went down in the middle of the El Yunque National Forest?

His brother shoved the protein bar wrapper into his pack and zipped it closed. "We need to keep moving."

"Are you sure?"

"Yes. We have to go." Diego slid his arms through the straps of the pack.

Jax had to trust that his brother was right, and he wouldn't have a severe reaction to the bite. If he did, Jax would have no choice but to flag down a group of hikers and pray that trying to save Diego's life didn't end up making it a whole lot easier for whoever was after them.

They hiked a couple more hours with very few breaks and almost no conversation. The air was thick and heavy, and it was a lot quieter than Jax had expected, given that the rainforest was teeming with life. Although he'd been too tired to pay much attention last night, a lot of the wildlife here was nocturnal, so it would be a lot noisier after dark.

As the light penetrating the canopy overhead grew duller, the time between seeing or hearing any other hikers grew longer. It was probably close to the six pm curfew Diego had mentioned, although Jax had no way to check the time. The trail they were following was actually paved, with handrails on either side over the deep crevices. Thick foliage crowded in on both sides, but the smooth walking path felt like pure luxury. Diego must have deemed it safe to follow a more well-laid out and used pathway now that most people had left the forest. Whatever the reason, Jax was grateful for the reprieve from the rough trails they had followed to this point, especially since they were traveling on quite a steep descent and the mist had turned the ground on either side of the cement slick and shiny.

A river flowed by them to the right, and every leaf and plant to their left dripped with moisture. The dampness in the air was so thick it collected above the neckline of Jax's T-shirt and slid between his shoulder blades. The thick aroma of wet earth and the heady fragrance of—if memory of his fifth-grade trek through the forest served—over fifty different kinds of orchids drifted up his nostrils with every breath.

The thought of the time reminded him he had no phone. That got him thinking about Mikayla, something he'd been fighting all day, since it hurt his chest to think about her wondering why he hadn't contacted her. Now his thoughts wandered along that trail that was as winding as the one he and his brother were on. What was she doing now? She'd be praying, he knew that with absolute certainty.

The thought released a little tension from his tight muscles. *Dios, remind her that I am in your hands and help her not to worry.*

A sound that had been hovering around the periphery of his consciousness for a while grew louder, a distant rumbling that had become nearly deafening. Was that water? Jax was about to reach out to tug on the strap of Diego's pack to ask him, when he caught a glimpse of the source—a large waterfall dumping water into the pond below from a height of maybe thirty-five or forty feet.

Despite the grimness of their situation, Jax stopped to drink in the beauty. Given the lateness of the day and the rapidly fading daylight, no other people were around. They had the spectacular natural wonder to themselves.

"La Mina Falls." Diego slid the pack off his shoulders and set it at the base of a tree, its wide ferns swaying gently thirty feet above their heads. "Should be okay to go in, now that it is almost dark."

A bath—primitive as it might be—sounded pretty good after a couple of days of hiking in the intense humidity. Jax dumped his pack next to his brother's. In a couple of minutes, they had stripped to their boxers, grabbed soap and razors, and picked their way carefully over rocks to the edge of the pool. Diego waded in first and Jax followed, moving slowly to avoid losing his balance on the slippery stones. They made their way almost to the bottom of the falls before sitting down, submerged to their shoulders.

The coolness refreshed and rejuvenated Jax. He set his supplies on the rock next to him and cupped his hands to scoop up enough water to splash on his face before dumping a few more handfuls over his head and neck. After running his fingers through his hair and doing a rough job of shaving and washing with the soap, he gazed at the steep rock face rising on either side of the falls, plants and trees clinging stubbornly to cracks and crevices in the stone.

"Look." Diego pointed across the water.

Jax caught a patch of green flitting between the trees on the far side of the pool. "What is it?"

"*El higuaca*. Puerto Rican parrot. One of the rarest birds in the wild. There are only about forty or fifty left in the world."

"Wow." Jax watched the bird a moment. Another flash of green caught his eye, and he drew in a quick breath. "Two of them." The parrots flitted around the trees before swooping into the open and flying over the pool, close enough that he could see the blue tips on the emerald wings and the bit of orange above their beaks, the white rimming the large, dark eyes. The loss of his phone struck him again. He'd give anything to take a picture or capture the flight on video to show Mikayla when he got home. But maybe he'd miss out on the experience if he viewed it through the tiny screen. The rat-a-tat-tat sound of their calling to one another bounced off the rock walls and echoed around the canyon. He didn't move, barely breathed, as the birds flew over them, circling in front of the waterfall before disappearing over the tops of the trees. "That was amazing."

"It was. I have never seen them live." Diego sounded slightly out of breath. "This is the only place they live now."

Somehow the idea that this rainforest was the one bit of land in the world where the beautiful birds felt safe comforted Jax a little, as though he and Diego could experience the same thing. He splashed more cool water over his chest and shoulders. Hopefully Diego was finding it equally refreshing, especially on the arm that had been bitten. The reminder punctured the cloud of euphoria he'd been floating in since witnessing the rare species overhead. Was that why Diego had sounded that way? Was the poison affecting his breathing? Jax shifted a little on the rock. "How is the bite?"

Diego pulled his arm from the water. Jax winced at the raised bump surrounded by circles of fiery red. "It is all right. The water is helping."

"How are you feeling?"

His brother stuck his hand into the water again. "Not too bad."

Yet. The unspoken word shimmered in the air between them. How long would it take for the poison to circulate through Diego's body, and how would it affect him?

Jax couldn't think about that. There was nothing he could do about it. If the situation got bad later, he would deal with it then.

They soaked beneath the thundering falls for twenty minutes, until Diego stood, water dripping from his body.

A mark on his brother's shoulder caught Jax's eye. "You've been shot?"

Diego glanced at the scar. "Oh. Yeah." He brushed the tips of his fingers across his left ribcage where a similar scar marked his skin. "A couple of times."

"Want to tell me about it?"

"Later. We better get out now while we can see well enough to get across the rocks and find a good place to spend the night."

"All right." Jax rose too, reluctantly, and grabbed the soap and razor. For a few minutes, he'd been able to relax, to almost forget about everything that was happening and simply enjoy the company of his brother.

The rocks were incredibly slippery. At one point, a few feet from shore, his foot slipped and he nearly went down, but Diego shot his arm out and grasped his elbow, steadying him. In the twilight, Jax caught the flicker on his brother's face before Diego let him go. Even if he wouldn't admit it, he was clearly in pain.

When they reached the shore, Diego unzipped his pack and pulled out his water bottle. "Better fill these while we're here."

Jax nodded, grabbed his bottle, and followed his brother to the water's edge. Clouds had drifted across the thin moon and a light mist had started to fall. As though the looming darkness and rain had summoned it, a symphony of sound—the singing of a million coqui—rose to fill the forest.

They dressed quickly in dry clothes from their packs although, given the droplets of water hanging heavy in the air, they likely wouldn't stay dry long. By the time they made their way to the trail, it was almost completely dark. Would they be able to find a sheltered area to get a little sleep?

"We better not go far," Diego said, crossing over the trail and down the small, plant-covered slope on the other side. "The canopy is fairly thick here—should keep most of the dampness off us."

Jax tried to watch out for the *manzanillo* he'd almost brushed against earlier, but soon gave up trying to distinguish one plant from another in the gathering dark.

After a couple more minutes of pushing their way through the thick foliage, his brother stopped beneath a tree where there was a bit of a clearing. "We'll have to make this do for tonight."

"It's fine." Jax dropped his pack to the ground and lowered himself next to it, his back to the trunk of a tree. He shifted a little, trying to find a spot free of roots. Since they couldn't grow deep in the rainforest, the roots of the trees stretched out largely above ground. Diego settled against the trunk next to him, their shoulders nearly touching.

It was too wet for a fire, not that it would be smart to light one anyway. As much as Jax would have loved the warm comfort and the ability to cook something, the feeling he'd experienced when they were kids lost in the woods wrapped itself around him now. Even damp and hungry, having his brother next to him filled Jax with a security he wouldn't have expected. The sense that, as long as they were together, watching out for one another, everything would be okay.

Diego dug around in his bag and pulled out two packs of jerky, two protein bars, and a KitKat.

Jax's mouth watered at the sight of the familiar red packaging. "You've been holding out on me." He unscrewed the cap of his water bottle and took a swig.

Diego's smile was grim. "I was saving it for a special occasion."

"Which is?" Jax swiped a few drops of water from his chin.

"We are halfway to our destination." Diego held up his own bottle and Jax tapped his against it.

Again, his brother flinched. The pain in his arm was clearly getting worse, which tempered his news that they were making progress. Jax didn't bring up the subject, only accepted the food his brother passed to him, setting half the KitKat bar on top of his water bottle to savor after eating the rest of their meager meal.

It was going to be a long night, and he had no idea if Diego would be fit to travel the next day.

Might as well enjoy the bit of pleasure the chocolate would bring and then hunker down and wait to see what the morning would bring.

Chapter Twenty-Eight

Okay, that's it. Mikayla dropped her paintbrush into the jar, hard enough to splash water onto one corner of the largely blank canvas she'd been staring at for two hours. She couldn't wait a minute longer. She'd managed to get through the day yesterday, but another full day had passed without hearing from Jax. For once, painting had failed to draw her away from the thoughts racing through her mind. Even if he had lost his phone, he would have had lots of time to get another one by now. Something had definitely happened.

She pushed off her stool and strode to the window. A cloud of mist had draped itself over the city, and a light rain pinged against the glass. Was it time to let Daniel know what was happening?

Her phone vibrated and Mikayla snatched it from her pocket. A text from Nicole. *Elle's fever high. Taking her to the hospital. Jordan is at a friend's until tomorrow. Will update you ASAP.*

Mikayla's stomach twisted. Elle was sick? Mikayla couldn't ask Daniel what she should do now. If he knew how concerned she was about Jax, he'd be torn about whether to go after him or stay with his wife and sick child. No way she was putting him in that position. She typed in a response to her sister. *So sorry Elle is sick. You and Daniel focus on her. All is well here. Please do send an update when you can. xoxo*

Mikayla bit her lip. If she couldn't talk to Daniel, who should she call? *Chase.* Jax's former partner might have advice for her. He'd know the steps to take to find a missing person.

Missing person. Burning bile rose in the back of her throat. Was that what Jax was?

Mikayla shook her head. She couldn't get caught up in

thoughts like that. She needed to stay calm so she could think clearly. Tapping the contact icon, she called up the list of numbers and scanned it for Chase's.

Jax's friend answered after two rings. "Mikayla?"

"Yeah. Hi, Chase."

"Something wrong?"

That was the problem with private investigators—it was impossible to hide anything from them. A sad smile quirked her lips at the thought. "I don't know. I hope not."

"Jax?"

"Yes. He went to Puerto Rico a few days ago, following up on a lead that his brother was there. He texted me the night before last to say he found out Diego was dead, and he had just been to his grave."

"Oh no." Chase sounded genuinely distressed. "That's really sad. I know he's been searching for his brother for years, hoping to see him again one day."

"Yes, he has. He was pretty upset, but he said he wanted to follow up on one more lead, going to a restaurant in Candelaria where apparently friends of Diego worked. He was hoping to get answers about what happened and then he planned to fly home. He promised to call me yesterday, right after he went to the restaurant, but I haven't heard from him."

"And you're getting worried."

"I am. He always calls when he says he's going to, so I thought for sure I would hear from him yesterday. Even if he'd lost his phone, he should have been able to get another one and call me today. I have a bad feeling something is wrong."

"You're right, that isn't like Jax. He's always good at communicating, not wanting anyone to worry about him. Especially you."

"So you think something might have happened?"

"Don't jump to any conclusions. It's only been a couple of days, and he might have a good reason for not getting in touch with you."

Mikayla didn't answer. What possible reason could Jax have

for not making any attempt to let her know he was all right? None that didn't send waves of trepidation crashing through her.

"You want to go to Puerto Rico, don't you?"

As soon as Chase said the words, she knew they were true. Not only did she want to, she *had* to go. If Jax was fine, no harm would be done if she flew there, met up with him, and accompanied him to Toronto. If he wasn't fine, there was nowhere else in the world she could be but there, with him. Or at least somewhere she might be able to find him and help him if he was in trouble. "Yes."

A long pause met that word.

"Do you think I'm crazy?"

He sighed. "Probably. But if you are, so am I. I'll go with you."

Mikayla blinked. "You will?" She hadn't considered that possibility, only hoped that Chase would give her advice on where to start searching once she arrived in San Juan. "I didn't call to ask you to do that, Chase. Don't you have a case you're working on?"

"Nothing that can't wait a few days. Pete, the new guy, doesn't start for a couple of weeks, so I haven't taken on any big cases recently."

"Well, if you're sure …" It would be helpful, not to mention comforting, to have a friend with her, especially one with PI skills. And someone who cared about Jax, not a stranger she had hired.

"I'm sure. I'll throw a few things in a bag and drive to Toronto in the morning. I'll text when I'm on my way."

"Okay." The load that had been pressing down on her shoulders lightened a little. "Thanks, Chase."

"Of course. Jax wouldn't hesitate to do the same for either of us."

"No, he wouldn't. I'll see you in the morning."

"You bet."

Mikayla disconnected the call. Although her heart raced a little, the feeling of extreme helplessness had abated. She was moving forward, not sitting around waiting to hear from Jax. Or to get news about him. Maybe he would still call before she got on a plane the next day, but knowing a plan was in place would keep her from losing her mind between now and then.

Clutching the phone tightly, she stared out the window at the hazy gray night. *Father, watch over Jax. Keep him safe. Help Chase and me to find him, so we can bring him home.*

The clouds drifted past a pale quarter moon, and a few twinkling stars appeared in the sliver of clear sky beyond the veil of mist. The spectacle filled Mikayla with inexplicable peace.

Although she had no idea what tomorrow would hold, for tonight, she would leave it—and Jax—in the hands of the One who did.

Chapter Twenty-Nine

A light rain sifted through the canopy of branches overhead. Jax huddled against the tree next to his brother and wrapped his hoodie tighter around him. The temperature had only dropped slightly with the darkness, but the moisture seeping through his clothes made it feel cooler than it was. They'd been sitting there for a couple of hours, and Diego had started to shiver. Jax nudged him in the shoulder. "Are you okay?"

"I'll be fine."

"Is it the spider bite?"

"I said I'll be fine."

Jax uncrossed his arms and pressed the back of one hand to Diego's forehead. His brother jerked away, but it was too late—Jax had already felt the heat radiating against his skin. His heart plummeted. "You're burning up."

"I'm—"

"Don't say it. You're not fine. What other symptoms do you have?"

For a moment, Diego didn't reply. Then his shoulders slumped. "Body pain. Headache. Nausea. The usual. They'll pass."

The usual? "You've been bitten before?"

"Once. I survived then, and I'll survive now."

"But—"

Diego twisted to face him. "Look, Jax. As I said, we're halfway to our destination. We have to keep going; we do not have a choice. As soon as we arrive somewhere safe, I can get medical treatment if I need it. Until then, what I have isn't going to kill me. I've pushed through worse, believe me. Stop worrying, okay?"

It wasn't okay, not by a long shot. Still, his brother was right. All they could do was keep pushing forward. Tiny green lights blinked among the plants and trees, casting a jade glow around the area. Jax contemplated them a moment, mesmerized. "What are those, fireflies?"

"*Cucúbano*, actually. Click beetles."

Jax watched them a little longer, before another soft glow, emanating from the forest floor this time, caught his eye. Glow-in-the-dark mushrooms. He'd heard about them but hadn't seen them since he'd never been here after nightfall. He wrapped his arms around himself again. "Have you had to flee from a threat like this often?"

After a short pause, his brother said, "This is the first time in three years."

An image flashed through Jax's mind—of his brother lifting the backpack from the hook and brushing off the dust. "Are you telling me no one has tracked you down since Diego Rodríguez supposedly died and you became Tomás Santiago?"

"That's right."

His mind whirled. His arrival on his brother's doorstep and someone coming after Diego the next day was not a coincidence, then. "You're saying someone followed me here, to you."

His brother sighed. "That is what I have been trying not to say ever since I got that text."

"Why not? If this is my fault …"

"It's not your fault. You had no idea how I have been living the past few years. Why would it even occur to you that someone could be following you?"

Diego was being gracious, but Jax was a PI—he should have been more aware of being watched.

His brother pulled his backpack closer and rested an arm on it. "Think about this. When you were at home, did you ever have the sense that someone was watching or following you?"

"No, I …" The quick response died on Jax's lips. The silver Matrix.

"I take it that is a yes?"

"I was moving out of my apartment last week—the same day I got your postcard, actually—and I did notice a silver car parked across the street for several hours with two men in the front seats. I thought it was odd, but then I left town and moved to Toronto and didn't see them after that, so I had completely forgotten about it. Is it possible that whoever is after you wanted to find you so badly they would target your family in Canada?"

His family. The thought sent daggers of ice shooting through Jax's chest. Had those two men come here after him or did they contact others in Puerto Rico? If they were still in Canada, Mikayla may not be safe. Or their mamá. If these people couldn't find him and Diego, would they go after the two of them, trying to get information about where they might be?

Jax planted his elbows on his knees and pressed his fingertips to his temples. He had no phone, no way to contact Mikayla or his mother and warn them to be careful. The one he'd really like to call was Daniel, since Mikayla was unlikely to let her brother-in-law know she might be in danger. Jax would give anything to be able to ask his friend to watch out for her and his mother.

Diego nudged his arm. "What is it?"

"I'm worried about Mamá. What if they go after her next?"

His brother didn't answer.

"Are you going to tell me why they want to find you so badly?"

For a long moment, the only sound was the humming of the coqui and other tree frogs. The vibrating hoot of a screech owl briefly drowned out the chirping sounds before dying away. Finally, Diego pulled the backpack onto his lap and wrapped his arms around it. "I told you I could not stay with Papá, but I wasn't ready to return to Canada either. I decided I would try to find work in San Juan. I had no car, so I started out on foot. One night, cold and tired, I stopped at a restaurant to eat."

The blond man's whispered words rocketed through Jax. "Wait. Was that in Candelaria?"

"Yes, actually." Diego rested his head against the trunk of the tree. "How did you know that?"

"Ernesto only knew that you had gone to Puerto Rico, not where to find you, but he told me he would contact a friend who might have more information. That guy texted me the next day, after I'd flown to San Juan, and I met with him. He showed me your grave and told me you had been killed three years ago and that I should accept that and move on. When I insisted I couldn't, he relented and told me you'd had friends who worked at a restaurant in Candelaria. I was headed there when I stumbled across your place."

"Who was the guy?"

"He wouldn't give me his name, although one of his men called him *Señor H.* Someone important, because he had a couple of massive bodyguards with him and was incredibly secretive. In fact, he made me swear I wouldn't tell anyone he was the one who'd sent me to Candelaria. I assumed he was high up in either the drug world or some corporation."

Diego's eyes narrowed in the dim moonlight. "Where did you meet with him?"

"Behind a church in Lirios, *Iglesia Primera de 1 Samuel 22:2*, it was called."

"Was he blond? Glasses?"

Jax nodded. "*Sí.*"

A wide grin spread across his brother's face. "That wasn't a drug lord. That was General Sergio Huertas, the Commander of the Puerto Rico National Guard."

Jax's jaw dropped a little. He'd been casually chatting with the senior military advisor to the governor of Puerto Rico? He pressed a palm to his forehead. "You have got to be kidding me." No wonder the security guards had been so thorough in checking him out, so quick to come to their boss's defense when Jax had stepped toward him in a somewhat threatening manner. He groaned, heat crawling up his neck. "I think you better tell me how you came to be friends with the Commander of the National Guard."

Diego laughed. Despite his mortification, the sound relieved Jax a little, although it was at his expense. His brother couldn't be too ill if he was laughing, could he?

"I take it you did not treat him with the appropriate amount of respect."

Jax lowered his hand to his knee. "I did get a little frustrated with him when he told me I shouldn't go around Puerto Rico asking questions about you."

Diego sobered. "That was good advice, actually."

"Why? What were you involved in?"

"I am getting to that. The night I went to the restaurant, I got talking to the waitress, and she introduced me to a group of people who invited me to sit with them at their table. Turned out they were part of a resistance movement fighting to undermine the hold the drug cartels have on this country. When they heard about my past, they invited me to join them."

"Wow." A breeze brushed by and Jax tugged his hood a little lower over his forehead. He was beginning to understand what Diego had meant when he said that he had essentially moved from one dangerous situation to another. "You were a freedom fighter?"

"Kind of, although we were not fighting against the government. In fact, we had the unofficial and unacknowledged approval of both the government and the military and essentially operated as a black ops division of the armed forces. I spent a year at boot camp, receiving military-grade training in everything from recon to weapons to interrogation to withstanding torture. Then they assigned me to a unit and sent us into the field. We would intercept drug shipments or get to the kids they used as dealers, try to convince them to leave the business. If they agreed, we'd help them and their families relocate, that sort of thing. We had an extensive, well-trained group and managed to cut into the cartels' business quite a bit. We cost them a great deal of money. Our primary target was a drug lord named César Torres."

"Puerto Rican?"

"Colombian. The major cartels here are from the Dominican, Colombia, and Venezuela. The cartels love using this country to traffic through because it's close to the US and is a major port. And there's a lucrative local market too. In a country of less than three million, it is estimated that more than sixty thousand are users of illegal drugs like heroin and fentanyl."

“Oh, man.” Jax had no idea drugs were such an issue here. His heart ached over the toll that had to take on his people.

“Yeah. It is a massive problem. Several years ago, Torres took a serious run at the country and pretty much took over as kingpin of the drug world. Other than a few months’ break in 2017 when we were deployed to help with hurricane relief and clean-up after Maria tore through the island, we went after him hard. Until …”

“Until what?”

Diego didn’t answer for a moment, long enough that Jax wondered if he would. Then he blew out a long breath. “The waitress I mentioned? Her name was Leya, and she was a fighter too. We worked closely together and ended up falling in love. Four years ago, we got married.”

“You have a wife?”

“I did.” A heavy sadness had crept into his brother’s voice.

Jax gave him time, not sure he wanted to hear what happened next.

After a moment, his brother wrapped his arms tighter around the backpack. “Three years ago, Torres’s people ambushed our safe house one night and there was a massive exchange of gunfire. Leya was at the window a few feet from me and she … she got shot. I tried to get to her, but she had been hit in the chest by more than one bullet, and she was already gone. Before I could reach her, I got hit too. Somehow, despite how injured I was and how much I was resisting because I didn’t want to leave my wife behind, a couple of my friends managed to drag me onto the fire escape and up to the roof. A number of us were able to get out that way. They found someone to treat my gunshot wounds in secret and announced to the world that I had died. And I had, in more ways than one that night.”

The heaviness in Diego’s voice settled in Jax’s chest. His brother had been through so much, suffered so deeply, and Jax hadn’t had any idea. And he’d lost so much fighting for his country. That made him a hero in Jax’s books. Which was taking a bit of a mind shift.

After another lengthy silence, he turned slightly to contemplate his brother. Diego's cheeks were wet, although Jax wasn't sure if that was tears or the mist that continued to drift around them. His brother had tipped back his head. Jax followed his gaze through the rooftop of branches—not nearly as thick now as it had been when he'd been here as a kid, something else the hurricane had stripped from this country—to the few stars that had managed to break through the cloud cover to glitter across the dark sky. A crane glided overhead, silhouetted for a moment against the golden glow of the moon. More beauty shimmering above the pain and heartache below. The two of them stared at the sky for a long time, enveloped by the echoing symphony of the tree frogs.

Then Diego spoke again, so quietly Jax had to strain to hear him over the night sounds of the rain forest. "She was carrying our child."

Jax closed his eyes and leaned his shoulder against his brother's. His own cheeks were wet, tears trickling down to mingle with the dampness on his skin. "*Siento mucho todo lo que has perdido.*"

He *was* sorry for all his brother had lost. Sorrier than words could express. The thought of losing Mikayla was more than he could bear, so Jax couldn't imagine what Diego had been through. He'd not only lost the woman he loved but his son or daughter as well. How had he survived?

Diego swiped his fingers over his face. "Torres has been on a mission to hunt those of us who got away that night and eliminate us. I know of two friends who have already been found and killed, although others were able to flee the country. Somehow Torres must have found out that I did not actually die that night. Maybe his people have been watching you or they have the postal service on their payroll, which isn't impossible."

"Why did you send that card?"

Diego ran his hand over his damp hair. "You and Mamá have been so much on my mind since I left home. When I was about to get married, I was missing you both terribly; it felt so wrong that you would not be there. I contacted Ernesto and asked him to send me a postcard from Venezuela. I drew the fish on the back, knowing you would understand it meant I was alive, even if I couldn't tell you where I was. Then I returned it to Ernesto. I don't know why it took so long to get to you."

"He said he mailed it to me four years ago, but that the country was in chaos at the time, and he wasn't surprised it got held up." Jax stuffed his hands into the pocket of his hoodie. "How did Ernesto know my address?"

"He traveled to Canada a lot on business, and whenever he was there, he checked on you and Mamá for me. Sent periodic updates, even pictures sometimes." Diego chuckled. "Including one of you all tall and gangly at your high school graduation."

The idea that Diego had been keeping tabs on them the entire time Jax was searching desperately for him tangled up Jax's emotions like the necklaces in Mikayla's jewelry box he often teased her about. The truth—that his brother hadn't discarded his family as cavalierly as Jax had believed he had—released a little tension from his muscles, but the idea of his brother knowing where they were and that he could have easily contacted them coiled them up again, until Jax had no idea how he was supposed to feel. "I will have you know that my date to graduation found me extremely handsome."

His brother let out a short laugh. "I am sure she did. From what Ernesto told me, a lot of women have over the years. Although he did not seem to think you dated many of them and no one for very long."

Jax's hands fisted in his pocket. "I don't think I like the idea of being watched that closely for years without my knowledge."

Diego started to shrug then stopped, as though the movement hurt him. "He did not watch you as much as I make it sound. A couple of times a year he would go to your neighborhood, see if he could catch a glimpse of you. All I really wanted to know was if you were okay. He would drive past the building in Toronto where Mamá lived as well and let me know if he saw her and how she seemed. That is all. But if his doing that, or the postcard I sent, is how Torres connected you and me, that makes me the one to blame, not you. Which is why I tried to avoid involving you in all of this. I have already put you at more than enough risk."

Jax shook his head. "You have been through so much and I wasn't there for you, but I am here now. And there is nowhere else I could possibly be."

Diego clasped Jax's forearm. "I admit that, as much as I do not want anything to happen to you, I am glad you are here, *conejito*."

Jax reflected on everything his brother had told him, everything he had lost. "I should not have hit you."

"Yes, you should have." Diego let go of his arm. "I may have been through a lot the last few years, but before that, from the time I left you and Mamá until I came to Puerto Rico, everything I went through was the result of my bad choices. And those choices not only hurt me, they hurt the two of you. Probably much more. So having it out with you did help ease the guilt a little. Besides," his brother's smile was faint in the dim moonlight, "I hit you first."

"That is true." Jax withdrew a hand from his pocket and touched his knuckles to his jaw, still a little swollen.

Diego crossed his arms on top of the backpack. "I wasn't completely honest with you before. I meant it when I said I have wanted to call you many times, let you know I was alive. And that most of the time it was not safe to do so. But other times, when I could have, I was too ashamed. I had no idea what to say to you, how to begin to ask for your forgiveness. Not when I have never been able to forgive myself."

"I hope you can one day."

"So do I."

"And I am working on it."

"*Gracias, hermanito.* That is all I ask." He rested the side of his head on his folded arms, as though it was becoming too heavy to hold up. "Did you say the church where you met the general, which is actually the church he attends, had 1 Samuel 22:2 in its name?"

"Yes. Do you know what that verse says?"

"I do, actually. A few months before we were attacked by

Torres's people, I was promoted to commander of our unit. General Huertas commissioned me, and he gave me the first part of that verse, which says, 'All those who were in distress or in debt or discontented gathered around him, and he became their commander.' It didn't used to be part of the name of the church, though."

"You think he added it when he thought you had been killed? As a tribute?"

"I don't know. Maybe." Diego set the backpack on the ground and clambered to his feet. "I am going to get ready for bed and then we should get some sleep." He stumbled a little and caught himself by planting a hand against a tree trunk. "Long day tomorrow."

Jax pressed his lips together to keep from commenting on Diego's state. Despite his assertions to the contrary, his brother was not okay. *God, help him. Don't let him get worse, please, or I don't know how we'll get out of this mess.*

Between the night noises of the forest and the bombshells Diego had dropped on him, Jax had no idea how sleep would be possible. Still, now that he had a better understanding of what the two of them were up against, getting some rest so they could travel as far away from César Torres and his people as they possibly could did seem like a really good idea.

Chapter Thirty

Mikayla opened the passenger door of Chase's red and black Mustang. Jax hadn't contacted her the night before or this morning, and she was struggling to keep a rising panic under control. She slid onto the front seat and settled her overnight bag on her lap before reaching for the seatbelt. What was it with these PI's and their fancy sports cars? Did they have to be so incognito when they were on the clock that they felt the need to go the other way when they were off duty? "Nice car."

"Thanks." He ran a hand over the dashboard, his face beaming. "It's a Mach 1."

Despite her angst, Mikayla managed a smile at the obvious pride in his voice. "Wow." Was that good? She had to admit it was cool. Maybe even cooler than Jax's Porsche, although she'd never tell him that.

Her smile faded. Would she be able to tell Jax anything again? Mikayla slammed the brakes on that train of thought. Of course she would. Jax was likely fine. It had only been three days since she'd heard from him. She was probably over-reacting, jumping on a plane to fly to Puerto Rico to try and find him like this. And no doubt he'd tell her that as soon as he saw her. Maybe he'd even sent a message to her that she'd missed while walking to the car. She tugged the phone from her bag and checked the screen. Nothing.

"I'm sure he's okay." Chase pulled the Mustang onto the street before glancing over.

"Oh yeah, me too." She waved a hand through the air. "I'll feel better once I see him, though."

"He won't know you." Chase grinned.

Mikayla touched a hand to her hair. She'd colored it dark

brown last night, wanting to at least minimize how much she stood out when she was traveling around Puerto Rico.

"It looks good, don't worry. And it was a smart idea, doing something to blend in a little."

"Thanks."

"How do you propose we find him? It may be a small country, but it's not like we can simply walk around and hope to run into him."

"I know. But Jax sent me a picture of his brother's gravestone with a small piece of metal artwork set in it. He said he saw a shop with similar pieces about forty minutes from there. Maybe we can find it and see if they know anything about either Diego or Jax."

"Not a lot to go on."

"No, but better than nothing. Like you said, it's a small country. Hopefully someone will have heard of Diego Rodríguez."

"You know it's a Spanish-speaking country, right? There could be dozens, maybe hundreds, of people named Diego Rodríguez there."

Mikayla hadn't thought of that. Of course there could be. She bit her lip. This really was a fool's errand, wasn't it? Why did she think she could do it? She was no private investigator. Of course, that's what Chase was here for. "Jax also mentioned a restaurant in a place called Candelaria where friends of Diego's worked. We could start there."

"Do you know the name of the restaurant?"

She thought back. Jax hadn't said the name, had he? At the time, it hadn't occurred to her that she might go there, so she hadn't asked. Foolish. "No. But I researched the town. It's fairly close to San Juan, and it's not that big."

"Still could be a number of restaurants." Chase reached over and touched the back of her hand with his knuckles. "Sorry. I don't mean to discourage you. We'll do everything we can to find him. I only want you to know that it isn't likely to be easy. And judging from what happened to Diego, it may not even be safe. Although the restaurant lead is a good one, we'll need to be careful how freely we toss out Jax's brother's name."

"That's true." Mikayla stared out the window. A morning fog drifted between the skyscrapers and businesses lining the busiest stretch of highway in Canada. Traffic was heavy, as usual, but her frenzied thoughts kept her so distracted that before she knew it Chase was pulling off the highway and approaching the departures terminal of Pearson airport.

A silver car exited the highway behind them, and Mikayla studied it in the side mirror. Two large men sat in the front seats. Was that the same car with the driver who had bumped into her in the street? Another memory struck her, one she hadn't thought of since the day Jax had moved. The car that nearly ran her down outside his apartment was silver too, wasn't it? Was it possible it was the same vehicle? Were they following her and Chase? She pressed a hand to her abdomen. No reason they would be, unless they thought she might lead them to Jax.

If they were tailing him, no doubt they'd followed him to the airport as well. Had he noticed? If they hadn't flown to Puerto Rico after him, had they notified someone there that he was coming? Was that why communication with him had been cut off?

Mikayla shifted on the seat. *Rein it in.* She needed to slow down and think so she didn't make a mistake that would put Jax in even more peril. Or herself.

"You okay?" Chase turned into the underground parking lot and lowered his window so he could take a ticket from the dispenser.

"Yeah, sure." Should she tell him about the car? If he thought someone was following them, no doubt he would call off this crazy trip and suggest they go straight to the police. Mikayla studied the mirror. No other cars entered the lot behind them, and she tore her gaze from the side mirror. She was being paranoid. No one was following … A flash of silver caught her eye and she checked the reflection again. The car that had been following them on the ramp had entered the underground parking lot. Okay. That was weird. But short of changing her mind about flying to PR, what could she do about it?

Chase parked the car and killed the engine. "Sure you want

to do this?"

Mikayla grabbed the straps of her bag. "I'm absolutely sure. But you don't have to come with me if you're not. I'll be fine."

He reached for the door handle. "Well, I wouldn't be fine if I let you go alone. Jax would kill me. Or Daniel would. Or they'd take turns. In any case, I think I'd rather face whatever we encounter when we get to Puerto Rico." He shot her a look. "Which I'm sure will be nothing but palm trees and spring breezes. And Jax enjoying both."

While not communicating with her? That was unlikely. "I'm sure you're right." Mikayla pushed open her door. The silver car drove by slowly. Both men stared straight ahead. She pretended to do up the zipper on her bag while keeping an eye on them in her peripheral vision. Consumed by trying in vain to catch a decent glimpse of their faces, she forgot to check the license plate until the car had driven too far past her and Chase for Mikayla to see it.

The vehicle wended up and down aisles until it reached the exit and drove out of the lot. Extremely weird. At least they weren't going to follow her and Chase into the terminal. Either she was wrong and the silver car being at the airport had nothing to do with her, or they only wanted to make sure she was actually flying somewhere. Cold chills ran along her spine, but Mikayla shoved thoughts of the men out of her mind. While she'd be careful to watch for anyone who might be showing particular interest in her when she arrived, nobody would keep her from going after Jax.

Chase met her at the rear of the vehicle. "Hey. I should mention that I might have a bit of trouble at customs. There's another Chase Washington on the no-fly list and that sometimes causes issues. So far I've been able to work it out with them, prove we're not the same guy, but you never know what could happen."

Chills brushed over her skin again. What if they didn't let Chase on the plane? Should she still go? "Good to know."

He opened the trunk and reached for his bag. "We should also see if we can find Jax and Diego's dad. Maybe Jax will be there and so busy catching up with him that he's forgotten about keeping in touch with us."

"Maybe." Mikayla gripped the straps of her bag tighter. That would have been an intense meeting, if Jax had ended up going to see his father after finding out his brother was dead. It made sense that he would, but would he have forgotten to contact her because of it? That wouldn't be like him, although it would be understandable if a reunion with his dad after decades apart occupied all his mental space for a couple of days.

Chase slammed the trunk closed and the two of them strode towards the terminal. No sense wasting time driving herself crazy with all these questions. No one but Jax could answer them, so the only way to ease her mind was to get to Puerto Rico, find him, and ask him herself.

Mikayla checked her messages one last time before getting in line at the ticket counter. She hadn't booked online in case Jax did message her this morning that he was fine and about to come home.

Still nothing. She bit her lip as she tucked the device into the pocket of her bag. Whatever was keeping Jax from contacting her couldn't be good.

Chase lowered his duffle to the ground as he joined the line behind her. When Mikayla had checked the website last there had been quite a few seats available. Hopefully that was still true, and they would be able to sit next to each other, do a little strategizing on the best course of action to take once they landed. The decision to come had been so spontaneous she hadn't thought much past getting to the country. Chase's idea to contact Jax's father was a good one.

Although it wouldn't likely be easy to narrow down all the men named Juan Miguel Rodríguez in the country either, especially since Mikayla had no idea what town he lived in. The person at the front of the line finished and walked away, clutching a boarding pass in one hand. Mikayla shuffled forward behind the four people ahead of her as the next person stepped to the counter. She had to stop thinking about how little they had to go on, how much like searching for a needle in a haystack this crazy trip was, or she would abandon the idea altogether.

And she couldn't do that. Even if it had only been three days, Jax's silence was filling her with a dread she couldn't explain. Something was wrong. Something more than him losing his phone or getting distracted by a visit with his papá.

The person in front of her in line moved to the counter. When he strode away two minutes later, a laptop case slung across his chest and his ticket in hand, Mikayla strode forward, motioning for Chase to join her. They managed to get seats next to each other, and the ticket agent didn't comment on Chase's name when he showed her his ID. Hopefully things would go as smoothly with customs.

They got into different lines to go through the security check. The airport was busy, and it took so long to reach the conveyer belt that Mikayla was starting to get a bit nervous about reaching their gate in time. She set her bag on the belt, loaded her phone, wallet, and shoes into the gray bin, and walked through the metal detector. The security guard waved her along and she grabbed her stuff and bent to slip on her running shoes. Chase's voice caught her attention as she finished tying her second shoe and she straightened. He was arguing with two security guards, both standing in front of him, their faces stern. Mikayla's heart sank. *Please let him through. I can't do this alone.*

"You'll have to come with us, sir." When Chase didn't move, the larger of the two men grasped his elbow.

"Wait." Chase twisted toward Mikayla. "Mik. I need to straighten this out. Don't get on the plane without me."

Mikayla didn't want to make this worse for him, but she wasn't about to make any promises she didn't plan to keep. "I'll wait as long as I can."

"Mikayla. If you get on that plane, I'll call Daniel and tell him where you're going." Chase sounded desperate, which, given how the jaws of both security guards had tightened and the one who held his elbow had already started to pull him toward a long white hallway, was not helping his cause any.

Mikayla wouldn't blame him if he did call Daniel. He was trying to protect her, like Daniel would want to do if he knew about this crazy quest of hers. She took a couple of steps closer, until another security guard held up a hand to stop her. "Elle is really sick, and I don't want to pull Daniel away from her. Give us both as much time as you can, then do what you have to do."

He sent her a last, pleading look, but didn't speak again as the guard dragged him away.

Mikayla watched until the three of them had disappeared through a set of doors. *God, help them to let him go in time*. This time she didn't add the thought that she couldn't do this alone. Whether or not she wanted to, and whether or not Jax's former partner made it to the plane on time, she wouldn't have a choice.

Like Chase, she would have to do what she had to do.

Mikayla headed for the waiting area at the gate where she would board the flight to San Juan. Her mind churned as she attempted to process everything that had happened since Chase had picked her up that morning. The smart thing would be to wait for him, which would probably mean taking a different flight, but sitting around the airport doing nothing would drive her crazy.

She tightened the grip on her bag. She wasn't a helpless child. The last few years had been rough, but with the help of God, she had made it through. Her experiences had strengthened her, and although she occasionally needed to remind herself not to worry, to give her anxieties up to God—especially those that involved losing someone else she loved—it had become easier to do that as she persevered through the shadowy realm of grief and loss. While it had been the most painful experience of her life, it had also taught her a valuable lesson. There was no place she could go where she would not find God waiting there for her.

Maybe the people in her life wouldn't like her going off to a strange country on her own, but that was the thing. She wasn't on her own and never would be.

The thought fortified her as she approached her gate. The memory of the two men in the silver Matrix drifted through her mind and her steps slowed. Who were they and why were they following her and Chase? And watching her and Jax outside his old apartment building? The answer came to her in a blinding flash of light.

Diego.

It wasn't impossible that someone Jax had investigated might be after him, but if they were following her to the airport when she was trying to get to him in Puerto Rico, it made sense that this was about his brother. Still, if Diego was dead, why were they continuing to tail Jax? And how could she ensure they didn't use her to do it?

Her phone. She barely resisted the urge to smack her head with a palm. Why had she brought it? She knew better than that. Jax hadn't taken his; he'd bought a burner phone when he arrived, and she should have thought to do the same thing, even if it meant he could no longer reach her. She had his temporary number—she could text him from her new phone once she had it.

Mikayla had almost reached her gate. If whoever was following her was tracing her, even now, with her phone, she was about to confirm her destination to them. She reached gate 27 and passed by. At the waiting area on the opposite side of the long hallway, a sign announced the imminent departure of a flight to Jamaica. The plane hadn't boarded yet, and Mikayla slipped into the waiting area and settled on a hard seat two away from a man and woman. They were clearly tourists in their shorts and matching Hawaiian shirts. The man even had a camera around his neck.

Under other circumstances, she would have smiled, listening to them chatting to each other about everything they would do and see. They held hands as they discussed the excursions they had booked and what restaurants they planned to visit. Was this a second honeymoon for them?

Her throat tightened. Would she and Jax ever have a second honeymoon? Or a first? She gave her head a little shake as she set her bag on her knees and unzipped the end pocket. She needed to stay focused. If she could keep her wits about her, the chances of them both surviving whatever situation she was about to walk into might go up. Mikayla dug around in the pocket and withdrew her phone.

Aware that she was running out of time to board her own flight, she quickly deleted her contact list and any personal information. The photos she sent to her computer so she could download them when she got home, whenever that might be. After erasing those from her device, she clutched the phone in her cold fingers. What should she do, throw it in the garbage? That might stall the search for her, if one was actually being carried out and she wasn't being paranoid.

A voice crackled over the loudspeaker, announcing that the flight to Montego Bay was about to start boarding. Mikayla stared at the large red and white striped bag on the floor next to the woman two seats over. Maybe she could do a little more than simply halt the search.

When the announcement had been made, the man in the Hawaiian shirt had begun rifling through the documents he clutched in one hand. The woman leaned close as they checked to make sure they had their boarding passes and any other documents they might need. In seconds, they would begin gathering up their bags and preparing to board.

Mikayla set her bag on the ground, as close to the woman's as possible. Unzipping the top, she dug inside with one hand while casually reaching out with the other. She slid the phone into a small, open pocket at the end of the woman's bag. When she tapped it down, it was barely visible from above. Would the woman notice it when she picked up the bag?

Mikayla zipped hers closed and straightened. She held her breath as the woman scooped up the handles of the bag and stood. Still chatting away to her husband, she flung the straps over her shoulder and the two of them started for the line. Hopefully the woman would discover the phone during the flight and turn it in to a ticket counter at the airport when they landed. The last thing Mikayla wanted was to cause trouble for that poor couple by having someone with nefarious intentions follow them around Jamaica.

She didn't take a deep breath until the man and woman had disappeared into the tunnel. Then she grabbed her bag and hurried to the gate for her flight to San Juan.

It hurt to lose her phone and any opportunity Jax might have to contact her in the next few hours, but if passing it off to someone else meant throwing whoever was following her off her trail—and Jax's—then the loss would be well worth it in the end.

Chapter Thirty-One

Jax dozed off and on all night, jerking awake when a thin ray of light worked its way through the canopy overhead. Morning. The mist had deepened to a drizzle. His gaze fell on an Emerald, a small hummingbird, clinging to the rough bark of a tabonuco tree and appearing as wet and miserable as Jax felt.

In the light of day, the forest had grown quiet again, the only sounds the occasional call of a bird and the patter of rain on the broad leaves and bright orange blossoms of the False Bird of Paradise plants. Jax straightened and ran his fingers through his damp hair. Might be just as well that Mikayla wasn't here, as much as he missed her. If he looked as bad as he felt, he wasn't sure he wanted her to see him that way. Of course, if they were going to get married, they'd have to be able to show each other the worst of themselves, physically or in any other way. The thought of that—of seeing her again, of committing himself to her for life—warmed him despite the dampness.

Speaking of Mikayla, he'd give an awful lot of money for a good cup of coffee right now. His stomach growled and he pressed a palm to it. And a hot meal. They'd been subsisting on protein bars, beef jerky, and water, and his body was protesting hiking the rough, mountainous trails of El Yunque on such little food.

He shot a sideways glance at Diego. His brother was still asleep, his breathing shallow, beads of moisture dotting his forehead. Could be mist, but Jax suspected it was the fever gripping him as the poison raged through his body. How long did symptoms of a black widow bite last, anyway? Could they get worse? If he'd known they were going to be trekking through the rainforest, Jax would have done some research on the wildlife or any other potential hazards. Like the boa their teachers had warned them about when his class came here.

Jax scrutinized the overhanging canopy of trees. The boas, which were typically six or seven feet long, blended in well with the tree trunks, since they were brown with spots. One could be coiled above their heads, even now. Although he scrutinized every branch, he saw nothing but a pair of bananaquit, the national bird of Puerto Rico, a small warbler with black and white head and yellow breast, flitting around the wet, heavy leaves.

Jax tried to estimate what time it was. The light was dull, but the thick cloud cover and steady drizzle made it difficult to tell whether that was because it was early or because the sun wasn't making any attempt to break through the thick haze. Either way, they should likely get going. Although Jax was loathe to wake his brother, they hadn't gone far off one of the main trails through the park last night. Hikers would likely be starting to walk by before too long, although the rain might keep the numbers lower today.

Before Jax could decide what to do, Diego stirred next to him. His dark eyes, when he opened them and met Jax's, were slightly bloodshot, and Jax could still feel the heat shimmering off him, but he was alive. That was something.

"*Buenos días.*"

Diego managed a faint smile as he straightened. "*Buenos días.*"

"*¿Cómo te sientes?*"

His brother closed his eyes again, as if assessing how he felt. "Not too bad."

A little vague, but Jax didn't push him. They needed to move. As Diego had said the day before, if he still needed medical attention when they reached their destination, he could get it then.

They ate another protein bar, took a few gulps of water, then started off. Diego led him to the paved trail they'd taken the day before, which Jax was grateful for. In case the spider bite was making his brother a little less alert, Jax would pay close attention for any sound that could indicate other people were approaching.

They hiked for an hour before the drizzle morphed into a more serious rainfall. Jax tugged up the hood on his sweatshirt, for all the good it would do him as it was completely soaked through. Diego wasn't complaining or showing any signs of slowing down, so Jax wasn't about to either. Being wet was uncomfortable, miserable, even, but not deadly. Not like, say, falling into the hands of a notorious drug dealer.

The thought made him pick up his pace a little and tug his hood away from his ears so nothing would block the sound of voices or approaching footsteps.

The day passed slowly. As Jax had expected, they encountered only a handful of people, and each time they had enough warning to vacate the path and duck behind trees or fallen logs.

The rain never let up, only grew heavier as the hours dragged on. When twilight draped like thick cobwebs over the forest, they left the paved trail and started along another rough one, a steep incline fraught with roots and fallen branches. Jax trudged along, his hiking boots heavy with rain, water splashing beneath them with every step. Once he fell, going down hard on one knee. Diego stopped and half-turned toward him. "Are you okay?"

His knee throbbed, but if Diego could press on in his condition, so could Jax. "Fine."

His brother nodded and continued the climb. What little light had struggled to penetrate the cloud cover and canopy of ferns flickered and threatened to go out like a candle in a breeze. How much longer would they go today? Jax didn't ask, only kept planting one foot in front of the other. The Mina River flowed forty or fifty feet below them, a gray and brown boa winding through the canyon.

A few more minutes and Diego stepped off the trail onto a thin ledge. Jax edged along after him until they reached an opening in the rock. A cave. He nearly wept. Was it possible they could spend the night out of the elements? That they might be able to find dry clothes somewhere in the bottom of their packs and change out of the sopping ones that clung to both their bodies? Hardly daring to hope, he followed his brother a couple of feet inside the cave, breathing in the musty smell of their shelter. "Are we spending the night here?"

"Seems like a good place." Diego shrugged off his pack then offered Jax a wry grin. "Unless you would like to go farther?"

"No, this is good." Jax tugged his pack off too and dropped it on the floor. It was too dark to see how far back the cave went, but as they were already in out of the rain, it didn't much matter.

Diego dug around in his bag and pulled out the flashlight. When he shot the thin beam around the space, Jax caught a glimpse of a pile of twigs and logs piled against one wall of the deep cavern. A sudden rush of wings, accompanied by high-pitched squealing, filled the air along with a cloud of black flapping around Jax. A bat brushed against his shoulder, and another skimmed the top of his head as hundreds—maybe thousands—of the tiny, winged creatures swooped past him. Startled, he stumbled back a few steps.

"*¡Cuidado!*"

His brother's warning cry came a little late. Jax's last step fell on air, and he dropped several feet, landing on his hands and knees on a steep incline. Gravity and the sharp angle tugged him toward the canyon. He grabbed wildly at a sapling to keep from sliding, but it snapped in his hands. Suddenly, he was tumbling and rolling down the incline, crashing over sparse foliage that did nothing to slow his descent.

A few seconds later he landed at the bottom, thumping to a stop on his back on a patch of plants and dirt inches from a field of rocks that likely would have killed him on impact. A few feet away, the river flowed gently on. The air had been knocked out of him, and Jax stared up at the darkening sky a moment, desperately willing his lungs to remember how to function. Finally, he drew in a shuddering breath. A few more of those and he was able to start assessing how the rest of his body was doing, as Diego had done upon waking that morning.

"Jax!"

Diego sounded even more frantic than he had when Jax first stepped off the rocky ledge outside the cave. He shouted something else that Jax couldn't make out over the ringing in his ears and another sound, a deep rumbling like the Mina Waterfall when they approached it the day before. Was there a waterfall around here? He couldn't remember hearing it when they were hiking up the side of the mountain.

Diego shouted again. The desperation in his voice as he scrambled down the side of the rock face finally broke through Jax's daze.

"The river!"

Jax forced himself to roll onto his side. What about the river? He peered in the direction of the roaring sound. Through the murky dusk, he could barely make out a wall of water hurtling toward him, crashing against one side of the canyon and then the other. He froze.

Flash flooding was the biggest threat in the rainforest. Somehow, although it had been raining all day, he hadn't considered that possibility. Likely Diego had, which was why he had taken them off the lower, easier trail and up the rougher one to the cave. If Jax hadn't fallen into the canyon, the two of them would have been perfectly safe there as the water roared by.

Now, though … His heart in his throat, he scrambled to his feet and threw himself against the side of the mountain, fumbling for finger and toe holds as the wall advanced like a train barreling along the tracks.

"Jax."

He looked up. A few feet above him, Diego held tightly to the thin trunk of a tree with one hand and stretched his other one out to Jax. Could he reach it?

The roar of the water shook the ground like an earthquake. Jax dug his fingers into a crevice and hauled himself up a few more inches. The water reached him, swirling around his boots and splashing off the rock face onto his jeans and sweatshirt.

Jax flung an arm above his head and Diego's fingers closed around his wrist. His brother yanked him up as Jax scrabbled to push off rock with his toes, dig the fingers of his free hand into dirt, anything to help Diego haul him out of the ravenous mouth of the watery monster.

When he reached his brother's side, Diego waited until Jax had a good grip on a root and then released his wrist and jerked his head for Jax to go on ahead. He made his way cautiously upward, testing the strength of every root, every foothold, before putting his full weight on it, trying not to think about how, if one of them gave way, he would hurtle into the black, swirling water below and be swept away, likely taking his brother with him.

At last they made it to the ledge. He and Diego crawled over the lip of the rock and collapsed, panting, on the floor of the cave.

Neither of them spoke for a few moments, until Diego sat up. "Are you hurt?"

Jax had no idea. Every inch of him pulsed with pain, but were any of the injuries serious? "I don't know. Give me a minute." Breathing still required effort. Had he hit his head? He didn't think so. Although he had struggled to draw in air, he hadn't blacked out, which was a good sign. His legs weren't broken either, or he wouldn't have been able to sprint to the rock face or climb it.

He ran through a mental checklist, moving body parts as he did. Finally, he eased himself to a sitting position and pressed his back to the wall. "I think I'm okay."

"*Gracias a Dios*." Diego swung around to sit next to him.

Yes. Thanks be to God. Once again, He had proven His presence and protection over Jax in snatching him from the jaws of near-death. Jax never should have escaped either that fall or the roaring flood waters as unscathed as he had. He should have broken something. Like his neck. Mikayla must be praying very hard for him. A wan smile crossed his face.

Diego expelled a breath. "I could use a drink."

Jax almost laughed. His entire body ringing with shock and pain, he could use a drink himself, something he rarely indulged in. He rested his head against the cold, damp stone. "How did you not drink when Leya died?"

"I nearly did, believe me. I had to lean with everything I had on my higher power and the one-day-at-a-time principle, or my version of it, anyway. Every day I told myself *just not today*. You can have a drink tomorrow, just not today. And the next day I would tell myself the same thing. But I knew, if I had even one, it would be like you falling down the mountain. There would be no way to keep myself from dropping all the way to the bottom. Only I wouldn't have escaped the raging river below—it would have sucked me in, swallowed me up. I never would have gotten free of its clutches. Certainly not on my own." He picked up a pebble from the floor of the cave and tossed it against the far wall. "Some days, when all I could think about was Leya and our child, it was a battle to remind myself why that would even matter. Then I'd throw myself on God's mercy again and make it through one more day."

Jax's chest ached for his brother. The fact that he had been able to stay sober and clean during a period of such intense pain, grief, and loss was a testament to how far he had come. Still, it must continue to be a battle for him.

He lifted his arm, partly to assure himself that he could and partly to press his hand to Diego's forehead again. His brother didn't pull away this time. To Jax's relief, Diego's skin was cool against his. "You feel better."

"I am. I told you I would not die. Not from the spider bite anyway."

That sobered Jax. The elation of his death-defying climb to the cave dissipated into the mist drifting past the mouth of the cave. He might have escaped a fall and a flood tonight, but he and Diego weren't out of the woods yet—literally or figuratively. They were still being pursued by a deadly enemy, and no one in the world knew where they were. Like those four days when they were kids. They'd survived then, but something told him it wouldn't be as easy this time.

God, help me not to worry about what might come next and simply be grateful for how far you have brought us. That really was something to celebrate. "Got any more KitKats?"

His brother clasped Jax's arm. "*Hermanito*, after what we went through tonight, I think we can do a little better than that."

Chapter Thirty-Two

Mikayla had grown up in Chicago and lived in Toronto the last couple of years, so she was used to driving in big cities. Still, maneuvering through the streets of San Juan when she had never been to the country before had her clutching the steering wheel of her rental car so hard her knuckles ached.

Even in the light of the streetlamps, the palm trees lining both sides of the streets were intriguing and definitely not something she'd seen in either of the cities she had lived in, but she kept her eyes on the road in front of her, determined not to be distracted by the foliage, interesting buildings, or colorful storefronts. She wasn't here to sightsee—she was on a mission.

That meant she needed to get to Candelaria and find out if Jax had ever reached the restaurant where Diego's friends worked and, if he had, what had happened to him after that. She had no idea how many restaurants there were in the town or how perilous it might be to go around asking about either Diego or Jax. The sudden break in communication from Jax suggested it might be extremely dangerous, so she would have to proceed with a great deal of caution.

Mikayla had always preferred to have a clear plan, to know exactly where she was going in life and how she was going to get there—something she believed was rooted in her abduction as a toddler. Dating Jax had helped a lot. He was much more spontaneous than she was, and part of getting involved with him meant she'd had to let go of her compulsive need to see far down the road in front of her. God was in control, not her. That truth had become a life motto over the past year.

Still, a little more foresight than she possessed at the moment would bring her a lot of comfort. *Father, help me let go of my need to know what will happen and simply trust you. You've proven yourself worthy of that trust over and over. Give me courage. Please, please help me to find Jax. And let him be okay.*

She refused to let the thought that he might not be take root in her heart and mind. Not when she'd just committed him—and her worries—to God.

Mikayla followed the GPS and managed to find her way out of the city. With each mile that clicked beneath her wheels as she headed west on PR-22, she prayed that Jax wasn't in San Juan. The airport was incredibly busy—what if he'd been there at the same time she was, on the departures level, and they'd missed each other?

If he was anywhere else in the city and couldn't get to a phone, she would never be able to find him there. Not to mention that the distance between them would be growing with every passing second. Mikayla straightened in her seat. Although she wasn't sure how much faith she could put in her intuition, as obscured as it was by her concern for Jax, she didn't believe that he was in San Juan. So where was he?

Did someone want to keep Diego's death a secret for some reason? Enough to permanently silence anyone who might stumble across his grave?

Mikayla let go of the wheel with one hand then straightened and bent her fingers a few times to get the blood flowing. She couldn't think that way. Jax was alive. He had to be. And the tip about Candelaria gave her a place to start. Slightly better than nothing.

"Look at me, Jax." Mikayla managed a shaky smile. "Striking off into the unknown with no real idea where I'm going or what will happen when I get there. You'd be impressed." He might not be happy when he found out she'd put herself at risk to come to Puerto Rico after him, but part of him would be proud of her for launching into an adventure without a plan. Like she was proud of him for never giving up on his brother, for going after him, whatever the cost.

A light rain pattered against her windshield, and she switched on the wipers, straining to see in the waning daylight and heavy mist. What time was it, anyway? She twisted her arm a little to check her watch. Almost seven o'clock at night. Eight o'clock here, since she hadn't changed her watch from Eastern to Atlantic Standard time yet.

Her stomach grumbled. She hadn't had anything but water since she'd left for the airport. No wonder she was hungry. Thankfully, Candelaria was only half an hour away. She would head there, find a place to spend the night, then begin her quest by choosing a restaurant for a late dinner. Or not that late here, apparently, as Jax had told her it wasn't unusual for people, even kids, to eat at eight or nine at night. She could feel out her server, see if he or she knew anything about Diego. If not, she would go from one eating establishment to another tomorrow. It might be risky to ask about the Rodríguez brothers, but at this point, she wasn't sure she cared. She had to find Jax, and if this was the way to do it, she'd take whatever chances she needed to take.

Maybe she could pull over once she reached the town and find a hotel on her … Her thoughts trailed off. She had no phone to search for hotels on, and she didn't want to pull over here and try to enter a request for the GPS to direct her to one. Hopefully it would be easy to spot a place as she drove through the town.

The poor weather and visibility slowed her a little, but forty-five minutes later she was driving through Candelaria. She'd completed the first leg of her journey.

After traversing the streets for several minutes, the *Hotel* sign on the front of a white stucco building with teal trim caught her eye. Mikayla turned into the small lot and parked her rental car. For a moment, she sat and contemplated the place. It appeared to be well-kept up and the signs were in English, which was promising. Mikayla's Spanish was rudimentary, and while she knew that at some point she would have to try and communicate that way, she was hoping to put that off as long as possible.

With a curt nod, she grabbed the overnight bag she'd set on the passenger seat and pushed open her car door. Even this late in the evening, a blast of humid air hit her as she stepped out of the air-conditioned vehicle. She closed her eyes, listening to the sounds of crickets and frogs, light traffic, voices calling to each other in Spanish. Her chest ached suddenly with a ferocity that stole her breath. Although Jax had been born in Canada, he'd told her once that his heart would always belong to Puerto Rico. Being here, in his family's native country, made her feel so connected to him that the idea that she might never see him again sent a pang of grief twisting through her. Her eyes stung, but she blinked away the tears and opened her eyes.

She'd come this far. She wouldn't give in to emotion now. Mikayla hit the remote to lock the car door and strode toward the entrance of the hotel.

The man behind the front desk smiled as she approached. "*Hola.*"

Mikayla returned his smile. "*Hola. Hablas inglés*?"

His smile widened. "Yes, madam. Of course. How can I help you?"

His accent was strong, but Mikayla had no trouble making out what he was saying. "Do you have a room available for the night?"

He clicked a few keys on the laptop on the desk. "*Sí.* Yes. We have a single room."

"*Está bien.*" Mikayla set the bag on the counter and unzipped the pocket. After tugging out her wallet, she opened it and withdrew her credit card.

The man clicked more keys and the printer on a shelf behind him whirred to life. He fetched the piece of paper it spit out and set it on the counter. "That will be sixty-eight dollars. U.S., of course." He reached for a pen in the holder on the counter. "You are from America?"

"Canada, actually." She handed him her credit card then bit her lip. How much information should she give out to strangers? Of course, he could access the billing address attached to her card and see for himself where she was from, but she really needed to think before she answered any questions. Being here alone instead of with Chase meant she had to be extra careful.

As Mikayla signed the form, the man ran her card through the machine then handed it to her along with a door key card and instructions on how to get to her room.

"*Gracias.*" Mikayla stuck the key in her pocket and then returned the card to her wallet and stuffed the wallet into her bag. "Can you tell me if there is a restaurant nearby?"

"Of course. There are two I would recommend: *Restaurante de Esmeralda* and *El Pescado Rojo*. *El Pescado Rojo* is across the street and two blocks east." He pointed in the general direction of east, which she appreciated. "Esmeralda's is three blocks west of here."

"*Gracias*," she repeated.

The man, dark curls framing his young face, flashed her another smile. "*De nada.* I wish you a good night."

Mikayla nodded as she heaved the bag off the counter. Should she leave it in her room or go straight to the restaurant? Her stomach rumbled again, settling the question for her. She left the office, hesitated a moment, and then turned west. Esmeralda's Restaurant. Maybe a woman owned the place, someone Mikayla could ask about Jax or Diego.

El Pescado Rojo. The meaning flitted on the periphery of her mind. *Rojo* meant red. And *pescado*? It took a minute to come to her, but when it did, she halted abruptly. *Pescado* meant fish. The Red Fish.

Diego had signed the postcard he'd sent to Jax with a fish. Was that a sign? She spun around and headed east. Whether or not it was, something inside her told her this was the way to go.

And, as she had little else to go on at this point, she'd follow her gut tonight and see where it might lead her.

Chapter Thirty-Three

In the thin beam of light from Diego's flashlight, Jax contemplated the wood piled against the wall. "Could we take a chance on a fire?"

Diego nodded. "I think it would be okay if we build it far enough back in the cave. It'll get a little smoky, but it might be worth it to be able to cook our food and dry our clothes."

Jax tossed his wet hoodie over a rock. After the day they'd had, both of those sounded worth the gamble. "No chance this rainforest is populated with rabbits, is there?"

Diego snorted. "No chance at all. We are going to have to go a little more Puerto Rican with our dinner."

"Mongoose?" Jax had seen a couple of the furry mammals scurrying away from them as they'd approached. Some of them were pretty big, twenty-five or thirty pounds, but a smaller one would feed the two of them.

"No, you do not want to get too close to those—they are liable to have rabies. I have something else in mind."

"What do you want me to do?"

"Get the fire started. Here." Diego unzipped an outside pocket on the backpack, dug around, then tossed a box of matches in a plastic bag to Jax.

Jax caught it. He'd managed to find a dry T-shirt, jeans, and socks in his pack and was starting to feel almost human again. A fire and a little hot food would no doubt take him the rest of the way. He'd even started to feel optimistic about the possibility of them reaching their destination and getting somewhere safe, out of the reach of Torres and his men.

Diego tugged a small net and an empty canvas bag out of his pack. "Wish me luck."

"*Suerte.*" Jax studied the net in his brother's hand. What did that mean, fish for dinner? Some kind of bird? Before he could ask, Diego had dropped his pack near the entrance of the cave, slung the canvas bag across his chest, and disappeared onto the ledge, clutching the net. A surprise, then. Jax shrugged. His brother knew the country and these woods a lot better than he did. Whatever he brought back would be edible. Really, anything that would help ease the gaping hole in his abdomen would do.

He wandered over to the pieces of wood and twigs propped against the wall of the cave and grabbed a couple of handfuls of the kindling. After depositing it on the spot Diego had indicated, he hauled over several pieces of wood then pulled the box of matches from his pocket. He and Diego had learned how to start a fire without matches when they were Boy Scouts, and Jax had demonstrated the technique to Mikayla once, but the process was long and tedious. After a strenuous day, he was thankful all he had to do was strike a match and drop it onto the kindling.

A few minutes later, flames flickered in the middle of the stone floor. Jax scanned the opening of the cave, straining to hear over the crackling of the fire and the night sounds in the forest for any sign that his brother might be returning. He'd found a couple of longer sticks they could use to hold something in the fire. After rummaging around his brother's pack and finding a knife, he reached for the sticks and whittled one end of each to a sharp point.

That was about all he could do until Diego returned with food. The snapping of a twig outside the entrance brought Jax's head up sharply. What if that wasn't his brother? He still held the knife in one hand, and he clutched it tightly as he rose and melted into the shadows at the side of the cave, away from the light of the fire.

His shoulders relaxed and he lowered the knife as Diego stepped into the cave. The canvas bag across his chest bulged, which was promising. Jax folded the blade of the knife into the holder. "What did you catch?"

"A few anoles."

"Anoles?"

"Yes." Diego reached into the bag and pulled out a bright green reptile.

"Ah. Lizards."

"Yep." His brother returned the lizard to the bag. "Want to give me that knife you were ready to impale me with when I came in?"

His neck warm, Jax held out the tool. Diego took it and carried it and the canvas bag to the opening of the cave.

Jax followed him. "Could you smell the smoke outside?"

"A little, but the mist is doing a pretty good job of smothering the smell." He pulled a lizard from the bag and made quick work of skinning it. It had been twenty years since Jax had prepared a meal this way, and the display did temper his appetite a little. He shoved away his squeamishness and forced himself to watch in case he needed to do it himself next time.

While Diego finished taking care of the four lizards he'd brought back, Jax retrieved the sharpened sticks. "Will these work?"

"Those are great." Diego reached for one and skewered two of the little beasts he'd just cleaned. Jax exchanged the full stick for an empty one and Diego did the same with it. The two of them carried their sticks to the makeshift campfire.

Jax squatted next to the flames and held the stick a couple of inches above the hot coals. "Are these good?"

"They are better deep fried, but they're not bad. They taste a little like bacon."

The mention of bacon sent a fresh wave of hunger rumbling through Jax's stomach. Memories of Saturday morning bacon and egg breakfasts across the table from Mikayla at Joe's, the diner Nicole owned, sent a wave of another kind rolling through his chest. Although he'd missed her constantly during the week when they'd been separated over the past year, this was a whole new level of longing. At least then he always knew it would only be for a few days. Now, given the precarious position he and Diego found themselves in, there was no guarantee when—or if—Jax would hold her in his arms again. He shoved the thought away so he could concentrate on cooking his dinner.

It took a few minutes, but finally the food was ready, and they both pulled the sticks from the fire and settled onto the cold stone floor to eat. Jax tugged off a strip of meat and stuck it in his mouth. A little chewy, but Diego was right; it tasted vaguely of bacon and maybe a hint of chicken. Not bad.

When the gaping hunger was at least partially sated, Jax wiped a spot of grease from his chin. The black grooved into the crevices of his brother's fingers caught his eye. "Where did you learn to work metal like that, anyway?"

Diego took a swig from a water bottle and set it next to him. "Prison." He offered Jax a wry grin. "I told you it was hellish in The East, and in a lot of ways it was. I meant it when I said it straightened me out, though. It did scare me, enough that I knew I never wanted to go back there. It also gave me the chance to go to rehab, which provided me with the tools I needed to stay sober once I got out, since alcohol was always a bigger problem for me than drugs. And they offered a lot of different classes, including metal work. I had no idea how much that would interest me until I tried it one day and I was hooked."

"You're really good. The piece you have on display outside your shop caught my eye, and even the small one set in the stone on your grave is impressive."

"Oh yeah." Diego looked a little sheepish as he dug at the coals with the tip of his stick. "That was a vanity, I admit. If I actually was killed and that stone was all that was left for anyone to remember me by, I wanted it to hold a small piece of my work, leave something behind that would remain after I was gone. I knew it was a risk, but when my friends set up my grave, I asked them to cover it with weeds the best they could. I assumed they had, since no one connected the stone to my shop. Not until you did."

Diego stoked the fire with the stick before adding a couple more pieces of wood. The orange glow from the flames flickered against the stone walls of the cave, a barrier against the dampness. Like it had when they were kids, the warmth of the fire made it easier to believe his brother's assertion that nothing bad could happen to them if they stayed together. Having a full stomach was helping too.

Diego tossed the stick onto the floor next to him. "I picked something else up in prison, something that changed my life."

Jax tore his gaze from the flames and shifted to face his brother. "What's that?"

"God."

"Really." That was it, the thing that Diego had said the other night that had been niggling at the back of Jax's brain ever since. "So that is what you meant when you said that if it weren't for the grace of God, your life would have spiraled out of control again after you'd had that whiskey with Papá."

"Yes. Exactly." Diego bent his knees and wrapped his arms around them. "I know Mamá took us to mass when we were kids, but it was not until some people from a church in Toronto came to talk to us in prison that it started to make sense to me. Began to be real."

"I get it."

"You do?"

"Yes. About a year ago, I had a conversation with a friend about God. A few conversations, actually. And I came to believe that God was real and cared about me and what was happening in my life. I have been following Him ever since."

Diego tipped his head and contemplated Jax. "And what is her name, this friend of yours?"

The warmth creeping up Jax's neck again had nothing to do with the flickering flames. "What makes you think it is a her?"

"I told you. I know you, little brother. I can see it in your eyes. It is a woman, and I am guessing she is more than a friend."

Jax leaned against the damp cave wall. "All right, her name is Mikayla Grant. She is an amazing artist, like you, only she paints with watercolors. You would like her."

"I'm sure I would." Diego waited a moment and then grinned. "Are you going to tell me more or do I need to pull it from you piece by piece? I am trained in interrogation techniques, you know."

Although Diego was asking, Jax hesitated. Did his brother really want to hear about the woman Jax loved when he had lost his pregnant wife so brutally not that long ago?

"It is okay."

Jax met his brother's eyes. "What is?"

"Talking about her. I want to hear it, honestly."

It was disconcerting how well his brother could read him. Good though, at the same time. As though time and distance had not severed their connection as completely as Jax had thought. "I was visiting a good friend of mine, Daniel Grey, a former partner in our PI firm. His wife's sister came to dinner one night, and I was drawn to her right away." He rubbed his forehead with the side of his hand, remembering. "She did not feel the same way."

Diego snorted a laugh. "No doubt you are an acquired taste. Like anole."

Jax sent him a heated look. "Thanks a lot."

"How did you win her over?"

"Daniel had been searching for a missing child for several years, and that night at his condo Mikayla saw an artist's drawing of how the boy might have aged. She recognized him as a kid who had lived in her neighborhood in Chicago. She and I and another friend, Holden Kelly, whose brother, Gage, had abducted the child in the first place …"

Diego's eyebrows rose and Jax shook his head. "Long story. Anyway, Gage had died, but because he rescued the boy from an abusive home, Holden was driven to find out if the kid, Matthew, was okay. The three of us went to Chicago for three weeks and found Matthew. Turned out things weren't great with his new family, so CAS took him. Holden and his wife, Christina, are now in the process of adopting him."

Diego let out a low whistle. "I was not expecting a telenovela when I asked about this woman."

"That is exactly what I said it felt like. Anyway, I did manage to, as you put it, win Mikayla over while we were in Chicago, although it wasn't easy. Not," he shot his brother another look, "because I am an acquired taste, but because she had lost her parents in a car accident the year before and was afraid to get close to anyone again in case she also lost them." And now she could lose him, given the recklessness with which Jax had followed his brother into this situation.

Diego gazed into the flames. "I understand that."

Of course he did. "I'm sorry, Diego."

"Don't be. I am happy for you. But she will be worrying about you now, when she doesn't hear from you."

"Yeah. She definitely will. If I had known you were going to toss my phone into the fire, I would have sent her a quick message first."

"I'm sorry."

"It's all right. I know it was the smart thing to do. I will get another one and call her as soon as it is safe."

Diego nodded. "Will you marry this Mikayla?"

"I want to, more than anything. I have the ring, but the timing has not been right for me to ask her yet."

His brother continued to stare into the fire. "Take it from me, little brother. Do not wait too long. Life is precious and fleeting, and you never know what could happen." The sadness that had infused his voice when he'd told Jax what happened to Leya thickened it again.

Neither of them spoke for several minutes, until Diego unclasped his arms from around his knees. "I am glad that you found your way to God, Jax, and glad that you have found this woman. I look forward to meeting her."

The suggestion that he would, that the two of them might make it out of this situation alive and that Jax would see Mikayla again, warmed him as much as the coals glowing red on the cave floor. "I look forward to that as well."

Diego picked up the stick and stoked the fire until small flames flickered. "I have always been fascinated by fire, the good it can do and the destruction. I think that is why I was so drawn to metal work. After I became a believer, I was drawn even more. When I heat the metal in the flames, it is to make it pliable, yes, but also to refine it, to cleanse it of impurities so that it can be used to make something beautiful. It struck me when I was working one day that that's what God does with us. He allows us to go through the fire, like He did with those guys in the Old Testament, you know?"

"Shadrach, Meshach, and Abednego, yeah." That had always been one of Jax's favorite stories, even as a kid.

"Right. God did not stop the king's men from throwing them into the flames, but they were not alone. A fourth man was there, walking next to them." Diego rested his hands on his knees. "That is how it has been for me, Jax. Through everything—prison, having to leave Canada, not being able to stay with Papá, then, most of all, losing Leya and our child—I have been through the fire. But I have not been alone. That is the only reason I have been able to keep going."

Jax had a feeling his brother was telling him that story not only to share more of his past and his faith with him, but to remind him that, whatever they faced in the future, God would be with them. The promise straight from the Bible did ease a little of Jax's tension.

Still, he couldn't help but hope they didn't encounter a fiery furnace of their own in the hours to come. If they could get to wherever they were going soon, maybe Jax would be able to spare Mikayla the pain of losing someone else close to her.

There was pretty much nothing he wouldn't do to make that happen. Knowing that so much of what might transpire in the next day or two was out of his control, he sent up a fervent prayer that God would take them the rest of the way safely.

And that He would watch over Mikayla until Jax arrived home and the two of them could be together again.

Chapter Thirty-Four

"Nature calls. I will be back shortly."

Jax nodded as his brother stepped outside the cave. Branches rustled, followed by a silence broken only by the chirping of the coqui and the dripping of rain. Jax dug through his pack and wrestled a pair of track pants free. None of his clothes were clean. As soon as they were somewhere safe, he'd find a place to do his laundry. And shower.

The thud of a footstep at the entrance to the cave announced his brother's return. Still crouched in front of the backpack, Jax grasped the zipper and tugged the bag closed. "So how far do you think we have left to travel before we reach—"

The faint scent of cigar smoke drifted around him. Jax let go of the pack. His brother didn't smoke. He started to rise, but something cold and round dug into the base of his skull, pinning him in place.

"Before you reach where?" The Spanish words came out deep and raspy. When Jax didn't answer, the man pulled the weapon away. "Stand up and turn around slowly. Keep your hands where I can see them."

His heart thundering a staccato rhythm against his ribcage, Jax did as he was told. *God, help us. Get us out of this somehow, please.* Thoughts of Mikayla consumed him. Was it possible he would never see her again? That she would never know what had happened to him or Diego?

The man in front of him was tall and solidly built with short, spiky dark hair. His stone-cold stare passed over Jax head to toe like a CT scan. When he met Jax's eyes, confusion flickered across his features. "You are not Diego Rodríguez."

"Of course not. I heard that Diego Rodríguez is dead."

Before he could move, the man whacked him across the jaw with the gun. Pain shot from his chin to his right ear, but Jax worked to keep that off his face.

"We know he is alive. What we do not know is where he is. Which is what you are going to tell us unless you want things to go much worse for you."

What could he tell them? Had Diego seen or heard the man enter the cave? Would he stay away? Jax wasn't sure whether to hope his brother would take off so at least one of them could survive this encounter or that he would show up and somehow be able to help.

"Nothing to say?"

"I cannot help you." Jax couldn't give up his brother, not even if it saved his own life. Which it likely wouldn't. Besides, he had little information to give. That lack of knowledge might offer protection, but in this case, it likely meant Torres or his men would torture him until he was dead or they gave up in frustration. Judging from the coldness in the eyes glaring at him, Jax was pretty sure he would die first.

The man's eyes hardened even more as he snatched a walkie talkie from the holder on his belt. "Backup is two minutes away. We will see how long you stick to that story."

Jax swallowed. He hadn't been trained to withstand torture like his brother had. How long could he hold up under that kind of treatment without telling them where Diego was?

Keeping the pistol trained on Jax, the man pressed a button on the side of the walkie talkie. If he got through to his friends, Jax and Diego would be outnumbered in a matter of minutes. Jax had to do something. He tensed his leg muscles. When the man held the walkie talkie to his mouth, Jax sprang at him. The walkie talkie clattered to the ground as Jax drove his body into the chest of the Colombian, propelling him against the wall of the cave. The man still clutched the gun, and Jax grasped his forearm and slammed it against the stone repeatedly, until the weapon dropped to the ground. Jax let go of the man and dove for the gun, but before he could reach it, the man barreled into him and knocked him onto his back. He snatched a dagger from a holder on his calf and slashed it across Jax's forearm. Driven by the sudden hot stinging, Jax heaved the man off him and flung out his left arm, searching for the gun. His fingers closed around it.

He started to lift it, but the man stomped his boot down hard on the weapon and Jax's hand, pinning both to the cold stone. Jax pressed his lips together to keep from howling in agony. He met the hard gaze of the man towering above him. A cold smile crossed the guy's face as he raised the knife. "This is more fun anyway."

Trapped and unable to roll out of reach, Jax stared at the blade. This was it, then. He would never see Mikayla again. The steel blade glowed orange in the light of the flames. Refining fire. *God, help me. Give me courage. Take me home quickly.* He held his breath as the knife arced through the air toward him.

A muffled bang echoed off the walls of the cave. A splotch of crimson spread across the chest of the man towering above him. The Colombian crumpled to the floor of the cave like a marionette whose strings had been cut, landing sprawled on his stomach across Jax's legs.

Jax scrambled free and stumbled to his feet, bracing himself with his uninjured right hand against the damp stone wall.

Diego stood just inside the entrance to the cave, his arms out straight in front of him, a 9 mm pistol with silencer attached clutched in both hands. Jax stared at his brother for a few seconds before glancing at the intruder lying at his feet. A deep chill spread from his chest to his extremities. "You killed him."

"If I hadn't, he would have killed us both. Or his friends would have."

"Do you know him?"

Diego stalked over and used his hiking boot to heft the man onto his back. The dark eyes stared, unseeing, at the roof of the cave. "That's Angel Ramirez. Torres's right-hand man." He shot a look at the cave opening. "He doesn't usually travel alone. His people must be nearby."

"He said they were a couple of minutes away." Jax couldn't tear his gaze from the man's lifeless features. Too bad the man his brother had shot wasn't Torres. Not that he would have wanted anyone to die at their hands, but if someone had to, killing the head of the cartel might have shut down or at least slowed operations temporarily. Including the manhunt for Diego. This death would only make things worse for him and his brother if Torres did manage to capture them. For now, it might buy them a few minutes to get away from the vicinity, depending on how far the muffled gunshot had carried over the sounds of the wildlife and the roaring water below.

Diego shoved the pistol into the back of his jeans. "Help me with him." He bent down and grabbed the man by both wrists and dragged him to the opening of the cave.

Realizing what his brother planned to do, Jax strode over. Gritting his teeth against the nearly blinding pain in his fingers, Jax grasped the man by the ankles. Together, they hoisted up the body, swung it past the opening to the cave, and dropped it. A few seconds later, the distant sound of Angel Ramirez splashing into the swollen river reached the cave.

Diego's open backpack sat on the floor a few feet from the opening, and he snatched it up. "We need to get out of here, now."

Jax didn't have to be told twice. He scooped up the gun Ramirez had pointed at him and shoved it into his own pack, zipped it closed again, and slung a strap over his shoulder as he strode toward the entrance after Diego.

When he stepped outside, Jax paused to stare into the forest. The rough, muddy trails were difficult enough to maneuver in the daytime—how would the two of them fare in the thin light of the moon trickling between the canopy of branches?

Likely better than if they stayed in the cave, waiting for more of Torres's men to arrive. With that powerful incentive driving him into the dense underbrush, Jax swiped aside a branch and fell into step behind his brother.

Chapter Thirty-Five

El Pescado Rojo pulled Mikayla in and wrapped her in its embrace like her adoptive mother used to do when Mikayla came home from a long trip. The place was small and dimly lit. Dark wooden shutters covered every window, but the flicker of the candle-like bulbs set into the holders of the chandeliers hanging above every table cast a warm glow over the room that made the place feel like home.

The server, a large man with dark hair and dark eyes and the kind of muscles that required many hours a week in the gym, was patient with her faltering Spanish. He pointed out items on the menu and tried to explain them to her in his equally faltering English, leaving them both laughing.

Finally, she managed to order *bistec encebollado*, which the server assured her was their signature dish and responsible for the rich aroma of roasting meat hanging in the air. Mikayla still wasn't sure what it was, but any dish that smelled like that had to be good.

"You are eating alone, *señorita*?"

She blinked. Why was he asking her that? She would rather no one know that she was in the country on her own. Maybe it had been a mistake, coming here tonight.

As though he realized his question had made her uncomfortable, he held up a hand. "*Perdón.* I only ask because …" He pointed to the menu he'd set at the spot across the table from her. "I may take this, yes?"

"Oh." Warmth seeped into her face. "Yes, of course. *Sí.*"

He nodded and grabbed the menu. After the man had disappeared through the swinging doors of the kitchen, she pressed both palms to her heated cheeks. She was being paranoid. Just because she was in another country didn't mean she was any more vulnerable than she would be at home. The server had been nothing but friendly and hadn't given off any vibes that merited her suspicious response to his question. Lowering her hands to her lap, she leaned against the chair and surveyed the small space.

Every table had at least two people at it, and most were filled. The room hummed with voices and laughter. A middled-aged couple walked by. Both nodded and said, "*Buen provecho*" as they passed. Mikayla smiled at the greeting. Jax and Risa always said the same thing before eating. The memory of all the meals she had shared with them surged back so forcefully her smile faded quickly.

It took a few minutes for Mikayla to register that eight different servers worked the place, all men, every one of them as big as the one who had taken her order.

Mikayla pursed her lips. Was that a prerequisite for working here? Like one of those chains in North America where all the women fit a certain type? Maybe it was a Latino thing. Bemused, she watched them for awhile, until her server returned and set a plate in front of her. "You will enjoy, *señorita*."

The sentiment, worded as it was—more like a command than a wish—sent a smile flitting across her lips. "Thank you."

"You are welcome. *Buen provecho*."

Mikayla nodded. "*Gracias*."

"Is there anything else you need?"

As a matter of fact, there was. Information. But did she dare? Chase's warning, that they likely shouldn't toss Diego's name around too freely, drifted through her mind.

Still, she had to take the chance. "Did you happen to know a man named Diego Rodríguez?"

Something flitted briefly across the man's features. Confusion, maybe? Did he understand what she was asking? As Chase had suggested, she might need to be more specific if she wanted to pin down which Diego Rodríguez she was referring to. "*Está muerto*." On the flight here, she had practiced saying that Diego had died, in case she needed to say it to someone. "He died three years ago, when he was thirty-four. *Treinta y cuatro*."

Whatever it was that had briefly crossed the server's face had disappeared. He shook his head. "I know no one by that name. *Lo siento*. I am sorry."

Mikayla waved a hand. "It's fine." She almost added *it was a long shot* but figured the colloquialism might lose something in translation. He nodded and left her, and Mikayla leaned closer to inhale the tantalizing aroma of the dish. No doubt she *would* enjoy it, as he'd ordered her to do. She grabbed her fork and dug in. It was clearly a beef dish, with rings of onions on top and some sort of sauce coating it. Mikayla didn't recognize the spice when she stuck the first bite into her mouth, but it was delicious.

The rice and vegetables were good too, and she took her time eating, savoring every bite before setting her knife and fork on the empty plate. When she pressed her napkin to her lips, her heart sank a little. She'd been so preoccupied with the food and her thoughts that she hadn't realized the place had largely emptied out. Mikayla eyed a large clock on the wall behind the bar. Almost ten pm her time, eleven pm here. No wonder everyone had left. And now she had a late walk home alone in an unfamiliar town in a country she was visiting for the first time. Not smart.

The man who'd brought her the food stood outside the door to the kitchen, his head bent close to two other servers. One of the other men held a small child in pajamas, hair slicked down on the head resting on the server's shoulder as though maybe the little boy had recently gotten out of the bath. What was he doing up so late?

When the server glanced in her direction and said something else to the two men, chills traveled along her spine. Were they talking about her? Maybe she'd been right to be paranoid earlier.

The man broke loose from the group and strode across the restaurant toward her. The smile on his face would have eased her concern if it wasn't a little strained. He reached for her empty plate. "I can get you anything else?"

"No, *gracias*. Just the bill, please."

The man's forehead wrinkled. Mikayla bit her lip. How did you request the bill in Spanish? She'd asked Jax that the last time they'd gone out for dinner, but the word escaped her now. She clawed through her memories, trying to hear his voice. Gradually, it came to her. *Cuenta.* "*¿Uh, la cuenta, por favor?*" Was that right?

His face cleared. "Ah. Of course, *señorita.* I will be right back."

She watched as he wended past tables and through the opening in the bar to a large cash register. Struck with the sudden urge to leave the place, Mikayla grabbed her bag and strode after him. Should she use her credit card? She frowned. If anyone was trying to track her, that would make it easy for them. Of course, she'd had to use it for the hotel room. And she likely wouldn't be in this town for very long, so hopefully it would be okay.

Even so, when the server printed the bill and handed it to her, Mikayla fished a few American bills from her wallet and set them on the bar. The smaller the paper trail she left, the better. "*Gracias.*"

When she pushed outside, a warm breeze brushed across her flushed cheeks as she started for her hotel. The streetlamps were spaced a little farther apart than she would have liked, and she held her breath when she was forced to walk through puddles of darkness before reaching the next circle of light.

When the hotel sign came into view, Mikayla fixed her gaze on it. She strained to hear any sounds behind her, but the only footsteps echoing along the quiet street were her own. When she reached the hotel, she started to pull open the front door, then remembered the clerk had told her that she had to walk along the side of the building to get to her room. She should have tried to find it earlier, so she'd know exactly how far it was from the front door.

Mikayla scanned the area and, seeing no one, dove around the corner of the building and started along the dimly lit walkway, fumbling in her pocket for the key card as she walked. Her room was the fourth one, and as soon as she reached it, she slid the key into the slot, pushed open the door, then stepped inside and turned the lock.

The room was draped in shadowy darkness, and she felt along

the wall until she found the switch. Only when light flooded the space did she take a breath.

Mikayla berated herself for her nerves as she tossed the overnight bag onto the bed. Without thinking, she reached for the pocket in the bag to pull out her phone to check for a message from Jax. Disappointment flooded through her when she remembered she'd dumped it at the airport. First thing tomorrow she would pick up a disposable phone and try calling him again. And she'd call Chase to let him know what was happening and make sure he was okay.

Until then, the best thing she could do was get some rest. The bed appeared comfortable, and now that her stomach was full and the effects of the long day of travel were hitting her, no reason she shouldn't be able to grab a few hours of much-needed, uninterrupted sleep before she continued her search in the morning.

Chapter Thirty-Six

Jax followed his brother through the trees as noiselessly as possible. Thankfully, a half moon had broken through the cloud cover and pale light fell across the rough pathway, enough to see a couple of steps ahead. He hadn't taken time to grab his hoodie, and the rain, which had lightened to mist again, was damp against his bare arms. Countless insects buzzed around his head. Although he was warm enough, he wouldn't have minded being able to pull up his hood to ward them off. After about twenty minutes, Diego held up a hand and they both stopped, straining into the darkness for any hint of someone following them.

Nothing but the calling of the tree frogs and the incessant buzzing around Jax's ears broke the stillness.

"Sit." Diego hissed the command as he gestured to a log.

"Shouldn't we keep moving?"

His brother didn't answer, only slid the pack off his shoulders and dropped it on the ground. Jax held out for a couple of seconds before exhaling and lowering himself to the log. Diego yanked something out of his bag that Jax couldn't make out in the dim moonlight. When his brother carried it over and set it on the log next to him, he realized it was a first aid kit. "Diego, I'm fine. We need to get as far away from here as we can."

Diego unzipped the bag. "First of all, we should not use each other's names anymore. And secondly, you are not fine. If you lose much more blood, I will be carrying you over the mountain. Not to mention that you're likely leaving a trail that will be as easy to follow as if we posted signs along the way." Although he spoke barely above a whisper, his brother's voice held barely contained rage.

Jax studied him, but Diego concentrated on rooting around in the kit and didn't meet his eyes. Was he angry at Jax for getting injured?

Now that his brother mentioned it, the pain he'd been blocking from his mind blazed across his arm as though Diego had drawn that hot poker he'd threatened Jax with over his skin. Jax inspected the wound. His forearm was covered in blood. Diego might have been right about how much he'd been losing without realizing it. And about how much was dripping onto the forest floor like crumbs left by Hansel in that fairy tale his mamá used to read him and Diego before bed.

He might have summoned a smile at the memory if the direness of their situation hadn't fully struck him in that moment. If Torres's men couldn't follow the trail of blood tonight, they would certainly be able to as soon as the darkness lifted even slightly. Enough to know which direction to head in anyway.

Diego pulled a roll of gauze, tape, and a pair of scissors from the bag. He set the scissors and tape on the log then unrolled a few feet of the gauze and pressed the end to Jax's arm. Jax hid a wince. His brother worked silently, winding the gauze around and around his arm and then reaching for the scissors. He cut the gauze then taped the end down securely before returning everything to the first aid kid. "You probably need stitches, but that's the best I can do for now."

"I'm all right."

"Do you have any other injuries?"

His hand throbbed, but they couldn't take any more time. Torres's men might have already found Angel's body and started after them. "No."

The brief second of hesitation didn't slip past his brother's radar. "What is it?"

Jax sighed and held out his left hand. "He stepped on my fingers. I think one might be broken."

His brother took Jax's hand in both of his, feeling along each finger and the back and palm. Jax gritted his teeth to keep from crying out at the pain.

When Diego finished his inspection, he let go of Jax and

leaned back on his haunches. "One is broken for sure, maybe two. I'd splint them, but if we do run into Torres, I'd rather not make it obvious that you are injured."

"Why?"

"Because they will use any weakness to their advantage." Diego pushed to his feet, zipped the kit closed, and stuck it into his backpack. "Let's go."

Jax pushed off the log and followed his brother, who made a ninety-degree turn from the direction they'd been moving and started into the trees. In case Diego had gotten turned around in the dark and thick mist, Jax hazarded voicing a question. "We are not taking the same route as before?"

"No. That was to throw them off if they are following the trail of blood. This is the way we need to head."

Jax had to hand it to his brother. He could think quickly under duress. How had he even thought to head twenty minutes in the wrong direction to throw their pursuers off? Even if it meant it would take them that much longer to get to where they were going, Jax was impressed with his brother's shrewdness.

They moved as quietly as possible through the dense forest. Their progress was much slower than it had been in daylight. Twice Jax caught the toe of his hiking boot on a root and nearly went down, and several times a branch, damp and cold, slashed across his cheek. He had no idea how his brother was faring, since he was concentrating on watching the ground and ducking under any low-hanging branches coming at him.

Every half hour or so, they would stop and listen in the darkness. When Diego was satisfied no one was following them, he'd gesture for them to continue.

Jax lost all sense of time as they moved steadily forward. A slight dizziness assaulted him periodically, no doubt from the blood he had lost. He ignored it and forced himself to keep moving. Finally, after a couple of hours, Diego nearly tripped over a log that had fallen across their path. He caught himself on the thick trunk before dropping onto it and whispering, "Let's take a break."

Jax lowered himself onto the wood next to his brother. He

slid the pack off his back, set it on the ground in front of him, and tugged the water bottle from a side pocket.

Neither of them spoke as they drank, then Diego set his bottle onto the trunk between them. "That was very foolish of you." His voice was low, quiet, and vibrating with the same rage Jax had caught in it earlier.

Jax narrowed his eyes. Had he heard his brother right? He lowered his water bottle to his knee and spoke, keeping his own voice low. "What was?"

"You, not giving Ramirez the information he wanted."

Jax slid around a little to face his brother. "You would have preferred I give you up?"

"To save your own life, yes. Every time."

"Is that what you would do if our positions were reversed?"

Diego didn't meet his gaze.

"I didn't think so." Jax took another swig of water.

"Even so, do not do it again. If they catch us, tell them what they want to know."

Jax stared into the darkness. "I won't."

"You will, one way or the other. They know how to get the answers they want. The sooner you give them what they are after, the less you will have to suffer. They may even let you live."

"I—"

"No." His brother did meet his gaze then. In the glow of the watery moonlight, his eyes were intense. "I mean it. This is my problem, not yours. And you have a lot more to live for than I do." The anger had seeped from his voice, replaced by pleading. "Do not be a hero. If they order you to give me up, give me up. If they ask you for information, supply it. If not for my sake, or yours, then for Mikayla's. And Mamá's."

Jax contemplated that. The thought of what their mother and Mikayla would go through if he never returned to them did tear at his chest. But Diego was his brother … He clutched the cap tightly between two fingers, letting the bottle dangle between his knees. "If it's your problem, it is my problem."

"I know." Diego clasped his forearm. "But if it comes down

to it, if only one of us can live, it has to be you. Promise me." The same desperation that had carried along his words in the blacksmith shop when he'd begged Jax not to come with him flowed through them now, like the streams flowing through these mountains.

After a few seconds, Jax shook his head. "I can't promise that."

Diego expelled a long breath. "Just think about it. And we will both pray it is not a decision either of us has to make." His fingers tightened around Jax's arm briefly before he pulled his hand away. "We should go."

Although his legs felt as though they each weighed a hundred pounds, Jax put the water bottle away and pushed to his feet. "Are we anywhere near our destination?" Did his brother even know? He didn't appear to be using a compass or any guide other than memory, or the stars, maybe, to lead them to where they were going.

Diego shoved the water bottle into his pack before hefting it onto his shoulders. "Not too far now. Three or four hours, maybe, until we reach the edge of the rainforest. A friend will be waiting there to take us to Fajardo."

Which should bring this insane flight through the rainforest to an end sometime around dawn. Was that good? Would they need to hide all day until they could emerge from the trees under the cover of darkness? Jax fell into step behind his brother. That wasn't his call. Diego seemed to know exactly what he was doing, so Jax would trust that and do whatever his brother told him to do. Except turn him in if and when Torres or his men demanded he do so. He couldn't do that, not even to save his own life.

Although he did have at least two details to supply, since the name of the man driving the truck was Jorge, and now Diego had told him where they were headed. Likely for that very reason. Would passing that bit of information along to their captors expose whoever was waiting to take them there? Jax wasn't sure he could do that either. Although he'd never been tortured before, so he really had no idea what he would do.

Dios mio, help us get to our destination safely so I don't have to find out. The prayer eased a little of his angst, and he lowered his head and concentrated on putting one foot in front of the other.

They hiked another hour or so, the only sounds breaking the heavy stillness of the forest the occasional snapping of a twig and the ever-present song of the coqui. Then Diego stopped in a small clearing, so abruptly Jax nearly ran into the back of him. His brother held up a hand, calling for silence.

Jax worked to keep his breathing slow and steady. Had Diego heard something? He listened but could detect nothing in the trees, no sound or movement other than the frogs and insects that had been the soundtrack of their journey since fleeing the cave. What did Diego think—

Blinding lights flashed all around them. Instinctively, Jax covered his eyes, the light so intense after the near darkness they'd been practically feeling their way through that pain shot behind them. What was happening?

His heart pounding, he lowered his hand and blinked in the brightness. When his eyes adjusted, his chest tightened until he had to force himself to draw in a breath. A dozen men in camouflage surrounded them. Each held an AK-47, and the barrel of every weapon was pointed directly at the two of them.

No wonder it hadn't seemed as though anyone was following them—Torres's men were ahead of them, waiting.

And he and Diego had walked right into their trap.

Chapter Thirty-Seven

Something slapped across her face, jerking Mikayla from the deep sleep she'd sunk into after changing into her flannel bottoms and navy T-shirt and crawling between the sheets. Her eyes flew open. The lamp she'd left burning in the corner had gone out, leaving the room in a thick blackness she could practically feel pulsing against her skin. A cry rose in her throat, cut off by the duct tape or whatever it was covering her mouth.

Mikayla bolted upright. What was happening? Who was in her room? *Father, help me.* Blood pounded so loudly in her ears she could barely hear the whispered words of Spanish being exchanged above her. At least two people were here then.

Someone grabbed her arm, but she yanked hard, freeing herself, and shoved her feet against the mattress, scrambling away from the grasp of the intruder. She backed into another body. Strong arms wrapped around her torso, pinning her arms to her sides as whoever it was hauled her off the bed. Mikayla kicked wildly, driving her heel into a knee. The man holding her grunted and tightened his grip around her.

"*¡Para!*" he hissed into her ear. "Stop."

Yeah. That wasn't happening. Mikayla flung back her head. When it connected with his face, a shower of prickling stars shot across her skull. Hopefully she'd hurt him a lot more. A stream of Spanish words filled the air and the grip on her body loosened. Jax hadn't taught her any swear words, but if she had to guess, those were spewing from the man's mouth now. Good. She *had* hurt him.

"*¡Usa la jeringa!*" the man gasped out.

What did that mean? Mikayla struggled to free herself.

Footsteps thudded on the tile floor. Someone was coming toward them. Seconds later, something sharp pricked her arm.

What …? The room spun around her. Mikayla clung to consciousness, but her thoughts grew fuzzy, and her body wouldn't respond to any of the frantic commands to resist that she was issuing it. If she passed out, she would be completely at the mercy of whoever had broken into her room. And no one would be able to help Jax. She fought to hold on to those two thoughts, to use them to resist the weakness sweeping over her, but her eyelids drooped, and she slumped into the arms of the man holding her.

Father, help me …

Chapter Thirty-Eight

Someone yanked the pack off Jax's back. The heavy bag thumped against his swollen hand and fire shot up to his elbow. Mindful of Diego's warning not to let Torres's men spot any weakness, he worked to keep the agony off his face. When strong hands gripped his arms, forcing them behind his back so whoever it was could wrap a tie around his wrists and yank it tight, he had to clench his teeth until they ached so he wouldn't cry out.

He only managed it by seeking out his brother's eyes and fixing his gaze on them. Someone tied Diego's wrists too before patting him down and yanking the pistol out of the back of his jeans.

Jax scanned the circle before lasering in on Diego. He raised an eyebrow. His brother shook his head slightly. Torres wasn't here. Which might buy them a little time. Jax had no idea if Torres preferred to pull the trigger himself when they managed to catch one of the members of Diego's unit, but even given what little he knew about the man, he suspected he did. So, what would they do with the two of them, take them to their leader?

The old line, usually spoken by aliens on the cartoons he and Diego had watched as kids, might have made him smile if the situation they found themselves in wasn't so ominous. *Mikayla.* Two men grabbed him and forced him to start walking between them. Not for the first time since he'd left Toronto in search of Diego, Jax understood that his life could end any moment. *God, help her. And Mamá.*

He didn't regret coming here. He'd found his brother and the two of them had come a long way in re-establishing the close relationship they'd had when they were growing up. That deep need to find Diego that had driven him to become a private investigator, to travel the globe chasing down every possible lead, had been satisfied the moment Diego had turned him around and he'd come face to face with the brother he'd thought he had lost forever. If they died here, at least they would die together. Diego wouldn't be alone at the end of his life, something that would have haunted Jax forever.

Even so, the thought of never seeing the two women he loved the most in the world again did send pain twisting through him that far surpassed the throbbing in his fingers. He tripped over a tree root and one of the men jerked him upright. The tie dug into his sore hand at the sudden movement, and he bit back another cry.

They stumbled through the forest for twenty minutes before coming out of the trees at the edge of a rough gravel road. Several jeeps were parked on the shoulder, and the men grasping Jax's arms directed him over to one of them. The man who had been holding his left arm let go and pulled open the door, and the other one pushed him inside. Jax had to duck quickly to avoid banging his head against the metal frame.

As the two men who had brought him to the car slid onto the back seat, one on either side of him, he caught a glimpse through the front window of Diego being forced into the jeep in front of his. In seconds, both vehicles had spun off the shoulder and onto the rough, rutted road. Every bounce sent fresh pain coursing through Jax's hand until, in an effort to avoid throwing up, he forced his mind to take him far away, to the dinner party at Daniel and Nicole's place where he had met Mikayla for the first time.

He closed his eyes as memory after memory played across his mind like a home movie. Sitting in the park with her across from her childhood home as she told him about her disastrous prom night experience. Crawling under the old table in the laundromat so Mikayla could show him the picture of herself and her mother she had drawn when she was nine years old and waiting for their clothes to dry. Going to the warehouse to rescue her after she'd been abducted, only to find that she was about to escape through a basement window and hadn't needed him at all.

And that night after they'd visited Ciana in the hospital and she'd leaned against the brick wall of her building and told him she loved him. The joy that coursed through him at the memory tempered the ache, and Jax opened his eyes. What was Mikayla doing now?

His brow furrowed as a heaviness he couldn't explain settled in his chest. Was she okay? Was anyone checking on her, making sure she remembered to eat and sleep, something she could forget to do when she was immersed in painting? Nicole, hopefully, although she might be exhausted from taking care of little Elle and trying to grab sleep whenever she could.

God, could you watch out for her? Make sure she's all right? The heaviness didn't lift as he'd expected. Maybe it had more to do with the situation he and Diego were in, but somehow it seemed connected to Mikayla. Was she worrying about him? He prayed that was all it was, and that nothing had happened to her. If it had, there was nothing he could do about it now. Except pray. Pray that she was okay and that, if he and Diego didn't survive whatever happened in the next few hours, that God and the people she loved would surround her and help her get through it.

Maybe it would have been better if they had never met. Or if he hadn't worked so hard to convince her to give them a chance. He shook his head slightly, unable to bring himself to regret the year they had spent together or the love they shared.

Whatever happened now, Jax prayed that Mikayla would not regret it either.

Chapter Thirty-Nine

Pinpricks of light—like the first stars flickering in the night sky—gradually broke through the thick darkness. Shivers gripped Mikayla. It was so cold. Had she turned the air conditioning in her room up too high? Her eyelids fluttered, but for a moment she couldn't open them. Why were they so heavy? And why was her mouth …?

Memories flooded back and she forced her eyes open. She sat in a wooden chair, both wrists tied to the arms with thin rope. An empty chair faced her, as though someone planned to sit on it to interrogate her. What did these people think she knew? She tugged on the ropes, but it was no use—they were too tight. Condiments and various containers lined the shelves around her, close enough that, if she hadn't been restrained, she could have reached out and touched them on either side. Was this a walk-in fridge?

A movement a few feet away captured her attention. Two men stood inside the open doorway, talking in Spanish too quietly for her to hear most of the words. Not that she would have necessarily understood them, but she would have loved to try.

Both men were dressed in black from head to toe, including a mask pulled down over their faces, and one of them held a serious-looking weapon in his hands. Another gun that appeared to be an automatic rifle leaned against a shelf next to the second man, who had propped a shoulder against the side of the refrigerator and crossed his arms.

Mikayla gritted her teeth. Who were these guys and what right did they have to grab her from her bed and drag her here? Wherever *here* was. She hadn't done anything to hurt anyone.

The man who'd been slumped against the shelving straightened. "*Está despierta.*" He jerked his head in her direction.

Mikayla recognized those words. Since she worked on her art much of the night, Jax often teased her about how late she slept in the morning. When he visited her on weekends, he'd come to her apartment early in the morning, let himself in with the key she'd given him, then put on a pot of coffee while he waited. When she emerged from her bedroom late in the morning, still sleepy and with disheveled hair, he'd laugh and announce, "*Está despierta,*" which he'd told her meant, *she is awake*.

When Jax said it, she didn't mind, especially since he always followed up the pronouncement by setting a hot cup of coffee in front of her. Coming from the man grabbing his automatic weapon from the floor and swinging it in her direction, it wasn't cute. In fact, it sounded distinctly like a threat.

Clutching their weapons, the two men advanced on her slowly. When they reached her, one of them stuck the butt of his rifle against her neck. Mikayla glared at him, although all she could see were dark eyes peering through the holes in the mask. Did they speak English? Would she even be able to understand what it was they wanted from her?

One of the men held the gun on her while the other grasped the end of the tape covering her mouth. "*¿Se queda callada?*"

What did that mean? The man held a finger to his lips. Ah. He wanted her to be quiet. Fine. If it meant they'd remove the tape, she could keep her mouth shut. Not that she had a lot of choice in the matter. They were in a walk-in refrigerator. If she made too much noise to suit them, they could simply walk out, close the door, and let the oxygen slowly seep out of the room.

Likely why they had brought her here.

Mikayla nodded. With one quick movement, he ripped off the tape. Although she'd braced herself, the shocking sting that followed took away her breath for a few seconds. She grasped for the words she wanted to say in Spanish. When they came to her, she said, quietly, "*¿Qué quieren?*" She studied the man. Would he tell her what they wanted with her?

"*Dinos porqué preguntas sobre Diego Rodríguez.*" The man dug the rifle a little deeper into her neck.

Mikayla jerked away. Diego? Was that why they had brought her here, because she'd asked about Jax's brother in the restaurant? Was this the man who'd waited on her earlier? He'd said the rest of the words too quickly for her to pick up on any after the first few, which she knew meant they wanted her to tell them something. Something about Diego. Did they want to know why she had been asking about him? That would make sense. But what could she tell them, that she was searching for his grave? For his brother? The last thing she wanted to do was drag Jax into this if these people were malicious. Which they gave every indication of being.

"*Estoy …*" she fumbled for the words *looking for his,* "… *buscando su …*"

He prodded her with the weapon. "*¿Su qué?*"

His what? Good question. She hadn't learned the word for grave yet. If this was her server, he did speak a little English. Might be worth trying to say it that way. "Grave? Tombstone?"

The two men exchanged glances before the one who'd been asking her questions leaned closer. "*¿Por qué?*"

Mikayla fished for a good reason to give them for wanting to find Diego's grave. "*Es …*" She stopped and shook her head. Not present tense, past. He *was* a friend. Or the brother of a friend, anyway. Close enough. "*Era un amigo*."

Through the holes in the mask, his eyes narrowed. He didn't believe her. Would he shoot her? Lock her in here? *Father, help me. Give me the words to say. I don't know what else to tell them.* Mikayla met his slitted gaze steadily. After a few seconds, he jerked the weapon toward the door. The other man followed him to the opening. They spoke quietly for a few seconds, until the man who hadn't asked Mikayla the questions stepped into the doorway and called out, "Amaya."

Was that a woman's name? Hope rose in Mikayla as she straightened on the hard chair. Even a cruel woman didn't pose the same threat to her as men did. And maybe she would be easier to reason with.

Light footsteps sounded outside the unit but stopped before

the woman came into view. The man who'd called her disappeared through the opening. Once again, she caught the low murmur of voices—a man's and a woman's this time—but couldn't grasp what they were saying. After a moment, the man's voice rose a little, and Mikayla caught the odd word—*Diego* again, and *peligroso*, which meant … dangerous, maybe? Did they think she was a threat to them somehow? She did not feel like a threat at the moment, strapped to this chair and still woozy from whatever they'd shot into her arm.

The woman sounded calm but firm. When the murmuring stopped, the man still holding the weapon on Mikayla peered into the hallway and then lowered the rifle to waist level, clearly trying to block someone from entering the small space.

"*No le muestres tu cara*," he said, gruffly.

Cara. Mikayla knew that word. Face. What was he saying, that he didn't want Mikayla to see the woman's face?

The woman—Amaya—pushed the weapon away. "*Estaré bien.*"

Mikayla's shoulders relaxed slightly. The woman was insisting she would be fine. That didn't sound like someone about to come storming into the room, firing a weapon. The way the man stepped aside suggested he respected her enough to do what she told him, even if he had hesitated before doing it.

Mikayla studied her as she appeared in the doorway and walked to the empty chair. She was tall and slender, with long, dark hair caught up in a high ponytail and big, almost black eyes. In jeans and a fitted white T-shirt, she appeared far less intimidating than either of the masked men. Until Mikayla met her strong, steady gaze and realized why neither man, although they had protested a little, had been able to stand up to her for long.

For several seconds they only stared at each other. Then the woman spoke, in lightly accented English. "You broke my brother's nose."

Mikayla lifted her chin. "You should tell your brother not to abduct strange women from their beds at night."

A slow smile spread across Amaya's face. "I will pass that

along."

"Good."

She crossed one long leg over the other. "Who are you?"

Mikayla mulled that over. Should she tell her? She was getting a little tired of trying to figure out what she should and shouldn't say. Clearly these people recognized Diego's name, so maybe if she shared a little about herself—keeping Jax out of it if possible—they would give her the information she was seeking. "My name is Mikayla Grant. I'm trying to find the grave of Diego Rodríguez."

"Why?"

There appeared to be no way around mentioning Jax, not if she wanted to get anywhere with this conversation. *Father, give me wisdom. Help me to know what to say. I don't want to make things worse for him.* She did want to find him, though. And if these people could help, Mikayla would tell them anything they wanted to know. "A friend of mine came to Puerto Rico to search for Diego. He texted me when he found Diego's grave, but that was nearly four days ago, and I haven't heard from him since. I'm worried something has happened to him, so I'm trying to get to the last place he was, or might have been, so I can find him."

The woman's intense gaze rested on Mikayla's face a moment, as though she was trying to ascertain the truth of her words. "Who is your friend?"

Mikayla sighed. "Diego's brother, Juan Miguel."

Amaya blinked, her long lashes sweeping the top of her cheekbones. "Jax?"

Mikayla's head jerked. All right, now she had a few questions of her own. "How do you know Jax? And who are you, anyway?"

"Wait." The woman rose gracefully to her feet and walked to the opening. "Adrián. *Ven aquí.*"

The man who had called for her earlier appeared in front of her. "*¿Todo bien?*"

"*Sí. Quiero que la sueltes.*"

"*Pero—*"

"*Ahora. Por favor.*"

Mikayla struggled to follow the conversation. His sister wanted him to do something that he clearly didn't want to do. What was it? What did *sueltes* mean?

Adrián hesitated before resting his weapon against the shelving and bending to lift his pant leg. When he tugged a jagged-edged knife out of the sheath strapped to his calf, Mikayla drew in a quick breath.

He stalked over to her. Her heart thundered, but he used the knife to saw the rope holding her left arm to the chair. When it snapped free, Mikayla pressed her hand to her chest, watching as he sliced through the ropes holding her other arm in place. As soon as he finished, he spun around and strode to the door. He stopped in front of the woman, who reached up and tugged off his mask. One of the two men who had been talking to her server outside the kitchen door earlier. The one who'd been holding the child. What kind of father carried around an assault weapon?

And did that mean the server was the one whose nose she had broken? A small twinge of regret worked through her. He'd been so nice to her at dinner. But then he'd scared her half to death by drugging and abducting her. The twinge vanished.

"*Es amiga del hermano de Diego*." Amaya planted the hand clutching the wool mask on one hip.

Mikayla rubbed her arms where they still burned a little. The woman believed she was a friend of Jax's. That was a good start. Now Mikayla wanted to know exactly who this Amaya was.

Adrián shot a look at Mikayla. "*¿Segura?*" Doubt flickered across his face, which explained his question—was Amaya sure that Mikayla was who she said she was?

"*Sí.*" She shoved the mask against the man's chest, directing him into the hallway. "*Ella y yo vamos a hablar*."

Mikayla's fingers closed into fists. Yes, they were going to talk. After the way these people had treated her, they owed her answers. She waited impatiently for the woman to return to her seat. As soon as she had settled on it, Mikayla crossed her arms. "Are you going to tell me why you drugged me and brought me here?"

"Yes, of course. I am sorry for the way my brothers treated you. The three of them, as well as all the other servers in the restaurant, are members of an elite, highly trained security team. And they can be a little … over-protective."

"Why?"

"Some people are after me. If they find me, they will kill me. When you showed up asking questions about Diego, my brothers assumed you were working for those people."

"Then you knew Diego?"

"Yes. We worked together."

"These people who are after you, did they kill him?"

"Yes."

Mikayla pressed her knuckles to her lips. If someone had killed Diego and was still hunting the people who had worked with him in some capacity, was that what had happened to Jax? The room started to spin around her again.

The woman rested a hand on Mikayla's arm. "Are you all right?"

"I'm worried about Jax. He didn't come here in the last few days to talk to you or your brothers?"

Amaya shook her head, her dark hair swishing against her back. "No. Definitely not."

Mikayla's stomach lurched. "When I spoke to him four days ago, that was his plan. Do you think the people who are after you did something to him?"

The woman hesitated. "It is possible. They are extremely ruthless."

Mikayla stood and took a step toward the opening. "I need to find him."

The woman rose and moved into her path. "You can't start out tonight, on your own. Wait until morning and I will go with you."

"You will?"

"Yes. I know the country and I can take you to where Diego is buried. It is not that far from here."

"But …" Mikayla cast a longing glance at the doorway.

Everything in her wanted to return to the hotel, jump in her car, and start driving.

Amaya grasped her arm. "We will leave as soon as it is light. I promise."

Her shoulders slumped. "All right."

"My brother Eduardo is still recovering from his encounter with you, but I will have my other brothers, Berto and Adrián, return you to your motel."

Mikayla shot her a look and the woman grinned. "They will be on their best behavior. I promise you."

"How did they know where I was staying? I made sure no one was following me."

"They did not need to follow you. There are not many hotels in town. Adrián called Giancarlo, the man who checked you in, who is a friend. He told Adrián you were there and gave him your room number and a key card."

"Is your name really Amaya?" Somehow, she doubted the woman's brother would have used it in front of her that freely if it were.

"No." A sad smile crossed the woman's face. "I have not been completely honest with you, and I am sorry. Everything that has happened the last few years has made us extremely cautious. Too cautious, sometimes."

"I understand."

The woman nodded, slightly. "Even so, if you are a friend of Jax's, then you are a friend of ours. Family, even." She held out a hand, and Mikayla took it. "My name is Leya Rodríguez. Diego was my husband."

Chapter Forty

The jeeps sped through the gates of a high stone wall that extended in either direction as far as Jax could see. The eastern sky had begun to lighten, and in the dull gleam he could make out two rows of barbed wire lining the top of the wall. Was this a prison? A high-security compound? It appeared to be the latter, as the silhouette of a mansion at the top of a set of stone steps came into view on his left. Jax stared out the window as they passed by. The thought of all that money its occupant had amassed on the backs of Jax's people chafed far more deeply than the tie around his wrists. They drove past the house and continued along a paved lane. A row of small cement cabins flashed by his window before the jeep lurched to a stop. Jax stifled a moan as he was thrown against the seat. Now what? If Torres was here, would they be executed immediately?

Dios, help us. Give us courage. Jax uttered the pleas silently over and over as the men on either side of him climbed out of the vehicle and one of them reached in to grab Jax's arm.

He managed to maneuver himself out the door—not an easy task with his hands restrained. The other man rounded the rear of the vehicle and they each grabbed one of his arms again.

Two other men in black T-shirts and gray and black camouflage pants extracted his brother from the vehicle and flanked him as they fell into line behind Jax. Their captors directed them up a rough pathway and into one of the cabins. The interior was dim, the only light the dull gray dawn filtering through the tiny slats that had been set periodically into the walls up near the ceiling in lieu of any real windows. Not nearly big enough for a person to crawl through.

A bucket sat in one corner, their bathroom, apparently. And two thin mattresses with no sheets, blankets, or pillows lay on the floor against the walls. Clearly this was a holding cell. The question was, how long would it be holding them?

The tie around his wrists tightened. Jax winced as one of the men sliced through it with a knife and freed his hands. Another man released Diego's wrists before they all tromped out the door, leaving Jax and Diego alone. The door slammed shut and the sound of at least three locks sliding into place echoed around the small room.

Jax rubbed his left wrist. His skin was raw and bleeding a little, but the ache of that paled in comparison to the throbbing in his fingers. Still, they were alive.

So far.

Diego shot him a grim look. "Home sweet home." He walked over to the wall and lowered himself onto one of the mats.

The exhaustion of their night without sleep and the long trek through the woods before being captured hit Jax like a truck and he stumbled to the other mat and sat, cradling his left hand. "Torres's compound, I take it?"

"I assume so." Diego rested his head against the wall. "I've heard about it but never seen it."

"How do you think they found us?"

His brother blew out a breath. "A drone. I'd been listening for one since we entered the forest but hadn't heard anything. Torres uses the best, and the military-grade drones are almost silent. I didn't catch the hum of it over the sound of the coqui until we stepped into that clearing, and then it was too late."

They sat in silence for a few minutes, until his brother nodded at Jax's primitive bed. "You should try to get some sleep."

Diego was right. Nothing might happen for hours yet, maybe even days, if Torres wasn't around. They needed to keep up their strength as much as possible. Jax stretched out on the thin mat, bending his good arm beneath his head.

Against the other wall, Diego did the same.

For a long time, his whirling thoughts kept Jax from giving in to oblivion. Thoughts of Mikayla, mostly, although also of their mother and his other friends—Daniel, Nicole, Chase, Holden,

Christina. And Matthew, Jordan, Elle, and Ciana. A sad smile flitted across his lips. He would have loved to have seen the four of them grow up, been an uncle to them and involved in their lives as Mikayla would always be. He hoped that spending time with them would bring her joy and comfort. And that maybe, someday, she would find love with someone else.

That thought twisted in his gut even as he wished it for her. As much as it hurt to think of her in the arms of another man, Jax didn't want her to be alone forever, not if someone else could bring her joy. As long as he was good to her—and he would be. Daniel would make sure of that.

The thought appeased his restlessness a little and the prayer he'd uttered before, for courage for him and Diego, drifting through his mind, Jax sank into a shallow sleep.

Chapter Forty-One

Mikayla propped a shoulder against the trunk of a palm tree and crossed her arms over her chest. Impatience gripped her and she tapped a foot against the grass, staring at the back door of the restaurant where she'd dined—and later been held against her will—the night before. The impatience was a little unfair. Only the faintest hint of pink lightened the eastern sky. Leya had told her they would leave as soon as it was light, and Mikayla couldn't claim that it was yet, not with a myriad of stars still twinkling overhead. Still, morning was coming, and she could barely stand to wait a moment longer before starting after Jax.

Especially now that she had connected with someone who might be able to help her find him. Leya. Mikayla's chest squeezed. The woman had already experienced Mikayla's greatest fear—losing the man she loved. The intense sorrow in her eyes when she spoke of Diego proved how deeply she had loved him and how desperately she continued to experience the pain of his loss, even now, three years later.

And Mikayla would feel the same if something happened to Jax.

She uncrossed her arms and ran her hands up and down them, trying to ward off the chills that skittered along her skin, despite the warmth already hanging heavy in the air.

Twenty minutes later, the back door cracked open, and she pushed away from the tree. Four men, dressed in black but not wearing masks this time, stepped out the door. Two of them clutched an assault rifle in both hands. They stopped a couple of feet from the exit while the other two strode toward two beige Range Rovers parked behind the restaurant next to a dark blue Honda.

The two men with the rifles scanned the area around the restaurant. Mikayla studied them. Seriously, what kind of people were after Leya that they needed to be this careful? Obviously, whoever they were, they were extremely ruthless, as Leya had claimed. Which meant that, if Jax had fallen into their hands, they needed to get to him fast. Although how many people would they be up against if they found him? Would the four men be enough to take them on and free Jax?

You need only to be still.

The thought rippled through Mikayla like a flowing stream, driving away her chills and unclenching her muscles. The reminder that God fought on her side and all she had to do was trust, chastised and comforted her as Mikayla walked toward the restaurant.

When her hiking boots crunched on the gravel of the parking lot, both men swung their rifles in her direction. Thankful for the light of the streetlamp, she held up her hands, and after a couple of seconds they lowered their weapons.

Leya stepped outside, the child her brother had been holding the night before in her arms. She brushed the little boy's hair away from his face and kissed his cheek. The man who'd waited on Mikayla stepped outside behind them. In the light of the dim bulb attached to the wall next to the door, she could see that his nose was taped and bruises extended across his cheeks and below his eyes. He reached for the little boy. Leya held the child close a moment longer before releasing him to her brother.

She clutched the man's arm and spoke to him in Spanish. "Take care of him."

"You know that I will." He leaned in to kiss her on one cheek and then the other. "You be careful too."

"*Siempre*. Always."

Mikayla caught enough of the exchange to surmise that Leya had begged her brother to take care of the little boy. She was a good aunt to be that concerned about her brother's son. Of course, Mikayla felt the same way about Jordan, so she got it.

Leya turned away. Her gaze fell on Mikayla and a smile lit

her eyes. "You are here already."

Mikayla offered her a wry grin. "I have been here half an hour."

"I understand. You are anxious to find Jax. We will do everything we can to help you." She gestured to the blue car. "You and I will ride together."

Mikayla followed the woman to the Honda. Like the men, Leya was dressed in a long-sleeved black shirt and black pants. Only after the two of them had slid onto the front seats of the car and slammed their doors—Leya immediately hitting the button to lock them—did the two men patrolling the back of the building lower their rifles and jump into the Land Rovers.

Leya started the car and followed one of the Rovers out of the parking lot, the other one falling into place behind them. Their little convoy wasn't exactly inconspicuous, but hopefully it would keep them secure.

Neither spoke for a few moments, then Leya sniffed. Mikayla gazed at her. "Are you okay?"

"Yes. Sorry. It is just the first time that I have left Mateo."

"Mateo?"

"My son."

Her son. The truth darted through Mikayla. The little boy was not her brother's. "Is Mateo …?"

"Diego's child? Yes."

Which meant he was also Jax's nephew. A nephew he didn't even know he had. Mikayla slumped a little in the seat. "How did you and Diego meet?"

"He came into my family's restaurant one night, as you did. He said he was drawn to the name because of a game he and his brother played together."

Mikayla's eyes widened. "That's why I went there. Jax had somehow found out that Diego had friends who worked at a restaurant in Candelaria, but he didn't tell me which one. I asked the man at the hotel—Giancarlo—which restaurant he would recommend, and he mentioned two. As soon as I translated the name of yours into English, I knew I had to try there first, like maybe it was a sign."

"I guess it was. In any case, I was a server then, not hidden in the back like I am now. We got to talking and it hit me that he would make an excellent recruit."

"Recruit for what?"

"My brothers were military, and I belonged to a black ops group working against the drug cartels operating in this country. Diego was keen to help. He went through training and quickly rose in the ranks. At the time of his death, he was one of our top commanders."

Her voice had thickened, and Mikayla gave her a moment before saying, softly, "You don't have to talk about him if you don't want to."

"No, I do. It hurts, yes, but it is good at the same time. Brings back the wonderful memories along with the hard ones."

"What happened to him?"

"We had been married for one year and I was four months pregnant. One night we were in a safe house, a large group of us. César Torres, a cartel head we had been targeting, stormed the house with an army of his people. We were outgunned and outmanned and many of us were shot and killed, including Diego. I was shot as well, and Torres's people must have thought I was dead, because they left me there when they took off. My brothers heard about the attack and rushed to the site. They did not expect to find me alive, but I was, barely.

"For many weeks, my life—and Mateo's—hung in the balance, but in the end, I recovered. For my safety, my brothers insisted I change my name, that we not let anyone know I had survived. Since Diego was gone, I did not care whether anyone believed I was alive or dead, so I agreed. Mateo was born a few months later, and we have lived in hiding ever since, because Torres has continued to hunt down the members of our group."

They were the good guys, then. She and Diego. Did Jax know that? Mikayla prayed he did, or that he would have a chance to find that out and not die thinking his brother had stayed on the wrong path. That he would somehow know that, far from remaining in the drug world, Diego had sacrificed his life fighting against it. "I'm so sorry, Leya. I can't imagine what you have been through."

"It has been hard, yes. But I have Mateo. He brings me joy every day and reminds me so much of his father." She regarded Mikayla a moment. "Diego spoke often of his little brother. He loved him deeply."

Mikayla smiled faintly. "Jax loved him too. He became a private investigator specializing in missing persons because he was so determined to find his brother. When he found out a few days ago that Diego had died, he was devastated."

"And what is he to you, this Jax?"

"He is my …" She hesitated. *Boyfriend* felt so juvenile, such a trite label to describe what she and Jax shared, how she felt about him. No other name for it was accurate, though. She wasn't his fiancée, or wife, as much as she would gladly have been. Would gladly be.

Leya reached across the console to touch her arm. "You love him."

"Yes."

"That almost makes us sisters."

"Yes, it does." Another sister. Another gift from God. Whatever happened with Jax, the two of them had loved the Rodríguez brothers fiercely, something that would always bind them together.

Leya returned her hand to the steering wheel. "I have never been to Diego's grave."

Mikayla pressed her fingers to her mouth. "I didn't realize. I'm sorry. You shouldn't be taking this chance, not for me."

"I am not only doing it for you. I am doing it for Diego, and for his brother, my brother-in-law. And for our son. And I am doing it because it is time—past time, actually—for me to go to my husband's grave and say goodbye."

Chapter Forty-Two

When Jax woke up, light poured through the high slits in the wall. Forty-eight straight hours of rain and *now* the sun chose to shine? Diego sat on his mattress, arms folded on the knees he had pulled to his chest.

Jax sat up and ran a hand over his face. "Did you get any sleep?"

"A little."

His stomach growled. The anoles he'd eaten the night before weren't going to sustain him much longer. "I don't suppose they have brought food or water."

"Not yet. Sorry."

"It's fine."

"It's not fine. None of this is fine." Diego pressed his fists into his forehead. "I never should have dragged you into this."

"Dragged me? As I recall, I had to force you to take me with you. It was my decision, not yours."

"Still, if I had not made the choices I have made, including sending you that postcard, you'd be safely at home with the woman you love right now."

"And if I hadn't shown up at your door, you would still be working on your art and Torres would not have tracked you down. And maybe we would never have found our way to each other."

Diego lowered his hands and contemplated him. "Maybe not."

"I am not sorry I came."

His brother managed a weak smile. "I should be, but, selfishly, I am not sorry you did either."

Jax reflected on their exchange. He hadn't lied to his brother—he wasn't sorry he had come. Still, he was very aware that things did not look good for them. As he'd promised, he had given a lot of thought to whether he could forgive Diego for everything he had put him and their mamá through. What he kept coming back to was that he couldn't refuse to forgive him. Not when God had forgiven him. And not when God had forgiven Jax more than he could ever be called upon to forgive anyone else for.

If they survived this, he and Diego would still have much to work through, but there was no way Jax was going to die—that he was going to let his brother die—while withholding forgiveness from him.

"Diego. I want you to know that I forgive you."

His brother shifted to face him. "You do?"

"Yes. And I need you to forgive me."

"For what?"

"For turning you in. For not doing more to try and help you."

Diego clasped Jax's knee. "Jax. You were fourteen. You should have been thinking about girls and baseball, not how to help your stupid, drug-dealing brother escape the mess he'd gotten himself into."

Jax nodded. After a moment, he said, "I was also thinking about girls and baseball."

Diego pulled back his hand. "You are thinking about a girl now as well, no?"

"Yeah. I am."

"Me too."

"Tell me about her. Leya. What was she like?"

His brother's eyes glowed in the dim light as he pulled back his hand. "She was the bravest person I ever knew. One night we were walking along the sidewalk and had almost reached an alley when we overheard some men talking. We stopped and listened and soon realized it was a group of Torres's men, eight or ten of them at least. I literally had to wrap an arm around her waist and hold her back, or she would have gone storming down that alley with her little pistol against all their automatic rifles." He chuckled. "She was really something. Smart. Beautiful, too. And she had this huge heart and the best sense of humor. We laughed a lot."

"I wish I could have met her."

"So do I."

They were silent a few minutes. Lost in thought, Jax jumped when his brother's hand landed on his knee again. "Thank you, *hermanito*. Your forgiveness means more to me than I can say. And if you make it home, please tell Mamá how sorry I am." His voice cracked and he let go of Jax and covered his eyes with his hand.

"I will. Although she forgave you a long time ago."

His brother lowered his hand. "She did?"

"Yes. She told me that she has prayed for you every day since you were born, and that it is impossible to hold on to bitterness and unforgiveness toward someone you love and who you continually bring to God."

Diego's shoulders slumped. "I do not deserve your forgiveness, either of you. But I am deeply grateful for it. And—"

The sound of a lock turning cut him off. They scrambled to their feet. The other two locks clicked before the door flew open. One man, red curls sticking out beneath his black wool cap, stood in the doorway holding a tray. Four others congregated behind him, all holding assault rifles pointed at Jax and Diego. "Hands where I can see them."

They held their hands up. The man set the tray on the ground to the right of the opening and then slammed the door shut. The locks clicked into place again.

Diego walked over and picked up the tray. Jax sank onto the mat again as his brother set it on the floor between them. It held two water bottles and two apples. Not the most filling meal, but better than nothing.

Jax reached for a water bottle, twisted off the cap, and took a drink.

"Save as much as you can. No telling if or when they will give us more."

At his brother's warning, Jax lowered the bottle and screwed on the lid. Although he longed to chug it all, that was probably good advice.

He finished every bit of the apple, including, at Diego's urging, the core. His brother didn't say so, but Jax knew Diego was thinking ahead to what the two of them might have to endure. The thought made the apple churn a little in his stomach, but Jax forced himself to keep it down as he lay back on the mat.

He had no idea how much time had passed before the sound of a car door slamming and loud voices calling out disturbed the stillness of the compound. Diego stared at the door of the cabin.

"That's Torres's voice, little brother. I don't know what will happen now, but I do not believe we will have to wait much longer to find out."

Chapter Forty-Three

They'd been driving about an hour when the Range Rover in front of them skidded to a halt in the middle of the road. Leya managed to bring the Honda to a stop behind it. Mikayla held her breath, watching in the side mirror as Adrián's vehicle fishtailed a little before he brought it under control and stop a few inches from their bumper. She leaned to the right to try and see ahead of Berto's vehicle. A small herd of cattle meandered across the gravel road ahead of him. They showed no interest in the vehicles as they wandered in front of the Land Rover, down into the ditch, and into the field on the far side.

Mikayla peered over at Leya. She lifted her slender shoulders and offered Mikayla an apologetic smile. "It happens."

When the animals had all cleared the ditch, the convey surged ahead. Shortly afterwards, Berto turned onto a gravel road. Leya followed the vehicle and they bounced along the rutted road for a few minutes before the Rover turned into a rough parking lot.

A small plot of land, dotted by headstones and crosses, sat to Mikayla's right. She studied the small cemetery through her window as Leya pulled the Honda up behind the Rover and shifted into park. "This is the place."

What a lot of courage this woman had, putting her own life on the line to say goodbye to the man she loved and help Mikayla find his brother. "How did you know this was where Diego was buried?"

"Although everyone we fought with believes I am dead, my brothers have kept in touch with several of the other survivors. One of them let Adrián know this is where they brought Diego's body."

Mikayla stared out the window. Jax had been on this land only a few days earlier. Her heart rate increased. Was it possible they might find some clue here as to what happened to him after he'd called her that night?

Static filled the air. Leya reached over the back seat. When she straightened, she held a walkie-talkie. She pressed the button on the side. "*¿Sí?*"

She let go of the button. Through the crackling static, Mikayla made out a man's voice, likely Berto or Adrián. "*Espera en el coche hasta que te diga que todo está seguro.*"

"*Está bien.*" Leya rested the walkie-talkie on her knee. "Berto says to wait until he gives the all-clear."

Mikayla had caught enough to figure those had been the instructions. And they made sense to her, given what Leya had told her about Torres. She was glad that Leya's brothers and the other two men had agreed to accompany them today. Knowing what little she did about how Leya had been living the last three years, Mikayla guessed she'd had to do some fast talking to convince them. Or maybe she'd simply looked at them with that way she had. In any case, they likely weren't happy with Mikayla for showing up and disrupting their lives. For putting Leya at risk, even if unintentionally. Mikayla hoped they would still be willing to defend her should the need arise, although they would save their sister first—as they should. Especially as she had a child who needed a mother after already losing his father.

Mikayla watched through the front windshield as the four men picked their way through the grass, spreading out to cover the perimeter of the cemetery. The land was hilly and covered with tufts of grass and weeds as far as she could see. No one was around, so hopefully they could search the cemetery and be gone before anyone drove by. The walkie-talkie crackled again, and Leya and her brother exchanged a few words.

Leya tossed the device into the back and pushed open her door. Mikayla did the same. The two of them swished through ankle-deep grass to the first row of headstones. Three of the men had taken up positions around the edge of the cemetery. Adrián stood at the far corner of the plot of land. As Mikayla and Leya approached, he nodded at a stone set into the ground. Mikayla stopped midway along the row, wanting to give Leya time alone at her husband's grave. Adrián must have felt the same way, as he slid his rifle under one arm, wrapped his other arm around Leya, kissed the top of her head, and then let her go and strode a couple of rows away to take up his post.

Leya dropped to her knees. For a moment, she didn't move, then she ran her fingers over the small stone. When she pressed her eyes shut, a tear slid down one cheek.

Even though she stood ten feet away, Mikayla was deeply aware that she was intruding on an intimate moment, witnessing a grief she was not meant to. She turned, facing away from the stones like the men who'd accompanied them were doing, giving Leya privacy. A warm breeze blew across Mikayla's face as she gazed out over fields dotted with palm trees. The chirping of birds and crickets filled the air like a lullaby. A peaceful place for Jax's brother to be laid to rest. The thought comforted her a little. Hopefully it had comforted Jax as well.

Caught up in thoughts of Jax, Mikayla jumped when someone called her name. She whirled toward Leya, who had risen to her feet. She gestured for Mikayla to join her at Diego's grave. As Mikayla approached, Leya swiped the last of the moisture from her cheek. Although her eyes were red, she appeared composed, and when she spoke, her voice was steady. "I want to show you something."

She crouched again and Mikayla knelt on the grass next to her. Leya pointed to a small round piece of metal artwork set into Diego's stone. "What do you think?"

Mikayla ran her fingers over it. "Jax sent me a picture of this. He said he'd seen similar pieces at a blacksmith shop in a town forty minutes from here."

"Did he say which town or in which direction?"

Mikayla thought back. "No. I'm sorry." She rose and swiped dirt from the knees of her jeans.

"It is fine. There can't be that many blacksmith shops around here. We don't carry phones, though. Do you have one?"

Instinctively, Mikayla reached into her pocket then made a

face. "I dumped it at the airport in Toronto so no one could use it to follow me."

"That was very smart." Leya linked her arm through Mikayla's as they started for the car. "It is not a problem. We will go into Humacao. It is big enough that the hotels should have a business center. We can use a computer there."

"Will your brothers be okay with that?"

Despite her sorrow, a hint of amusement sparked in Leya's dark eyes. "No, but they will come around." When they reached the Honda, Leya patted Mikayla's arm before letting her go. "Give me a moment to let the boys know what we are doing, and then we will be on our way."

Mikayla nodded and climbed into the car. She didn't have to hear the conversation to tell that the men, especially Adrián and Berto, were unhappy. As before, though, it did not take long for Leya to convince them, and in moments the three vehicles were on the road again.

"Will they actually drive to Humacao?" Mikayla contemplated the back of the Rover in front of them.

"They will, because they know if they do not, I will go there without them." Leya's voice still held humor, but also, running beneath it, a core of steel. Not a woman to be taken lightly. As her brothers—and maybe Diego—had no doubt found out the hard way.

Ten minutes later, the houses grew closer together and businesses lined the sides of the road. They passed a sign indicating that they were entering a town called Lirios. Mikayla gazed out her window at the pale pink and green and yellow houses and shops. They passed a church—*Iglesia Primera*, according to the sign—with a large cross attached to the blue stucco front of it. She fixed her gaze on the cross, the symbol calming her, until it disappeared behind them.

They drove for nearly an hour. Heavy traffic and potholes slowed them down, and Mikayla fought the urge to drum her fingers on the door handle in frustration. What if they were heading in the wrong direction? If they were forced to get back onto the highway and retrace their route past Lirios, she might lose the tenuous grip she had on her sanity. Finally, they exited, following signs for Humacao. When the Range Rover in front of them slowed and then turned into the parking lot of a hotel, Mikayla shook her fingers, trying to dispel a little of the nervous energy coursing through her. *Father, help us locate the shop and get the information we need to find Jax. Please. Before it's too late.* She breathed the fervent prayer over and over as the three vehicles parked.

When the men congregated outside the Honda, they had shed their assault rifles. Regardless, they were a formidable team, given their size and the fact that they were dressed in black. Hopefully their presence would keep anyone from approaching her or Leya. If not, Mikayla had no doubt they were armed with more discreet weapons, and the four of them would do whatever they needed to do to protect them. Not that Leya appeared to need a lot of protecting. The image of Eduardo's bruised face drifted through Mikayla's mind. Maybe she didn't need all that much protecting either.

The thought cheered her as they followed Adrián and one of the other men into the hotel, Berto and the fourth member of the team bringing up the rear.

A business area sat to the right of the lobby, and the group headed straight for it. Although the two people behind the front desk, a man and a woman, did glance over, no one made a move to stop them as they made their way to a bank of computers. The one man already seated before a monitor abruptly exited whatever he was working on, grabbed the briefcase he'd set on the seat next to him, and left.

Three of the men halted in the opening between the lobby and the computer area as Leya settled in front of one of the machines. Mikayla pulled a chair over next to her, while Berto stood guard behind them. In thirty seconds, Leya had logged on and entered *blacksmith shops in Puerto Rico* into the Google search bar. When a short list came up, she clicked on one of the names, but the shop only advertised metal pieces for machinery. The next two she dismissed. "These are more than an hour away. If Jax said forty minutes, then this one, Tomás Santiago Designs," she clicked on the link, "is the only possibility. Except that it does not give a location, only an email address."

Several pictures came up on the screen, and Mikayla drew in a quick breath. The art pieces were very similar to the one on Diego's stone, except larger. "That has to be the place Jax mentioned to me." She shifted her chair closer and leaned in. "What about this?" She pointed to the photo of a small building, smoke pouring from the chimney. "Is there any way to tell what area this might be in?" The shop took up most of the picture, but if she squinted, she could make out the street behind it for a couple of blocks, with a few other shop fronts. The signs were blurry, though, and most were too far away to read.

Leya studied the monitor for a moment before shaking her head. "I don't recognize it. Maybe Berto will." She half-turned in her seat and spoke to her brother in Spanish. "Berto? Do you know what town this shop is in?"

He bent over Mikayla's shoulder for a few seconds and then straightened. "*Eso es Mariana.*"

Leya twisted to peer up at him. "Are you sure?"

"*Sí.*" He tapped the screen with his index finger. "*En ese bar conocí un amigo.*"

Mikayla grasped enough to understand that he recognized a bar a block or so from the blacksmith shop, almost cut out of the photo. Even with that little to go on, he sounded sure it was the one he'd been to. Mariana, then. "Is that far from here?"

Leya exited the site, cleared the search history, and pushed back her chair. "Only a few minutes. Mariana is a barrio in Humacao."

Mikayla jumped to her feet and followed Leya out of the business area. A few minutes. Soon, they might have another clue about what had happened to Jax. A mixture of apprehension and excitement twined through her, but she attempted to keep both in perspective.

She needed to think clearly and not allow emotions to cloud her judgment. If she did, it could be Jax who paid the price.

Chapter Forty-Four

Footsteps approached the cabin, and Jax and Diego rose. Diego held up a hand and Jax clasped it with his good one. "Remember the fourth man, little brother. Whatever happens now, we are not heading into the fire alone." When Jax nodded, Diego pulled him close and smacked him on the back a couple of times.

Before Jax could say anything, the locks clicked, and the door flew open. Diego let him go and stepped back.

Four men stormed inside. Four others stood outside the door, rifles pointed in their direction. The four who had come into the cabin grabbed Jax and Diego by the arms and dragged them outside. *Dios, ayúdanos. God, help us. Give us courage*. The prayer that had dug itself into his heart and mind since arriving in Puerto Rico filled Jax again as the men directed him across the rough yard in front of the cabin and over to a cleared area. More armed people stood in a semi-circle there behind a tall man with dark hair and a closely trimmed beard.

The men holding him stopped a few feet from the one Jax assumed was Torres, but the other two forced Diego over to the cartel leader, halting in front of him.

"Well, well. Diego Rodríguez. Back from the dead." Torres spoke in Spanish as he grabbed a handful of Diego's hair and yanked back his head. "It is a miracle."

A few of his men chuckled obligingly. Diego didn't respond. Torres shoved his head away and spun toward Jax. "And you must be Juan Miguel."

The men shoved him forward. Torres's gray eyes swept over Jax. "My men have been watching you for a long time. Thank you for making it so easy for us to find your brother."

"Let him go, Torres." Diego spat out the words. "I am the one you want, not him."

"Actually, I want you both." His cold gaze settled on Jax's face. "And not only the two of you, but your beautiful lady friend as well, Juan Miguel. We have also been watching her. We thought she was flying here yesterday to join you. Instead, she went to Jamaica. Meeting another man, no doubt. But we will find her."

Jax's eyelids flickered a little. Mikayla had gone to Jamaica? Why? As far as he knew, she didn't know anyone there, and he doubted she would take a spontaneous vacation. Not when she'd be worrying about him.

His stomach lurched. Why was Torres threatening to keep searching for her now that he had him and Diego? Would he go after Mikayla even after the two of them were gone?

"Leave her alone." Jax ground the Spanish words out between clenched teeth. "She has nothing to do with this."

"She is involved with you, which means she is involved with this. My men found Angel's body in El Yunque early this morning. If you had not killed him, I might have let her go. But Angel's loss was very personal to me. And he will be difficult to replace. So, she will have to pay too, like you and your brother will." Still glaring at Jax, Torres said, "You caused me a lot of trouble, Diego Rodríguez. And cost me a great deal of money."

"That was the idea."

Torres took the bait and whirled away from Jax to stalk over to Diego and drive a fist into his abdomen. Diego groaned and bent forward as much as the tight grip on his arms would allow.

Torres planted his fists on his hips. "I know I have already taken one thing from you—your pretty little wife."

Diego straightened, his jaw tight. "Do not talk about her."

"How will you stop me?"

When Diego didn't answer, Torres let out a cold laugh. "Even so, that was only a small down payment towards the debt you owe me. Maybe your brother will make the next payment. Or Mikayla Grant will. Not only for your debt, but because you both have Angel's blood on your hands." Without making a move in Jax's direction, he snapped his fingers. The men holding Jax forced him closer.

Torres spun around and snatched Jax's left wrist, lifting his hand as though examining it for evidence. Jax worked to keep the pain off his face, but it was useless. His fingers were swollen and red. No way to hide that they were broken.

Torres met Jax's gaze, his eyebrows arched. "It is true what my men told me then. Angel did not go down easily. We will see how much fight you have in you when I ask you about who helped you escape into the forest and who was planning to assist you when you reached the other side." He squeezed Jax's wrist slightly before dropping it. The man who'd been holding Jax earlier grabbed his elbow. "Carlos. Bring me the hammer."

Dios mio, ayúdame. Help me. How much pain could Jax withstand? He had very little to tell Torres; would the man continue to torture him even if he gave up those sparse details?

One of the men jogged over to Torres and handed him the tool. "Bring him." Torres stalked to a small white table under a tree. The men dragged Jax after him. When Torres rapped on the wooden surface with his knuckles, one of them shoved Jax's wounded hand onto the table, holding it in place by tightening his fingers around Jax's wrist. Instinctively, Jax tried to jerk away, but he stopped resisting when the man shoved harder, pressing his fingers into the wood. He bit back an agonized groan. What use was there in fighting? He and his brother were completely outmanned and outgunned. Barring a miracle, nothing could stop what was about to happen.

Jax tried to brace himself as Torres raised the hammer in the air, although he knew the effort was useless.

"Wait." Diego struggled to free himself from the men who had brought him over to witness what Torres planned to do to Jax. "Do not do this. I will tell you what you want to know."

Torres pursed his lips, clearly reluctant to stop what he had already put in motion. Slowly, he lowered the hammer, disappointment flitting across his features. "All right. Who has been helping to keep you out of my sight for so long?"

Through gritted teeth, Diego ground out, "Jeraldo Ibares and

Frisco Alcarez."

"And where do they live?"

"Jeraldo is in Salinas and Frisco in Guayama."

"Who were you going to meet when you came out of the forest?"

"Alejandro Montoya from Luquillo. He owns a boat and was going to take us to Miami."

Torres contemplated him a moment, hefting the hammer in one hand as though still thinking about using it. Finally, he dropped it to his side and nodded at the men standing behind Jax. "José, Alix, Lorenzo, each of you take one of those men and check it out. Report to me as soon as you have confirmed you have them in your custody." He swung his attention to Diego. "If you cannot find even one of them, we will return to this spot tonight, and it will be even less pleasant for our two guests—and for Mikayla Grant when we find her—than I'd been planning for it to be."

Diego returned Torres's intense stare until the man waved a hand through the air. "Take them to their cell."

The two men jerked Jax around and followed Diego and his guards to the cabin. When the door clanged shut behind Jax and Diego, neither of them moved for a moment, until Diego stumbled to the mat and sank onto it. He propped his elbows on his knees and dropped his forehead onto his palms.

Jax lowered himself to his own mat and gave his brother a few minutes. His hand throbbed, although it could have been a lot worse. Finally, he broke the thick silence. "You should not have given up your friends."

"I didn't." Diego spoke quietly, as though Torres's men could be hovering outside the cabin. Which they likely were.

Jax shifted closer. "You didn't?"

"No. I gave them fake names. I hope."

"Torres is only going to be angrier when he finds out."

"I know. And I am aware I may have done nothing except make this situation worse. It was the only way I could think of to buy us a little time."

Time for what? Jax didn't voice the thought, but it hung in

the stale air of the cabin between them.

"*No sé*. I don't know," Diego responded, as though Jax had spoken aloud. "All I know is that I could not let him do what he was about to do to you. Not without trying to stop it." He raised his head. "I have done what I could. Only One can save us at this point. Like Daniel's friends said, if He chooses not to, He is still good and He will not turn His back on us. We are in God's hands now."

The cold chills that had plagued Mikayla in Toronto had coalesced into a thin coating of ice that covered her whole body. The urgency to find Jax had deepened, and she leaned forward a little in the passenger seat as Leya drove toward Mariana, as though the movement could compel the vehicle to move faster.

Leya reached over and touched her hand. "You feel something, don't you?"

"Yes." Mikayla forced herself to sit back. "I can't explain it, but something is telling me that Jax is in terrible trouble, and I need to get to him now."

"God."

"You think so?"

"Yes. Absolutely." Leya returned her hand to the wheel. "Do you have a faith, Mikayla?"

"I do. So does Jax. I've been praying for him every minute since he left Canada."

"That is good. It is the most powerful thing you can do for him."

A good reminder. Mikayla contemplated the woman behind the wheel. If she had a faith, did that mean … "Was Diego a believer too?"

"Yes, his faith helped him to overcome his addictions and turn his life around. And my one comfort, since he died, is that he is with God, and I will see him again one day."

Mikayla would have that comfort too if something happened

to Jax. She pressed her eyes shut. She couldn't think about that. Not yet.

According to the small screen set into the dash, they were a mile from Mariana. What would they find when they got there?

It was a beautiful, sunny day. Palm trees swayed in a gentle breeze. Mikayla had always wanted to come to Puerto Rico. Now that she was here, she was so focused on Jax and what might be happening to him that she couldn't take in the sights. Someday she and Jax needed to come back here for a holiday, when they could enjoy everything there was to experience about this beautiful place.

The thought warmed her even more than the blazing sun filtering through the tinted windshield. Leya flipped on the turn signal and slowed the vehicle. Berto was driving the Land Rover in front of them, and he had pulled onto a side street. Mikayla's breath caught at the building ahead of them on the right—the blacksmith shop from the picture online.

Would the artist or blacksmith or whoever worked there be able to tell them anything about Jax? She studied the roof of the building as Leya parked the car. No smoke drifted from the chimney. A wave of disappointment crashed through Mikayla. What if no one was around to talk to them? This was the one lead they had to Jax, the last thin hope that they might be able to find him before it was too late.

Two of the men headed up the empty driveway in front of them, and the other two fell into step behind. As they had when they'd gone into the hotel, the men left their rifles in the vehicles. Likely for the best, given the people walking by. Still, Mikayla hoped she was right about them carrying other weapons on them somewhere.

When they reached the shop door, Berto rapped lightly. Nothing appeared to move inside, and after a few seconds, he tried the handle. The door swung open.

Mikayla followed the two men into the small, dark building. No fire burned in the forge, although the aroma of smoke still emanated from the walls. As her eyes adjusted to the dim lighting, she drew in a quick breath. The place had been torn apart. Pieces of wood and metal littered the ground. The floor was covered in a thick layer of ash and coal, as though someone had shoveled out the contents of the forge and dumped it there. Had they been searching for something? For someone?

A piece of twisted metal caught her eye and Mikayla flipped it over with the toe of her shoe. A phone, melted almost beyond recognition. Was that Jax's burner phone? She scooped up the device and brushed the ash off it. No way to tell who had used it or what the history had been. Likely why whoever had torn through the place had left it on the floor. If it had been one of the last things Jax had touched, she couldn't leave it here to be swept up and tossed into a landfill somewhere.

A huge cupboard sat at the far end of the room. The doors had been flung open and the drawers pulled out, their contents strewn across the floor. Did this upheaval have anything to do with Jax? Had whoever turned this place upside down taken him somewhere?

Argggh. So many terrifying questions and scenarios poured through her mind that Mikayla barely resisted the urge to snatch debris off the floor and pelt it at the wall. The worst part was, the temperature, while uncomfortably high, was the same in here as outside. If there'd been a fire in the shop in the last day or two, it would have been even hotter in this room. No one had been here for a while. Not with the forge running, anyway. Which increased the likelihood that Jax's visit—and very likely his disappearance—was connected to whatever had happened here. The prickling of the thin layer of ice coating her skin intensified.

Leya rested a hand on her back. "There is a house on the property. We will go there and see if the occupants can tell us anything."

Mikayla nodded woodenly and followed her across the shop floor. Before they reached the door, she tripped over something sticking partway out beneath an overturned drawer. She crouched and tugged a shoe free of its prison. Tiny dots of blue paint splashed across the logo shortened her breaths. Jax's running shoe.

Why was it here? She doubted he'd have packed any other footwear when he was traveling so light. She couldn't tear her gaze from the splotches of blue. When she'd grabbed a rag to clean the paint off the fabric the day she'd spilled it, Jax had stepped back, out of her reach. "Now I'll take a bit of you with me wherever I go," he'd said, flashing her that grin of his that always left her a little weak in the knees.

Only now he'd left even that bit of her behind, wherever he had gone. Or been forced to go.

Leya touched the shoe. "You recognize this?"

Mikayla swallowed around the lump in her throat and nodded. "It is Jax's."

"Then we know he was here. That is helpful."

Was it? Why had he abandoned his shoe? The implications twisted her stomach. She shoved the drawer out of the way with her foot, unearthing the other shoe. Mikayla grabbed that one as well and, clutching both, followed Leya out of the building.

The pathway to the house was rough, although the yard was otherwise neat and the small flower beds well kept, and it appeared as though someone had recently applied a fresh coat of pale green paint to the small, stucco house.

Adrián and his partner led the way up onto the small porch. Mikayla set Jax's shoes and what was left of his phone on the bottom step to pick up on their way out and then waited next to Leya as Adrián rang the doorbell. After a few seconds of silence, Adrián tried the knob. Locked. He peered over his shoulder at Leya. When she nodded, he tugged a gun from the holster strapped to his chest, stepped back, and aimed a kick at the door, right below the knob. His boot cracked loudly against the wood and the door flew open. Holding the gun up next to his head, Adrián entered the house, the other man on his heels.

Leya went up a step after them.

"*Amaya, espérese,*" Berto hissed sharply behind them.

Clearly, his sister had no intention of waiting. She waved away his protests and stepped onto the porch. Mikayla followed her. Jax might be in this house, hurt or trapped. She had even less inclination than Leya to stand around outside doing nothing while others searched the place.

When she stepped over the threshold, her heart sank. Whoever had trashed the shop had done the same to the house. Worse, if possible. The couch and chair cushions were slashed and the stuffing pulled out. Pictures had been flung from the walls, and from what Mikayla could see through the opening into the kitchen, every dish lay smashed in pieces on the floor. Someone had been searching the place for something and had clearly taken delight in doing so by inflicting as much damage as possible.

Who had decimated the place and why? Everything in Mikayla told her that it had something to do with Jax and his decision to stop here, but she had no idea how or why that visit had precipitated the disaster that followed.

Where are you, Jax? She ran trembling fingers across a table littered with pieces of glass. *Father, be with him, wherever he is. Protect him and help us to find him.*

The annihilation of the house continued from room to room. The mattress in the bedroom had been cut open and all curtains torn from the rods. Far more carnage had been wreaked than necessary.

They found no evidence of life, however. Whether or not he had left the premises willingly, whoever had lived here—Tomás Santiago, Mikayla assumed from the name of the business and a few bills scattered around an overturned desk in the living room—was gone.

By the time they reached the kitchen again, Mikayla's stomach was churning, and she pressed a hand to her abdomen, trying to still it. Now what? Leya nodded toward the back door. "We will check the yard." They exited the building the way they had toured the shop and the house—with two men in front of them and two behind.

The fenced-in back yard was small, with a row of palm trees lining the metal fence and a tiny cement shed in one corner. Adrián and Berto, weapons still drawn, checked out the shed while the other two men inspected the perimeter. A minute after they'd gone in, her brothers exited the little outbuilding. "*Nada*." Adrián shook his head. "*Vamos*." He and Berto started for the house.

Go? Mikayla swallowed a wave of bitter disappointment. If they did, they would leave empty-handed, with no more leads or any idea where Jax might have gone—or been taken—after he'd been here.

"I am sorry, Mikayla. But we will not give up. We will keep searching." Leya took a last look around, stopping to peer into the small space between the concrete shed and the fence.

"That is a very bad idea." A rough, male voice, thickly accented in Spanish, uttered the ominous words in English.

Leya held up her hands and took a step backwards as a man came out of the space, aiming a pistol at her face.

Behind Mikayla, a series of clicks indicated that the four men with them had all cocked their weapons, but as she and Leya both stood between them and the stranger, it was unlikely any of them would have a clear shot. Mikayla focused on the person threatening them. A tall, muscular man with short brown hair. She couldn't tear her gaze from the gun. Had he used it on Jax?

Clearly, he had no intention of standing down, despite the firepower aimed in his direction. Which left them all at an impasse. What would happen now?

For a few seconds, no one moved. Then Leya slowly lowered her hands. "Marcelo."

"Leya?" The man shoved the pistol into the back of his jeans. Then he stepped forward and grasped her upper arms. "I thought I must be seeing a ghost." He kissed her on one cheek and then the other.

Mikayla blinked. What was happening? Leya and this man knew each other?

The four men moved toward them, weapons still at the ready as though none of them was sure yet that everything was okay. Leya held up a hand and they stopped but didn't holster their guns.

Marcelo let her go. "I am sorry for pointing a gun at you. I thought Torres or his people might have come back."

"So Torres did this to the house and shop?"

The man nodded. "Yes. His lackeys, anyway. They were here three days ago."

"Why? Who is Tomás Santiago and why is Torres interested in him?"

The man studied her a moment, his brown eyes turbulent. Then he scanned the small yard before grasping Leya's elbow and turning her toward the house. When he spoke, he had lowered his voice. "We need to go inside. I have much to tell you."

A little dazed, Mikayla followed the two of them past the four men still closely watching what was happening, wariness on their faces. Berto entered the kitchen last and closed the door behind them. When he straightened, his dark eyes sought out his sister. "*¿Qué está pasando, Amaya?*"

Although Marcelo had used his sister's real name, Berto was clearly still being cautious. And of course he wanted to know what was happening. Mikayla felt for him. For some reason, maybe for her sake or out of caution, Leya and Marcelo had been speaking in English. Her brothers, who appeared to know a little English but not much, were no doubt having trouble following the flow of conversation.

"*Lo siento.* I apologize." Leya introduced everyone to Marcelo. "*Luchamos en la misma unidad, con Diego.*" She touched Mikayla's arm. "We fought in the same unit, with Diego."

When Mikayla nodded, Leya turned to Marcelo. "And this is my friend Mikayla. She is here trying to find Diego's brother."

"Ah yes, Jax. He was also here four days ago, before Torres's people arrived."

Mikayla sucked in a breath. Marcelo had seen Jax? "Is he okay? Do you know where he is now?"

"He was fine when I saw him last. As for where he is now, that is part of what I have to tell you." Marcelo shifted his gaze to Leya. "I cannot believe you are here, that you are okay. Diego believes you are dead."

Leya's head jerked. Shock jolted through Mikayla too, and she pressed a fist to her mouth. What was he saying, that Diego wasn't dead after all?

"What do you mean?" Leya's voice shook, one of the few times Mikayla had seen the woman's iron composure rocked. "Diego is dead. He was killed in the shootout that night, at the safe house."

"No, Leya, he is alive. Or was, when he left here with his brother a few days ago. He was shot that night at the safe house, yes, but he survived. We told everyone he had been killed to protect him from Torres and his men. Since he thought you were gone, he did not argue. He has been living in hiding ever since, here. *He* is Tomás Santiago."

Leya swayed on her feet. Mikayla grasped her elbow to steady her. Adrián holstered his weapon and strode to her other side, pressing his hand to her back. "*¿Qué pasa, Leya?*"

Mikayla didn't blame him for wondering what was going on. She understood the words the man was saying, and even she couldn't wrap her mind around most of it.

"He says that Diego is not dead," she answered, in Spanish.

"*¿Qué?*" Adrián swung his gaze to Marcelo. "*¿Dónde está?*"

Yes. That was the question Mikayla wanted answered too. If Diego was indeed alive, where were he and Jax?

A shadow passed over the man's face. "*No sé*. I do not know. Torres must have been tracking his brother somehow, because the morning after Jax showed up here, we got an alert that Torres's men were on their way. Diego and Jax took off into El Yunque. They were supposed to meet up with Marc-Antoine on the north-east side of the forest earlier today. The plan was for him to drive them to Fajardo to meet up with a friend who would take them by boat to Miami. Only they did not show up when they were supposed to. Marc-Antoine knew their route as we had practiced this escape several times, so he hiked an hour or two into the woods, hoping to meet up with them. Instead, he found a clearing with many boot prints. He followed the trail, and it came out at a road where he could see the tracks of jeep tires in the mud."

Leya's arm trembled slightly beneath Mikayla's hand. "You think Torres has them."

He hesitated, then nodded. "*Sí.*"

The cold that had been shimmering around her for days penetrated Mikayla's skin and went deep inside, freezing her to the core. A ruthless, bloodthirsty drug lord bent on revenge had Jax and his brother. How long had they been in his custody? Was there a chance they were still alive? A shudder moved through her.

"*¿Leya?*" No doubt Adrián could feel his sister trembling as well.

She quickly translated everything Marcelo had told her before returning her attention to her friend. "You don't know where he is holding them?"

Okay, good. Leya was staying optimistic. She knew Torres much better than Mikayla did. If she believed Jax and Diego were still alive, so would Mikayla.

Marcelo shook his head. "No. We think we know the approximate area, but we have not been able to pinpoint the location of Torres's compound. The army likely knows, but as they do not officially recognize our existence, no one has been willing to talk to us."

Leya held out her hand. "Do you have a phone?"

Marcelo didn't hesitate, only tugged a silver device from his shirt pocket and set it on her palm. Leya closed her fingers around it and spun around. "I will call General Huertas while we are driving to Fort Buchanan. He will speak to me. And if not, we will storm their headquarters and refuse to leave until they agree to help us find Jax and Diego."

Chapter Forty-Five

Leya spent the drive on speaker phone, being passed from one person to the next as she repeated her urgent request for a meeting with General Huertas over and over. Mikayla had no idea who that was, but judging from his rank, and given what she already knew of Leya's fierce personality, Mikayla guessed he was someone high up in the Puerto Rican military. She clasped her hands in her lap as they hurtled along the highway, sending up an endless stream of silent prayers that God would keep Diego and Jax safe and that the army would be willing to help them find the two brothers. Leya wove in and out of traffic, the two Land Rovers somehow managing to keep pace. They had just passed a sign indicating that the place Leya had mentioned, Fort Buchanan, was ten miles away, when she finally reached an aide to General Huertas.

Leya spoke to him for a couple of minutes in rapid-fire Spanish that Mikayla couldn't decipher, then Leya disconnected the call and signaled to get off the highway. The Rover that had been traveling ahead of her veered across two lanes of traffic, narrowly avoiding clipping the front of a truck to skid onto the ramp ahead of her. Mikayla grasped the door handle and checked her side mirror. The second Land Rover had followed them both off PR-22.

"The General doesn't want us to come to Fort Buchanan. He's waiting for us at a place along the canal where Diego and I met with him once." Leya grabbed the walkie-talkie and spoke into it in Spanish, relaying that information to her brothers.

Mikayla nodded, her mind spinning. Part of her was starting to wonder if she was still asleep in her hotel room the night she had arrived in Puerto Rico. Believing that everything that had happened since she awoke to Leya's brothers in her room was a dream was easier to accept than that all of this—including her upcoming secret meeting with a top general in Puerto Rico—was actually transpiring. She pinched her arm. Nope. This was real. Jax was in trouble, and if she had to meet with a Puerto Rican general or the queen of England or the pope himself to help him and his brother, she would do it.

They drove along quiet streets for several minutes, Leya relaying instructions to Berto through the walkie-talkie, until she told him to turn into a small parking lot on their right. The lot was empty except for two army jeeps and a black Lexus. A soldier in full khaki camouflage from head to toe stepped in front of the vehicle Berto was driving and he stopped. Another soldier strode to the driver's side window and spoke to him for a moment before waving him into the lot. The soldiers stepped aside and let all three vehicles pass, although they did peer through the windows, watching them as they drove by before resuming their posts at the exit to the street.

After they'd parked, another soldier waited for Leya and Mikayla outside the Honda. The general had indicated that he would only meet with the two women, which had to be driving Leya's brothers crazy. Even so, they didn't get out of the Land Rovers, only waited, their vehicles idling, as Leya and Mikayla followed the soldier to the rear of a small building. In a clearing between rows of palm trees, a man with short blond hair and wire glasses sat on a bench, gazing out over the canal. He stood as they approached and met them halfway across the clearing.

"Leya." He took her hand and held it between both of his. "It really is you."

"Thank you for meeting with us, General Huertas."

His lips twitched. "I rarely refuse a request to meet with someone who has come back from the dead." He let go of her and ran a hand over his shorn hair. "I could hardly believe the things I was being told. I needed to see you to make sure they were true."

"I understand." Leya touched Mikayla on the arm. "General, this is Mikayla Grant. She has come to Puerto Rico to find Juan

Miguel, Diego's brother."

"Ah yes, Jax." He shook Mikayla's hand as well. "I met with him a few days ago."

"You saw Jax?"

"I did. A mutual friend set up our meeting. Impressive and very determined man. Not surprising, given his family connections."

Leya cleared her throat. "General …"

"I know. Time is of the essence. But tell me this, is it true that Diego is still alive?"

"Apparently he is. At least, he was, four days ago."

"What do you need from me?"

"We believe César Torres has him and Jax, and we need to know where his compound is."

The general scrutinized the area, although the chances of anyone getting past the massive, heavily armed men in the parking lot was miniscule. "I'm sure you can appreciate that is classified information. There is an ongoing investigation and—"

"General."

At the pleading in Leya's voice, the general's stern features relaxed a little. "Give me a moment." He pulled a phone from the inside pocket of his jacket and strode a few feet away from them, stopping beneath a palm tree to press the device to his ear. His grave voice carried a little way on the breeze but not enough for Mikayla to make out the words. Not that she would have understood them.

Next to her, Leya clenched and unclenched her fists. Of course, she was as desperate as Mikayla to obtain the information they needed. She'd only found out an hour earlier that the husband she thought had been dead for three years was alive, and now she might lose him again before she had the chance to see him, speak to him. Hold him.

Mikayla's arms ached at the thought of holding Jax. Would they get to him in time?

Terror rose like flickering flames, torching her insides in a rush of heat and agony. *Father, please. Let him agree to help us.*

She nearly groaned the words. They'd gone to the top. If the general couldn't or wouldn't help them, then no one could. Jax and Diego would be on their own.

General Huertas tucked the phone under his chin and pulled a notebook and pen from his pocket. He scribbled something in the notebook then finished his call and shoved the phone into his pocket as he returned to them. "Here." He tore the sheet out of the notebook and handed it to Leya. "The coordinates."

Mikayla stared at the piece of white paper. The answer to the question that had been ringing through her mind for days—*where are you, Jax?*—was on that three-inch by two-inch rectangle. They could get to him now. *Father, don't let it be too late.*

Leya took the paper from him. "Thank you, General. I will not forget this."

"I have deployed a unit to head there immediately. Tell your people to wait for them to arrive before launching a rescue attempt."

Leya didn't respond.

"Leya."

She met his gaze. "We will wait as long as we can."

He nodded and offered her a salute.

Leya returned the salute before spinning around and heading for the parking lot. Mikayla matched her stride, her heart thrumming with every step. *We're coming, Jax. Hold on.* Prayers flowed from somewhere deep inside, pleas so intense she couldn't put them into words. All she could do was trust that God understood the cries of her heart.

Leya stopped outside Berto's window long enough to pass along the coordinates to him and then she and Mikayla jumped into the Honda. Leya punched the numbers on the paper into the GPS before turning the key in the ignition and sending gravel shooting out from beneath their wheels as she spun out of the parking lot after Berto, Adrián's vehicle right behind them. As soon as they were on the road, Leya began making phone calls. From what little Mikayla could pick up, Leya was coordinating a team to meet them outside the compound.

Mikayla studied the small screen in the dash. Fifty-five minutes. Fewer, given the rate at which they were driving. Or maybe more, given the road conditions and the possibility of having to stop for animals in the road. She'd only been in Puerto Rico a couple of days, and she'd already learned that it usually took a lot longer to get anywhere than the GPS suggested. Still, God willing, they would arrive at Torres's compound before too long.

One question—the answer to which she could barely stand to contemplate—pulsed through her mind over and over like the blood pounding through her veins.

What would they find when they got there?

Chapter Forty-Six

Diego had been right. As the hours dragged on, Jax was thankful he'd eaten every bite of the apple Torres's men had brought them, although even that wouldn't hold him much longer. As the temperature rose in the cabin, the need for fluids rose correspondingly, although Jax tried hard to keep from thinking about it. He and Diego had nursed their bottles of water for hours, but as shadows lengthened across the cabin floor, they both drained the last few drops.

What did it matter? Likely they would be dead from causes other than thirst long before the need became desperate. Jax slumped against the wall, his brother next to him. Silence hung as thickly as the hot, moist air in the cabin. They needed to conserve what little energy they had left, and even talking felt as though it would require more than Jax had in him.

Mikayla consumed his thoughts, so completely that he could see her shimmering in front of him and had to clutch the empty water bottle in both hands to keep from reaching for her. No doubt the lack of sleep and food and the poor oxygen quality in the cabin was causing him to hallucinate a little. Fine with him, if his hallucinations meant he could spend his last few hours or minutes gazing at the woman he loved.

He propped his elbows on his knees and pressed the cap of the bottle into his forehead. *God, be with her. Give her strength. If we do not survive, help her to be able to move on with her life, like she did, finally, after her parents died.*

How long would that take? He lowered the bottle and slid a glance over to his brother. "Did you ever get involved with another woman?"

The question seemed to draw his brother back from some

deep place he'd retreated to. He ran a hand over his face. "After Leya?"

"Yeah."

"No. I mean, Tomás Santiago wasn't exactly hitting the town every night. I laid pretty low after what happened at that safehouse. The few times I did cross paths with a woman and the thought flitted through my mind, something—my head or my heart—immediately shut it down. Although I knew she was gone and I would never see her again, I couldn't conceive of being with anyone else. What Leya and I had was too irreplaceable." He shifted a little to face Jax. "Do you believe in soulmates?"

Jax reflected on the night he'd met Mikayla at that crazy, strained, awkward, completely magical dinner party at Daniel and Nicole's. He never had been one to buy into the whole soulmate thing, the idea that God might have one person He intended for someone to spend their lives with. Only maybe, on a subconscious level, he had, because he'd lost any interest in dating a couple of years before he'd met her. As though he knew somehow that he was waiting for her. "I think I do, yes."

"You feel that way about Mikayla?"

"From the moment I first saw her. I walked into the kitchen and she was standing at the sink doing dishes, and it was like …"

"The heavens opened up and angels started singing."

"Exactly. I knew instantly that she was the one I was meant to spend my life with."

"The same thing happened to me." Diego had been clutching his empty bottle too, but he tossed it into the corner of the cabin where it bounced off the wall and spun around in a circle on the floor. "You know, in a way you were responsible for the fact that we met that night."

"Me? How?"

"I think, when I first came to Puerto Rico, I went to see Papá because I was searching for connection, for family. After I had to leave, when I was hiking across the country, all I could think about was Mamá and you and how much I missed you both. That night in Candelaria, when I saw a sign pointing to *El Pescado Rojo*, the memory of those days in the woods with you came flooding back. The way we caught and cooked those fish and how good it felt, the two of us facing everything nature could throw at us and surviving it together. I did truly believe that, as long as the two of us were together, nothing bad could happen."

"I believed it too."

Diego touched Jax's knee with his. "I keep going over and over that in my head. And I know that what is happening is bad, but on a bigger, spiritual scale, those words are still true. Even if the worst happens to us, we will be together. We'll be in the presence of God. Forever. And we will be with Mamá again one day."

"And you will see Leya. And your child."

A smile crossed Diego's face. "Yeah. I will."

"So you're right. Ultimately, it will all be good." It still hurt his chest, thinking about what Mikayla and his mother and the other people he cared about in the world would go through. But what Diego had said about the Shadrach, Meshach, and Abednego story was also true. Whatever happened next, he and his brother wouldn't be alone. God would be with them. He would still be sovereign, and He would still be good.

The tension knotting the muscles in Jax's body eased and he drew in the first deep breath he could remember taking in a while. He'd barely exhaled when the tromping of boots on the hard ground outside the cabin rose above the growing chorus of the tree frogs. Diego clasped his forearm. "God may choose to deliver us. But if not …"

Jax nodded. His brother had clearly been thinking the same thing he had. Hopefully those thoughts had brought Diego the peace they had brought Jax. They both pushed to their feet and waited as someone unlocked the door. As before, when it was flung open, four men stormed in while four others waited outside, AK-47s trained on Jax and Diego.

"*Vamos*." The men grabbed their arms and forced them from the cabin.

Torres waited for them by the table under the tree where his men had dragged Jax earlier. This time they took him and Diego straight there. As they approached Torres, a beam of rose-colored sunlight worked its way through the branches of the tree to fall across the implement in the man's hand. Torres had traded the small hammer he'd threated to use on Jax's hand earlier for a short-handled sledgehammer that appeared capable of doing even more damage.

The drug lord's gaze riveted on Diego as their captors jerked him and Jax to a stop a couple of feet in front of him. Torres's eyes were an unusual silver-gray color—as cold and hard and unyielding as the steel Diego had forged to create his works of art. Contempt flickered in them now as he gazed at Diego and spoke in Spanish, his voice as cold and hard as his eyes. "As I'm sure you know, we did not find any of the men you mentioned earlier." He smacked the end of the sledgehammer against his palm a couple of times. He stepped closer to Diego. "I'm not surprised you lied to me. Only very, very disappointed. And disappointing me always carries a heavy price, as Rodrigo, the man I tasked to tail your brother and then Mikayla Grant, found out earlier today. Rodrigo clearly got cocky and tipped his hand, letting her know he was following her, or she would not have had the foresight to lose him at the airport. But I dealt with him and his partner, and now I will deal with you. Your brother will pay first and, as promised, it is going to be extremely unpleasant for you both."

Jax's fingers ached in anticipation of what was to come. At least Torres hadn't found Mikayla. Maybe she really was in Jamaica—which would make him happy, given what was happening in Puerto Rico. *Dios, watch over her please. Keep her safe and far, far away from here.*

Torres nodded at the men holding Jax. They shoved him forward and, as before, one of the men grabbed his left arm and pressed his injured hand to the top of the table. Jax couldn't tear his gaze from the sledgehammer. His breath came in shallow gasps as he mentally tried to prepare himself for the pain. Was Torres even going to try to get information out of him? Or did he simply plan to whale away on Jax's hand—and knees and ankles, maybe—until he felt his *disappointment* had been appeased? Or until Jax passed out. How long would that take?

He sought out his brother's gaze. Diego's dark eyes reflected a tumultuous storm of impotent rage and horror and he'd clenched his jaw tightly, as though trying to hold in a torrent of words.

Don't beg, Jax pleaded with his brother silently. Torres had taken everything from Diego—his wife, his child, his identity, his freedom. If Diego begged him to spare Jax's life, Torres would have stolen all that his brother had left—his pride, his dignity. And throwing themselves on Torres's mercy would do nothing but give the drug lord exactly what he wanted. Nothing would stop him from doing what he planned to do, certainly not feeding his ego by debasing themselves before him.

As his brother had reminded him earlier, they were in God's hands now.

Chapter Forty-Seven

"We can't wait any longer." Leya clutched the rifle in both hands that she'd pulled out of the trunk of the Honda when they arrived outside the compound an hour earlier. Even with the coordinates, they'd had trouble finding the place. The road leading to it branched off two others so rutted and nearly impassable they could barely be considered roads at all. The entrances to both were almost completely hidden by trees and foliage, enough that they'd driven past the first one twice and the second entrance once before circling back and eventually ferreting them out. No wonder Marcelo said they'd never been able to pinpoint the exact location.

Mikayla eyed the intimidating weapon. Leya hefted it slightly into the air. "M107. Sniper rifle. That was my role in our unit."

It was becoming increasingly clear why the other fighters, including her brothers, tended to defer to Leya. Apparently, there was nothing the woman couldn't do. Hopefully they would listen to her now as well. They'd waited until twilight with no sign of the military unit General Huertas had promised to send, and every second that passed increased Mikayla's trepidation that something was happening to Jax and Diego.

"Here they come." Leya tilted her head in the direction of the man and woman dressed in black and gray camo patrolling the fence. They'd passed by every ten minutes while the fighters had been waiting, but Leya's team had left their vehicles two hundred yards down the road and hidden themselves in the scrub brush outside the compound, and neither of them turned in their direction. When they were fifty yards away, Leya gestured for Marcelo and another man to come closer. "*Cuando pasen de nuevo, desármenlos y luego únanse a nosotros.*"

The two men nodded.

Mikayla attempted a translation in her head. Something about the guards coming back. They were to do something to them and then join the rest of the team. Maybe it was just as well Mikayla didn't know what Leya had told them to do.

Leya leaned closer. "I told them only to disarm the guards. We will not kill anyone unless we have to."

Meaning when any of their lives were at stake. Including Jax's or Diego's. Mikayla shoved away the thought so she could stay focused on their mission.

"Let's move in." Leya slung the rifle over her shoulder and started for the metal fence surrounding the compound.

Adrián and the man who had traveled with him both carried wire cutters. In seconds they had snipped through the metal and peeled back an opening large enough for all of them to crawl through. As she and Leya waited outside the fence, the four men they had been traveling with and eight others from Leya and Diego's former unit—five men and three women—crawled through one at a time until all twelve stood inside the compound.

When Mikayla started to go through the opening, Leya stopped her with a hand on her arm. "This could be extremely dangerous. Why don't you wait in the Land Rover?"

Mikayla shook her head. If Jax was somewhere on the other side of this fence, she wasn't about to sit around waiting for others to go in and help him. "I'm coming."

Leya pulled back her hand. "You will need to stay by my side and do exactly as I tell you then."

"All right." Not wanting to waste any more time talking about it, Mikayla hauled herself through the opening. Marcelo and his partner melted into the brush near the entrance to the compound to wait for the security patrol to return.

The rest of them jogged along the laneway leading into the compound from the front gates. The entire area appeared to have once been forest, but parts of it had been cleared to form a rough road and, to their left, space around a massive white house set up on a hill. Leya gestured for half the team to head into the woods and circle around behind the house. The rest of them, including

Mikayla, followed her into the trees to the right.

They moved nearly silently through the brush. Mikayla kept her eyes on the ground, determined not to be the one to give them away by snapping a twig beneath her shoes or tripping over a root. They skirted a cleared area carved into the trees. Voices drifted from that direction, and Leya motioned for them to take up positions where they could see without being seen. She led Mikayla over to a large tree and crouched behind it. Mikayla lowered herself to the ground next to her. "I'm going to climb the tree, try to see what is going on," Leya whispered. "Wait for me here."

When Mikayla nodded, Leya adjusted the strap of her rifle more securely over her shoulder and then reached for a branch. In seconds she had made her way fifteen feet up and stood on one branch while leaning forward against another, peering toward the clearing.

A noise from that direction snagged Mikayla's attention and she scrambled to her feet and peered around the trunk of the tree. Through a break in branches, she glimpsed a tall, bearded man with short dark hair striding toward a tree on the far side of the clearing. A large man flanked him on either side, both clutching a rifle. They made their way over to a white table set up under the tree.

Who were those men and what were they planning to do?

Boots pounded on the lane running along the far edge of the clearing and she swung her gaze in that direction. Seven or eight armed men tromped over to a cement cabin. One of the men unlocked the door and flung it open and he and three others disappeared inside. When they reappeared, Mikayla drew in a quick breath. *Jax.*

Two of the men had grabbed his arms, and when they reached the door of the cabin, they directed him outside roughly. What were they planning to do to him? Mikayla slid farther around the tree.

"Wait."

At Leya's whispered command, Mikayla stopped, her heart thumping against her ribs. Everything in her wanted to cry out for the team to move in, to stop the men from doing whatever they were thinking of doing. She trusted Leya, though. So she would wait. For now.

Two more of Torres's men appeared in the doorway, another man—a slightly taller, bigger version of Jax—between them. Diego. Mikayla tilted her head, seeking out Leya. She had rested the rifle in the crook of the tree, at eye level, although she wasn't yet peering down the sights. Her gaze appeared to be laser focused on her husband.

The men hauled Jax and Diego over to the tree where the three men Mikayla had seen earlier stood waiting. She concentrated on the bearded man who had picked something up from the table and now clutched it in one hand. Mikayla squinted, trying to make out what it was. It didn't appear to be a weapon, but she couldn't see it well enough to identify it.

Unlike the others, the man with the short dark hair didn't carry a rifle, and he wasn't dressed in a black shirt and gray and black camouflage pants. Instead, he wore khaki green cargo pants and a navy T-shirt. Despite the casual attire, he radiated authority.

Was that César Torres? Ice prickled across her skin again. How long would Leya wait before ordering her people to move in?

The men holding Jax and Diego directed them under the tree and yanked them to a stop in front of Torres. They were too far away for Mikayla to hear what they were saying, but after a moment, Torres brought the object he was holding down onto his palm a couple of times. Was that a hammer? Horror threatened to close her throat. What did he intend to do with that?

The men holding Jax shoved him forward a little, and one of them took hold of his arm and pressed his hand to the table.

A wave of dizziness struck Mikayla. Torres was going to slam the hammer down on Jax's hand. They had to stop him. She craned her neck to peer up at Leya. Using the crook of the tree to stabilize the M107, she had leaned in to peer down the sights of the rifle.

Could she get a clear shot from here? What if she hit Jax or Diego? Blood pounded so hard through Mikayla's veins she could feel the throbbing in her neck and temples. *Help her. Help her. Help her.* The fervent prayer beat out a rhythm in her mind in rhythm to the pulsing of her heart.

Torres raised the hammer.

From the corner of his eye, Jax caught the movement of the sledgehammer as Torres hefted it into the air. He kept his gaze steadily on his brother. Diego didn't speak or turn away from Jax. Which helped. Even so, Jax instinctively strained against the man pinning his injured hand to the table. The muscles along the man's arm bulged as he gripped Jax's forearm with one hand and his wrist with the other. As the hammer arced toward him, Jax gave one last tug.

The tight grasp on his wrist eased and Jax yanked his hand back. A deafening crack echoed through the air, and then the head of the sledgehammer landed on the table with a sickening thud, so close the cold metal brushed against the tip of his middle finger.

The man who had been holding him in place crumpled to the ground. The rest of Torres's men spun around. One of them rounded the table and shoved Torres behind a tree, shielding him with his body.

"Jax." Diego grabbed his elbow and yanked him in the direction of the row of cabins. A second shot echoed around the compound. Jax cast a look over his shoulder as another of Torres's men dropped to the ground. Who was attacking them?

With the drug lord's men occupied, he and Diego sprinted for the cabins and dove around the rear of one of them. They stopped, backs pressed to the cement, as more shots filled the air. The sound of shouting and of boots thudding across the hard ground suggested that more of Torres's men were joining the firefight.

"Who's shooting at them?" Jax whispered.

"I have no idea." Diego peered around the corner of the building, then whipped behind the wall again as a flurry of shots from an automatic weapon shattered the brief stillness. "But I—"

"Diego." A man emerged from the bushes behind the cabin. He clutched a rifle in one hand and tossed another one towards Diego. Jax recognized him as the man he'd given the keys to his rental car to in his brother's driveway. A friend of Diego's then. Excellent.

Diego caught it. "Marcelo. How did you know where we were?"

The man slammed his back against the wall next to Diego. "Long story. I'll fill you in later. There's something you need to know, though. Ley—"

Gunshots peppered the air. Footsteps crashed through the underbrush of the woods in front of them. From the sounds of it, a number of people were advancing in their direction. Rapidly. Given the look Marcelo shot Diego, Jax guessed they weren't with him. More gunshots echoed from the area he and Diego had just vacated. The shouting of Torres's men grew louder. Were they retreating toward the cabins?

If so, and if the people storming through the woods weren't on their side, then the drug lord's fighters had formed two groups and were running toward the same location.

And Jax, Diego, and Marcelo were about to be caught in the middle.

Chapter Forty-Eight

The man who'd been holding Jax's hand in place had dropped to the ground as the hammer came down on the table with a ringing thud. Mikayla struggled to draw in a breath. Had Torres hit Jax? The other men surrounding the drug lord whirled toward the woods where Leya and her team were staked out and began firing in their direction.

"Mikayla. Get down."

She ducked behind the tree and sank to the ground, her back pressed to the trunk. One crack of gunfire followed another until Mikayla couldn't tell whether they were coming from the clearing or if it was Leya's team returning fire. A bullet whizzed past her and lodged in the trunk of a nearby tree. Mikayla stared at the spot where a chunk of wood and bark had flown out.

Above her, Leya continued to fire in the direction of the clearing. After several minutes, the shots echoing off trees and buildings and vibrating in the air died away, and Mikayla stole a quick peek around the trunk. From her vantage point, she couldn't see much. Only three bodies sprawled around the clearing. None of the men who had been standing under the tree were there any longer. Including Torres.

Had he been shot?

Had Jax and Diego?

"Leya."

Mikayla twisted back around. Twenty yards away, Adrián stumbled toward them, his arm around a man whose head lolled against Adrián's shoulder. Berto.

Leya scrambled down the tree and landed next to her. "Stay here."

Mikayla slumped against the rough bark of the tree as Leya

ran toward her brothers, the sniper rifle bouncing against her side with every step.

Adrián stopped and lowered Berto to the ground and Leya dropped to her knees next to him. Feeling as helpless as she ever had in her life, Mikayla clutched the tops of her knees and sent one barely coherent plea after another heavenward. What else could she do?

She wasn't trained in military tactics like Leya and her people—and probably Torres's guys. She was an artist. The only weapon she could wield effectively was a paintbrush. What good would that do Jax or Diego or the rest of them if the drug lord or any of his thugs came after them?

The only thing she'd been able to do to help Jax was to let Leya know that he and Diego were in trouble. Mikayla tucked a recalcitrant chunk of hair behind one ear. That had been something, at least, although if they weren't able to get them away from Torres unharmed, then it all would have been for nothing. And at least one of Leya's people would have been injured, maybe worse, in the process.

Her stomach twisting, she peered over to where Adrián and Leya knelt on either side of Berto. Their brother lay on the ground, unmoving.

The sound of gunfire, more distant than the shots that had rung through the air after Leya's first volley, punctured the silence. Who was shooting now? Was that the other half of their team, the ones who had circled around behind the large white house? Were they still engaging Torres's men? Which side was winning?

Were any of the other people who had come with them injured? Mikayla pressed her eyes shut. It didn't bear thinking about, all the people who might have been hurt because of her rash decision to come to Puerto Rico. But how could she not have come?

She propped her elbows on her knees and lowered her face to her hands. All she wanted was to head in the direction she'd last seen Jax, but Leya had told her to wait. She wouldn't go against those instructions, not while Leya was tending to her injured brother. Still, she longed to see Jax. Had he and Diego escaped and found a safe place to hide?

Be still. Be still. She moaned, the questions pounding through her head as painfully as the blood had rushed through earlier.

A footfall, barely crunching the foliage, broke into her frenzied thoughts. Good. Leya was coming back. Now they could go see if—

Something cold and hard pressed against her temple. Mikayla looked up. The dark-haired man she'd seen under the palm tree, the one who had hit Jax with the hammer, stood in front of her holding a finger to his lips.

"If you alert them, I promise you it will be the last sound you ever make." He tipped his head slightly in the direction of Leya and her brothers. Her heart beating out a rapid, uneven drum solo against her ribs, Mikayla shifted her attention to the three of them. Leya and Adrián still bent over Berto, their backs to her, unaware of what was happening a few yards away.

Keeping the gun pressed to her head, Torres bent down, grasped her elbow, and hauled her to her feet. "Mikayla Grant, I presume?" A cold smile writhed across his face like a venomous snake. "My name is César Torres. You will come with me, please. You have destroyed everything I have worked long and hard for, so now, if you wish to live, you will do one favor for me. You will get me the man I thought I had killed three years ago. If I am going down today, I will be taking Diego Rodríguez with me."

"You're hit." Diego strode over to Marcelo. Jax stared at the crimson stain spreading across the man's ribcage and hip just below the bulge of his bulletproof vest. That was not good.

Marcelo stumbled backwards until he rammed the side of the cabin. He lowered his gun to the ground.

"We need to get him inside." Diego handed Jax his rifle and pressed his palms to the top of the frame of the window set into the rear wall of the cabin. The window eased up a few inches, and he slid his hands beneath the frame and shoved it up a couple more feet. Jax helped him get Marcelo to the window then Diego climbed in and assisted Marcelo the rest of the way. This was a different cabin than the one Jax and Diego had been held in and clearly not designed as a cell. It was bigger and the door had a lock in the handle as well as a deadbolt. Diego slid an arm around Marcelo and assisted him to one of the two single beds in the large room before striding over and locking both.

The windows in the front and back left them vulnerable, but it did make Jax feel better to know it would take Torres's men extra time to get through the door if they came after them. And they were armed themselves now, so they could use the windows to fire out of to keep anyone at bay who came too close to the building. Until they ran out of ammunition, anyway.

Diego returned to the window and Jax handed him his rifle. Then he grabbed the one Marcelo had set on the ground and swung one leg over the window ledge. Footsteps crunched along the side of the cabin. Jax hesitated. Was that a good guy or a bad guy?

"What are you doing?" Diego whispered.

Jax held up a finger. "One minute."

"Jax. We're safer in here."

"I know. I just have to check something out."

Diego glanced at the rifle Jax clutched in his good hand. "Do you even know how to use that thing?"

"I carry a gun for work. I'll figure it out."

"But …"

Marcelo groaned, and Jax nodded toward the bed. "Take care of him. I'll be right back."

Diego was clearly not happy about it, but he returned to his friend's side.

Jax dropped lightly to the ground and sidled along the cement wall. He froze when he caught stealthy movement deep in the woods behind the cabins. A flash of beige camouflage and blond hair and glasses. General Huertas? Did that mean the military had found out he and Diego were here somehow and come to rescue them? If so, why was Marcelo here? He shook his head. Time enough to sort all that out later.

When he reached the corner, he took a deep breath before peering around the edge of the building. A man clutching a weapon had pressed his shoulder to the wall near the front of the cabin, his back to Jax.

Red hair curled out beneath his black wool cap. The man who had brought them food that morning. One of Torres's guys, then.

Jax contemplated his options. He could easily put a bullet in the guy right now. He hadn't lied to his brother—he did carry a gun for work and practiced with Daniel at the shooting range all the time. Even so, he'd never actually used a weapon on a human being and didn't relish the idea of doing it, particularly in the back of someone who wouldn't see it coming and who wasn't an immediate threat. If Jax could get close enough, he might be able to take him out another way.

Blocking out the blazing pain that shot across his injured fingers, he flipped the gun around and closed both hands around the barrel. One step at a time, his gaze darting continually to the ground so he could avoid stepping on anything that might alert the man in front of him to his presence, Jax advanced toward the front of the cabin. The redhead appeared fixated on something happening in the clearing and didn't move as Jax approached. He held his breath when he drew close enough that, if the man whirled around, he'd be able to shoot Jax before he had time to even spin the weapon around and point it at him.

A couple of feet from Torres's man, Jax pulled the gun back and then swung it with all his might at the guy's head. As soon as it connected, the redhead dropped to the ground. His weapon tumbled onto the grass. Jax squatted next to him and pressed two fingers to his neck. The pulse beating beneath his skin relieved him, and he picked up the man's gun and straightened.

Silence had fallen over the compound. Was it over, then? Had Torres's men either been killed or taken into custody? He should return to Diego, see if he could help with Marcelo. Jax took a couple of steps toward the rear of the cabin.

"Juan Miguel." Torres's voice rang out across the road, and

Jax turned around, slowly. Had the drug lord seen him or was he only trying to pinpoint his and Diego's location? Either way, clearly this wasn't over yet.

Several of Torres's men lay on the ground around the clearing. Torres stood beneath the palm tree next to the white table. He wasn't alone. His arm was around someone's neck as he pressed the barrel of a handgun to her head. Jax went numb all over. Was that …? "No." The word came out in a raspy whisper, shot through with terror. She had dyed her hair dark, but it was definitely Mikayla. What was she doing here?

He shook off the temporary paralysis and stalked toward them, the numbness replaced with a scorching heat like the billowing flames in his brother's forge. "Let her go, Torres."

"Weapons down."

Jax tossed the rifles onto the ground. When he was ten feet from the tree, Torres cocked the pistol he still held to Mikayla's head. Jax froze. Mikayla's eyes locked on his as she mouthed the words, *I'm sorry*.

He shook his head. No way she should be sorry for anything. This was all Torres's doing. "Let her go and take me. She's not the one you want."

"No, she isn't. But neither are you. There's only one I want now, and as soon as you give him to me, you and your girlfriend will be free to go."

Jax's chest squeezed. He'd sworn to his brother that he would never betray him, never give him up. But he couldn't let Torres hurt Mikayla.

"Jax, no. Don't—"

Torres tightened his hold around Mikayla's neck, cutting off her agonized words. She grasped his forearm with both hands as though fighting to breathe.

Jax had to tell him where Diego was. He had no choice.

Before he could speak, a cabin door behind him thudded against the wall and a voice called out, "I am here."

His chest aching, Jax stayed where he was, his eyes not leaving Mikayla's as the footsteps behind him drew closer.

Everything he and his brother had gone through the last few days—the long talks, the flight through the forest, surviving spider bites and falls down mountains and flash floods, risking their lives for each other—had been for nothing.

Diego's strong hand landed on his shoulder. "It is all right, little brother. I am ready. Take Mikayla home and marry her, and one day you can tell your kids about their uncle and the life lessons he learned the hard way. And let Mamá know I am sorry and that I love her."

Jax nodded.

Diego squeezed his shoulder. "*Te amo, conejito.*"

"I love you too."

His brother let him go and strode toward Torres. The drug lord waited until Diego stopped in front of him before he let go of Mikayla. She stumbled toward Jax. He met her halfway to the tree and pulled her into his arms. She was trembling, and he cupped her head in his hand and held her tightly against his chest. He watched, his throat tight, as Torres pointed the pistol at his brother's face. The drug lord had positioned himself so that his back was to the tree. With Diego in front of him, no one could get a clear shot.

Jax eyed the rifles he'd dropped in the grass. He didn't trust for a second that, after he killed Diego, Torres would simply allow him and Mikayla to walk away. They had to get to those weapons.

Before he could move, a woman's strong, steady voice shattered the stillness. "Diego. Ground."

She'd barely finished saying the words when his brother dropped like Jax had when he'd stepped out of the cave onto thin air. A single shot rang out.

Jax stared in fascinated horror at the round red mark in Torres's forehead. Blood splattered against the trunk of the palm tree behind him. The pistol clattered to the ground as the drug lord slowly collapsed, sprawling on his face in the dirt next to Diego.

Members of the military, led by General Huertas, poured into the clearing, although it appeared as though Torres's men were all either dead or had fled.

His brother pushed to his feet. "Leya?" He searched the trees in front of him wildly.

Jax shifted his gaze to the woods. Leya? How was that possible?

A woman with long, dark hair caught up in a ponytail appeared at the edge of the woods and stepped into the clearing, still clutching a sniper rifle in one hand. Diego let out a startled cry and started toward her. When they met, the woman dropped the weapon and flung herself into his arms.

Mikayla pulled back a little and offered Jax a tremulous smile. "Oh yeah. Leya's alive."

Jax let out a short, incredulous laugh, partly at the news and partly at her ability to joke so soon after peering directly into the face of death. "I see that. What about …?"

"Your nephew? Mateo? Absolutely adorable."

"*Gracias, Dios*."

Her face grew serious. "*Sí. Gracias, Dios*."

Jax ran his fingers across her cheek, unable to comprehend that she was real and not the hallucination he'd seen in the cabin. "I heard you went to Jamaica."

A faint hint of humor sparked in the green eyes he loved. "Not me, only my phone."

His fingers stilled on her soft skin. "You are a formidable woman."

"I was not alone."

"No, you weren't. Neither was I."

"I know." She wrapped her arms around his waist. "Speaking of Jamaica, after all this, I'm thinking we might need to go there for a vacation."

Or a honeymoon. He kept the thought to himself. Definitely not the right moment. "Done." Jax kissed the top of her head before pulling her to him again and resting his cheek on her hair. The faint scent of lilacs mercifully drifted over the acrid scent of gunpowder hanging in the still air of the clearing. He couldn't wrap his mind around everything that had just happened. All he knew with any degree of certainty was that Torres was dead, his brother's wife and son were somehow, miraculously, alive, and so were Diego and Mikayla.

In this moment, that was all he really needed to know.

Chapter Forty-Nine

Their late dinner that night at *El Pescado Rojo*, closed to the public, was a loud, raucous affair. Salsa music pulsed from the speakers as platters of enchiladas, rice and beans with amarillos, and red snapper were passed around and glasses were filled again and again.

Jax sat next to Mikayla, still unable to believe that she was here, in Puerto Rico. Their fingers brushed when she handed him a dish or he refilled her water glass, and he rested his knee against hers beneath the table. He was gripped with a deep need to keep touching her, to assure himself that she was real and that she was safe and unharmed. Every time he did, she flashed him a smile, until he began to wish fervently that the room wasn't full of people, that they could have a few minutes alone.

Whenever Jax had glanced his brother's way during dinner, Diego was doing the same thing—touching Leya or Mateo over and over. His wonder and disbelief had to be that much more profound and overwhelming than Jax's, given that, until a few hours ago, he had believed his wife and son died three years ago. Jax wasn't even sure Diego had eaten, as he had one arm around his wife and the other around the toddler sitting on his lap throughout the entire meal.

Jax studied his sister-in-law. Although she was extremely beautiful, her appearance was not as compelling as her presence. She radiated strength and confidence but, as Diego had said, she laughed often and gazed adoringly at her husband and son. Any lingering anxiety Jax might have had about his brother's future dissipated. No doubt the two of them would have a long and happy life together, especially now that Torres was gone.

A couple of hours into the festivities, Diego pushed back his chair and stood. His young son had fallen asleep in his arms, his little head, covered in dark, tousled curls, resting on Diego's shoulder. A hush fell over the table as he reached for his glass and spoke in Spanish. Jax translated quietly for Mikayla as Diego made his speech.

"I want to thank all of you for coming after my brother and me today. I know the risks you took, and I am deeply grateful to every one of you. To my brothers Berto, Adrián, and Eduardo, thank you for watching out for Leya and Mateo for me."

Jax contemplated Berto. He'd taken a bullet to the shoulder and his arm was in a sling, but he'd insisted on joining them for dinner, likely against doctor's orders. The same doctor who had set and splinted Jax's fingers and wrapped them up for him. The process had been painful, but with Mikayla next to him, clutching his good hand in both of hers, he'd barely felt a thing. The doctor had cleaned and bandaged the slash on Jax's arm as well but didn't think he needed stitches since the wound was no longer bleeding and had started to heal.

Marcelo had been rushed into emergency surgery but was expected to recover. General Huertas had met with them before they left the compound area and, after throwing his arms around Diego and expressing his joy that he was alive, he informed them that none of the soldiers had been seriously injured. A number of Torres's men had been killed or taken to the hospital, a few had fled. One drug lord's hold on the country had been broken, which was cause for rejoicing, even if others would attempt to rise up and take his place. That was a worry for another day.

Diego gazed at Leya. "Of course, I am well aware that my wife is fully capable of taking care of herself." His wife reached for his hand, and he squeezed her fingers before facing the room again. "And speaking of women who can take care of themselves: Mikayla Grant." He tipped his glass in her direction.

Laughter at Eduardo's expense rippled through the room as Jax translated for Mikayla and then pressed a kiss to her temple. Leya's brother, his eyes and nose still swollen and bruised, offered Mikayla a sheepish smile as Diego continued his toast.

"We all owe you an enormous debt of gratitude. I will leave it to my brother to try and express his appreciation to you, but I wish you both all the joy and happiness in the world."

Mikayla smiled as Jax tightened his hold on her hand.

Diego cleared his throat. "Over the last few days, I have received some incredible gifts. My wife and my child." His voice broke and he stopped and rubbed his eyes with two fingers. Leya stood, slid an arm around his waist, and kissed him on the cheek. He shot her a grateful look before continuing. "And I got my brother back. Jax, I will never be able to thank you for coming after me and for not giving up on me, even though I gave you and Mamá so many reasons to." He held up his glass. "*Por la familia.* To family."

Jax, his own throat tight, raised his glass in his brother's direction before clinking it against Mikayla's.

Diego set his water on the table. "And now, I need to take my son to bed."

"And then his wife," Leya added.

Diego grinned and kissed her before reaching for her hand.

More laughter and a few cat calls echoed off the walls of the small restaurant as Diego and his family headed for the back hallway that led to a set of stairs to the suites above the restaurant. Although Diego had barely slept for days, Jax doubted his brother would sleep much tonight either. More than likely, he would spend the night making up for lost time with his wife. As thrilled as Jax was that Diego had gotten his family back, a twinge of jealousy worked its way through him. He'd love to make up for lost time with Mikayla too, hold her in his arms all night so he could ward off any bad dreams—for either of them—and assure himself that she was okay.

The timing wasn't right for them, though. Hopefully soon. In the meantime, Jax watched as his brother, holding his sleeping son close in one arm, his other arm wrapped around Leya, left the dining area. Jax froze the image of the three of them in his mind to carry back to Canada with him. The thought of leaving his brother, so soon after finding him and when they still had so much to work through, filled him with a melancholy sadness.

Mikayla leaned close. “We’ll come back often. I want to get to know them too.”

Jax touched the side of his head to hers. How had she known exactly what he was thinking? Was she starting to read him too? Like a book? “Did you call Nicole?”

“Yes, and I’m glad I did. Chase told them I’d come to Puerto Rico, and Daniel was about to leave for the airport.”

“Are they upset you didn’t tell them you were coming?”

“A little. But I couldn’t have. I didn’t want Daniel to leave when Elle was so sick.”

“Is she all right?”

“Yes, thankfully. She has an ear infection, but the antibiotics are already clearing it up.”

“Good.” Jax ran a finger down Mikayla’s cheek. “Want to get some air?”

Her smile was warm and helped melt a little of the cold that had settled in his core when he realized she was the one Torres was holding a gun to. She nodded and they rose and slipped out the door of the restaurant and around to the small patio at the side of the building. Music and light spilled from the windows. The salsa song that had been playing ended and “*Mi Razón de Ser*” by Banda MS started up. The name translated as “My Reason for Being,” which felt perfect for this moment.

Jax held out his hand. “May I have this dance?”

Mikayla slid her fingers into his, and he wrapped his arm around her waist and pulled her close, the fabric of her pale pink sundress soft beneath his fingers. He guided her around the patio, thankful she’d returned his running shoes to him so he didn’t have to dance in his sodden, too-large hiking boots. And that he and Diego had been able to retrieve their backpacks after the battle with Torres. His wallet had still been in the front pocket of the pack, untouched, which, given his adventures over the last few days, was a minor miracle. Pulling on a clean T-shirt and jeans after finally being able to wash the damp, dirty clothes they’d stuffed into their backpacks seemed like one as well. Between the long, hot shower he'd taken after seeing the doctor, and the dry, fresh-smelling clothes, Jax felt like a new man.

For several minutes, they moved to the slow rhythm of the music. Mikayla rested her head on his chest, and Jax drew her closer. What would he have done if he'd lost her?

He would have survived, as Diego had done, by trusting in that fourth man to walk with him through the flames. Still, it would have been the hardest path he'd ever had to traverse.

The song ended and Mikayla lifted her head. In the moonlight, her eyes glowed like the last embers of a fire. Jax cupped her cheek with his good hand. "Why did you tell me not to let Torres know where Diego was?"

Her face softened. "I didn't want you to live the rest of your life regretting giving up your brother."

He stroked her cheek with his thumb. "Do you think it would have been any easier for me, living with the fact that I stood there and watched you die?"

"Maybe not."

"There is no maybe about it." Jax touched his lips to her forehead. "Those few seconds were the most terrifying of my life. I know, with God's help, I could survive if I lost you, but I don't even want to think about that happening."

"I get that. When we figured out you'd been taken by Torres's men and I knew there was a good chance I might never see you again, I felt the same way. But I also experienced a peace that I would never have expected to feel. I knew that, if the worst happened, I would not be left alone."

Every time he thought he couldn't possibly love her more, she said something like that, and he fell for her even harder. She'd come a long way over the last year in trusting God—and Jax—with her life and future. A future he knew with absolute certainty he wanted to share with her, however much time God gave them.

The countless stars twinkling over their heads caught his eye, and Jax tipped his head to contemplate them. Mikayla followed his gaze and let out a quiet sigh. "Under the stars, like the night you took me to prom."

He lowered his gaze to meet hers as another slow song drifted from the restaurant. "Mikayla Grant, *te amo*. I love you with all my heart. These last few days with my brother reminded me that life is short and precious and only God knows what the future holds. All I do know is that I want to spend every minute of that life with you." He ran his fingers lightly over her face, brushing a strand of hair from her cheek. "*¿Te quieres casar conmigo?*"

Before he could translate the proposal into English, she covered his hand with hers. "*Sí, mi amor. Me casaré contigo.*"

For a few seconds, he couldn't form the words to reply. How did she even know what he'd asked her, let alone how to respond? And in perfect Spanish.

Mikayla squeezed his fingers. "I've been practicing. When you finally asked me, I wanted to be able to give you the right answer."

He grinned. "And you did." Hopefully. Probably a good idea to check. "You do know what you said yes to, right?"

"If I agreed to spend my life with you, to be your wife and have your children and love you in sickness and health, for better or worse, then *sí. Lo sé.* And my answer is still yes."

Jax kept his wounded hand wrapped around her waist but slid the fingers of his other hand along her jaw and into her hair as he lowered his mouth to hers. He was usually pretty good with words—in two languages—but in this moment his heart was so full that no words would come. Instead, he poured everything he was feeling—his joy, relief, love, and hope for the glorious future she'd described—into his kiss, praying she would understand.

Finally, reluctantly, he raised his head. "I'm sorry I don't have a ring to give you. I mean, I do, but it is in Toronto."

A gleam lit her eyes. "You bought me a ring?"

"Yes. Awhile ago."

"That's okay. I can wait until we get home to get it. Do you know when you'll be ready to leave Puerto Rico?"

Jax hadn't thought that far ahead, but as soon as Mikayla asked the question, he knew the answer. "If you're all right to stay here a few more days, then before we leave the country, there is one more thing I really need to do."

Chapter Fifty

Jax stood under the awning extending along the length of the hotel and rapped lightly on Mikayla's door. The day was hot and sunny, and he drew in a deep breath filled with the aroma of the *flor de maga* growing in large pink blooms on the trees dotting the yard.

As soon as Mikayla opened the door, Jax pressed both palms to the frame, leaned in, and kissed her. "I sincerely hope that you are open to a short engagement."

Although they'd spent the entire day together the day before, strolling around Candelaria and taking time to recover from everything that had happened, the few hours they'd spent apart, sleeping in their respective hotel rooms, had felt far too long. Leya had called Giancarlo before their dinner party the other night and arranged for Jax to have the room next to Mikayla's, but the thin wall between them might as well have been a mile wide, he felt so lonely for her.

Mikayla laughed. "The shorter, the better."

Jax fingered a strand of her dark hair. She touched the other side of her head in a self-conscious gesture. "I wanted to try and fit in a little better."

He pulled her to him. "You fit perfectly." He found her mouth again, losing himself in the taste and feel of her.

The clearing of a throat drew him back to the present, and he let her go. Diego leaned against the driver's side door of Leya's Honda, which they planned to take on their road trip, his hands clasped on the roof of the car, a smirk on his face.

Jax reached for Mikayla's hand as they strolled toward the vehicle.

"You drive, little brother." Diego held up the car keys. "I would like to sit in the back with my family." Jax nodded and held the passenger door for Mikayla, waiting until she had climbed in before closing it and rounding the front of the car.

"Sorry to interrupt." Diego lowered his voice as he handed him the keys. "It was starting to appear as though we might be waiting all day for the two of you if I did not do something to get your attention."

Jax elbowed him in the ribs. "You are one to talk."

Diego grinned. "I admit that, after four nights of sleeping next to you, it has been very sweet to wake up with my wife in my arms. Kind of like the difference between having anole or Eduardo's *bistec encebollado* for dinner."

Jax made a face at him. "That is a little insulting but understandable, I suppose. I am happy for you, *mi hermano*."

"I am happy also."

Jax didn't doubt that. Diego and Leya hadn't even come out of their room the day before. Eduardo, who had prepared the amazing meal they'd all shared the night they returned from Torres's compound, had assumed chef duties while Adrián and his friends took care of Mateo and waited tables at the restaurant, giving the two of them time to re-connect. In the afternoon, as Leya's brothers were starting to prepare for the dinner rush, Jax and Mikayla offered to take Mateo to the park. They had sat in a sand box for hours, helping Mateo build a castle while Jax attempted to comprehend how much his life had changed in only a few days.

And from the way his brother radiated joy today, Jax was pretty sure he and his wife would be able to help each other through the process of dealing with everything they had gone through the last three years quite effectively.

They took PR-22 westbound toward Arecibo on the northern coast of Puerto Rico. According to Diego, their father still lived there, although in a different place than he'd lived when he'd brought them here as boys. The memories Jax carried of that time were mixed—the strongest feelings he could recall were missing his mother and forging an unbreakable bond with Diego. As they had while lost in the woods as Scouts and while fleeing through El Yunque, the two of them had been forced to rely on each other for survival when their papá began drinking more and more heavily. Likely why Jax never had been able to let go of his mission to find his brother.

He hadn't seen his father since he and his brother had been returned to Mamá two years after being taken, when Jax was ten. Would he even want to see him and Diego? Would he have any interest in meeting Leya and Mikayla and his only grandson?

Whatever Papá's reaction, they had to try to see him before they left the country. To take the first step in the long journey back to each other. They were family.

Even though it left him to steer with his bandaged fingers, Jax couldn't bring himself to let go of Mikayla's hand as he drove. After they'd danced under the stars and he'd asked her to marry him, they'd settled on a bench behind the restaurant and talked for hours. He shared with her his experiences in Venezuela and Puerto Rico, even about being robbed in the alleyway, as well as everything he and Diego had been through in the rainforest.

She told him how close she'd come to losing her mind after he broke off contact and she had no idea where he was or if he was okay. The story about her walking to the store alone at night and being accosted by a strange man nearly drove him out of *his* mind, but he couldn't be upset with her, not after the chances she'd taken, coming after him. If she hadn't, Torres would have killed both him and Diego, likely after hours of torture. Diego would have died without knowing that his wife and young son were alive, and Mateo would have grown up without a father.

Although it would take a long time for Jax to get the image of Torres holding a gun to Mikayla's head out of his mind—if he ever did—he would always be grateful to her. He tightened his grip on her hand and she smiled. Thankfully, so far she seemed almost miraculously unaffected by the trauma of the past few days. Likely it would hit them both in the weeks or months to come, but at least they would be together. They could help each other through it like Diego and Leya were. Maybe even as husband and wife, if Mikayla was as willing to cut their engagement short as she said she was.

They had to stop twice and maneuver their way around aging vehicles stalled in their lane on the two-lane highway, so the trip that should have taken less than an hour took closer to two. At last, Diego leaned forward to direct Jax along a winding road, eventually instructing him to stop in front of what appeared to be a four-unit building painted teal blue with a slightly sagging front porch. Like many of the houses in Puerto Rico, metal bars lined every window, which were otherwise open to the hot, muggy air.

"Papá's unit is on the second floor." Diego climbed out of the back seat and reached in for Mateo. Leya came around to join the two of them, and Diego held their son as she tugged a white sunhat over Mateo's dark curls and tied it under his chin.

Jax stopped next to Mikayla and watched the three of them. Mikayla leaned closer to him, her breath warm against his cheek. "Amazing how they already seem like an incredibly close family."

It *was* amazing. Mateo was remarkably comfortable with Diego, as though he had an innate sense that the father he had never met already loved him and would do anything to keep him safe. Jax sent up a quick prayer for them, that Diego would stay sober and never again set foot on the same path that had taken their father from them.

His son balanced on one hip, Diego stepped up onto the curb next to Jax. "*¿Listo?*"

Good question. *Was* he ready to see the father he hadn't spoken to in over twenty years? Ready or not, it was time. "*Sí.*" He ran his palms over the front of his jeans before capturing Mikayla's fingers in his and following Diego and his family through a gate in the wrought-iron fence that surrounded the house.

They passed through an archway and up a set of stone steps clinging to the outside of the cement building. The door at the top opened into a hallway with one unit to the right and another to the left. Diego led them to the door on the left, halfway down the tile in the hallway, worn and scuffed by years of being trod underfoot by countless tenants. He rapped lightly on the door, and they waited in silence. The aromas of cilantro and sofrito drifted on the air. From what Jax could remember, their papá didn't really cook, although it had been a long time. Maybe his dad had picked up a few life skills in the last couple of decades that Jax didn't know about.

When no one answered, Diego knocked again. The door across the hallway from them creaked open and an elderly man in an oversized cardigan called out, in Spanish, "The family is not home. Can I help you?"

The family? Jax pursed his lips. That didn't sound right.

Diego swung around. "*Hola, Señor Fuentes.*"

Clutching a wooden cane in one hand, the man stepped into the hall and squinted a little in the dim lighting. "Diego?"

"Yes, it's me." Diego shifted Mateo to his left hip so he could hold out his right hand. "Good to see you again."

The man took it in his gnarled one. "You too. It has been a long time."

Diego acknowledged that with a nod. "Too long, I know." He introduced his wife and son and Mikayla, then tilted his head toward Jax. "And this is my younger brother, Jax. We were hoping to speak to our father. Do you know where he is?"

A shadow passed over the old man's face. "I am very sorry to tell you this, but your father passed away a year ago. Liver failure."

The air rushed out of Jax's lungs. Their papá was gone. He had waited too long to try and see him. Why hadn't he come sooner? He'd convinced himself it was out of loyalty to Mamá, but if he were being honest, she had never asked him not to see their father. That had been his decision alone.

Mikayla rested a hand between his shoulder blades. Like a warm compress pressed to a gaping wound, her touch drew out a little of the toxic cloud of self-recrimination and sorrow billowing through him, and he drew in a shaky breath.

Diego sent him a stricken look as Leya slid an arm around his waist. He didn't speak, though. What was there to say?

Señor Fuentes held up an arthritic finger. "*Un momento.*" He disappeared into his apartment. While he was gone, Jax translated the news for Mikayla. A minute later, shuffling footsteps and the thump thump of a cane on the tile floor grew louder. The old man stepped into the hallway and held out a long white envelope to Diego. "Your father left this with me to give to you or your brother if you ever showed up here."

Jax gazed at the envelope. In vaguely familiar handwriting, their father had scrawled *Diego y Juan Miguel Rodríguez* across the front of it. Papá had written them a letter? What could he possibly have to say?

When Diego didn't move, Jax reached out and took it. "*Gracias, Señor Fuentes*." He folded the envelope and stuck it in the back pocket of his jeans.

The old man leaned on his cane with both hands. "I want you to know that, in his last few years, your father was a changed man. He started going to church and stopped drinking. He found peace, although he carried regrets with him to his grave. Mostly about the two of you and your mother and how he abandoned all of you. I don't believe he was ever able to fully forgive himself for that."

Diego cleared his throat. "Do you know where he is buried?"

"He attended the Presbyterian church three blocks east of here, and they laid him to rest in their cemetery."

Diego nodded. "I know where that is. *Gracias, Señor*. And thank you for being such a good friend to Papá."

"He was a good friend to me. I hope you can forgive him one day." With a final dip of his head, the man went into his apartment and closed the door.

Jax relayed the conversation to Mikayla as they walked back to the car. When they reached it, Leya lifted Mateo out of Diego's arms. "There is a park across the street. Mikayla and I will take Mateo there. You and Jax go to your father's grave and say goodbye."

Diego leaned in to kiss her on the cheek. "*Gracias, mi amor*." He turned to Jax. "*¿Estás listo, hermanito?*"

The answer came to him immediately this time. No, he definitely wasn't ready. Jax had prepared himself for a difficult conversation with their father, but he hadn't braced himself for the possibility that he would never have a conversation with his papá again.

His throat tight, he nodded. Maybe he wasn't ready, but he had let his father down by not coming to see him sooner. He would not let him down again by refusing to go to his grave and say goodbye.

Chapter Fifty-One

Jax followed Diego through the opening in the metal security gates surrounding the church and along the walkway winding around the side of the white cement-block building. A large cemetery was set back twenty yards from the church, overlooking the ocean, and they headed toward it. The memory of rounding the car and spotting the cemetery where he believed his brother had been buried rocketed through Jax, and he pressed a hand to his stomach.

"You okay?" Diego's steps slowed.

"Yeah. Just remembering when General Huertas took me to the cemetery where he thought you were buried."

"I'm sorry."

Jax shrugged. "That turned out all right. This time it is for real, though."

The same sorrow drifting through Jax crossed his brother's face. "Not what either of us had hoped for, I know."

The two of them wound their way through blocks of cement surrounded by small patches of grass, burial plots raised above the ground so they wouldn't be affected by the water level. This close to the water, the familiar smell of salt and brine he'd inhaled when he arrived in Luquillo greeted him, and Jax took a deep breath. Not that his father could enjoy it, but it comforted him to know that Papá's final resting place was this close to the ocean he had loved.

The first few rows contained large, ornate sites covered with flowers. They continued on to a section of smaller, plainer sites where they found the one with their father's name carved into a cement cross.

When they stopped in front of it, Diego draped an arm around Jax's shoulders. Jax gazed at their father's name and the dates of his life, struck again by the pitiful inadequacy of that little line to convey the depth of a human being's existence. He had been named after his father, and seeing that name, his name, etched in stone, shook him a little. Reminded him of how close he'd come over the last few days to needing a stone like this himself. Although, if they had died at Torres's hands, they likely would not have had one as their bodies would probably never have been found.

The simple words carved beneath the numbers—*At Peace*—echoed what Señor Fuentes had said about Papá. Although their father had left them and never been the presence in their lives he should have been, Jax was glad he had found peace. That he'd had friends and a church community surrounding him at the end of his life. That he hadn't been alone.

Diego nodded at the cross. "Can you do it?"

"Can I do what?"

"Forgive him, like Señor Fuentes said he hoped we could."

Jax reflected on that. Despite everything, he didn't have strong feelings of animosity or resentment toward his father. Those years of living with him in Puerto Rico had shown Jax that what Ernesto had said about Diego was true—addiction was bondage, and the man his dad was when he'd been drinking was not truly him. Certainly not the person God had created him to be.

If what his friend and neighbor had said was also true, that Papá had turned to God and been freed from that bondage in the last years of his life, then God had forgiven him. So how could Jax not? Especially when he might have been able to help his father if he had gone to see him earlier. It would take longer to forgive himself for that than it would take to forgive their papá.

"I think so, yes." Jax turned to face his brother. "Can you?"

Diego's smile was sad. "If anyone knows about needing forgiveness, it is me. God and you and Mamá have shown me far more mercy than I deserve, so I cannot withhold that mercy from anyone else." He touched the cement cross at the head of the stone lightly with his fingers. "Do you want to read that letter?"

Jax drew in a deep breath as he tugged the letter from his back pocket. The envelope was sealed, and he slid his thumbnail under one corner of the flap and carefully ripped it open so he could remove a folded sheet of paper. His fingers shook slightly as he unfolded the thin, lined page. The last words he and Diego would ever receive from their father. Would they help with the healing they would both need to do in the months and years ahead?

The words had been written in a spidery Spanish that suggested Papá had not been well at the time of writing. The letter was dated eighteen months earlier. How long had his father suffered?

Pushing away that thought, Jax began to read.

My sons,

There are no words to express to you how sorry I am for not being a better father to you. It is the greatest shame of my life that I left your mamá and that I tried to take you both from her. I have never had the courage to ask for her forgiveness or to try to tell the two of you how much I regret my actions, as much as I have wanted to over the years.

Diego, I know I passed along my weaknesses to you. When you came to see me a few years ago and then left because you did not want to be dragged back into that life, I realized that you had done something I had never been able to do. Found the strength to overcome. Your visit changed something in me. It gave me hope and started me on a journey to find the source of that strength. It took me a long time, but I finally realized that the freedom you had experienced could only come from God. Thank you for showing me the way to find that for myself.

Juan Miguel, you were always the strong one in the family. I am so grateful to you for taking care of your mamá. Although I have not seen you for many years, I know you will have grown up to be the kind of man I always wanted to be. A man of courage and integrity who will always be there for his family. I hope and pray you have found the kind of faith that has given me such peace and hope, despite the regrets I will always carry. I wish you both every happiness—good wives like the one I had but never realized the value of until it was too late, beautiful children, success in whatever you choose to do. Above all, may you experience the deep joy that I found late in life and that has been a truly undeserved gift from a merciful and loving God.

I love you both,

Papá

Slowly, Jax folded the paper and returned it to the envelope. Diego's hand still rested on the cross. When his dark eyes met Jax's, they held grief and regret. Jax got that. The tsunami of sorrow washing over him took him by surprise. He wouldn't have expected to feel this deep ache of loss after living most of his life without his father.

Hope too, though. That one day he would see Papá again. The God they had both given their lives to was a God of second chances. While Jax had lost any opportunity to reach out to his father in this life, one day they would stand face to face. Grief with hope, as the Bible promised.

He clasped his brother's shoulder. "Are you okay?"

Diego offered him a weak smile. "I have much to process."

"Me too."

"I need my wife."

"I get that. I need my fiancée."

Diego raised his brows. "Fiancée?"

Jax grinned as he let go of him. "A lot happened while you and your wife were locked in your room. I asked Mikayla to marry me and she said yes."

Diego planted a hand between Jax's shoulder blades and directed him toward the church. "That is excellent news! When will this happen?"

"Soon, I hope." Jax stepped onto the walkway leading to the front of the building. "Will you and Leya come?"

"Of course we will." They reached the front of the church and started along the sidewalk toward the park where Mikayla and Leya and Mateo waited for them. "General Huertas has promised to vouch for us with the Canadian consulate in San Juan and do what he can to expedite the re-issuing of our passports. He thinks it will only be a couple of days before we can pick them up, and then we can go to Canada."

"We?"

"Yes. Leya and I would like to fly back with you and Mikayla if it is okay. I need to see Mamá, ask for her forgiveness in person. And I would very much like for her to meet her daughter-in-law and grandson."

A myriad of emotions swirled through Jax, like the wall of water crashing from one side of the canyon to the other as it advanced toward him. One he hadn't expected to feel while walking away from his father's grave rose to the surface. Joy.

The moment he had dreamed of for years—seeing his mother and brother reunited at long last—was within reach. "It is a lot more than okay. Nothing would make me happier than to see Mamá's face when she realizes you are alive and well."

"Except maybe marrying the brave and beautiful Mikayla and beginning your lives together." His brother's voice held teasing laughter as he slapped Jax on the back.

Jax couldn't argue with that. The dream of seeing his family together again had been superseded—if only slightly—by the dream of starting a family of his own, with Mikayla.

And now both of those dreams were closer to becoming reality than he had dared to hope. While he would need to grapple with his failure to be there for his father when he was sick and dying, Papá's last words were coming true for Jax as well.

He was being blessed with the undeserved gifts of a loving and merciful God.

Chapter Fifty-Two

Diego was uncharacteristically quiet as Jax steered Mikayla's car through the streets of Toronto. It had taken three days for them to get their passports. Jax and Mikayla had spent a lot of that time with Diego and Leya and her family, but they'd also been able to do a little touring around Puerto Rico. As Jax had imagined it would, it brought him incredible joy to show Mikayla his country, a place that had endured so much but remained resilient and breathtakingly beautiful.

They had arrived in Canada this morning and gone straight to Mikayla's apartment. Mikayla had suggested that Leya and Mateo stay with her while Diego and Jax go see their mother for the first time, so Risa wasn't completely overwhelmed.

He and his brother had left the two women drinking coffee and chatting away as though they had known each other forever.

Diego's fists rested on his thighs. "Mikayla is an extremely talented artist."

Jax doubted that his fiancée's artwork was uppermost in his brother's mind, but likely he was trying to get his mind off the coming visit with their mother. Jax didn't blame him. Diego had caused Mamá a lot of sorrow. Although Jax knew his mother would be thrilled to see her elder son, to know he was alive, that didn't mean their initial conversations wouldn't be difficult. He'd indulge his brother and help distract him.

"Yes, she is. And so are you. What are you planning to do about your shop?"

Diego straightened his fingers and rubbed them across his jeans. "I'll sell it. There's a building behind the restaurant that Leya says we can install a forge in so I can keep doing my metalwork if I want to. Which I do since, crazily enough, Tomás

Santiago was starting to do quite well. Lots of international attention. Which was making me nervous, but hopefully it will be okay now."

"It's not crazy. Your work is beautiful; I am not surprised you're doing well with it." Jax slowed the car as they approached their mother's condo building.

"*Gracias*." Diego stared out his window. "Did you tell Mamá you were coming after me?"

"No." Jax signaled to turn into the lot. "I couldn't get her hopes up until I knew something for sure, so I only told her I was traveling for work." He wheeled Mikayla's car into a parking space. After killing the engine, he studied his brother. "Are you ready for this?"

They had asked each other that a lot lately. And it was a silly question, really. How could one possibly be ready to face a parent he hadn't seen in decades?

Diego took a deep breath. "As ready as I will ever be." Which was the only answer to the question.

Neither spoke on the elevator up to the sixth floor. When they'd walked the thickly carpeted hallway to their mother's door, Jax touched his brother's elbow. "Could you wait out here, give me a minute to prepare her?"

Diego nodded and slumped against the wall. Jax rapped lightly on the door before pushing it open. He'd texted to let Mamá know he was coming by but hadn't mentioned the reason for the visit.

His mother slid a marker into the book she'd been reading and rose from her chair in the corner of the living room as he walked in. "Jax." As always, her face lit up when she saw him. She crossed the room and grasped his upper arms as he leaned in to kiss her on the cheek.

"Mamá. It is good to see you. How are you?"

"I'm fine." Her smile faded as she ran her fingers over his jaw. Between Diego's fist and Angel Ramirez's gun, it was a mass of fading bruises. Her gaze dropped to his left hand, and she grabbed it so she could examine his fingers. "But what happened to you?"

"It's a long story, but I'm okay, really. I will tell you everything, but first, I need to let you know where I was the last few days."

Her dark eyes searched his intently, as though she understood that what he was about to tell her might shake the foundations of her world. "All right."

"Can we sit?" Jax pointed to the couch with his injured hand.

His mother settled on the couch cushion, facing him. "*¿Qué es, Jax?*" Her voice trembled slightly, and he reached for her hand and held it in his good one.

"I told you I was going after a missing person, but what I didn't say was that the person was Diego."

She drew in a quick breath. "And?"

"I found him."

Mamá tugged her fingers from his and pressed her palms to her cheeks. "Is he … okay?"

"Yes. He's fine. He is doing really well, actually. He is clean and sober and has a strong faith in God. And it was because of you that I was able to track him down. When you showed Mikayla the pictures of Ernesto last week, she reminded me he was in Venezuela. I went to see him, and he told me Diego was in Puerto Rico, so I flew there. With God's help, I was able to locate him."

His mother's fingers slid to her mouth. "Where is he now?"

"He came to Canada with me this morning." Jax inclined his head toward the doorway. "Now he is waiting in the hallway. Do you feel ready to see him?"

Mamá lowered her hands to her lap where she clasped them tightly. "*Sí.* Of course I want to see my son."

"All right then. I'll get him. And I will be here."

She nodded, her gaze shifting to the doorway. Jax rose and strode across the room to open the door. Diego appeared as shaky and uncertain as their mother as he pushed away from the wall.

"She wants to see you."

He dipped his head. When Jax stood back, his brother brushed by him and stepped into the condo. His mother let out a soft cry as Jax followed him in and closed the door. Diego went straight to her, dropping to the floor in front of her and lowering his forehead to her knees. "Mamá."

She closed her eyes and rested her hands on his dark hair, the curls his son had inherited from him. A tear slid down her cheek. Jax leaned a shoulder against the wall, his own eyes pricking as he watched the two of them. After a moment, Diego straightened, his cheeks glistening like they had the night he'd told Jax about losing his wife and child. "*Lo siento, Mamá. Perdóname*. I don't know how to tell you how sorry I am. How much I regret leaving you and Jax."

She took his face in her hands. "Coming home is a good start."

"I know I caused you terrible pain."

"Yes. You did." Her voice was gentle but firm. "But I forgave you a long time ago."

"I don't deserve your forgiveness."

Mamá shook her head. "None of us deserves forgiveness. It is a gift." She let go of him. "Here." She patted the cushion.

Diego pushed to his feet and sank onto the couch next to her. Not wanting to interrupt them, Jax lowered himself onto the armchair in the corner. Mamá reached for her elder son's hands and held them in hers. "Jax says you have found God."

He offered her a weak smile. "I think it was more that He found me, but yes, I gave my life to Him." He hesitated before adding, "In prison."

A sigh escaped Mamá. "We have much to catch up on."

"Yes, we do. And I will tell you everything—anything you want to know. For now, other than my faith, the biggest thing I want to share with you is that I have an incredible wife, Leya. We have been married for four years, although …" He shot a helpless look at Jax, who could only shrug. Where did they even begin telling that crazy tale?

Diego turned back to Mamá. "It is a long story, but we both thought the other had been killed three years ago. Only when Jax came and set a series of events into motion did we discover that we were both alive. And now we are together again. She is here in Canada with me. And so is our son."

Mamá clapped her hands together in front of her chest. "*¿Tengo un nieto?*"

Diego nodded. "Yes, you have a grandson. His name is Mateo, and he is two and a half years old."

"May I meet them?"

"Of course." Diego's voice broke a little, as though he'd been worried she wouldn't want to after everything he had put her through. "I would like that more than anything."

Mamá wiped a tear from his cheek with her thumb. "Do you have a place to stay?"

"We will get a hotel room nearby."

"Would you stay here? That would give us a chance to talk and for me to get to know your family."

Diego shot another look at Jax. Jax had been staying in his mother's guest room while hunting for a place of his own in Toronto, but he had no problem with his brother and Leya and Mateo joining them. "It is fine with me. You and Leya can take the second bedroom. I will crash on the couch."

"We cannot kick you out of your room," Diego protested.

"I don't mind. I would like to spend time with you and get to know my sister-in-law and nephew better before you need to return home." Besides, if Jax had his way, it wouldn't be for long.

"Okay then." Diego squeezed Mamá's hands. "I do have a lot to tell you. And I want to hear about everything that has happened in your life since I left."

"Then it is settled." She let go of him and rose. "Go and get your family and bring them here so I can meet them."

"Yes, ma'am." Diego grinned as he stood and kissed his mother on both cheeks. "*Gracias, Mamá*, for welcoming me home. It is far more than I deserve."

She rested a hand on his back as they walked to the door. Jax followed them. When Diego had stepped into the hallway, their mother stopped in front of Jax. Grasping his forearms, she said, "Thank you for bringing your brother home, for never giving up hope that you would find him."

The joy he had longed to see in her eyes flowed through them and Jax nodded, his throat too tight to speak. In the days to come, they would have a lot to talk about. There was still so much about the last twenty years of Diego's life that Jax didn't know, and Jax needed to tell Mamá about all that had happened to him since he left Canada. Had that only been a week ago? It felt like a lifetime.

But for the first time in many years, they would be together under one roof, the three of them. For a few days, at least. They would have time to talk and share and work through all the pain and joy of the time they had missed out on. And they would. They were family. God had put them in each other's lives and now He had brought them back together.

Through the grace of God, they had come through the flames and emerged refined and ready to be molded by Him into something even more beautiful than Diego's exquisite works of art. A masterpiece that would be a testament to God's faithful presence and protection over each of their lives every day that they had been apart.

Chapter Fifty-Three

Mikayla tried to prepare herself as she approached Nicole and Daniel's condo. Her sister had assured her she was thrilled Mikayla had arrived home safely, but Nicole had been desperately concerned when she couldn't get hold of her—which Mikayla understood perfectly.

Although she felt badly about worrying her sister and brother-in-law, a smile crossed Mikayla's face. Two years ago, she had been completely alone in the world. No one except her agent, Leigh, would have been concerned if she'd gone missing. Now she had a lot of people in her life who cared deeply about what happened to her, who loved her unconditionally.

They reached the door and Mikayla lifted her hand to knock. "Hey." Jax came up behind her and caught her fingers in his. She faced him, grateful for the reprieve.

He pressed the palm of his injured hand against the wall next to her head. "By the time we leave this condo …"

"I know." Mikayla smiled up at him.

"No second thoughts, Grant?"

She shook her head. "*Ni uno.*"

His eyes darkened, and he leaned in and pressed his lips to hers. After thinking she might never see him again, every moment she spent with him, every touch, had become so meaningful, so powerful. Mikayla slid a hand around the back of his head and pulled him closer, deepening their kiss. For a few seconds, she let herself revel in the feel of his mouth on hers, the faint hint of wood and earth and rain that still clung to him, as though he carried part of Puerto Rico on his skin now. She could happily lose herself in that scent, in his touch, forever. After a moment, he brushed his fingers across her cheek. "We should probably go inside."

"Probably." Or they could stay out here all night, just the two of them …

He smiled as though he could read her thoughts. Which he likely could, since he'd had the uncanny ability to know what she was thinking and feeling from the moment they had first met. "After you." He rested his hand on the small of her back and guided her to the door. Mikayla rapped lightly on the wood. She could still hardly believe that she and Jax were engaged, although the ring he'd given her a few nights earlier, after Diego and Leya and Mateo had left for Risa's condo and they were finally alone in her apartment, did help it feel more real. She fingered the diamond ring with the large stone in the middle and a smaller one on each side—the exact one she would have chosen if she had been with Jax when he was shopping for it.

Daniel opened the door. "Mik. Good to see you." He kissed her on the cheek.

"You too." Mikayla slid off her jacket and hung it on the hall tree behind the door.

"Jax." Daniel held up a hand and Jax clasped it. "I can't tell you how happy I am that you are both home safe and sound."

"We are happy as well, believe me."

"I want to hear about everything that happened."

"Yes. We will talk."

Daniel slid an arm around Mikayla's shoulders. "You know I would have come with you if you'd told us what you were planning to do."

"I know." Her cheeks warmed a little. Although she still believed she'd done the right thing by not putting him in the position of having to choose between helping her and being with his family when his baby girl was so sick, she didn't blame him for being hurt that she hadn't asked. "I'm sorry for not letting you know."

"Promise to keep us in the loop next time and I'll let it go."

She smiled weakly. "I genuinely hope there is no next time."

Daniel inclined his head toward the kitchen. "Your sister might not let you off the hook so easily. She wants to talk to you."

Jax touched her back lightly again. “Good luck.”

Mikayla trudged toward the swinging doors between the living room and kitchen. Walking into the brightly lit room to see her twin stirring a pot on the stove brought back a rush of memories. She’d walked into the same scene a year before, her sister preparing for a dinner party at which Mikayla would meet Jax for the first time. That night had changed her life. And so would tonight. Shivers skittered across her skin, although the feeling that accompanied them was the opposite of the one that had rippled through her when she was so afraid for Jax. “Hey, Nic.”

Her sister swung around, sauce dripping from a ladle onto the tile floor. “Kayla.” She dropped the ladle into the pot, stepped over the drops, and strode over to Mikayla. “Honestly, I don’t know whether to shake you or hug you.”

“I won’t blame you, whatever you decide.”

Nicole shook her head before wrapping her arms around Mikayla. “I’m just glad you’re okay.” She stepped back. “You are okay, right?”

Mikayla smiled. “I’m fine. Honest.”

Nicole touched Mikayla’s hair. “I almost didn’t know you.”

“I know. I was trying to fit in a bit better, although I’m not sure I pulled it off.” Torres had guessed as soon as he saw her who she was, although for all Mikayla knew, he’d seen pictures of her. Maybe his people had been following her for weeks or months and reporting her activities back to him. She repressed a shudder. Tonight was for celebrating, for looking forward, not dwelling on the past.

“I can’t believe you took off without telling me.” Nicole grabbed a couple of paper towels from the holder on the counter, wiped up the drops, then returned to the stove and picked up the ladle.

“I can’t either.” Mikayla sank onto a stool at the island, grateful that the worst of the lecture appeared to be over. “But you had enough to worry about, with Elle. How is she doing?”

“She’s fine now, thankfully.”

“Are she and Jordan here?” Come to think of it, the condo

had been quiet when Jax and Mikayla came in, which was unusual.

"Mom and Dad took them this afternoon so I could get ready. They'll drop them off in a couple of hours." Nicole gave the pot a final stir and turned off the burner. She held a hand under the ladle as she carried it over to the sink and ran it under a stream of water. When she turned off the tap, she shook the utensil in Mikayla's direction. "No changing the subject. I need to know everything that happened to you while you were gone."

Did she? Should Mikayla tell her about being abducted from her bed at night, or gagged and strapped to a chair in a walk-in refrigerator, or having a drug lord hold a gun to her head? "Nic, I promise I will tell you everything, but for tonight, could we relax and enjoy our dinner?"

Her sister pursed her lips. "Okay, fine. We'll leave it for tonight. But only if you promise that you'll tell me everything—and I mean everything—soon."

Mikayla nodded. Being a twin was a beautiful gift, but it had its drawbacks. Clearly her sister could tell that she'd been contemplating holding back on a few details, and she wasn't having it. "I promise. Now what can I do to help?"

"Actually, there isn't much to do. I was working today, so Daniel refused to let me make dinner. He ordered Thai food from that amazing place near the diner, and it should be here soon. Do you think Jax's family will be okay with that?"

Daniel and Nicole had invited Risa, Diego, Leya, and Mateo to join them for dinner so they could get to know them, which Jax deeply appreciated. Mikayla and Jax had come early, but the rest of his family should be here soon. "They'll enjoy whatever you serve them. They're great, Nic. I don't know Diego that well yet, but Leya is incredible. And little Mateo is so cute."

"I can't wait to meet them." Nicole settled on a stool next to her. Her gaze dropped to the hands Mikayla had folded in her lap. "Wait. Is that …?"

Mikayla held up her left hand. "We're engaged."

"Kayla!" Nicole snatched her hand and pulled it closer. "I can't believe you didn't tell me on the phone."

"I wanted to do it in person."

"And you've let me go on for ten minutes without saying anything." Tears glistened in Nicole's eyes as she clasped Mikayla's hand between both of hers. "I'm so happy for you and Jax."

"Me too." Warmth wafted through Mikayla's chest. She *was* happy. Happier than she had been in her life. Happier than she would have ever believed she could be again after losing her parents. The thought of them drew a lump into her throat and, to distract herself, she nodded toward the stove. "What were you stirring when I came in?"

Nicole released her hand. "Sauce for a cake I baked last night. I thought I could at least make dessert."

"How is Connie?"

A sad smile drifted across her sister's face. "She's doing all right. She came home a couple of days ago. We've had some good talks since her latest incident, and although I don't want to lose her, I think I'm getting to the place where I will be able to let her go. She's ready. She wants to be with Jesus and Joe, and I don't want her to feel as though she needs to hold on for my sake. I told her that, and it seemed to lift a burden from her."

"You gave her a wonderful gift, Nic. I'm proud of you."

"Thanks."

Someone knocked on the condo door, and Mikayla slid off the stool. "If that's Jax's family, I want to introduce you."

"It could be Chase or Holden and Christina and the kids. Daniel invited them to join us too."

"That's so great. I'm dying to see Ciana again. And to apologize to poor Chase for abandoning him at the airport."

When they came through the swinging doors, Leya, Diego, Risa, and little Mateo had come into the condo. As Daniel was taking their jackets, Holden, Christina, and the son they were in the process of adopting, Matthew, came in behind them. Mikayla took the baby carrier from Holden and set it on the couch. Ciana was sleeping, and for a long moment Mikayla gazed at her, drinking in the sweet round cheeks and the floral headband that matched the baby's pink onesie. Would she and Jax have a little one like this one day? When she finally tore herself away and joined Jax and his family, he sent her a knowing smile that brought heat into her cheeks again.

He had barely finished introducing everyone when the food arrived. Daniel took the paper bags from the delivery guy and was about to close the door when Chase appeared in the opening. Daniel gave him a one-armed hug before carrying the food into the dining room. Jax hugged him too and slapped him on the back a couple of times. "Thank you for being willing to come to Puerto Rico with Mikayla, brother. That means a lot to me."

"I would have been happy to. I'm sorry I couldn't."

Jax shook his head. "It wasn't your fault."

Mikayla wrapped her arms around him. "I apologize for leaving you at the airport. I know you wanted me to wait, but I had to get to Jax."

"I get it." Chase grinned. "I'm glad it all worked out."

Jax held out an arm toward the dining room. "Shall we?"

When they walked into the room, Daniel had set the various dishes in the middle of the table. The enticing aromas of ginger and sweet basil wafted from the takeout containers, and Mikayla breathed in deeply.

Once they were settled, Jax reached for Mikayla's hand under the table as Daniel said grace. Her brother-in-law thanked God for the gift of family and that Diego and Leya had found each other and Jax and his Mamá had been reunited with the brother and son who had been missing for so long. When Daniel finished, *Amens* echoed around the table.

Jax's family seemed completely at ease, and the conversation around the table was lively. They didn't share too many frightening details about what had transpired in Puerto Rico, but Diego did keep everyone laughing by telling them about Jax being startled by a colony of bats and tumbling down a mountainside and of how he'd met with the highest-ranking military officer in Puerto Rico without realizing it. Some of the stories Mikayla had heard already and some she hadn't, and she listened with a mixture of amusement and barely contained terror, knowing how badly things could have turned out. *Thank you, Father. For answering all our prayers.*

Before Mikayla knew it, her plate was empty. Two hours had passed since they arrived at the condo. Someone knocked at the door and she glanced at Jax. Was that …?

Nicole excused herself to answer it, and a moment later Mikayla caught the sound of Jordan's excited chatter. Her shoulders relaxed. Her parents. "Excuse me a moment." She wiped her fingers on a napkin and pushed away from the table.

"Aunt Kayla!" Jordan flung himself at her as she approached the door.

"Hey, buddy." Mikayla hugged him and ruffled his curls. "I missed you."

"Missed you too."

"Come on, Jordan." Nicole settled her daughter on one hip and rested her other hand on her son's shoulder. "I want to introduce you and Elle to some new friends of ours."

They headed into the dining room, leaving Mikayla alone with her parents. Her father gave her an awkward hug. "Good to see you, Mikayla."

Although it clearly required effort, she appreciated him calling her by her name. "You too. How did it go with the kids?"

Her mother's face lit up. "We had a great time. They are such wonderful children."

"Yes, they are. I'm glad you're getting to know them better."

Her father nodded. "We are as well." He cleared his throat. "Nicole mentioned you were in Puerto Rico. Did you have a good trip?"

Clearly Nicole hadn't told them much about why she had gone or the threats they had faced. Maybe someday Mikayla would fill them in, but this wasn't the time. "I did, actually. Jax was there, searching for his brother, Diego, who's been missing for a long time, and he managed to find him. In fact, Diego's here tonight with his wife and son." She hesitated. "Would you like to come in for dessert, meet everyone?"

Her mother rested a hand on Mikayla's arm. "Thank you for

the invitation. But we don't want to intrude."

Her father nodded and reached for the doorknob.

"Wait." Mikayla took a step closer to them. "Mom. Dad." Although the words tripped a little over her tongue as they came out of her mouth for the first time, they felt right. "You wouldn't be intruding. I'd really like for you to stay."

Her parents exchanged a look before her father let go of the knob. "All right then."

"Great." Mikayla led the way into the dining room and introduced her parents to Chase and to Diego and his family.

Jax had met them a couple of times, and he stood now and shook hands with her dad and hugged her mom. "I'm glad you could join us Mr. and Mrs. Hunter."

"Marion and Roy, please." Her father pulled out one of the chairs Daniel had carried over to the table and held it for her mother.

Before Jax could sit, his phone buzzed, and he touched Mikayla's arm. "I will be right back."

She nodded before returning to her seat and looking around the table. Holden's arm was slung across the back of Matthew's chair as Matthew cradled his new baby sister in his arms. Holden said something and he and Matthew chuckled. Holden squeezed his son's shoulder before turning to Christina. She smiled at him and he kissed her on the cheek. Mikayla averted her gaze, not wanting to intrude on the intimate moment.

Mateo was still awake on Risa's lap, but his head rested on her chest and his eyelids had started to droop. Diego sat next to them, Leya on his other side. When Leya's smiling eyes met Mikayla's, the look that passed between them held the promise of a deep, lifelong friendship. Mikayla held the feeling close as she continued her perusal of the room.

Jordan was perched on a stool at the corner of the table, close to Daniel, whose fingers rested on his stepson's back. Nicole had settled Elle on her lap and was running her fingers through her daughter's blonde curls. Her parents appeared slightly uncomfortable, but they were here, and suddenly that mattered very much to Mikayla.

The door to the condo opened and closed, and everyone's attention shifted to the opening between the living and dining rooms. Jax appeared in the doorway. "Can we squeeze in a couple more friends?"

"Always." Daniel gestured for them to come into the room.

Jax stepped to the side to allow the man and woman with him to pass by. Diego drew in a sharp breath and shoved back his chair. As he rounded the table toward them, Jax said, "Everyone, these are Diego's friends. And mine. Ernesto and Camila Rivas."

Ernesto strode toward Diego. When they reached each other, Ernesto clasped Diego's upper arms. "*Mi amigo*. I cannot believe it." He kissed Diego on both cheeks before pulling him into a hug.

When he stepped back, Diego reached for Ernesto's wife's hands. "Camila. So good to see you."

Tears sparkled in her dark eyes. "And you."

Diego glanced from her to Ernesto. "I cannot believe you are here."

Ernesto lifted a palm. "I cannot believe *you* are here."

"I'm sorry I could not tell you the truth."

"I am only glad your little brother didn't listen to me, just like when we were boys." Ernesto slapped Jax on the back. "That he went after you anyway."

"I never would have found him if you had not put me in touch with General Huertas. Although, it would have been helpful for you to tell me who he was."

Ernesto grinned. "That is what you get for showing up at my home uninvited."

Diego nodded toward the folding chairs Daniel had set up near him and Leya. "Come, meet my family. And tell us what you are doing in Toronto."

"I invited them." Jax walked to Mikayla's side and held out his hand. She took it and stood, her heart rate picking up a little as he tugged her closer. "As you have heard tonight, my brother and I and Mikayla and Leya had many interesting adventures in Puerto Rico. Some were a little scarier than the ones we shared, but we will save those for another time. These experiences reminded us that life is precious and that every moment spent with the ones we love is to be deeply cherished." He let go of Mikayla's hand and wrapped an arm around her. "When I saw Ernesto in Venezuela, he asked me to make sure to invite him to the wedding when Mikayla and I got married. Which is why he and Camila—and all of you, the people we care about the most in the world—are here. We are getting married tonight, in this place where we met one year ago."

Commotion broke out around the table, with everyone talking at once. Mikayla's gaze met Risa's warm one. She had pressed her fingers to her mouth as though, like Mikayla, so much joy filled her that she could barely contain it. She slid Mateo onto Diego's lap and then stood and came around the table to hug Mikayla and Jax.

Nicole's green eyes had widened. She smacked Daniel lightly on the arm. "Did you know about this?"

He chuckled. "Jax might have mentioned it earlier today, since he and Mikayla needed a little help smuggling clothes and flowers into the condo."

"I can't believe you kept it from me." She swung her attention to Mikayla. Despite her words, her eyes danced with laughter. "Or you."

"I know. I'm sorry. I hope you will forgive me and agree to stand up with me."

"You know I will. But …" Nicole scanned the room. "Who is going to perform the ceremony?"

Another knock sounded on the door. Perfect timing. Mikayla grinned. "That will be our pastor. Could someone let him in while Jax and I get ready?"

"On it." Holden slid his chair away from the table and headed for the door.

Mikayla came around the table and stopped next to her sister's chair. "Would you come help me?"

"Of course." Nicole handed Elle to Daniel and followed Mikayla to the master bedroom.

"Jax is using the guest room, so Daniel said he'd hang my dress in your closet. Could you grab it for me while I touch up my makeup?"

Mikayla's fingers trembled slightly as she ran the brush across her cheekbones and applied mascara and lipstick. In a few minutes, she and Jax would be married. The horror of the last few days was evaporating like the rain on a hot afternoon in Puerto Rico, replaced with a deep joy and hope for a wonderful life together.

When Mikayla came out of the bathroom, Nicole held up the gown Jax had dropped off to Daniel earlier. In a garment bag, of course, so he wouldn't catch a glimpse of it, although when she walked toward him tonight, it wouldn't be the first time he'd seen her in it.

"Kayla. This dress is gorgeous."

"You're the one who gave it to me." The night of her big gallery opening in Chicago a year ago, her sister had surprised her by sending the shimmering gold gown to her hotel, and Mikayla had felt like a princess in it all evening. Especially after the opening, when Jax had picked her up in a limo and driven her to the old bandstand he'd fixed up with twinkling lights and music for the redemption of one of the worst nights of her life. She'd realized that evening, dancing in his arms, the gold gown swishing around her ankles, that she was falling for him. That she could let go of her need to know what might happen and simply trust God and Jax with her future.

The months that followed had only deepened that trust and the love she felt for him. Wearing this gown for the second time, the evening she declared her love for him in front of witnesses and vowed before God to commit herself to him until death parted them, felt perfect.

"I know. I have impeccable taste." Nicole held the gown in front of her and swished it side to side.

"Yes, you do." Mikayla took off the blouse and dress pants

she'd been wearing, and her sister lifted the gown and let it slide over Mikayla's shoulders and waist until it fell in shimmering folds around her.

Nicole did up the zipper. When she came around in front of Mikayla, she pressed her clasped fingers to her chin. "You are stunning."

"Thank you." Mikayla hugged her. "And thank you for being my maid of honor. There is no one else in the world I would want by my side."

"I'm honored to stand with you." Nicole held her at arm's length. "Daniel and I love Jax, and nothing will thrill us more than seeing the two of you get married and start your lives together."

Mikayla grinned. "Then let's go do this." A slight twinge worked its way through her as she and Nicole made their way to the living room. The only thing that could have made this night more perfect would have been if her adoptive parents were here. She pushed away the sadness. She would see them again one day. In the meantime, her birth parents were present, and it felt as if she and Nicole had taken a few small steps toward re-building what the four of them had once shared. Mikayla didn't have a lot of memories of the time before she was taken from the park, but a few, ethereal recollections did drift through her when she thought back on her early years. Happiness. Love. Laughter. And a pair of pink running shoes with rainbow laces that she had adored.

When they reached the opening to the living room, Nicole whispered, "Wait here." She rounded the corner and disappeared. A moment later she returned to Mikayla, clutching a bouquet of flowers. "Daniel gave me this for you."

Mikayla took the bouquet. After numerous calls around the city, she had found a flower shop that carried *flora de maga*, the national flower of Puerto Rico that had grown on trees all around the motel where they'd stayed and which she had fallen in love with. She clutched the bright pink blossoms now, the soft, cottony scent wafting on the air taking her back to those last few glorious days in the country. Days that, after the terrors they'd endured, had felt so sweet.

Soft music started up. Mikayla smiled when she recognized the song—"Wonderful Tonight," the first song she and Jax had danced to at their prom under the stars. Perfect. Nicole touched her elbow. "Are you ready to get married?"

"More ready than I have been for anything in my life."

Her sister nodded and walked ahead of her into the living room. As soon as Mikayla entered and saw Jax standing on the other side of the room, Diego next to him, the slight nerves she'd been feeling disappeared. Jax was ridiculously handsome in a dark suit and steel blue shirt. What drew her up the aisle, though, past rows of chairs and people she was vaguely aware of but couldn't really take in as she passed by, was the way he was gazing at her. His dark eyes, glistening slightly, were fixed on her as she approached, and they radiated so much love she struggled to keep drawing in breaths.

What had she ever done to deserve that love? This man? All she knew was that he was another incredible gift from God. *Thank you, Father.* She kept her gaze locked on his as she handed the pink flowers to Nicole and reached for the hands he held out to her.

The pastor spoke briefly on the sanctity of marriage, but the homily, as inspiring as it likely was, was mostly lost on Mikayla. She forced herself to be fully present during the vows, wanting Jax to hear in her voice and see in her eyes how much she meant every word. When it was her turn, she repeated the ones she had practiced carefully so she could surprise him. "*Yo, Mikayla Grant, te recibo a ti, Juan Miguel Rodríguez, como esposo y me entrego a ti, y prometo serte fiel en la prosperidad y en la adversidad, en la salud y en la enfermedad, todos los días de mi vida.*"

Tears welled in Jax's eyes, and he lifted both her hands to his mouth and kissed them. Then, at the minister's prompting, he slid the wedding band onto her finger and held out his. He had taken the tape off so Mikayla could work the ring onto his fourth one, not one that had been broken, thankfully.

The pastor pronounced them husband and wife, and Jax took her face in his hands and pressed his lips to hers, a sweet and gentle kiss that held the promise of many more kisses and many years together. Years that, like their time in Puerto Rico, would hold challenges and triumphs, sorrow and joy, losses and unexpected gifts.

Neither of them could know what that future might hold. But as Jax had told her once and as Mikayla had finally come to understand, they didn't trust in the place their path would lead them to, they trusted only and always in the One who would take them there.

Author Note

Dear Readers,

And with that, the curtain closes on the series following the lives of Gage, Nicole, Daniel, Holden, Christina, Jax, Mikayla, Diego, and the people in their lives. My hope and prayer is that you have come to love all of them as I have, and that the way they changed and grew as their stories unfolded has encouraged you in your own walk with God.

The theme of all my books is that we are not alone—that whatever we are going through, God has promised to never leave us or forsake us. Because He is God and because He is good, He always keeps His promises, so we can trust that He will be with us every step of the journey He takes us on. As Jax and Diego discovered, God does not always deliver us from the flames, but He is always, always in the fire with us.

If you are carrying hurt or trauma or resentment from the past, my deepest hope is that you can lay it at the feet of Jesus and, with His help and strength, forgive as He forgave. As Risa said, "It is impossible to hold on to bitterness and unforgiveness toward someone you continually bring to God." As you do, may you find the burden of bitterness lifted from you, replaced by the incomprehensible peace of Jesus Christ.

Dear ones, whatever circumstances you may face now or in the future, I pray that you will be deeply aware of the presence of God with you. And that you will experience the truth that, whether or not God chooses to deliver you from whatever situation you are in, He is still good. He is still sovereign, and He loves us as a good father.

You are never alone.

Sara

If you enjoyed this story, I'd appreciate if you'd consider leaving a review on any of the book-selling sites.

I'd also love to connect with you on the following sites:

Website (where you can sign up to receive my short, once-a-month newsletter): www.saradavison.org

Facebook: www.facebook.com/authorsaradavison

Also, if you aren't aware, I have a number of other Christian romantic suspense books in print. You might be interested in checking out the following titles:

The Seven Trilogy - The End Begins, The Darkness Deepens, The Morning Star Rises

The Night Guardians Series - Vigilant, Guarded, Driven

The Rose Tattoo Trilogy - Lost Down Deep, Written in Ink, Sharp Like Glass (coming in 2023)

two sparrows for a penny series: Every Star in the Sky, Every Flower of the Field (coming in 2023), Every Bird that Falls (coming in 2024)

The Watcher (standalone)

Discussion Questions

1. After losing her parents in a car accident, Mikayla struggled with the fear of losing someone else she loves. Do you wrestle with the fear of losing something or someone precious to you? How is she able to let go of those anxieties? If you have, what helped you to do so?

2. This story is set in Canada, Venezuela, and Puerto Rico. Did you learn anything about any of these countries that you didn't know? Do you like books with international settings? What book set in a country that isn't your own have you enjoyed the most and why?

3. Nicole struggles to forgive the parents who abandoned her as a child. Mikayla tells her that, "I think all you can do is pray that God will give you the ability to forgive them since, humanly speaking, it's too hard." Do you have someone in your life that you struggle to forgive? If you have been able to, what helped you and how did you feel after you did?

4. Mikayla's adoptive mother gives her a key chain with Exodus 14:14, "The LORD will fight for you; you need only to be still" printed on it. What do the words "be still" mean to you in this context? Do you believe the Lord fights for us? What do you think this looks like in real life? Is this something you have personally experienced?

5. Ernesto tells Jax that Diego was an amazing person, but that addiction is bondage. As he puts it, "The alcohol, the drugs, those were not him. They were thieves, stealing him from us one bottle, one hit, at a time." Do you have someone in your life trapped in this type of bondage? If they have found freedom, how did they do so?

6. Mikayla's birth mother, Marion, tells her, "I know there's nothing I can say or do to make up for the past. But I want you to know how sorry I am. I hope that one day Nicole will be able to forgive us, although I won't blame her if she can't." Have you ever hurt someone so badly that they struggled to forgive you? What did you do or say to them to show them how remorseful you were? If the relationship was restored, how did it happen?

7. Mikayla contemplates the idea that, "Words mattered. Languages did too. And using the ones that showed you knew the person you were talking to, that you understood them, allowed you to connect with them on a soul-deep level." Have you found this to be true in your life? In what ways?

8. When Jax finds his brother's grave, it bothers him that nothing is engraved on it except Diego's name and his dates of birth and death with a hyphen in between. "That pathetic hyphen meant to somehow encapsulate a person's life on earth. Who they were. What they'd done. Who loved them. How could a small straight line possibly hope to convey the slightest hint of any of that?" What epitaph would you like engraved on your headstone to capture who you were in a way that a hyphen cannot?

9. When Jax is missing and Mikayla has no idea where he is, she tries to pray. "*Father.* She stopped, not sure what to ask for this time. Maybe she didn't have to know. God knew what she needed, even if she couldn't put it into words. And He knew what Jax needed too." Do you believe this is true, that we don't always have to put our prayer requests into words, because God knows what we need? Have you ever found yourself unable to express the cries of your heart to God? Did He answer your prayer even when you weren't able to form the request?

10. When Diego asks Jax if he believes in soulmates, Jax's initial response is, "He never had been one to buy into the whole soulmate thing, the idea that God might have one person He intended for

someone to spend their lives with." After meeting Mikayla, he changed his mind. I wasn't sure I did until the day I met my husband while playing baseball. I knew immediately that he was the man I would marry. We talked through much of the game, and before I left, he gave me his business card. I still remember standing in my parents' kitchen that evening, afraid to look at the card. He hadn't told me his last name, and I was worried I wouldn't like it, because I knew it would be mine. We were engaged ten weeks later, and after twenty-five years, he is still the love of my life and my best friend. How about you? Do you believe in soulmates? Do you have a good story of meeting yours?

Manufactured by Amazon.ca
Bolton, ON

27649496R00184